SON OF THE STARS

SON OF THE STARS

A MOTHMAR NOVEL
BOOK THREE

AMANDA AULER

SPIRELIGHT PRESS

SPIRELIGHT
PRESS

964 High House Rd #3042 Cary, NC 27513
Copyright © 2025 Amanda Auler
All rights reserved. No portion of this book may be reproduced in any form without permission
from the publisher, except as permitted by U.S. copyright law.

For permissions contact: amanda@authoramandaauler.com

www.authoramandaauler.com

Character Illustrations by Nemaiza Rhayne
Scene illustrations by Kateryna Vitkovska
Map Illustrated by Rebecca Paavo
Chapter Illustrations by Sarah Cools
Edited by Eva Campney
Cover by Fantastical Ink
Type set in Garamond EB

ISBN:

979-8-9865922-7-5 (paperback)
979-8-9865922-8-2 (hardback)
979-8-9865922-9-9 (ebook)

10 9 8 7 6 5 4 3 2 1

Library of Congress Control Number: 2025912962

Printed in United States of America
This book is a work of fiction. Any references to historical events, real people, or real places
are used fictitiously. Other names, characters, places, and events are products of the author's
imagination, and any resemblance to actual events or places or persons, living or dead, is entirely
coincidental.

GLOSSARY

- Aska – The essence of the Taka Reu

- Austur – The easternmost village

- Darlöh – A state of unnatural sleep

- Eldfall – The tallest mountain bordering the eastern side of the valley

- Eldur – Someone with Heitt skilled enough to wield flame

- Fera – The Gift, given by the Stars, that allows the Gifted to tether to an inanimate object

- Greater Mothmar – The mainland

- Häfa/Häfan – A Mothmari curse

- Heitt – The Gift, given by the Sun, that allows the Gifted to warm and heal

- Hekla – A volcano, also a Mothmari curse

- Leídín – Or "the Way" is the ancient religion of worshiping the Celestials

- Lesser Mothmar – The islands off the mainland

- Lóthkol – The advanced school that focuses on Gifts

- Sodur – The southernmost village, Pallah's home

- Ströndbar – A small fishing village set in northern cliffs

- Taka Reu – Worship of The Mother, the Dark Gifts and those who practice them

- Tala – The Gift, given by the Moon, that allows the Gifted to tether to an animal

- Vestur – The westernmost village, Solyana's home

GIFTS

- Acute Fera – The ability to manipulate only one specific type of object

- Acute Tala – The ability to manipulate only one specific type of animal

- Bein Fera – The ability to manipulate bone

- Blou Fera – The ability to manipulate blood

- Broad Fera – The ability to manipulate inanimate objects

- Broad Tala – The ability to manipulate all animals

- Feldur Fera – The ability to manipulate skin

- Gler Fera – The ability to manipulate glass

- Lakimi Fera – The ability to manipulate muscles

- Malmur Fera – The ability to manipulate metal

- Mann Tala – The ability to manipulate a human

- Predatory Tala – The Gifted's aptitude is a predatory creature

- Prey Tala – The Gifted's aptitude is a prey creature

- Stein Fera – The ability to manipulate stone

- Vatin Fera – The ability to manipulate water

- Vindur Fera – The ability to manipulate wind or air

- Vior Fera – The ability to manipulate wood

- Falki Tala – The ability to manipulate falcons

- Fiskur Tala – The ability to manipulate fish

- Fugali Tala – The ability to manipulate birds

- Heri Tala – The ability to manipulate hares

- Ulfur Tala – The ability to manipulate wolves

KALDUR OCEAN
PAHRNADEE
OCEAN
KAIZAAN
MOUNT HEKLA
THONETHREN
WEST END
LAKE ILLGRES
NORTHERN MOUNTAINS
THE PINES
ELDFALL
ELD PLATEAU
HYTAST
SHASKOL
LOTHKOL
VALLEY OF VATIN
VATINO SEA
SPRETTA RIVER
VESTUR
TEMPLE CELESTIAL
AUSTUR
SODUR
KANA FOREST
WHITE WOOD
SHADOW WOOD
LEIF'S CABIN
LESSER MOTHMAR
BELJA RIVER
SKRIM

GREATER
MOTHMAR
MOUNT ENDIRINN
ENDIRINN
CAVE OF CRYSTALS
THE WITCH HEALER
STRONDBAR
THE CAVE WOOD
EEP ORD
EAST END
ICE PLAINS
PASS
TAKANAH
S E A
M O U N T A I N S
SEA

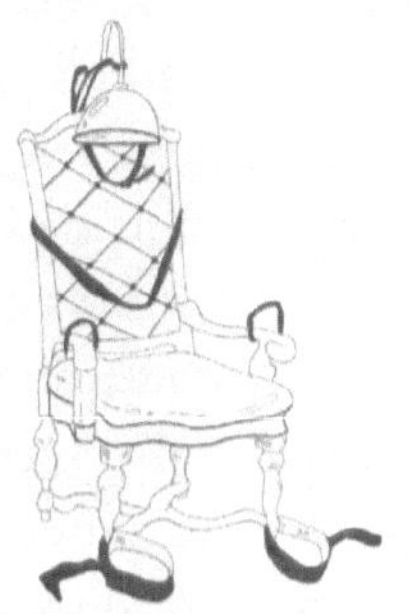

THE MACHINE

E RVAL'S RING-LADEN HAND RELEASED the ball toward the far side of the room at speed. *Rat-tat-pop!* It hit the stone of the basement wall and the ground near Phineas's feet before returning to Erval.

His old steward yelped, and a tool clattered to the floor. "Sire!"

Erval chuckled. "Just making sure you're awake, Phin."

The man grumbled, retrieved the tool, and continued his work.

It was almost ready. The machine he had spent so long working on, honing, and tuning. The device that would give him access to every beating heart, soul, and breath.

Erval squinted at his steward, whose hands worried over the gears and tubing at the back of the intricate contraption. Phineas had made promise after promise over the years, yet there was always something keeping it from working as it should. Erval recalled the first person he had ever positioned in the throne-like chair, other than himself, of course. She had been so young yet so stuffed with others' years. He had thought her preparations sufficient.

He was wrong. Strapped to the chair, she'd had no way to escape as the device sucked her dry until she was but skin stretched across cracked bones. Erval had been able to tether to hundreds in just those few moments, an all-consuming power like nothing he'd experienced before—at least until the girl expired and his tether snapped. It had left Erval chasing that rush of power ever since.

He knew it truly then: he could not be the one to secure himself to the device. Not only because of the danger it would present to his body, but more importantly, how fast it would diminish the souls he had accrued. So much time and effort spent, shoring up years for generations. To lose them in one fell swoop would not only be foolish but pointless. How would he be able to use his Taka Reu if he himself were the conduit? What a waste that would be.

But now... Erval studied his steward, calculating the amount of years stored in Phineas's stout body. Success would be guaranteed, but at what cost? Phineas was the closest Erval had to a confidant, something resembling a partner. And then there was Phineas's aversion to performing the Taking. Ever since the first time in the cells of Thonethren, Erval had known his steward hadn't been cut from the same shrewd cloth as he.

No, there was only one other person that could don the helm and imbue enough energy into the machine before him.

Pallah.

He ground his teeth and threw the ball again.

Rat-tat-pop! Back to his hand it flew.

"I found out where she's been hiding, you know," he told Phineas, and the tinkerer stilled. "All these years later." Erval wouldn't need to elaborate, Phineas knew of whom he spoke.

"Did you?"

Erval pulled the finnevel from his breast pocket, so conveniently small he usually carried it on his person. The device fit over his eye, a monocle of power. It amplified his tether far and wide until it could reach even the most obscure places on the map.

"Perhaps..." The steward held up a hand then seemed to think better of it.

Erval rolled his eyes, halfway to securing the device. "Problem?"

"Just...would you not kill her if you connected now? A straight connection to an adult has always proved fatal."

"I was able to connect to Solyana," he said with a shrug.

"Yes, but you had appeared to her in a physical form before latching onto her mind. Even if it was as a giant trapped in magma, it kept her alive."

Erval pursed his lips. He was tempted to reveal to his steward he had honed his Mann Tala to such a razor-edged point, adults no longer perished at the sound of his voice. Not all of them, anyway.

"Solyana had still been young," Phineas added, pushing his spectacles up the bridge of his nose. "I just wouldn't want you to kill Pallah, after all this time."

A laugh escaped Erval, so forceful he dropped his ball. "That would be hilarious."

"Quite." Phineas gave him a sideways look.

"Don't you worry your little head, Phin. If she's put in this much work to stay hidden from me, she's probably drinking the tea anyway."

"Right, sire."

"I'm sure there's a child around that cloaked valley, though." He fitted the finnevel over his eye and extended the metal arm behind one ear. "One that dislikes the taste of the tea. I'll just pay them a little visit is all." He relaxed into his chair with a sigh.

"You'd be showing your hand." Phineas didn't look at him, his eyes trained on his work. "She would know it's you."

"Well, that's the point, isn't it?" Erval's mouth curved into a languid smile. "Why should I waste any more time trying to track her down when one connection to some unsuspecting brat will convince her to come to me?"

Now Phineas turned to him, his eyebrows lifting in confusion. How could a man be so equally genius and daft at once?

"I'll spell it out for you, then." Erval pushed the finnevel up to his hairline, retrieved the ball at his feet, and began tossing it between his hands. "I cannot tether to her, as she's hidden herself so well. However, I've tethered in that valley before; I know where it is on the map. The news of my voice peppering thoughts would surely not escape her notice. Then she will come to me. It will be to kill me, but nevertheless…"

Phineas's mouth straightened to a grim line. "To kill you?"

"To finish the botched job she did so long ago, yes." A cold smile. "She's right to hide. She knows I'd make her life a living nightmare, even from this distance."

"Wouldn't she just keep running? It's been almost two centuries, and the tactic has served her."

"She won't run. Not if I tell her I have her brother."

The steward's eyes bulged from behind his spectacles. "You do?"

"Keep up with me, Phin! We just discussed Solyana, and you know she never returned from the mountain. Pallah's brother is a lost cause." He grinned wickedly. "However, she doesn't have to know that."

Erval waited on a laugh or at least a smirk from his steward—but none came. In fact, it looked as if the man was...sweating? Erval shook his head.

"What Pallah doesn't know won't hurt her—but it will hurry her."

Phineas wiped his hands on a small oily rag that hung from his apron. The torch protruding from the wall flickered, casting the small man a much larger shadow. "Brilliant, sire," he said quietly.

"Oh, don't flatter me." Erval rolled his eyes. "Are you quite finished?"

"I believe so. But until I have a suitable test subject, I won't know if—"

"Then what are you waiting for? Grab someone and test it out."

"Who do you—"

"The guard outside the door, a man from the cells, a woman off the street—do you think I care, Phineas? Do you think I lie awake at night feeling remorse or languishing in regret for the souls I have Taken and used?"

Phineas seemed to shrink into his skin.

"Grow up or get out. I have had enough of your sniveling." He turned and exited the dank basement, leaving his steward alone. He had felt discontentment from the man for years now, though he tried his best to ignore it. It was as if he purposefully wielded incompetence, as if he weaponized mediocrity.

He lowered the finnevel back over one eye as he ascended the staircase. Though the small device could be used just about anywhere, the connections it made occurred far more easily when he was in the observatory. High above spires and roofs, the device did its job with an efficiency lost in the basement of the castle. His boots clacked as he went, heralding his arrival and sending his guards scurrying like rats to attention.

He had toyed with the idea of a new steward over the years, with how much trouble Phineas seemed to enjoy injecting into his life. Sometimes the man's small rebellions were welcomed; it's not like Erval wanted zero resistance on his chosen paths—where was the game in that? But the persistent perspiring and quiet conflicts were beginning to truly grate. Erval considered. If he were to use The Taking on Phineas himself... He couldn't help the chill that shook him with pleasure—he would truly live forever. What was Phineas's lifespan up to now? Four hundred years? Five?

Erval's hair slid across his brow as he shook his head, dispelling the thought. He had, at some point, come to associate his own humanity with the rotund tinkerer. The steward reminded him where he'd come from, how long it had taken him to get here, and where he still intended to go. Doing away with him so quickly would be...irreverent.

Though, if the man continued to be so obstinate, not out of the question.

He wound his way through the stone hallways and corridors until he found himself at the highest point of his domain. Beneath the convex glass ceiling, plants trailed from hanging pots above a large map of Mothmar lain flat on a table. The sun streamed through the room, and Erval reveled in the warmth after having been underground for some time.

He cracked his neck side to side, and with the finnevel still fitted to his face, he settled into a high back chair that overlooked all of Thonethren. He focused his vision, closing one eye, the other staring straight into Kjarn's Eye.

Color, shape, and a vast stretch of land flashed before his vision as Erval covered distance like a falcon; over rolling hills and snow-sprinkled treetops his mind's eye flew. He searched, farther and farther south, until he found nothing but a land of fog and distorted reality. As if nothing were present—an empty void.

"Clever girl," he whispered to himself. "Hiding behind your masks. With all you told me of that place, I never counted on you returning to it. Though, I'll concede. Going back to the place of your birth, only to conquer it—we are more alike than you think."

His tether, amplified by the finnevel, failed to find whatever Pallah had created. What had she used? What Gift had she manipulated to make such a fortress? Then Erval felt him. A small boy, no more than four years of age, just at the edge of the barrier. Perhaps wandering without his mother? Erval grinned to himself and dove in, connecting to the boy's mind, to his soul.

There was a spark, a jolt, and Erval saw through the boy's very own eyes. "Hello there, son."

The boy's head whipped side to side, searching for the voice.

He was alone. Perfect.

"Listen close, boy. I have a message for you."

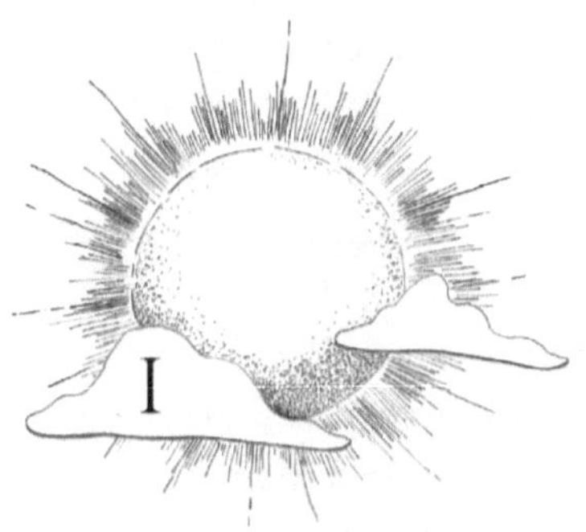

THE BOY ON THE MOUNTAIN

SOLYANA

HERE, ON THIS MOUNTAIN, surrounded by green, Solyana could easily believe she had completed her task. A blanket, not of white but of green, lay beneath her feet. A warm breeze tickled her face, pushing wavy strands of dark hair across her forehead. A meadow—a thing she'd only read about in historical scrolls—was history no longer. It was here, and it was real, and Solyana was standing at the center of it.

The boy before her walked a slow circle, taking in their surroundings, seemingly just as surprised as she. But he, wide-eyed and shaking, tethered no light. This boy had angered no Celestials. He was a prisoner, a victim.

"Ahren," Solyana began. "How long have you been here?" Fear began to creep in as all she had been told crashed against the rocks of reality.

"I..." Ahren shook his head, his dark hair matted on one side with...was that blood? "I don't know. One minute I was—" Terror shot across his face, and he sank to his knees, crushing the long stalks of weeds beneath him. "What did she *do*?" The words clawed their way from his throat. "Vámae!" Ahren's hands went to his chest, blood caked beneath his nails and dried in sprays up his arms.

Solyana froze. Had he murdered someone? Would he murder her? "Take a breath," she told him as he hitched and choked. "I have things to tell you, but you need to listen carefully."

"No, no, no!" Ahren's entire body shook, sweat beginning to soak his shirt. "She was just here!" His eyes were wild and bore too much white as he sat up and searched the grounds. "I want to go home. I want to go home!"

Solyana bit her lip and stepped back from him. She wouldn't be able to get him down the mountain, not like this. He needed time and space; he needed to grieve. She decided then she would not reveal any more information. If what Erval had told her was true, this boy was from an ancient time, locked in this place by a curse. And if Ahren's grief was this fresh, he was in no state to learn he had lost hundreds of years.

Thinking of Erval, the lava giant that spoke to her mind, caused Solyana to pause. He had promised to be her partner, to be alongside her, but since she had started up this mountain, Erval had been remarkably absent. Even now, she hoped by turning her thoughts to him, he would come back. But no. Where his voice had been now held only silence. She alone would have to explain to Ahren all that had happened, all that was happening. But how could she when she knew so little herself?

A sound rang from somewhere in the distance, like a cold wind howling through trees.

Ahren's head snapped up, and his eyes found hers once again. They were a beautiful blue, like Kana Ocean during whaling season, like a wave about to break. And suddenly, he was no longer a boy but a hardened man. She blinked, scanning his features. His jaw had sharpened, and his chin now bore a shadow that had not been there before. His eyes held hers with a greater depth. Had she just failed to get a good look at him at first?

The beard rippled darker over his jaw, growing fast—too fast.

She scrambled away from him, eyes wide with fear.

The ground beneath them began to quake, knocking Ahren off balance, and he fell. His fingers dug deep into the soft earth of the meadow as he pushed himself back up.

"What's happening?" Solyana shrieked.

But Ahren was in no state to answer; shock, fear, or both had overcome him as he stared at the grasses around them. As if it had been an illusion, something curated by a more powerful force than Solyana could ever know, the earth began to fold in on itself, turning over. Green grass and trees toppled and fell, evaporating into a dark and coiling mist—the *aska*, the physical manifestation of the Taka Reu. Its presence shook Solyana to her core.

Acting on instinct, Solyana grabbed Ahren's hand and started running, pulling him forward through the grass as it disappeared in their wake, turning all to ash as it floated away in smoky clouds of darkness.

Her eyes scanned the edges of what had become a crater, trying to find any features she could climb, any path of escape.

There! A crack in the wall!

Pulling Ahren behind her, they evaded the last of the turning ground and squeezed through the gap in the rock, hurling themselves into suffocating blackness.

They hiked blindly downward, their outstretched hands waving to warn them of any obstacles, feeling nothing but a cold that quickly dipped to freezing. Doubt and fear hammered through her thoughts, but Solyana grit her teeth, tugging harder on the hand in her grip. They had to keep going.

A final dip in a narrow crevasse opened up to light, and Solyana almost stumbled as she brought her hands up, squinting against the sun.

The rumbling behind them ceased, the gasp of their lungs and the crunch of snow beneath their feet the only sounds. Like unsatisfactory morsels of a long-chewed prophecy, they were spat from the mountain. Ahren fell to the ground beside Solyana, his fingers curling into the snow.

She turned back to the wall, blinking with shock as she surveyed the base of the frozen waterfall she had climbed, the ice smooth as rippled glass. Not so much as a scratch to denote the crack they'd come through, it was if it had never existed at all. She searched, too, for the evidence of her climb but none was found.

The air smelled different.

And then it hit her.

Heart thumping in her chest, Solyana charged away from the ice, intent on seeing the world as it should be, as the prophecy foretold.

"Wait!" Ahren cried, but Solyana hardly spared him a moment. She would see this new world; she would be the first to take in the future promised to her people. Only a row of trees stood between her and her view of a green Mothmar. A grin stretched across her face as Solyana burst through the foliage and onto the other side.

The stretching sky was a brilliant blue and filled with a bright yellow sun. Birds wove in and out of puffy white clouds that peppered the expanse. And just below those clouds was green, as far as her eyes could see. Trees, grass, hills, mountains, and valleys, all layered in colors Solyana had only dreamed about or seen in Jonas's paintings.

She choked out a laugh, falling to her knees at the edge of the tree line, hardly feeling the snow on her legs. "We did it!" she yelled into the echoing morning. "We..." She turned, half expecting to see Gamaliel, Lone, and Jonas standing behind her. Instead, a bedraggled man was stumbling through the trees, hand shielding his eyes from the sun.

"Did what?" Ahren examined his tunic and then his hands, which still shook. He looked wildly around.

Solyana's grin faltered, as she remembered everything in its fullness. She had left a sleeping Gamaliel, an injured Lone, and Jonas behind. Afraid the climb up the mountain would bring her friends to harm, Solyana had forged ahead to retrieve this boy alone. And Ahren, a victim to Stasis, a Taka Reu curse, had no idea he had been trapped for years. Solyana's eyes found the blood stains on his tunic and arms and wondered again what he'd been through, what he'd seen or done before he'd been spirited away to this peak.

How she wished she was with her friends now as they woke to a new spring day. They would forgive her the moment they saw the green, surely. The faster she got back down the mountain, the better it would be.

She straightened, a soft smile on her face, and shuffled over the snow to Ahren.

"Ahren," she said, and the boy—or man, she wasn't sure how old he was—looked up with red-rimmed eyes. "Let's get down to Endirinn as soon as we can. I lost my supplies, but we can find water and hunt—"

"Endirinn?" Ahren stared past her, surveying Mothmar. "How far are we from Sodur?"

Solyana blinked. Though she knew he was Priestess Avi's brother, it was strange hearing this ancient person speak of one of the villages from her valley. "We're quite a ways. The valley is about one moon cycle to the southwest. I'm from Vestur."

His mouth dropped open for a moment, but then he nodded curtly and said, "Are you going back home?"

"Like I said, we need supplies first."

"No." Ahren continued trekking down the overgrown path. "There's no time."

Solyana blinked. "Hold on! You can't go on your own." Or, in truth, not at all. She couldn't let him go back to Sodur. Not only had his people been gone for hundreds of years, but the deal with Erval still clanged loudly in Solyana's mind. She needed to bring Ahren in exchange for her sister's safety. "I have friends in Endirinn, Ahren. We can help you find your family."

He stopped walking so abruptly, Solyana barely kept herself from running into him. "How do you know my name? Do you know my sisters—my...sister?" he corrected.

Solyana nodded.

"But why are we *here*?" He looked around, a hand trying to run fingers through matted hair. "Why am *I* here? I don't understand." He took a shaky breath before focusing on Solyana once more. "Look, thank you for whatever you did, but my family needs me."

Solyana opened her mouth but closed it again. Anything she revealed would only distress him further. Gamaliel would have a plan on how to share information with Ahren, in time. "We both need to get to Endirinn first. We'll figure things out from there."

He shrugged and continued.

Solyana soon realized their trek down Mount Endirinn was going to be far faster than her path up. With the lack of snow and impassable ice, it just came down to winding around trees and boulders. She wondered if Björg had made it back to Gamaliel or if they would run into the mammoth along the way.

The snow was already thinning, though Solyana was curious how it had gone so quickly. During their travels, she and Jonas had speculated if the green would be something to happen overnight or if it would be a gradual change. Jonas had theorized if it were instantaneous, it would be an ecological nightmare: flooding, landslides, and destruction of people and animals alike. But the terrain didn't seem too terrible to Solyana, in spite of how quickly it had turned.

"Did you lose anyone in the battle?" Ahren's question stopped her, and she looked over at him, her mind running through the details she'd been given. She remembered reading something about a battle, a scroll Priestess Avi had given her. Was that what he was referring to?

"Oh *häfa*, you probably don't even know about it." He took a heavy breath. "Were you just hiking up here when you found me? By the stars..." He ran a hand down his face, his features in anguish once more. "I'm so sorry to have to tell you this. There was an attack by the Taka Reu on our valley." He reached out and grasped Solyana's shoulder. "They attacked our valley and the Temple Celestial. There was fighting and..." His eyes drifted away. They darkened.

Solyana braced herself. Ahren should know the truth. He needed to know the events he had left were centuries in the past, that the sister he spoke of was still alive and going to come for him in Thonethren. She had to tell him something.

"Look, Ahren. Before we get to Endirinn, you need to know..."

He blinked at her, his head cocked to the side.

"You've been up there for a while. People are going to be in shock when we arrive back in town...for a number of reasons."

He squinted at her. "For what reasons?"

"There's been a change in the weather, for one. Our land had been frozen over for...as long as I can remember."

Ahren gave her a look that conveyed just how crazy he thought she was.

"Why do you think I'm dressed like this?" She motioned to her parka and mukluks, which were altogether too warm. She began to take the parka off. "It's been a long time, and a prophecy has been fulfilled. Me coming back down this mountain with you is going to answer some questions and raise a whole bunch more."

Something shifted behind Ahren's eyes, and Solyana's stomach twisted. He scoffed. "I was just in the valley. Things weren't frozen—what are you trying to say?" His breathing grew rapid, his cheeks brightening a shade.

"Maybe we should get down the mountain fir—"

"How long have I been up here?" he asked, his eyes pinning her with a wildness from either panic or rage; they shone beneath the dirt and blood on his face.

Survival wrapped its hand around Solyana's throat and squeezed, trapping the answer in her throat. She couldn't tell him; she didn't know what he'd do.

"I know where your sister is," she said instead.

Ahren took a step back, his gaze softening. "Is she in the city?"

"Well..." Solyana resumed walking, trusting he would follow. "We know where she was last. And we think we know where she's headed next. That's why I need you with me, okay? We're going to find her."

"Who is 'we?'" Ahren's lips turned down into a frown. He felt his new beard with both hands. His brow furrowed.

"Let's just get down this mountain. My friends will explain every-thing soon."

They hiked until dusk before settling down, the air growing warmer as they descended. Solyana tried to make a fire using her Heitt, but no matter how much she beseeched the Father of the Day, no fire would come forth. Thankfully, Ahren stepped in, using his Vior Fera to gather wood to start a blaze the old-fashioned way.

Solyana's recent past wriggled like a worm in the back of her mind; her departure to the mountain alone, her use of the Taka Reu since her meeting with Erval. She knew a conversation with her friends was coming—a conversation she wished she could avoid. Was it too much to hope for forgiveness amidst the disgust and anger they were sure to feel? The weight of their judgment, the complications and delicacy Ahren presented, the beauty of the green... Solyana tried to simply enjoy the warm air, the sounds of birds, and the knowledge that Rhuth would be safe.

She woke to another full day of hiking, and by the time the two of them reached the northern gate of Endirinn, Solyana wanted nothing more than to eat a good meal and sleep.

"Wow," Ahren said, his eyes on the city. "This place is beautiful."

"It...is." Solyana's lips twisted as she led them both toward Temple Rinn. The city was more austere than she remembered. As if, in the few short days she had been gone, they had repaired and repainted. Stately white buildings, gilded in golden filigree, grew denser as they approached Endirinn's heart.

She reached for Ahren's hand, careful not to lose him in the bustle of the Main Square's marketplace. He was her ticket to keeping her sister safe, and she held on tight as she led him through the cobblestoned streets. Lanterns lined their way, hanging by rope strung between buildings. When had those been placed? Solyana hadn't remembered seeing them before.

At the heart of the Main Square there was music and lively chatter. The people of Mothmar were celebrating—but of course they were! She had brought the green! Their salvation from the eternal cold!

Dragging Ahren behind her, Solyana rushed closer into the Square, where she stopped dead in her tracks. In place of the simple stone fountain that had served as the marker of the center of the city, a statue now stood. A majestic figure, draped in a parka carved to look as though it were caught in the wind, a pack strapped to the shoulder of an outstretched arm, a flame held in its open palm. The face was a meticulous likeness, smooth feminine features marked by the stark carving of a scar—the same scar that was burned to the surface of Solyana's face now. She stared at her image in the stone before her eyes dropped to the candles and flowers strewn across its base, to the people who knelt there in prayer.

A gasp sounded from her left, then her right, and before long, there was a crowd forming a perimeter around her and Ahren.

"The Saint of Endrinn!" one cried out into the night air. "She has returned from the dead!"

ABANDONED

RHUTH

H ER FEET WEREN'T BLEEDING or bruised—that was her first thought. The circular door she'd discovered months ago proved to be almost impossible to open. She would have attempted to break it down before, but her captor had always been present, waiting. For what? Rhuth didn't know.

But the old priestess had been gone, first for days, then a week, leaving Rhuth alone to kick at the door until her soles were pulp and her fists were numb. It took every fingernail breaking and every aching bone to snap—but she made it through.

And that was her second thought. She was through…but to where? Blinking against a warmly lit room, Rhuth slowly propped herself up on her elbows, eyes searching the corners and shadows. It smelled like sweat and stagnant water. Water… Her tongue throbbed as she pulled it from the roof of her mouth, so dry her throat felt like it was lined with knives. She had to find water. Dust particles floated lazily in the stream of light coming through the window, and the stale air stuck in her lungs like honey.

She coughed, her chest contracting and spasming like she hadn't moved in years. Which could very well be the case, she knew. Rhuth spotted a pitcher of water on a dresser across from her bed and willed her body out from under the suffocating wool blankets.

Stumbling from her cot, she grasped at the pitcher and drank too quickly. Water dribbled down her chin and neck, soaking the light shift that fell to her knees. She wiped at her face with the back of her hand, feeling lucidity come with hydration.

Free.

She was free.

After biding her time for so long, she had control of her own body once more. She almost gave a shout of exultation when the smile that had begun its slow pull on her lips halted. The priestess surely wasn't gone for good, was she? How much time did she truly have before she was tossed carelessly back into the Maze?

Her hands shook as she set the pitcher back in its place. This wasn't the first time freedom had come—the first time, it had been stripped away from her. Her falcon, Halina, had been her means of independence. But Rhuth had known she couldn't allow her tethered creature to return to the valley, not with Priestess Avi lying in wait.

Rhuth had released her bird, steering her clear of the valley and most certain death. Losing Halina had sent her spiraling, her heart and mind unable to grapple with the loss. Time had become alien to her then, and she'd been unable to keep track of the sun without the use of her falcon's eyes. And just before that, she had seen Solyana in the Maze alongside her. Both caused fissures that broke her mind. Something feral had emerged, her body rocking back and forth, her aching throat screaming at her sister to escape, to save Rhuth. Had it been a hallucination? She couldn't know. But now, outside the Maze, she felt her mind returning, her understanding filling her, suffusing her with strength. She was no longer some caged animal. And she never would be again.

A small round mirror sat beside the pitcher and Rhuth felt a jolt of foreboding. What would she see when she peered into its frame? Would she recognize the girl that she was? Before she could waste any more time, fearing the priestess could be back at any moment, Rhuth lifted the mirror.

"Oh..." she whispered as her shaking fingers reached up to touch her face. Her voice sounded so different here on the outside. Her face was different, too. There were no mirrors in the Maze, but she had *felt* her face. Foolishly, she had thought the priestess had healed her. But it was not so. The smooth flesh she had felt in the Maze had been a lie. Fingers tracing the lines, Rhuth's eye welled with pressure. One eye, deep brown and whole, the other a mess of jagged scar tissue and angry pink flesh.

It hurt to cry.

Rhuth sniffed and slammed the mirror back down, turning it over on the wooden dresser. She wouldn't look at herself again.

Priestess Avi was not who she said she was. In fact, her true name was Pallah. It hadn't taken Rhuth long to figure out what was going on once she'd found the center of the Maze. From there, she'd been able to hear the priestess talk to herself as she piddled about the room. And what Rhuth heard had surprised her. Priestess Avi was not the same eloquent, self-assured leader that spoke to the masses of Mothmar; the woman was terrified. There was something, someone, hunting her. And staying in the valley kept her hidden from this threat. Rhuth hadn't been able to decipher who exactly it was, but she was certain about one thing.

Rhuth's people had been lied to.

She took a breath. She had to find her family. There wasn't much in the room, but she did find a couple of pairs of thick socks that she rolled up over her feet before heading to the door. Her hand shook as it grasped the handle, but she could not wait here, to be discovered and sent back into that pitch-dark Maze. No. She had waited too long, had worked too hard.

Cracking the door open, she peeked out. No one was in the hall. In fact, the entire place sounded deserted. Rhuth grinned to herself. Padding down the hall, and then the stairs, she found herself in the sanctuary of the Temple Celestial, and wariness began to take hold. The room was covered in dust. Parchment and refuse littered the floor. Rhuth slowed her steps, picking her way through the desecrated space, trying to keep the panic from clawing its way up her throat. There had to be an explanation, surely. A reason the valley's holiest place was left in disarray.

Reaching the double front doors, she opened them to the morning sun, expecting the market beyond to be filled with vendors. But the courtyard was empty. Wind whistled through forgotten booths and upturned carts. Piles of snow, usually cleared by Vatin Fera, were swirled into heaps by wind and time. The usual noise and bustle of children running amuck were replaced by a silence that chimed discordantly in her soul.

The valley appeared abandoned.

Mouth gone dry again, Rhuth stumbled from the temple, uncaring of the freezing air that whipped her hair and stung her face. Breaths coming in frantic gasps, she waded and slipped through piles of drift. Running, she had to keep running. Mama and Papa would be at home. They would know what had happened. They would hug her and tell her it was all going to be okay. Fridmey would be there, too; she would tease Rhuth, but Rhuth knew it was out of love. Solyana would be back from her journey, having heeded Rhuth's warnings and returned with haste. They would eat together. Rhuth's stomach rumbled. Maybe Mama had made some venison stew.

Blue-lipped and shivering, Rhuth finally arrived at her family's home in Vestur. No smoke rose from the chimney; no lantern flickered at the door. Stumbling through the seal skin flap, she fell, gasping for air. Snow dusted the floor beneath her palms, and there was no fire in the hearth. Her home did not feel like home, shadows lurking in its corners.

"Mama!" she cried. "Papa! Solyana! Fridmey!"

Nothing greeted her but the whispers of wind and the harrowing feeling that something was gravely wrong.

Hot tears sprung from her eyes as she curled up in a corner of the room, her only company a tattered blanket. She wrapped herself and rocked back and forth, her body attempting to soothe her heart but failing.

She was alone.

There was nothing here.

THE OBSERVATORY

PHINEAS

AFTER PACKING HIS SLIPPERS into the very top of his bag, Phineas's shaking hands moved to secure the leather straps. It took him four tries. He released a huff of air and wiped his sweaty palms on his robes when a single chime within a row of bronze bells hanging on the wall rang.

Phineas startled, eyes swinging across the row until he found the one listlessly bobbing among its brethren. It was labeled 'Observatory.' He glanced out his window at the full moon. The bell sounded again.

"It's not like you're getting any older," the steward mumbled. The bell rang a third time, incessant and jangling. "Oh, shut it!" he shouted and shuffled out of his rooms.

Moving through the halls of the castle, Phineas steeled his mind. After years of living with the most powerful Mann Tala alive—perhaps the only one alive—he had learned a thing or two about protecting himself. Erval had promised not to intrude into Phineas's mind, but the steward knew better than to trust a word from the king of Thonethren.

He whispered a prayer to the Mother Below, his face hot and red as he passed up the final stairwell to the observatory. He knocked gently on the door and cleared his throat.

"Come in!"

Phineas entered the circular room to find the King's face pressed to the cup of a telescope, one hand beckoning frantically behind him. "I think I found it, Phin!"

"And that would be?"

King Erval stood erect and raised an eyebrow.

Phineas knew quite well what he referred to, but he played the simpleton. He was good at that.

Erval steepled his fingers and pressed them to his lips, giving Phineas a once over. "The cluster. The grouping of stars I have been seeking to truly understand their *religion*." He blinked and spread his arms wide. "Phin! How can you be so daft?" Erval turned to look at the corner of the room, where someone sat, hidden in shadow. "*You* would never be so daft, would you, my sweet?"

"Never, my King," a feminine voice answered.

Phineas squinted but could see only a robed figure, legs crossed, holding a glass of something amber. The ice in it clinked as she turned it in her hand. It was not uncommon for Erval to bring his courtesans to observe his work, finding more pleasure in their minds than their bodies. Beside her sat a large cage containing a sabertoothed tiger. Phineas never understood Erval and his exotics. He pried his eyes away.

"My apologies, m'lord."

"I swear, your head is a brick." Erval turned back to the telescope and lowered it to Phineas's height. "No matter. Look here!"

Phineas shuffled forward and bent low, his spectacles coming into contact with the cup of the telescope, pressing them uncomfortably into his skin.

"Give me those," Erval said, reaching around and plucking the spectacles off his steward's face. "*Häfa*, these are dripping! Phineas, you sweat more than a pig on a summer's day."

Pigs didn't sweat, Phineas knew. But he bit his tongue, glad for the insult. It distracted the king from the real reason sweat soaked his garments. Things had been set in motion, and there was no turning back now.

Turning the wheel on the telescope, the viewport went from blurry to crisp, and he took in the constellation above.

"This is it, isn't it?"

Tension fell from Phineas's shoulders. "Afraid not, my King." And he was relieved. From his studies, Phineas knew the shape of the constellation, and this wasn't it. Over the past few years, chatter was rising of an ancient religion—different from the Celestials and the Taka Reu—that promised to hold power. And its central source seemed to hinge on a specific constellation.

Phineas would have to find it, and before Erval, to know what kind of havoc the king could wreak if he were able to access it. For Phineas knew that, given time, anything Erval pursued became a weapon in his hands.

"Perhaps if we find someone to teach us?" the steward intoned, stepping back from the eyepiece. He used a piece of his robes to rub the lens. "Another reason for my upcoming trip! For all we know, this could be the ever-elusive Hjörtur Cluster."

"Give me that!" Erval shoved Phineas from the telescope to look once more, spectacles protruding from his back pocket. "This resembles nothing of a stag! I swear you're blind, Phin."

Phineas plucked his spectacles from Erval's back pocket and worked on bending them back into shape. "In that, sire, you're not wrong." He fitted them onto his face, dabbed his forehead with his sleeve, and backed away a few paces.

"Well, I'm going to get Jothan up here for a second opinion. He's apt to see what I do." Erval turned to the shadow. "A bright lad, isn't he?"

"Much like a shooting star." The woman from the corner took a sip of her drink.

Phineas began to shuffle toward the door as Erval chuckled.

"Ha! Indeed. Brilliant and full of luck!"

Phineas mumbled, "All flash and no substance." His hand reached for the pull ring.

"What was that, Phineas?"

Phineas paused, a drop of sweat sliding into his collar. "Nothing, sir."

"Ring for him. And be off with you." Erval flicked a hand in his steward's direction, his face pressed back against the telescope. "You're leaving at dawn, yes?"

"Yes, m'lord."

"And where are you going again?"

"East Mothmar, to find that Seer I spoke of. He will know of the constellation we seek. He will understand what we must do to secure your reign."

Erval stood and turned to face Phineas. The steward couldn't help but feel it was the first time the king had truly looked at him in months. "That's quite a distance. Why don't you simply use the finnevel you made? It would be far easier to search through Kjarn's Eye than it would be to travel for weeks on end. Don't you agree?"

Phineas swallowed, his hands rasping over each other, as they were wont to do in times of distress. "I do it for you, sire, as you seem so intent on finding this ancient religion. I thought I could look for guidance regarding its source. Besides, I think it would be good for me. Good for..." Phineas took a breath and squeezed his eyes shut, not wanting to see his partner's face as he said, "The exercise would do me good."

Erval scoffed into a laugh. "That it would, indeed, Phin."

Phineas felt it then, the press of Erval attempting to tether to his soul. His eyes flew open and locked with the man across the room. "You said you wouldn't." He shifted his attention from the king to the woman in shadow behind him, feeling splayed open, raw. How dare he attempt it, and with a stranger present.

Lifting both hands in mock surrender, Erval began to walk about the circular room. "Yes, I did promise, didn't I?" The King's eyes roved across the ceiling, and Phineas turned and rang the bell for Jothan. Another body to focus on, someone else to manipulate or tease. Without looking back, Phineas opened the door to leave when Erval's voice came once more, all prior jesting dissolved. "Any faithful steward would trust his king fully. Would he not?"

Gulping for air, sweat beading across his lower back, Phineas's soft hand clutched the door handle like a lifeline. "Of course, my King."

Phineas had mere seconds before Erval would step into his mind, but too much lay there. Too much of which the king himself was unaware, much that Phineas had kept from him. The painstaking care he'd taken in every interaction over so many years, allowing Erval to grasp parts of the whole, but never the entire thing. Little by little, he had sated the man's efforts, creating a directed path on which Erval could tread. A path meant just for him, while Phineas waited just on the other side, fear threatening to choke him.

Erval smiled. "I'll keep my word, old friend."

Phineas sighed with relief. The steward turned to see the King's eyes filled with...was it love? Remorse?

"Stay safe."

"Of course, my King." And with a bow, he extricated himself from the room, still keeping the guard up in his mind, waiting anxiously for any intrusion. Pulling the door shut, he released the last of his breath, feeling nothing but the sweat pouring down his temples. He pulled a handkerchief from his pocket, closed his eyes, and dabbed.

"Hiya, Phin!"

"Jothan!" Phineas's hand flew to his breast as his eyes flew open. "You startled me."

"Clearly." Jothan's youthful features twisted into a crooked grin that turned Phineas's stomach.

Phineas's hand lowered of its own accord, the handkerchief dripping. "You will respect those in authority over—"

"Oh, are we speaking of you here?" Jothan interrupted him, one eyebrow arching. "Last I checked, we are both stewards." He circled Phineas slowly, a shark stalking its prey. "You're looking tired, old man. Perhaps you should rest up before your trip."

Phineas felt his face grow red and despised himself for it. "Erval and I have worked together for years, Jothan. You wouldn't begin to understand the loyalty a partnership like ours establishes." The words soured on his tongue, the lie of it.

"Yes, loyalty." Jothan rolled his eyes and puffed his cheeks in exasperation. "That's why he brought me into his inner circle, eh? Because he's so loyal...to you."

Phineas wanted to smack the smug grin off the young man's face but took a breath instead. It was good Erval had a new plaything—a direction to hone his ire. "Is *she* in there?" Jothan slicked back his hair. "She actually spoke to me last week."

Phineas's interest piqued. Erval did not keep his courtesans for longer than a day or two. He squinted at the boy. Jothan was young and had yet to see the evil that lay behind the door Phineas had just closed. He had yet to know the darkness that wrapped this city and choked the very life from it. Had yet to feel the evil that poured from the man they advised.

"A miracle, I'm sure." Phineas gave a curt bow. "You'll find the two of them in there. Good day, Jothan."

Jothan. The name curdled on Phineas's tongue. But he soothed himself, knowing if all went to plan, he would never have to entertain that horrible mollusk of a boy another day in his life.

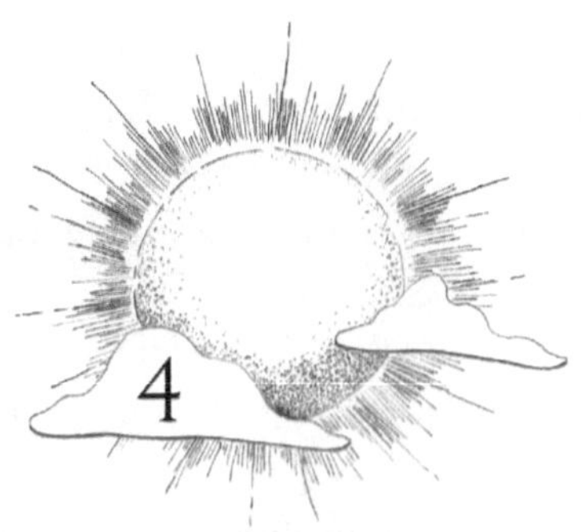

THE SAINT OF ENDIRINN

SOLYANA

"The Saint of Endirinn!"

"Solyana Marusda! She's returned from the dead!"

"Someone get the priest!"

"After so long! She returns!"

The echoing cheers and chants of the people of Endirinn muted to a din in Solyana's ears. She had been so concerned with Ahren finding out about how long he had been gone, she had never questioned the duration of her own absence.

Mind spinning, Solyana searched through the details of her climb up the mountain, her time in the meadow, the quake and its dissolution of the peak before they escaped the mountaintop. Nothing indicate a lapse, but the evidence before her refused to be dismissed.

Her eyes landed on Ahren, and she carefully positioned herself behind him, keeping his body between her and the people pleading for her attention. He had aged. The detail came again in full. Kneeling across from her in the meadow, she had watched as his face had lengthened, his shoulders had broadened, and his face had darkened with stubble. Had it affected her, too? Time had twisted somehow on that peak. The question was for how long?

"Solyana!" a commanding voice drew her back to the present, her head whipping around to see a large man holding a leather bag, rushing for them. She flung her hands out in front of her, barring him from touching her. "You live!" He knelt before her, his ice-blue eyes pale as the sky had been from the peak. His hook nose prodded familiarity in Solyana's mind before his long white hair braided into his beard, solidified it.

"Rorhan?" she asked, confusion and fear galloping up her throat. "How?" The word contained so much more than its simplicity suggested.

He squeezed her into a hug, lifting her from the ground and laughing great belly laughs. Just a few days ago, he and his sister, Pahlak, had helped save her from Orson's men. She remembered his suspicion when they first met over a fire, his tribe splayed out beneath the moon, asking to keep one of their mammoths.

"Gamaliel will not believe it." He lowered her to the ground, a grin stretching across his bearded face. "I see why you did not recognize me," he said with a wink. "I am much larger now." He patted his belly and laughed again. "My language has grown also."

"Who is this?" Ahren asked her quietly as he straightened his clothes, an edge to his voice.

"I am Rorhan! Great friend to Solyana." He clamped a hand down on Ahren's shoulder. "You are Ahren, yes? We have waited so long for you."

The crowd around them was still pressing in.

"How long?" Her voice held a note of panic she couldn't quell.

"Hey!" Rorhan barked at the people, their chattering increasing by the second. "Do not displease the Saint! She requires rest!"

The people backed away, bowing, whispering, and offering prayer.

The Saint? Solyana's eyes found the statue again.

"We go." Rorhan pulled the strap of his bag over his head and across his chest, securing it in place. "Before they get the priest and trap you in that temple."

"Rorhan—"

"Trap?" Ahren's gaze shifted from the temple to the market. "I just need supplies, and I'll be on my way."

Rorhan rounded behind them, resting a meaty hand on each of their shoulders, pushing them forward through the square. "It is late; the market is closing. Come have dinner. Lone is making stew."

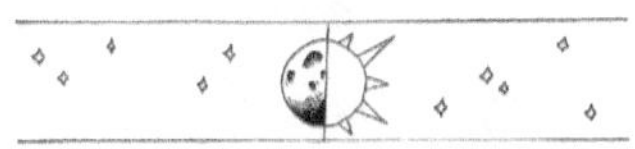

They hurried south, out of the city, following a winding path that shifted from cobblestone to dirt. Rorhan led the way, his stride threatening to leave Solyana and Ahren behind him.

"Where are we going?" Ahren whispered. "This guy is huge. You're sure you know him?"

"Yes."

"Because it kind of seemed like you didn't know him."

"I did." She shook her head. "I do."

"If you say so."

Solyana sighed. "Look, something is off, okay? I've only been gone a few days, but Rorhan... The city is..."

Older. It couldn't be denied.

Her heart thudded in her chest to the beat of her feet as she tried to catch up to the man before them. Would she even recognize Gamaliel? It burned in her heart; she had to know before she saw him.

"Rorhan?"

"Almost there!" he said over his shoulder.

Solyana sped up, leaving Ahren behind. "Rorhan," she said again. "Look, you need to tell me if...I don't know how to..." She took a breath. "How long have I been gone?"

Rorhan slowed to a stop, one hand clutching the strap across his chest, the other tugging on his beard. He squinted toward the setting sun, lips moving soundlessly before nodding firmly once. "Five."

"Five...what?"

His eyes softened. "Years. It has been five years, Solyana."

Any joy that had filled her for the prophecy's resolution evaporated. Her mouth fell open, and she heard Ahren say something but couldn't make it out. Rorhan continued walking and Solyana's own feet followed, though her mind could not proceed.

"No," she said with a shake of her head. "No. I only left a few nights ago, Rorhan. I was just here."

But she couldn't reconcile the things she had seen. The green returning so soon, Ahren's physical changes, Rorhan's growth, and the statue in town, the reaction of Endirinn's people.

"We thought the worst, Solyana," Rorhan said soberly. "All but Jonas." His head fell back as an unexpected bark of laughter burst from his mouth. "That little know-it-all was right!" He shook his head and placed a hand on Solyana's shoulder. "I know not what happened to you these last years. But I do know someone has been waiting to find out." He motioned with his head toward a small house set amongst tall grass.

Heart in her throat, Solyana watched as a tiny child ran through the front garden, squealing with delight. She wove her way through the green before scrambling up on top of a small boulder and launching herself headlong into the arms of a man, his back to Solyana.

"Again!" the girl cried as she twisted from the man's grip, tore back through the weeds, and threw herself from the rock into the air.

The man laughed as he caught her, his long hair swinging out behind him.

Solyana knew that laugh, the sound of it ringing in her bones.

He turned, bearded face grinning, the small girl in his arms. His eyes locked on Solyana's, and she could tell, even in the darkening eve, his face went white.

"Solyana?" The word was a breath as he stumbled forward.

The little girl squirmed from his arms and ran to Rorhan, who was encouraging Ahren into the small, firelit home. It became only the two of them beneath the dim sky, the warm breeze tossing Solyana's hair in the wind.

"You're alive," Gamaliel said, taking another step forward. "I always hoped, but I never...I never..."

Solyana ran to him.

She had lain in his arms just a few short nights ago, and her heart still beat to the rhythm of his own. His familiar face held new lines, his waterfall of dark hair was longer and bore a few glimmers of gray, his beard transformed him completely, but his eyes--his eyes. Those were the same. And in them she saw hope, love, and sorrow.

He wrapped her close, hands drawing around her head and waist. Solyana breathed him in, all wood smoke and cedar, the iron tang of a cave. And something else...something different that made her think of the few nights her father had come home after long meetings with the council.

Gamaliel sobbed into her neck, shoulders racking with grief. Solyana clutched him tighter, feeling the differences in him. His broadened shoulders, scratchy beard, a familiar stranger.

"We did it, Gam. We did it! The green!" she said as she pulled away, her eyes searching his for approval.

He nodded, his dark eyes scouring every inch of her face. His fingers gently trailed across her cheek, her forehead, down the tip of her nose. Chin quivering, he sniffed as tears pooled in his eyes. "You did, Sol. *You* did."

Solyana's heart wrenched at his emphasis. She had yet to ask for forgiveness, had yet to confess her sins. Her actions, unknown to her friends, was like a boulder gaining speed down the mountain, bringing her five years into the future, distant from everything she knew. She had to own up to her choices, come clean about her use of the Taka Reu.

Her own eyes filling with tears, Solyana found Gamaliel once more and it was then that it occurred to her; the little girl he'd been playing with could be his own.

She thought back to their journey to Endirinn, the tension with Lone at the start. Had they found solace in each other upon her disappearance?

Solyana took a step back, holding her arms tight against her chest. "Five years," she said, unsure she wanted to know the answer. "That's a long time."

He straightened his shoulders and wiped his eyes. "It is."

"Enough time to start a family."

He cocked his head, a single eyebrow rising. "Lone thought so."

"Oh..." The relief she had felt in seeing him dried up and was replaced with dread. "How old is she?"

"Marin?" He stuck a thumb in the direction of the small house. "She just turned three."

Three years. It had only taken him three years to forget her. "That's a pretty name," she said, averting her gaze.

"Rorhan's grandmother's or something." Gamaliel waved a hand. "I don't remember."

Solyana blinked at him. "Rorhan?"

Gamaliel's eyebrows scrunched together before understanding drew his eyes wide. "Heavens, Sol. She's Lone and Rorhan's daughter."

"Oh." Solyana stared at her feet, heat on her cheeks.

Gamaliel cupped her chin, bringing her gaze to meet his own. "You hungry?" He smiled and motioned for her to enter the small house.

"Famished." Solyana opened the door.

THE FALCONRY

RHUTH

WIND WHISTLED THROUGH THE slats of the boarded windows of the falconry, causing the dusting of snow near Rhuth's feet to dance. Sharp curved talons dug into Rhuth's shoulder, but she reveled in the pain. It meant she was free; she was alive. Her fingers, shaking from the cold, brushed through the bird's soft neck feathers.

Where to go? Alone, she had little means to survive but her own grit and tether to the birds. The valley's emptiness drew deep concern. Had the priestess done something more heinous than trapping a single girl? Or perhaps it was a turn of nature, a stroke of the Celestials' will, like a plague.

Only then did it occur to her Priestess Avi perhaps allowed her to escape, that she was biding her time. But why?

A creak came from the steps below.

Rhuth's eyes slid to the trapdoor in the floor, awaiting its rise, upward and inward, into the circular room.

"I thought I'd find you here." Priestess Avi's voice came from the floor. But when the woman stepped through, it was a different woman entirely. Rhuth took an involuntary step backward. "I know you care for the things."

"Who are you?" But Rhuth knew. Deep down, she knew. But how?

The old woman who had been the spiritual leader turned captor was now a much younger woman, not much older than Mama. Her long white hair was to her shoulders and the color of milky tea. The wrinkles that had dragged her face downward had disappeared, changing her face entirely.

The woman scrutinized Rhuth in a similar fashion, her gaze roving over Rhuth's damaged face.

"You're a little beast now, aren't you?" the woman asked.

"Who are you?" Rhuth repeated, unwilling to accept what she saw. "And where is my family? Where is everyone?" She ground her toes into the wood grain of the floor, wrangling the panic bubbling in her chest. The falcons nesting above her began to shake and shift, growing restless.

"Ah." The woman reached up to feel her own face and body before giving an impish smile. "I look nothing like the Priestess Avi you knew, do I?" The woman's knuckles turned white on the long metal staff the priestess always carried. Its presence was almost enough to convince Rhuth—almost.

"Because you defeated her?" she guessed.

"Because I *am* her." Priestess Avi released her staff, the rod remaining vertical of its own accord, and she began to slowly pace the room. "I hold many Gifts and many lives. I can change what I will. Keeping myself an ancient woman had been advantageous." She leered at the birds. "It's not anymore."

Rhuth's fear bit deeper and she tugged on the tether to her falcons. Two of them fluttered down and took perch on each of her shoulders.

"I checked your home first, of course," Priestess Avi said, wrapping her shawl closer around her shoulders. Frigid wind tore through the slatted wood of the falconry. "You must be freezing."

"I don't really feel it," Rhuth lied.

She chuckled. "You don't have to act tough with me, dear."

"If you're here to lock me up again..." Rhuth kept the trapdoor in her sights. One of the birds at her shoulder screeched. "I won't let you."

"I see that," Priestess Avi said. She slowed to a stop, eyes searching Rhuth's. "But there's no need to worry." She lifted her hands in mock surrender. "You're free to do as you please."

Rhuth narrowed her eye at the priestess.

Priestess Avi sighed and circled back to her staff. "I thought the purpose of the Maze would have been more clear, dear. Your power. Your way with your Gifts. It's unlike anything I've seen."

"I don't care what you've seen. Where is my family? What happened to Vestur?"

"But now, I don't know." Her scrutiny hardened as she ignored Rhuth's questions. "I don't think you even know what you're doing." Priestess Avi's lips curled into a sneer. "And if you don't know, then you can't help me. Perhaps I *should* do away with you. One less person for him to use."

Him? Fear lanced through Rhuth like a spear. She silently asked the Celestials for help, calling upon them to push wind into the room, to close the trap door, to bring the falcons to attention.

The Celestials must have heard her. The priestess whirled around at the sound of the wooden door slamming into the ground. Snow swirled like a tiny tornado throughout the room, and when Rhuth looked up, she found the falcons, their wings spread, beaks agape, chests puffed out in readiness to strike.

One of the falcons on Rhuth's shoulder released a scream, and the others joined it, dissonant notes forming a chorus of warning.

"You will not touch me, Witch. Now, tell me where my family has gone." As if the weather itself obeyed her, Rhuth felt her connection to the wind strengthen and grow, whirling the snow faster and faster until the older woman cried out.

Then it stopped by Rhuth's command.

The room fell silent, and Priestess Avi straightened, dusting errant flakes from her dress and shawl.

"I must know," the woman said, looking at Rhuth with avid curiosity, "the mystery that is your abilities."

"Tell me of my family!" Rhuth's patience was at its end, and the birds strained to act.

The priestess sighed. "Your father ran off some time ago. He searches for your sister. Your mother and elder sister journeyed with the others toward the coast. There was nothing left for any of them here."

Her shoulders fell, and the falcons took to the air and back to their roosts. Rhuth's skin throbbed where they had gripped her; she might even be bleeding.

"They left," she repeated.

They left *her*.

"Yes."

Rhuth tried to reason a course of action but came up short. Her village, her home, her family and her purpose within it, all empty. Abandoned.

"I suppose you can come with me. Unless, of course, you prefer to stay here." The priestess blinked at her, fingers trailing along her staff. "You could join my Serviseer, Phassa and her family. They've finally given up, too."

Rhuth caught the woman's eyes in her own. "The valley has become uninhabitable?"

"I have much to tell you, Rhuth, if you want to hear it. I still think you will serve a purpose within this prophecy, but I need you to decide where you stand." Priestess Avi took a breath. "Will you leave with Phassa and go east? Or will you come with me and go north?"

It was both too much information and not enough. "What's north?" Rhuth asked.

"A man," Avi said frankly. "A man from whom, for all these years, I have been hiding."

"Who?"

"The king of Thonethren. When I was a girl of your age, he sought to control me. Naturally, I was against the idea. I've done a good job of evading his notice until now. He's finally found me."

Rhuth's mouth went dry. "How?"

"Phassa's young son," she said with a shake of her head. "The king spoke into his mind. Someone must have shown him exactly where to look. My defenses were strong, but his power and dark will is stronger."

"I don't know what any of that means." Rhuth's family, at least her mother and Fridmey, were headed toward the coast. She would follow after them and get as far away from this priestess as possible. "It doesn't matter. I'm not going with you." Perhaps she could persuade Phassa to shift west and accompany her.

"You're right to be angry. But I have a final proposition."

Rhuth didn't want to hear it. Her hand gripped the strap on the trap door and pulled.

"Your sister, Solyana." Avi spoke loudly to be heard over the squeak of the hinges. "I believe the king has her in his grip or soon will. I'm not strong enough on my own to contend with him. But your Gifts, your power... If we leave now, we may be able to save her."

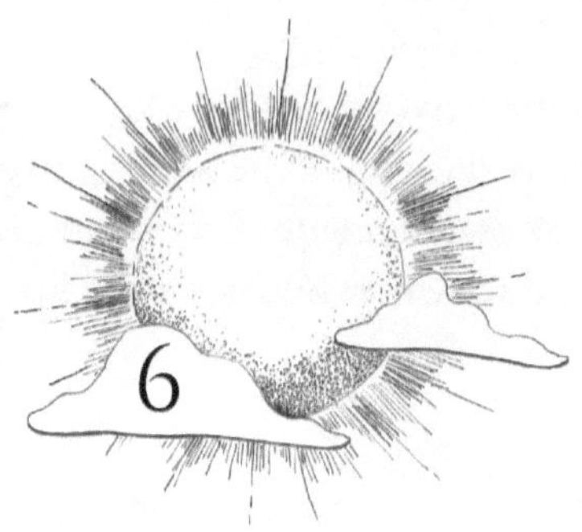

CONFESSION

SOLYANA

W ALKING INTO THE SMALL home, Solyana's eyes caught on the small child as she peeled out from behind the couch.

"Papa! Come get me!" she squealed.

Rorhan's voice rumbled from down the narrow hallway. "Where's my little *Elskan*?"

Ahren stood to the right of the door, hands by his sides, one arm clasping the other elbow. He gave Gamaliel a nod; the latter reached out to give the traditional Mothmari greeting.

The child giggled and ran, looking back over her shoulder at her father coming down the hall. She ran straight into Solyana's legs, gripping and pulling herself up on her tip toes.

"Up!" she cried.

"Oh!" Solyana pulled her into her arms, reminded of when Rhuth was little.

Marin's eyes widened as if only realizing then that she didn't know this stranger in her home and twisted out of Solyana's grip. Even in that small act, an ache stretched in Solyana's chest. So much life had been lived without her.

Ducking under a low-hanging beam, Rorhan came into the living space with a grin. "Come here my girl," he said as he dropped to a knee. Marin scrambled up his broad chest and cast Solyana a withering look.

"Stop winding her up, Han! She's got to go to bed soon and—" Lone, who was carrying a basket of bread, gasped and dropped it. The basket fell past her metal leg, its contents spilling out onto the floor.

"Mm, bread!" Marin squirmed out of her father's grip and began taking bites out of the rolls before placing them back in the basket.

Lone swayed a bit on her feet, and her metal leg creaked. "Y-you're alive."

Before Solyana could answer, Lone embraced her, her body shaking with tears.

Solyana felt her own eyes fill as she squeezed her back. "I'm here, Lone. I'm okay. Rorhan found us."

"How? I—" She pulled away, searching Solyana with her bright blue eyes before catching Rorhan's bicep with the back of her hand. "Way to warn me!"

"Marin wanted to play hide-and-seek! I could not refuse my only daughter." He shrugged and winked at Solyana. "Also, this is Ahren."

Fingers still gripping Solyana's upper arms, Lone peeked around her to see Ahren wave from the door.

"Hi," he said quietly. "I hope I'm not intruding. I'll be out of your hair in the morning."

"We are happy to have you," Lone said sweetly before lowering her voice to Solyana. "How much does he know?"

Solyana shook her head, biting her lip. Ahren wasn't the only ignorant one. Solyana had yet to tell her friends about her deal with Erval, but she shoved the subject from her thoughts.

"He wants to leave to find his family in the morning," Solyana said loud enough for Ahren to hear.

"Ah," Lone said with a click of her tongue. "Well, no journey was accomplished on an empty stomach. Let's eat!"

Solyana stirred the hearty stew, the potatoes, carrots, and meat swirling in the thick broth. It reminded her of the venison stew her mother used to make, though she'd never had access to so many vegetables. Another reminder that she had done it; she had brought the green. And with the prophecy completed, Solyana would get her sister back.

In the meantime, she had to know all that had happened in her absence. The most pressing of which was why her friends were still in Endirinn. Gamaliel sat beside her, poking at his stew, most of it untouched. Vinur lay at her feet, refusing to abandon her side, and it gave her the courage to ask the most pressing of questions.

"Why didn't you return to the valley?" Solyana asked Lone, who sat across the table stroking her daughter's hair.

"What kind of question is that?" Gamaliel interjected, his voice strained. "You were missing Solyana, we couldn't just—"

Lone placed a hand on Gamaliel's arm, her face softening. He quieted with a grunt, as if it were part of a song and dance they had done countless times before. But then he stood abruptly, knocking Solyana's knee to the side.

"Han, is that blueberry mead ready yet?" His hands scoured the top shelf in Lone's kitchen. "You said it would be done brewing this week."

"Not tonight, Gam." Han's voice held a firmness to it Solyana hadn't heard from the man before. Tension filled the room. "Solyana just got here."

Gamaliel turned back to the group, his eyes darting from Rorhan to Lone to Ahren, finally landing on Solyana. He clutched a mug, his arms and shoulders tight. "I don't want to have to go to Torny's, Han. Like you said, Solyana just got here." His fingers tapped an impatient rhythm on his mug.

"I wouldn't mind a cup," Ahren said lightly.

"See?" Gamaliel turned back to the kitchen, his hand scouring the upper shelves until glasses knocked against each other. "A-ha!" He pulled down a bottle, uncorked it with his teeth, and poured. He passed the mugs around the table and took a sip as he sat back down next to Solyana. "Your best brew yet, my friend." He lifted his mug and took a larger swig. "Don't you think?" he directed the question to Ahren, who sipped his drink and grinned. "Ahren likes it too."

Solyana averted her eyes and pushed her mug away. Much had changed in five years, it seemed.

Lone took a breath and locked eyes with Solyana. "At first, we didn't leave because we were waiting for you to return. But after six months, we had to decide. Did we want to travel back to the valley or try to make a life here? I was the only one with any family in the valley, but we were never very close, and Jonas wasn't about to leave after Seer Brotnur prophesied—"

"Jonas!" She felt ashamed she hadn't even thought of him. "He prophesied? What about?" She had only met the old Seer briefly the night before she had ascended the mountain. He had been able to detect Jonas's abilities as a Seer.

"We'll let Jonas explain that," Gamaliel offered between sips of mead. "He would kill me if I told you before he could."

"So, between that and the *Tungl* tribe dispersing—"

"My tribe," Rorhan said.

"When they started back, Han and Lak stayed behind. They'd disagreed with their chief's harsh assessment of you and wanted to help find you again. For the first year, we didn't stop looking. We tried to get messages out to your family, out to my own, but the rookery here refused. Austur, Sodur, and Vestur just aren't on their maps."

Ahren sputtered. "What?"

Lone turned to him, and Solyana was grateful. "Oh, sweetie." Lone placed a hand over Ahren's own. "You've been up that mountain a lot longer than Solyana. Hang tight, we'll explain everything in time."

Ahren's brow crumpled as he brought his mug back to his lips, and Solyana reached for her own. Perhaps the mead wasn't a bad idea, after all.

"Jonas can explain when he comes by later." Lone gave Gamaliel a sidelong glance. "But within that year, we really found a home here. We started working for coin, and before we knew it, we were moving into our own homes, becoming helpful members of Endirinn..."

"Falling in love." Rorhan's voice rumbled, his eyes on Lone.

"Yes," Lone said with a grin. "That, too. Can you bring the little *Elskan* to bed for me?"

Rorhan delivered his sleepy daughter to her bed and was back a moment later.

Lone continued. "Things began to shift after that year. The weather grew patterned, and year after year, it became evident that, yes, the seasons had returned. You really did it, Solyana! You brought back the green."

"What is she talking about?" Ahren's voice was hard, his eyes on Solyana.

Perhaps they wouldn't wait for Jonas. "You know of the Green Prophecy?" Solyana asked him, and he nodded. "I'm the answer to it. Ahren, you're from…" she struggled with her words, afraid of how Ahren would react. "You're from the past. A distant past. Whatever your sister did to you, whatever curse she performed on you, it kept you still for hundreds of years."

Ahren stared, saying nothing.

"For the last few centuries, Mothmar has been covered under ice and snow. Our people were dying, our food disappearing, blizzards prevented us from travel and trade. This is the first time I've ever seen…well, grass."

"I see." Ahren dropped his gaze to his hands. "I mean, not really, but…wow. Okay." He blinked, seeming suddenly weary.

"You will sleep tonight," Rorhan said. "Everything will feel better after sleep."

Ahren rubbed his temples.

"What happened with you, then?" Gamaliel asked. He let out a small burp. "You leave five years ago; now you're back."

Solyana didn't know where to look. Lone's face held hope and comfort, having found happiness settled here in this mountain town. Rorhan was much the same, though curiosity flickered behind his ice-blue eyes. And Ahren? He had a host of implications to sort through. She would look at Gamaliel. She owed him the most.

"I left only two nights ago," Solyana said. "I couldn't involve anyone else any longer. I'd watched…" She clenched a hand into a tight fist to steady herself. "Too many had died. For the prophecy, for me…" She looked up to see Gamaliel's eyes on his mug. "So, I took Björg and left. When I got to the top of the mountain, I found…" Solyana blinked and stared at her hands, unsure for the first time if anyone at the wooden table would believe even a word of her ludicrous story.

"It's okay." Lone reached across to give Solyana's arm a squeeze. "Take your time."

"Well," she whispered and cleared her throat. "I'm honestly not sure if you'll believe me. I'm not sure I would believe me if I hadn't been there." She surveyed the faces of those at the table around her, reminding herself these people loved her...or at least they loved the person they thought she was.

"There was a meadow, beautiful and lush, at the bottom of this icy slope. I found Ahren in the center of it...frozen." She looked back at Ahren again, worried what her memories might dredge up in him. Something flashed in his eyes, and he turned back to his mug. "But when I introduced myself, something odd happened. Ahren began...changing. And I guess I did, too. We were aging, very quickly."

Eyes flicking to Lone's, Solyana noticed the woman's demeanor. No longer was she watching Solyana with concern, but fear had etched itself into her features.

"As I've come to understand, Ahren was trapped on that mountain by means of a Taka Reu curse. I wasn't completely untouched by wrongdoing either, as I ascended without a third Gift."

Gamaliel let out something between a sigh and a grunt, but when Solyana's eyes flicked to him, he was taking another sip of mead.

"I also—" She stopped herself, afraid of the truth on the tip of her tongue.

Before she had left for Mount Endirinn, her mind had been occupied by someone else. Erval had been speaking directly to her, helping and directing her. She had kept his influence from her friends, thinking they would either believe her insane or put a stop to it. But it hadn't started with Erval. He had merely gained purchase in the cracks and crevices that had formed in her heart as they had traveled across Greater Mothmar. They had widened when she'd realized that, in order to become the savior her people needed, she would have to succumb to the force they most feared.

"Go on," Lone said.

Solyana blinked and pushed her mug away. Erval had yet to invade her thoughts again. Though he had promised to see her through her journey, he had grown silent as she'd scaled the ice wall alone, the storm at her heels. The more she tried to understand her encounters with him, the less she could make sense of them. She needed to be brave, consequences be damned.

"I have been practicing the Taka Reu."

The room went quiet, as if the space itself held its breath. Solyana forced herself to look each of them in the eye before settling on Gamaliel, whose brows furrowed, and his mouth turned down beneath his beard.

"It started after I was given the Gift of Tala."

Rorhan grunted.

"I knew it was wrong, but there was no other way to accomplish what I'd been tasked to do without harming more people!" The words spilled out, but they sounded like excuses, even to her. "Once I found out the giving of Gifts took lives—" Her eyes began to burn, and her hands covered her face. "I couldn't continue." Her palms pressed back onto the table. "Before we left the valley, Priestess Avi mentioned to me that I would possibly have to use the Celestials *and* the Taka Reu, in tandem." She looked at Gamaliel, his gaze filled with disgust. "I know now this is impossible, that she was likely only using the Taka Reu."

"I knew that woman couldn't be trusted," Gamaliel said through gritted teeth.

"Let her finish." Lone shot Gamaliel a look.

Solyana wiped at her eyes. "Things only got...worse." She wrung her hands under the table. "When I fell into that cave with Curry and Odie—"

The door burst open. Solyana jumped and turned in her seat to find a tall scruffy boy standing in the doorway. A leather satchel hung at his waist, stuffed full of scrolls. He wore short pants cropped at the knee and an intricate vest that looked out of place with the rest of him. His hair was wildly curly, the color of wet hide, and his face held perfectly round wire frames that seemed to make his eyes two sizes too large. An amethyst crystal sat in the hollow of his neck, secured by twine. The same crystal Solyana herself had pried from a cave wall to give to him.

"Did I miss dinner?" the boy asked, a tome in his hand.

"Jonas?" Solyana said through a choked laugh.

His eyes found hers, and he let out something between a gasp and a yelp. The charcoal pencil he'd been holding clattered to the floor along with the tome. "Solyana?"

TO FIND A KING

PALLAH

S NOW HAD NO PLACE so close to Thonethren. The city was built at the base of Mount Hekla, a dormant volcano, the lifeblood of the Taka Reu. Pallah could feel the raw warmth emanating from the ground, the power of the Mother Below just beneath her feet.

Issha, Pallah's friend—her only friend—stepped beside her with a grunt. "This it?"

"Yup." Pallah's voice came from within the hood of her cloak.

"And you're sure we're welcome here?" Issha had taken her cloak off, revealing a purple tunic beneath, though it was covered with enough grime, it could have passed for brown.

"Erval promised we'd be safe."

The girl beside Pallah snorted. "Vil said the same thing before the attack."

Pallah let out a slow breath. Her mind flashed an image of Vil, broken and bleeding beneath Vámae's hands. She had spent the last week trying to forget the Taka Reu's attack on the valley and the ruin it had wrought—her mother's dying breaths, her father's spiteful words, Tinloh's body in the snow, her sister's blood on her hands, the pain in Ahren's eyes as he disappeared in a haze of floating *aska*. All of it refused to be dispelled.

"This will be different," she assured Issha.

"Name and homeland!" A voice came from high above them.

Pallah peered up and her hood fell back. She squinted against the afternoon sun. "Pallah Bogson, Sodur."

She waited with trepidation, raising her hand to block the light. Erval had been absent for two days, her mind swimming in nothing but her own thoughts. What if he had changed his mind?

But the gate creaked open, the doors swinging in to reveal a cobbled street lined with simple homes.

"No welcome party?" Issha asked with a smirk.

"The gate opened, at least." Pallah gave a nervous laugh.

Issha gave her a long look. "At least."

The two women stepped through and continued north up the busy streets of the city. Thonethren was expansive, from rows of teetering tenements to plots of once-manicured manors, it seemed to hold every sort of person. Her eyes found patches of a dark, sticky substance plastered on walls and roofs and wondered at its intent. The people that milled about her bore signs of neglect—unwashed, unkempt, and unwanted. She remembered her father calling the city a place of darkness, a place of evil. Pallah breathed a sigh of relief. She would blend in here.

They had burned Vámae's body at the edge of the Pines, the Northern Mountains looming before them, the landscape covered in snow. It was important to Pallah that she not use Gifts to procure the fire but to do it by hand, rubbing two sticks together until her forearms were sore and her hands blistered. It was her penance for committing a deed she never knew she had been capable of. When the pyre was fully aflame, Issha had turned to Pallah, waiting on her to issue any final words. But Pallah had nothing to say. For what could be said to the person with whom she had shared a womb, only to end up killing her?

She had told Issha of Erval and his ability; she'd owed her that much. And as Pallah had expected, her friend held nothing but suspicion for someone with Mann Tala. So, Pallah didn't reveal how long Erval had been tethering her, how he had spoken to her since she was but a child. She herself didn't like to think on that and pushed it from her mind. He had promised her safe harbor. And that had been enough.

Only a few more days, Pallah. He had crooned into her mind one night as she lay shivering before a smoldering fire. *You'll be safe here with me. Remember, stick to traveling at night. If they send anyone after you, it will be when their god is high in the sky.*

Night after night, Pallah's emotions crusted over into calluses, closing her into a hardened box. Her mother had died, comforted by the presence of her daughter who had been missing—trapped in a maze—for two years. Confronting her father, she had killed him with Erval's help. His Mann Tala had ripped through her like a lightning bolt, doing away with her father with such ease, it had shaken her to her core.

And Ahren was gone, though not for long. The Taka Reu charm would keep him safe until she could find him.

But Tinloh... Just when she had gotten him back. Just when their tether had been regrowing its roots, deep and secure.

His blood was on Vámae's hands.

A hand clamped down on her upper arm, yanking her backward just as a horse-drawn carriage barreled past. Issha's fingers released their hold, and Pallah nodded in thanks. This bustling place, somehow both grand and dilapidated, beckoned her forward, closer to the castle at the center and Hekla in the north.

Pallah guided Issha through the streets, hoping against all hope she wasn't leading yet another one of her family to a place of death.

No, she told herself. This would be different.

Hello, young one. Pallah heard his voice in her mind—finally, after two whole days of silence. She looked up and into the distance, the castle's balconies barely in view. And there, on the highest of them, set far above the city itself, was a dark figure.

"Hello, Erval."

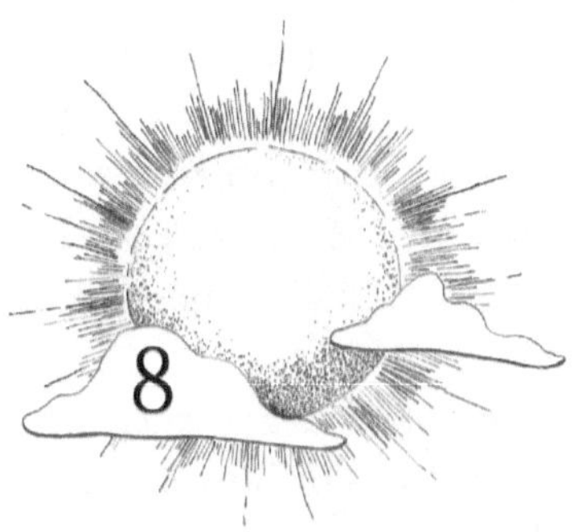

A WARNING

SOLYANA

"I KNEW IT!" JONAS shouted as he rushed around the table.

Solyana stood, laughing through tears, as the young man picked her up in a hug and spun her around.

"I told them you were coming back!" Jonas set her back on the floor. "And I have been *waiting,* Sol. I'm ready to go when you are. I have the plans drawn. We can set out first thing in the morning!"

"Wait, what? Hold on, Jonas." Solyana couldn't believe the boy who held her now was the same one she had left only a few days prior. Who was this man that stood in his place?

"Put her down, Jonas," Gamaliel said, his voice slightly slurred.

"Ah, my apologies," Jonas said as he lowered Solyana to the ground and ran both hands through his hair. His face reddened as he grinned. "How long has it been? Feels like days."

"I mean," Solyana began with a smile, "same."

Gamaliel grumbled something and tried to drink again from his mug, but he had reached the bottom of it. He set it back down on the table a little too firmly. "Are we out, Han?"

Rorhan's eyes went to the other side of the kitchen and Gamaliel followed his gaze. "It needs a few more days fermenting."

"Worth the risk." He beckoned for it.

Jonas lifted Gamaliel's mug and moved it out of reach. He found a seat beside Ahren. "We have a quest to embark on! A journey to traverse!" He began laying out scrolls, spreading them over the table. "Hi, I'm Jonas." He held out a hand to Ahren, who took it with a cautious squeeze. "You must be the kid from the mountain top. Well, you're not a kid anymore, I suppose. You're older than me! Much older...than all of us!" Jonas huffed a laugh and shook his head. "It's all coming together."

Ahren gave a quizzical nod.

"Solyana was just telling us about her experience on the mountain and a bit before," Lone said to Jonas before shifting her attention to Ahren. "If you feel comfortable, we'd love to hear from you, as well."

Ahren looked at the table.

The room settled, each person shifting and sipping from mugs before falling quiet once again.

Solyana cleared her throat. "When that blizzard hit on the ice plains, Curry bolted inside with Odie and I atop her. We were only a few steps in when we fell through the cave. When I came to, I found myself next to a pool of lava—"

"I think you mean magma," Jonas interrupted. "Magma runs underground; lava is on the surface."

"Just let her tell the story," Gamaliel said.

Jonas made a face but settled in his chair.

"Now, this is going to sound crazy," Solyana continued. "But a man rose from the fire, a giant. It might have been some kind of Gifted ability, something with the Taka Reu that allows him to use the...magma." She looked at Jonas. "To shape it, speak through it. He helped me...at first. The essence of the Taka Reu, or *aska*, had trapped me in place. I had attempted tethering to the Mother Below but hadn't truly given up my connection to the Celestials."

Jonas let out a small gasp, causing a blush of shame to bloom inside Solyana.

She squeezed her hands under the table. "This man encouraged me to beseech the Mother, and I did. The *aska* released me, and soon after that, I was able to use the Taka Reu without much hindrance at all. Odie had died in the fall, and Curry was... She didn't make it, either. I was the only one alive to be shown the exit."

Gamaliel sneered. "Who was this person? Did you find out their name? And why didn't you tell us this when you arrived in Endirinn?"

"You were using the Taka Reu?" Jonas asked.

"Give her a minute," Lone said.

"No, they're right. You all deserve an explanation." Solyana took a breath. "During the time I traveled through the caves—it seemed like ages—this man began speaking to me...in my mind."

Ahren's head snapped up.

"When I told him who I was, it was like he already knew. He introduced himself as Erval and started asking me about our valley, about Priestess Avi, in particular. And...about you." Solyana caught Ahren's gaze, his eyes as wide as twin moons.

Jonas stood from the table, face hovering over Ahren's head. "Wait a minute, Sol. This man spoke directly into your mind?"

"Yes," Solyana said, and her voice began to quiver. "I haven't heard from him since the night I was attacked by Orson's men, here in Endirinn. But I'd made a deal with him. He would save my sister, Rhuth. But he wanted me to bring Ahren to him. He wants Priestess Avi—he knows her as Pallah. And he thinks Ahren could convince her to—"

Ahren stood, his chair tipping, threatening to fall before it righted itself with a sharp *clack*.

Solyana looked up at him. "He wants you to convince her to—"

In two strides Jonas brought himself behind her, his hand clamping over her mouth. He whispered in her ear. "Is he speaking to you now?"

Solyana shook her head, body rigid in her chair.

"You must be on your guard. If he tethers you again—"

Solyana pulled away. "Tethers me? You can't tether people."

"You can." Jonas nodded curtly. "I've read enough. Trust me."

"He's right." Ahren's voice struck into Solyana like a spear, his eyes holding a new depth, a grief that hadn't been present before. "Someone did the same thing to my sister when she was young. I believe he did it again as she got older... It sounds like this is that same man."

"Over centuries?" Lone asked, shaking her head in disbelief. "That doesn't make sense."

"But it does..." Jonas said quietly. "If Priestess Avi—Pallah—has been alive for centuries, this man Erval could be doing the same. The question is how."

Their eyes locked, the unknown possibilities burning between them. Every nerve in Solyana's body revolted at the idea of having been tethered, like an element, like an animal. Bile rose into her throat. She needed his help to keep her sister safe, but Erval was not to be trusted. She had been naïve, had fawned when she should've been far more cautious.

A knock sounded on the door.

"Were you expecting someone else?" Rorhan asked his wife, already moving.

"No." Lone shook her head, pulling a knife from the kitchen counter as casually as if it were a napkin. Her metal leg creaked on her way to the door.

Rorhan was already by the back doorway that led to the bedrooms, arms crossed over his chest, guarding his sleeping daughter.

Gamaliel rose from his seat and passed in front of Solyana, picking up his staff along the way.

"Are we in danger?" Solyana asked, sweat breaking across her palms.

Jonas opened his mouth to speak, but Lone answered softly. "Just being careful," she said as she swung the door inward.

"Hello," said a voice, a man, and a nervous one at that. "Is this the home of Seer Jonas?"

Jonas craned his neck toward the door, and Solyana found herself doing the same.

"Who's asking?" Lone didn't hesitate.

"Please, if I could have just a moment of your time." The man's voice shook.

"Who is asking?" Lone repeated, her tone growing dangerous.

"My name is Phineas, and I'm here to warn you... I'm here to warn you all."

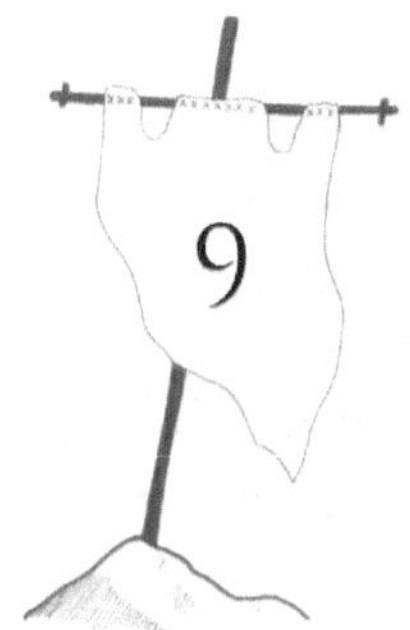

CONTENDER

HALLDORA

A KNOCK ON THE door shifted Halldora's eyes from her own reflection to the reflection of the canvas door behind her. "Yes?" She straightened the makeshift crown on her head. She would not be seen without a sparkling reminder to her men of her true position as Queen of Thonethren. Turning to examine her back in the mirror, she ran a hand down her thigh. Her tailor had done a fine job on the leather hugging her skin.

"We received a missive from the Crimson Chief." The muffled male voice came through the pliable wall.

Halldora rolled her eyes and gave her corset a tug. "And?"

"He's agreed to fight."

Her dark eyebrows rose, and she turned from the mirror, crossing her arms. "You may enter."

The soldier's face was a maze of red pock marks as he came into the light of the lantern hanging above the wooden table. Her army had grown unfairly young in the last few decades. While Halldora herself didn't look much older than thirty, it had come at a cost. The upkeep of her youth was taxing, but it wouldn't do to present an aging front to her men, energetic as they were.

"Did he mention where he's docked?"

Only when the boy pointed a shaking finger at the map did she smell the fear on him; the result of rumor taking root within the ranks. But she was not like her brother. She only performed the Taking on criminals, those most vile. Those loyal to her had nothing to fear. Her immortality would not to be built on the backs of innocents—Erval knew nothing of running a country properly.

The young soldier swiped his finger around the section of Kana Ocean between Thonethren and an island northwest of it.

"They're here, m'lady. Northwest of the Valley of Vatin there's a small island." His finger traced around the island, so close to the place she had once called home. "He's calling it Pahrnadee."

Halldora let a polished nail trace through the valley that contained the Vatino Sea. Collaborating with the Crimson Chief had been one of her wiser decisions. Not only did he claim to have an entire fleet ready and waiting to make a move on her wretch of a brother, but his knowledge of cartography was priceless.

"Pahrnadee." She arched an eyebrow before lifting her attention from the map. "So, he's already in Kana Ocean. Only a bit more travel until he's in prime position."

The soldier cleared his throat and removed his finger from the map, letting it hover over the table.

"Something else you'd like to relay?"

"Well, yes. I only worry about our own advance."

She looked into the boy's face and blinked once. "What's your name?"

"Corun, m'lady. I have—"

"And how long have you been in my army?"

"Joined up about a month ago," he said, straightening his shoulders.

"And your superiors haven't briefed you?"

The soldier's brow furrowed as he surveyed the map beneath Halldora's fingertips. Their location changed every month or two. Her brother, always on the prowl with his fancy devices, forced Halldora to maintain a nomadic kingdom. For now, they hid in plain sight, northeast of the city ruled by her new political friends.

"They did, my Queen." Corun's voice wavered.

Halldora eyed him again, this time with suspicion. A month of service and he dared to seek intelligence. "We have time," she said. "The Beast Riders will join us, and we will strike at the Red Moon."

The boy blinked rapidly, his mind turning beneath a layer of thick skull. "Yes, my Queen."

"To worry about our advance is to question my planning." She circled him like a panther. "Do you question me, Corun?"

The boy's breathing quivered. "No, my Queen."

"Do you question my authority? My legitimacy? My crown?"

Before he could answer, she slid a hand along his cheek, fingers spreading wide over his temples. The other clutched a dagger that she drove into his chest. The boy's eyes barely had time to widen in surprise as Halldora whispered the ancient words of the Taking.

He wheezed and slumped to the floor as a dark mist wound its way up and shot into Halldora.

"Joined up a month ago." She took a deep breath, accepting his life and his Gift. "I'm afraid that's impossible." Wiping her dagger on his shirt, she stared past the boy at her feet. "We're coming for you, brother. One way or another, Thonethren will be mine."

EMBER

RHUTH

R HUTH'S KNEES WERE TUCKED up into her chest as she watched the priestess from the corner. Priestess Avi—Pallah—whoever she was, packed furiously, her shawl discarded on the bed. The woman had promised Rhuth the only thing that would make her stay: information about Solyana. She hung on every word the priestess muttered while she worked.

"Sorry again about your face, dear. Like a lightning bolt gone wrong. I tried to patch it up as best I could, but my Feldur Fera is quite out of practice. Although it may mean it holds significance..." The priestess stood straight, eyes scouring Rhuth's face. "No, no, no..." She shook her head, returning to packing. "If living as long as I have has taught me anything, it's that nothing is ordained, nothing predestined. All is done and undone by the hands of man."

Rhuth's ire simmered beneath her skin. This woman had toyed with her and her people for so long. Outside, the moon was waxing, a steady snow falling on the empty grounds surrounding the Temple Celestial.

A small knock sounded at the door, and Rhuth watched as a small woman entered. Her face set in hard lines, she made no introduction or move to acknowledge Rhuth's presence, only addressing the priestess. "That voice has possessed my son again."

Priestess Avi shook her head and, for the first time since knowing her, Rhuth thought the woman might be scared. "You need to leave, Phassa. Leave and never come back. You shouldn't even be in my presence." Then she closed her eyes and took a deep breath. "Take the last of the dogs. We will be fine walking. Cross the Belja River and thread through the lower pass of the Hasta Mountains. I promise no unexpected weather will come. There is a city called Takanah just on the other side."

Phassa's eyes widened, and she backed away. "Takanah? That's not what you told the rest of the valley. Did you send them to their deaths? Or are you sending me and my family to ours?" Without waiting for an answer, the serviseer shifted her attention to Rhuth. "Child, this woman can't be trusted. Come with us! There is plenty of room, and we will move swiftly on sleds."

Sweat broke out on Rhuth's forehead as her eyes leapt between Phassa and the priestess—one woman promising salvation, the other had kept her a prisoner. It would have been an easy choice, yet what of Solyana? Rhuth would never forgive herself if she had the opportunity to save her sister and failed to.

Rhuth looked to the priestess, but the woman seemed apathetic toward her, ignoring her as she continued her packing. Something prickled at the back of Rhuth's mind, something she knew would make itself known, in time.

"I'll go with the priestess. But thank you, Phassa."

The woman opened her mouth to argue, but Priestess Avi spoke up.

"Take the sleds and go before I change my mind."

Serviseer Phassa skittered from the room, clutching her tunic at her sides.

"Why did you give her the sleds and dogs?"

"King Erval will assume I'm taking the fastest route from here. They'll serve as a useful distraction."

"So, you did send them to their deaths." Rhuth gaped.

The priestess didn't pause. "Our success is more important. And as a serviseer, she has vows to uphold. She is serving her priestess."

A firm ball of anxiety rested in Rhuth's belly. What if she had made the wrong choice?

Priestess Avi's eyes met Rhuth's, and there was a grin hidden within them, more malicious than kind. She slid her knapsack over her shoulder. "You're safe with me, Rhuth. I won't let any harm come to you."

"Like you didn't let any harm come to my people?"

"I never promised them anything."

Rhuth and Priestess Avi procured parkas, mukluks, dried foods, tools, and sleeping rolls before placing their supplies near the door. Rhuth was curled up on one side of the four-poster bed while the priestess sat by the fire, drinking what smelled like saxifrage tea. Rhuth had her own cup, but it was growing cold on the table.

"You should drink that," Avi told her. "There's a reason for all I do, girl."

"I don't like saxifrage." Rhuth thought of her sister. Solyana loved the taste of that plant.

"Even so, it will protect you against the King's meddling."

Rhuth sniffed the tea and took a sip. "What do you hope to gain in going toward this man you're afraid of?"

"I'm not afraid of him." The woman scowled.

"You're terrified." Rhuth drank her tea to hide her face which, she knew, looked a bit too smug. "Your hands are shaking."

Priestess Avi lowered her hands into her lap, resting the mug and leveling her gaze at Rhuth. "I've been away from him a long time... Yet I still remember the power he held over me for so many years." She bit at her lip. "I will admit, I am terrified—though not of the man, but of what I will lose forever should he find me."

"Power?" Rhuth guessed.

Priestess Avi shook her head. "Two things," she said. "Freedom is one of them."

"And the other?" Rhuth asked.

The priestess grew quiet. She took another sip from the trembling mug. "Forgiveness."

It was just before dawn, the stillness of the morning a stark contrast to the whirling storm in Rhuth's heart. She donned layers of clothes to guard against the cold.

The floorboards shifted outside her room as she finished lacing up her mukluks. "I'm finished, Priestess Avi. You may come in." Rhuth said it as if any unbreached boundaries existed between them.

"I'm through with the charade." The priestess strode into the room. "From here on, I'd prefer my real name."

"Pallah?" Rhuth clarified, who had known this from her time in the Maze.

The ghost of a smile drifted across the woman's face. "Yes. We leave now. The longer we linger, the greater chance he'll find us. Erval won't be fooled for long."

The two made their way out of the Temple Celestial, and a strange feeling began to wind its way around Rhuth's heart. It was something akin to loss or grief. "Is this the last time I will ever be in the Temple? In my valley?"

Pallah grunted. "Good riddance."

Falling quiet and stepping obediently behind her, Rhuth followed the woman to the foyer where their supplies waited for them. Pallah opened the doors, taking a quick glance at the mirror that had stood near the entrance since as long as Rhuth could remember. Something like disgust passed over the woman's face, though Rhuth wasn't quite sure why.

Snow sat on the ground, packed and hard, almost ice. It had been some time since the last blizzard. Rhuth shook her head to herself because Pallah didn't want there to be a blizzard. The woman before her had been controlling the weather, though Rhuth hadn't known such a thing to be possible. Perhaps she could spend their time traveling drawing more than just answers about Solyana from of the woman.

Shouldering their packs, the two made their way wordlessly over the icy snow and through the biting cold until they came upon the three buildings standing in a semicircle north of town. Rhuth's eyes found the falconry, and a familiar pulse of feeling came over every part of her.

Companionship. Loyalty.

Will you go with me? she asked the birds.

They were not human; she would not hear their answer as an audible voice. Instead, she heard them through feeling, she simply...knew.

Follow at a distance, then, she told them and took the reassuring peace that came over her as their acceptance.

The sun rose over the grounds slowly as they walked, casting shadows from Sháskol, Lóthkol ,and the Hytast.

"Well, Rhuth. I've debated how much to tell you," Pallah said between crunching steps up the slight hill.

"You told me you'd tell me all," Rhuth replied.

The priestess chuckled. "I did, didn't I? I'll reveal as much as I'm able, as long as you're amenable."

"And what do you want in return?"

Pallah glanced over her shoulder. "Your Gift, sweet child."

Her Gift.

Rhuth's Tala, she knew, went beyond a standard tether. She'd always believed it had stemmed from her respect for the animals she reached out to, her bids for relationship rather than control. But her time in the Maze had shown her just how different—how powerful—her Gift could be.

While trapped, Rhuth had started experimenting, not only with how she tethered to Halina, but tethering to inanimate objects. To her surprise, an energy within them responded.

Responded and obeyed.

A mug pushed off the table. A flame flickering without the presence of wind. Rhuth knew Pallah had begun to notice, but Rhuth herself was unsure of how such things were possible. If it was information the woman was after, she would be disappointed; Rhuth had none to give.

"I have seen the things you do with the falcons, and perhaps even with objects as well—though *that* is entirely lost on me. Such things I have only seen from people who possess the use of the Taka Reu, and not only that, but who have delved into the Taking."

Rhuth shuddered at the words. Though she didn't understand their meaning, their very cadence held darkness. "Well," she said quietly. "I don't use...that."

"Yes. Hence, why it's so interesting."

They entered the wood, following a path made by some animal. Rhuth eyed it for a moment. A fox. Yes, most certainly a fox.

"Who do you worship, Rhuth?"

Rhuth blinked. An odd question coming from the head of the Temple Celestial. Rhuth knew Gifts were tied to their religion, but she had never thought about such things in terms of worship. She simply loved the Celestials, as she had been taught to do since she was a girl.

"I worship the One who created everything," she said meekly.

"The Father of the Day? The Mother of the Night? The Children of the Sky?"

Rhuth shrugged, though Pallah, walking ahead of her, didn't see it. "Well, I mean that's what we call them. That's what you taught in the Temple Celestial. They're not really three separate beings; they're the One Above."

Pallah stopped walking. "You dare lecture the Speaker of the Skies on theology?" She gave a sly smile. "But it's an incorrect theology. They *are* separate beings."

Rhuth cocked her head. "They're Celestials. One thing made up of many."

Gray-green eyes narrowed in Rhuth's direction, full of depth and...curiosity?

But Rhuth hadn't the means to satisfy her. The knowledge of her Gift was almost instinctual. And if she knew anything about the animals she led, it was that instinct had no map but its own mind. She simply reached through with faith... Yes, that was how Rhuth understood it. A faith in something she could not see. A map that guided her soul.

Mind churning, Rhuth was comforted by the rhythmic click of her snowshoes against her pack. She wouldn't need them here, where the ground was so hard with packed ice. But in the Northern Pines some of the snow remained churned by its inhabitants. Rhuth's eye found a small scuff of snow, a potential trail that jut into some underbrush.

Her tether pulsed, and Rhuth stopped walking. There was a fox nearby, she was sure of it. It had been so long since she had tethered to anything but birds, the idea of a fox felt warm, inviting.

She reached out with her tether, just to see, and grinned. Rhuth tested her tether, pressing into the fox, requesting if she would join them on their journey. But even as she tethered to the creature, deep in the underbrush, she could feel an ache that almost brought her to her knees.

"Oh no." Puffs of white air curled from her mouth. Rhuth clutched her chest.

Pallah turned quickly. "What are you—"

"She lost her baby."

"Who are you talking about?" The woman cast wildly around.

A tear trickled from Rhuth's left eye, pressure building behind the scars of the right. She pressed her hand to it and pain shot up toward her hairline. Rhuth gasped.

A dark nose poked out from the brush, and Rhuth stilled herself, watching the whiskers flick and twitch.

"It's okay," she called to her. "You can trust me. I won't harm you." She crouched close to the ground.

The fox slowly revealed herself until she had fully emerged from the brush. She was a large animal, long-legged and graceful. Her black eyes shone as she approached Rhuth, sniffing her face and licking her once.

"I think I'll call you Ember," Rhuth said to the animal, reaching out to touch her rust-red fur. "Do you like that name?"

The fox released a chuff and trotted a distance away before stopping and looking back at Rhuth.

"We don't have time for pets," Pallah said, sparing not a glance in the animal's direction. "It will just exhaust you, maintaining your tether."

"No, it won't," Rhuth said honestly. "It never has. Does it exhaust you?"

Peering at Rhuth over her shoulder, Pallah narrowed her eyes. "I'll figure you out yet." The woman continued on. "But if you lag behind, the fox goes. We have little time to make it to the city, and we're in this together."

"I'm not going for you," Rhuth pointed out, letting her hand brush Ember's fur. "I'm doing this for Solyana."

"And what if I said so am I?"

Rhuth eyed her. "It's hard to believe anything after all you've done."

"You don't know half of what I've done."

A chill ran through Rhuth, but when she looked at the older woman, Pallah's eyes were tinged with sadness.

"It's a long story," Pallah said.

Ember trotted ahead of them, and Rhuth's eye followed her. "Better start talking, then."

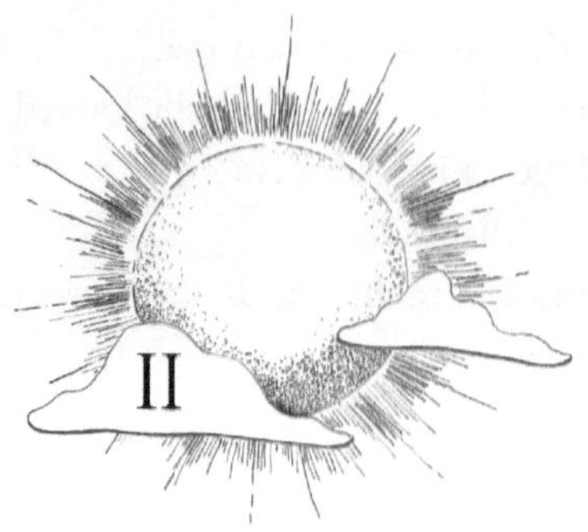

THE LEÍDÍN

SOLYANA

SOLYANA'S MOUTH WENT DRY as all heads turned to Jonas, his eyes still fixed on the scrolls strewn about the table. The name Phineas was familiar to her, spoken by Erval during their time in the cave. It had stuck in her mind like a thorn, and hearing it again finally loosened its hold. This man knew Erval, or Erval knew him.

In either case, they were no longer safe.

"Welcome, Phineas." Jonas barely concealed a grin. "I thought we were due to meet at Torny's Tavern tomorrow, but please, have a seat. Lone, if you would be so kind as to make this man some tea."

"Excuse me." Lone blinked, swinging an arm toward the door. "I believe introductions are in order."

"Phineas of Thonethren." Jonas was grinning now as he looked up from his scrolls. "He's early, but I'm sure he has reasons."

Panic drove Solyana to stand. Jonas didn't know, he couldn't. "I—" she began but then reconsidered. Phineas was not an uncommon name. This man could be anyone. She cleared her throat. "Why are you here?"

The stout man in the doorway made no move to cross the threshold. Instead, he stood with his head bowed, eyes peering over his spectacles, his scant hair sticking up in a few spots on his shining head. "I've traveled from the west to—"

"You work with Erval, don't you?" Solyana couldn't hold it in.

Phineas straightened, and Solyana couldn't miss the quick look over his shoulder into the dark evening behind him. "M-may I come in?"

The group remained silent, each seemingly waiting for another to accept or deny his request.

"Please?" Phineas extended a hand.

"At your own risk, I suppose," Gamaliel said, hands wound tightly around his staff. "As long as it's okay with you, Lone."

Lone lowered the knife and lifted a hand toward the door, pulsing her fingers ever so slightly.

Phineas teetered on his feet. "Oh!" he exclaimed, clutching at his robes. "Bein Fera?" he asked in a tone bordering awe. "A rarity."

Lone grunted and motioned him inside. He scuttled in as she closed the door behind him. Rorhan remained at his post near the back hallway, muscles rippling in his crossed arms. Phineas passed the enormous man to take a seat at the table.

Solyana glanced between Phineas and Jonas, who stared at each other, both through round framed spectacles. Jonas's eyewear was on the larger side, whereas Phineas's looked three sizes too small for his face.

"Does he know Solyana is back?" Jonas asked the man across from him.

Phineas shook his head. "Not yet, but it's only a matter of time. Have you all been drinking the blocking tea?"

Looking to everyone else, it was almost a relief to see they were all just as clueless as Solyana.

"Right, well..." Phineas pulled a few wrapped parcels out of the pockets of his robes. "Endirinn is quite sequestered from most everywhere else, and the king has snuffed out as many smugglers as he's been able. This is from my personal stores." The man spoke as he placed the parcels onto the table.

Jonas picked one up, sniffed it, then dug into his bag before retrieving a scroll. "I just saw a passage on medicinal teas..." He went quiet for a moment before raising a finger into the air. "Yes! A blend of saxifrage... Hey!" He leaned in closer. "This scroll has been tampered with. The other ingredients are scratched out."

Phineas nodded as if he already knew. "Saxifrage, rosebay, and arctic willow. Steeped at just under boiling for precisely four minutes. I would be surprised to find it written in any texts. Erval's reach is rather far. You see, this tea makes the drinker impervious to tethers. Whether through blood, skin, or bone." His eyes swung to Lone.

"Or in this king's case...man?" Ahren asked, unwrapping one of the boxes. "My sister could have used this."

"She did." Phineas's eyes gleamed behind round glass. "I was the first to give it to her. You must be Ahren."

Ahren gave a small smile.

Gamaliel snorted. "I'm not sure why we'd just drink something because you show up and say so."

But Jonas was already sprinkling the contents of his parcel into a mug and grabbing the kettle.

Solyana raised a hand. "Jonas, maybe we should—"

"There's no way of knowing until we try!" His fingers tapped his leg as the water warmed.

"But it could hurt you," Rorhan said softly.

Phineas huffed. "I would never harm a Seer."

Jonas pulled the kettle from the flames and poured himself a cup.

The group waited four minutes; the air in the room charging with anticipation.

Jonas lifted the cup to his lips and drank. "You ready, Lone?"

Her leg creaked as she sat beside him and nodded. She extended her hand toward him.

A chuckle emerged from Jonas's lips. "I feel nothing!"

"I can't... I can't get a hold on anything," Lone said with awe. "It's as if he doesn't have a bone in his body!" She shifted her attention to her husband whose eyes went wide.

"Hey!" he bellowed. "Do not touch my bones, Wife!"

She chuckled. "Sorry! I had to test if it was a problem on my end."

"Why help us?" Solyana asked.

"Because the king of Thonethren is planning something to which I cannot turn a blind eye. He desires full control of Mothmar and complete submission of its people. To stop him, I was hoping to acquire information of his future—if Seer Jonas would be so kind as to lend his abilities."

The group turned as one to Jonas, who looked a bit shocked. "My abilities?"

"Yes, you are a Seer. The last one, if the reports I've heard are true." Phineas's hands rasped over each other in succession. "You can help me understand how to stymie Erval on his path."

"How do you propose?" Jonas inquired.

"Using your Seer ability to show me a future where I can successfully stop Erval, preferably without him knowing of my betrayal."

Gamaliel's lip quirked. "He's not that kind of Seer."

Jonas's face contorted with a flash of anger in Gamaliel's direction but restored itself as it turned back to Phineas. "I receive visions at times, feelings to go one direction or another, but mostly I create maps of places I haven't seen. I haven't yet been able to see specific futures of specific people."

The man in stately robes deflated. "Ah, I see." His eyes scoured the table before him as if reading some unseen text. "I have other questions, information I seek. Perhaps I can be permitted access to some of your scrolls." He eyed Jonas's bag on the floor. "The tea will be payment enough, surely."

Jonas's lips twisted. "And for it, I thank you, but it is not my place to grant access to ancient texts. You would have to go to the priest."

"Ah, the priest..." Phineas nodded and leaned back in his chair, eyes flicking to Solyana, then to the mug in front of her. "I recommend *you* abstain from this tea. Though Erval doesn't know you're alive, I suspect news of your return would reach him quickly." He leaned forward and pulled her mug away. "If he tried tethering you again and found it to be blocked, he would know of your defection. However!" Phineas raised a finger. "He can be misdirected. I can teach you how."

"I need to recover my sister," Solyana emphasized, curious what else this man had to offer. "Erval has agreed to keep her safe if Ahren convinces Pallah to meet with him."

"Erval bargains with goods he does not possess."

Solyana's face twisted with confusion. "What do you mean?"

Phineas shook his head. "I don't doubt he knows where she is, but your sister is nowhere in Thonethren. I would know. I run that kingdom. That castle has been my home for centuries."

"What about Pallah?" Ahren interjected. "I mean...if she's still alive."

"She is," Phineas said, adjusting his spectacles. "But she is also not in Thonethren."

"Could Erval be keeping them somewhere secretly?" Lone asked.

"No." Phineas shook his head. "I'm his most trusted advisor. I would know."

Jonas pointed a finger at him. "Trusted but not trustworthy. As you're here...trying to glean information from us on how to stop the King."

Phineas's cheeks reddened but his eyes were clear and determined. "He is going down a path I cannot follow. And yes, I aim to stop him."

Solyana shuddered at the memory of him speaking to her through her mind. He had called her his partner, his words smooth in her ears. He had fooled her into believing she needed to use the Taka Reu, that she needed to leave her friends, that she needed to do things on her own. But she would not go alone any longer.

"If he knows of Rhuth, then she's in danger. I have to help." Solyana leaned forward over the table. "Can you start from the beginning? Who is Erval, truly?"

Phineas's tongue darted between dry lips before he cleared his throat and began. "Erval Mikkaelson, king of Thonethren, Iron Fist of the North, Herald of the Mother, was born into royalty. He would have taken the throne by natural succession, if not for his father converting to Celestial worship before Erval's announcement as heir apparent. This secured his sister, Halldora, as heir, and relegated Erval to nothing but her advisor.

"Rather than serve, he fled the castle and hid in the caves of Mount Hekla. He found me during this time, and I became his steward and closest advisor. He needed someone to keep him grounded, someone to keep him from losing himself in his own Gift. Because Mann Tala is a powerful Gift...one that causes even the strongest of men to stumble."

The room held its breath, and Solyana's heart picked up its pace. Though Jonas had said it just before, that Erval had tethered her, hearing it listed as an aptitude—Mann Tala—was terrifying.

"How could the Celestials give anyone such a Gift?" Solyana asked quietly, determined to understand.

Phineas leaned over the table to peer at her. "I don't believe they're the gods that gave it to him, my dear." He sat back again. "I went to Thonethren with great dreams of becoming an inventor, you see. And Erval, well—he had means. Not at first, mind you. He had cut ties with his father and sister, but the man has charisma. And little by little, he gained the trust of the people. Before long, we had the supplies and access to ancient scrolls we needed.

"I was able to concoct all sorts of inventions—many of which he still uses today. All the while, Erval strategized how to retake his throne." Phineas let out a sigh, the wind gone from his sails. "It was during this time we deciphered the true meaning of the Taka Reu."

Phineas held up two stubby fingers. "The first, one's relationship to the Mother Below is not mutually beneficial. Utilizing the Taka Reu takes directly from her source, her life. The earth is drained as we use its energy. What first appears to be lush and good, only turns to spoil and rot. The second is the discovery of the darkest act within the Taka Reu: the Taking of another life."

"You speak of murder." Rorhan sounded unimpressed.

"Not merely murder, no. It is a *Taking*." Phineas shoved his shaking hands into his lap.

Jonas's eyes finally left his maps, and he seemed to truly see the man across from him for the first time.

Phineas continued. "Murder would be a kindness. The Taking is one of years, of Gifts, of souls. The Taker becomes a collection of stolen Gifts and time. Take enough, and a man can make himself immortal." A single tear found its way out of his eye. He paused, seeming to collect himself.

"How many times have you Taken, Phineas?" Jonas asked.

Solyana watched Phineas carefully, certain he would deny it. No one would openly admit to doing such a thing amongst strangers.

"Too many times to count, dear boy." Phineas took a shaky breath. "And too many times to forget."

Eyes growing wide, Solyana felt Gamaliel tense beside her.

"If you, too, have claimed souls..." Rorhan surmised. "Then you are much older than you appear."

Phineas released a chuff of air. He removed his glasses, wiped them on his robes, and placed them carefully back on his face. "Yes. Quite old, indeed."

"Someone using this ability could live for centuries," Jonas said, pointing at Solyana, their earlier discussion settled.

"Living forever has never been a goal of mine. In fact, I'm uncertain when it became a goal of Erval's. I understood his desire to take back his kingdom, perhaps even all of Mothmar. But over the years, those dreams have grown dull to him. He's not the same man I met all those years ago."

"What is he now?" Lone asked.

"He seeks to understand the full depth of the power he's accrued. True, irrefutable control." Phineas straightened in his chair. "Control of every person, animal, and...god."

"The Celestials?" Solyana asked.

"To Erval, the Celestials are nothing but puppets of the True God, the Mother Below. We do live where she resides, Mount Hekla being the entrance to her chambers. If he could wield the deity beneath our feet? He would be revered. He would be—"

"A god himself," Jonas filled in.

Phineas nodded. "And that brings me here. I don't want to live in a world run by that man. Over the years, Erval has heard of individuals with the ability to manipulate all Gifts without the use of the Taka Reu. He has studied quite a few, both from afar and up close, and he's discovered... Well, essentially a new religion. And if you can't tell me expressly what our future holds, then I am indeed interested in those scrolls of yours."

"Ah! The use of all Gifts. That is no new religion, but a very old one," Jonas said with renewed vigor. He leaned forward in his seat, eyes never leaving the face of the man before him. "The One True Gift," he whispered.

Phineas blinked and shifted in his chair. "Yes, precisely. Even after countless years of searching, Erval has yet to find the constellation associated with this religion's worship. We've heard it called the Way or Pathway from many whom Erval has...questioned." Phineas's eyes slid to the men in the room. "And I have even had someone explain to me where to find it in the sky, during which season it is visible, and yet... It remains unseen. And I am grateful. Erval finding this information and wielding it would be the downfall of humanity."

Jonas shook his head. "He wouldn't be able to wield it, not truly, with his heart so blackened by the Taka Reu. It's more likely he would attempt to stomp it out. But I've done plenty of digging regarding the Way, and have also come up short. You will not find much else in these scrolls that I haven't already explored. I have plans to travel to—"

"Before we lay everything bare," Gamaliel interrupted, standing from his chair and eyeing Jonas. "We need to address the fact that Erval has been speaking directly into Solyana's mind. Well, five years ago, before she disappeared." His eyes flicked to Solyana. "He hasn't done so since, has he?"

Solyana shook her head. "No."

"We assumed you died in the storm," Phineas said. "I'm glad to see that isn't the case."

"Storm?" Gamaliel's eyes were on hers again. "What happened up there?"

Solyana placed a placating hand on Gamaliel's arm but addressed Phineas. "What do you recommend we do?"

"Exactly what you agreed upon: delivering him." Phineas nodded toward Ahren. "Erval will do anything to gain possession of this man."

"To bait my sister," Ahren said with a sigh.

Phineas nodded slowly.

"So, I'm to be traded?" Ahren asked with an edge to his voice, but then he continued. "What does he want with Pallah?"

"Your sister spent a long time with him. They were partners, or something that resembled partnership; Erval would never consider anyone his equal. I felt bad for the girl, really. I was relieved when she vanished. But Erval discovered her location in your valley five years ago, and everything changed. He's been attempting to draw her in ever since—though she remains elusive."

Solyana swallowed back the bile in her throat. She had given Erval that information, or had given him enough for him to make the connections himself. Had she doomed them all? Or maybe just Pallah?

She shook her head. "I'm sorry, Ahren, but you don't know the truth of what your sister has become. She has been masquerading as a priestess for decades. She's misled and killed countless people, she's held my own sister captive for...I don't know how long! Rhuth could still be trapped!"

Ahren's mouth hung open. "Pallah wouldn't—"

"No." Solyana shook her head. "I will not feel pity for this woman. She is nothing but evil."

Gamaliel nodded and pressed his knee against Solyana's under the table. Ahren's face hardened, and Solyana turned away from him.

Phineas sighed and leaned back in his chair. "I'm afraid that may be the result of Erval's influence. You see, he has been communicating with her since she was a child. His Mann Tala extends far and wide, and she had become his sole purpose for so long. He was obsessed. He is, still."

"That doesn't excuse her actions!" Solyana's breath quickened. "She's the reason our people starved! She's the reason we were trapped in our valley!" Though even as she said it, Solyana was singed with hypocrisy. The same man who had manipulated the strings of Pallah's heart had influenced Solyana, as well. Had she not fallen into the Taka Reu just as Pallah had?

Ahren opened his mouth to refute, when Jonas held up a hand. "I'm afraid I agree with Phineas. While Priestess Avi seems to be the reason for much wrongdoing in our valley, it sounds as if Erval is truly the one to blame." Jonas turned back to Phineas. "We get to the crux of it, then. If you've come for some answer as to what the future holds, I can't help you. But when it comes to information regarding the ancient religion you seek..." Jonas rolled up one of his maps and slapped it into his free hand. "I also can't help you."

Phineas blinked behind his wire framed spectacles. "Then I would like the Chosen One and Ahren to accompany me back to Thonethren. And I will teach them how to protect themselves from Erval's intrusions along the way."

"She's not going anywhere," Gamaliel said. "Not without me."

Solyana's cheeks burned.

"Funny you call her that." Jonas pulled his bag into his lap. "But in light of Solyana's return, Ahren's retrieval, and the green coming back to Mothmar—something even more important has been revealed. Two months after you left, Seer Brotnur—may he bask in the Father's eternal light—did, in fact, prophesy."

Solyana's head snapped up. Ahren raised an eyebrow.

Jonas rifled through his bag and retrieved a scroll. Unfurling it, he adjusted his glasses and began. "In five centuries, an uprising of darkness will consume the hearts of men. Desiring what is impossible to attain, they will capture the very souls of their kin."

Phineas stifled a gasp.

"Trapped, many will die at their hands, unknown to the one foretold. This continual dark will bring the cold. But when all hope seems lost, and the world knows nothing but white, there will come one who will bring green. One who must follow the paths of the sky. One who is all light, to stand to the one who is all dark, of which there will be two. One who possesses the three as one, who will save us all through the antithesis of darkness. Unaided by this world's gifts, filled with the one—the way that connects one to all, three in one. You will know this one by the mark, known by the one who brings the white."

The room fell to silence once more before Gamaliel stood to stoke the fire at the hearth. "They have been trying to interpret that these last five years."

"Trying? We have!" Jonas exclaimed as he launched to his feet and began pacing the room. "We believed for generations the prophecy, which was incorrectly recorded to begin with, was about *one* person. But it is, in fact, about five to seven."

Shaking her head, Solyana let out an exasperated laugh. "This makes no sense. How could we have gone on for so long without correction? Why would the Celestials allow such a thing?" The feelings and changes she had undergone while climbing up Mount Endirinn resurfaced, her need for truth rising above the confusion. No one knew the depths to which her faith had truly wavered, and even now, speaking it aloud filled her with shame. But her misgivings would not be silenced. "Why would they allow us to go so long without sending us this new prophecy?"

"You sound like me the last few years," Jonas said. "I hope to find those answers soon."

Solyana twisted her lips, eyes following Jonas. "So, who are these people? Am I even on the list?" Solyana refused to accept the possibility her entire life had been upended for a lie.

Chosen or not, spring had returned to Mothmar. The evidence was just outside their door.

"On the contrary," Jonas said. "Your return from the mountain answers that question for me. You, Solyana, are the one who brings the green. Releasing Ahren, although done incorrectly, brought the green...but with consequences. Your loss of five years is evidence of that. Then, there is someone who must follow the paths of the sky."

"But I thought that was us, following the Norlos!" Solyana said in disbelief.

Their entire journey to Mount Endirinn had rested on the belief they were being led by the waving lights in the night sky.

Jonas shook his head. "We thought so only because that is what Priestess Avi told us. But in cross-referencing the term Seer Brotnur used, I don't believe those are the paths the prophecy means. The word 'paths' translates back into ancient Mothmari as Leídín or...The Way. I believe this refers to the constellation Phineas speaks of. 'The way that connects one to all, three in one.' This refers to the religion we are meant to be following. The true worship of the Way."

"Alright, so I brought the green, someone else is supposed to follow the paths," Solyana said, ticking them off on her fingers. "What of the others?"

"Then we have the one who is all light"—Jonas held up three fingers—"to stand to the one who is all dark." He lifted a fourth finger. "Of which there will be two." He released his thumb. "One who possesses the three as one, who will save us all through the antithesis of darkness." He brought his second hand up with his thumb extended. "Known by the one who brings the white." He raised his pointer finger, for a total of seven. "Now, we don't know if any of these people are repeated, but I thought it best to assume we could be searching for this many."

"Do you have any theories for who might be whom?" Phineas inquired.

Jonas grinned, placing his hands on his hips, shoulders thrown back. "As a matter of fact, I do." The room stared at him in stunned silence. "I believe I'm one of them, and to fulfill it, I leave the day after tomorrow!"

HE LIKES RED

PALLAH

WHAT A SIMPLE BUT foreign concept—being cared for. Pallah rolled over, reveling within the down blankets, before her nose caught wind of something. She sniffed, eyes peering over a pillow to find a rolling cart piled high with plates of food. Food that neither she nor her siblings had to make in their tiny kitchen while their father breathed down their necks. She shoved the memory from her mind and scrambled from the bed.

A grin plastered to her face, Pallah stood before the cart. Between the steaming heap of fluffy yellow eggs, the thick cuts of bacon that still crackled atop a cast iron skillet, and entire plates of pastries, she didn't know what to eat first.

Piling her plate high, she jumped back into bed, a few of the items flipping from her plate onto the blankets. She giggled, thinking of the fit her father would have made if he could see her now, eating in bed, grease staining her covers. But Erval's steward had made it clear. She was the ruler of her own destiny here; there was nothing she couldn't do.

Pallah and Issha had arrived the evening before, though the glimpse of King Erval she'd had was her only one. He had yet to make another appearance. A litter had awaited her as they'd approached the city proper, and it had brought them swiftly through the streets. Women and children had followed, stopping every so often to search the ground. Pallah wondered what they were looking for.

"We stay together," Issha stated as they'd traveled from the outer huts and hovels to the more opulent mansions surrounding the castle itself. "I don't trust this king."

"I do," Pallah said, remembering his power weaving through her, the toll they'd struck together in the valley.

"I could never trust someone who could tamper with me."

"Interesting." Pallah gave her a hard look. "There is more than one way to manipulate a person, don't you think?"

Issha's eyes found the floor, and Pallah turned back to the window. She didn't need any judgment from someone who tethered blood.

They'd spent the rest of the litter ride in silence, but Pallah had faith. Issha would come to see Erval as she did, in time.

A robed steward had met them at the front gate of the castle. "Pallah! So glad to finally meet you. I'm Phineas." The man had given her a soft bow before turning to Issha. "And who is this?" The man was slightly out of breath, his face tinged red, his body more round than not. He fiddled with the wire frames on his face.

"Issha." She held out her arm for a traditional Mothmari greeting.

Phineas's lips turned down in a sort of backwards smile and gave her a half bow instead. "Greetings, Issha. Please, follow me."

They had followed the portly man into the castle until they reached a mid-level floor, modestly adorned with torches on the walls, the hallways made of simple stone. Pallah marveled at the beauty of it, even in its simplicity. Her valley was beautiful, of course, but this place held true majesty.

"Issha, you will be down the hall on your left. Pallah, you will be coming with me."

"We stay together." Issha's body shifted toward Pallah's, and Pallah suppressed a flash of irritation.

"Unless the king wishes us not to."

Issha had thrown Pallah a look over her shoulder, the color in her cheeks deepening. "I thought we agreed—"

"She's just worried." Pallah gave Phineas a demure smile. "I'll be fine, Issha."

Issha had turned away from Pallah without another word.

Phineas's beady eyes shifted from one girl to the other. He cleared his throat. "Please, make yourselves at home. His Majesty has made it clear this is just as much your home as it is his own. If you're hungry, cold, or tired, simply ring the bell in your room, and a servant will be there momentarily to attend to your needs."

"Can I see Erval?" Pallah had asked, eyes scanning for some obvious sign of him.

Phineas let out a squeaking laugh. "Heavens, no. He's a busy man. He will notify you when it's time."

Pallah's heart had fallen, a twinge of fear threatening to grow into an ache in her chest.

Leaving Issha, Pallah had followed behind the steward until they reached a hallway made of beautiful hardwood. Velvet curtains hung along the walls, creating a cozy ambience. Phineas pushed open a wooden door. This floor held even greater pomp than the level below. Pallah wondered for a moment why Issha had been assigned beneath her, but the thought was quickly pushed from her mind as she entered her room.

Now, here she was, the morning after her arrival, getting pastry crumbs on a down-filled blanket made from the softest fabric she'd ever felt in her life. Cocooned in her four-poster bed, she stared at the opulence of her quarters. She had clawed her way out from her father's house, from the mire of Sodur, to make it to the castle in this lofty city. And she had done it herself.

A row of bells lined the wall, each with a label affixed beneath it. She ambled over, admiring the craftsmanship and modernity of it. Never had she seen a system such as this. The labels read a litany, everything from 'kitchen' to 'stables' to 'bath.' She rang the last, and within ten minutes a servant was adjusting a lever at the copper tub in her room. Hot water sprang from the tap. The servant filled the bath with all sorts of earthy smelling liquids, and bubbles began to form on the surface of the water.

"M'lady?" She gestured to the tub.

"Oh!" Pallah gasped and laughed all at once. "Thank you." But the woman didn't leave. Instead, she stepped forward and began tugging at Pallah's clothes. "Oh, no, thank you," Pallah said, her face reddening. "I can bathe myself."

"As you wish." The servant bowed out of the room.

Crusted blood, dirt, and sweat flaked away into the water as she washed, and by the time she emerged, she felt like a new woman. Catching herself in the room's floor length mirror, Pallah surveyed every part of herself. Each time she was tempted to cringe away or dismiss a detail, she straightened her shoulders and took it all in.

No longer was she a girl, cowering under the wishes and whims of others. She was her own maker.

A bell rang and Pallah jumped, unaware the bells worked both ways. She skipped to it, her face breaking into a grin as she read the word beneath: 'Missive.' Below the bell, there was an open metal cylinder. Pallah squinted at it, getting on her knees to peer inside. Suddenly a scroll dropped into the tube, and Pallah gasped. She removed it with care.

Pallah,

I had to do a little guessing on your measurements but have procured a few options for our first meeting. Please dress and make your way to the upper balcony to join me for tea and cakes.

Yours, Erval

Ps. I prefer the red one

Heart thudding out of her chest, Pallah read the missive three times over before pressing it to her lips, folding it tight, and tucking it beneath her mattress—an old habit. She found the closet set into the wall, almost invisible, inlaid as it was. Pulling it open, she found at least ten dresses, each unique and jaw-droppingly beautiful. Though Pallah had never been one to wear anything but linen pants and a tunic, she was determined to make a good first impression.

Her hands gliding over the array of fabrics, Pallah stopped short on the red one. He liked red? She would give him red. She pulled the dress from its place and got to work.

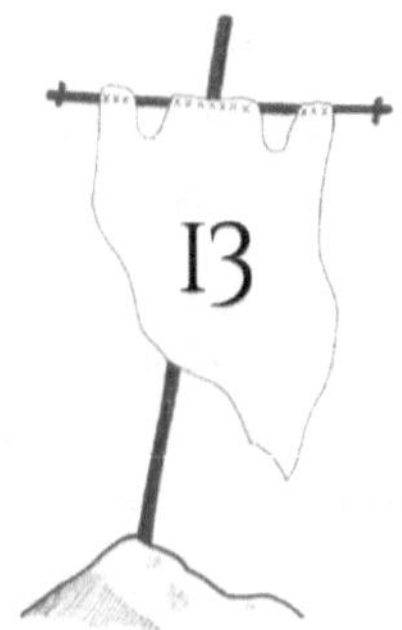

SNAKE TATTOO

HALLDORA

WOULD IT BE ENOUGH? The incessant gnaw of the unknown kept Halldora awake at night. She had gained ships from the Crimson Chief and Beast Riders from Chief Orson, but her spies' reports regarding her brother's martial capabilities remained inconclusive.

How many groundmen did Thonethren maintain? How many cavalry? Information was hard won, if it could be gleaned at all. When Erval had ousted her from her throne all those years ago, he'd had an army. And though it had not been large in number, he had effectively utilized his Mann Tala to poke strategic holes in her own retinue—as fragile as an unkempt wineskin.

Now, she had her own forces on a strict regimen of saxifrage tea—Erval would be hard pressed to psychically access her men now. But her stores were running low. They were going to have to move again, and soon, if they were to find more to keep up their supply. And to properly supply enough for the Crimson Fleet and Orson's men, too.

Halldora sighed, leaning back in her chair. The cost of being a leader was going to age her faster than any Taking could combat.

The moon was a wicked smile outside the window of her tent. She stared at it, listening to the chatter of crickets and toads.

And footsteps.

Halldora slowly straightened, ears piqued. The steps she heard were far too light to be those of her guard. Where were they? Young, impertinent pups. She trusted none of them.

Throwing a cloak over herself, she drew her longsword from its place near her bed and blew out her lantern.

The footsteps halted.

Häfa. She would have to move quickly.

Crouching, Halldora moved like a snake, quiet and invisible in the night. She exited her tent and snuck around the side, drawing her blade silently from its sheath. But when she rounded her tent, there was no one. She straightened, eyes and ears still on high alert. Perhaps she had imagined it.

A woman's voice sounded from behind her. "You must be Halldora."

Häfa!

Halldora swiveled, her hands up in surrender, sword hovering between two fingers. Innocence was her friend now. The appearance of submission would save her. Where were her guards?

But the question did not go unanswered for long. Stepping into the moonlight, a figure held a knife to one of her guard's throats. The hood of their cloak fell back to reveal the face of a woman, beautiful albeit hardened eyes shining from a mask of black paint.

Halldora took in the details. There were five total intruders including the woman, and only two of her own men. She carefully repositioned the hilt of her sword back into her palm. The work before her would not be easy. But before she could step forward to strike, the woman released her man and held the dagger to the side, eyes on Halldora.

"You have no reason to be afraid, Halldora. Even though you saw fit to dispatch Corun, I will show your servants grace." Her loose sleeves fell away from her wrists, revealing a long winding snake tattoo around her left forearm. "We only seek audience with the one bent on unseating the usurper."

Halldora relaxed her shoulders but kept her sword firm in her grip. Her intuition of the young pock-marked soldier had been right. "Spies in my ranks, hm?" She squinted at the woman, whose blonde hair was braided back in intricate weaves. "That's one strike against you. The second is this night business. I hold court during the day."

"If I had shown up earlier, your men would have brought me to you in chains. And no true queen would give a prisoner voice."

Halldora smirked as she slid her sword back into its sheath. "A fair point."

The blonde woman tilted her head with a matching smirk. "Your Majesty, I have a proposition for you."

"Do you, now?" Halldora's smirk became a smile. "And what would that be?"

"I've heard of your plans on working with Chief Orson of Takanah. I come to warn you against allying with him and to offer Your Grace my people instead."

"And what do you have to offer that Orson cannot?"

"A more potent army of Beast Riders."

Halldora rolled her eyes. "Chief Orson's beasts transform from people themselves, completely submitted to their riders. I don't see how yours could be an improvement. He has hundreds of them, an entire battalion."

Something like sorrow flitted across the woman's face before her hard eyes found Halldora's once more. "My Beast Riders ride *only* beasts. And we do not Take." Her shoulders straightened. "We do not practice the Taka Reu."

"You have something against it?"

"Without it, we are stronger, daughter of King Mikkael."

Halldora stilled, one eyebrow peaking. "Now that is a name I haven't heard in some time." If this woman knew of her father, then she knew the depths of Halldora's Taking. "I don't see how planting yourself firmly against my choice of religion will encourage an allyship."

The woman allowed a small grin to touch her lips. "Though I do not support the same Dark Gifts as you do, I see one who wields them yet darker. And if I were to choose..." She shrugged.

"And if I say yes?"

The woman clasped her hands behind her. "We have a supply of blocking tea that could keep your army secure for months. And we have a great number of Beast Riders trained to fight."

Halldora raised an eyebrow. She needed that tea.

"In return, you turn Orson away."

"And I'm assuming you require other payment. Are you looking to rule some part of Mothmar?" Halldora asked.

"No." The woman shook her head. "When this bloody business is done, my service will turn toward that of Solyana Marusda."

The name turned something in Halldora's mind. She had heard the whispers of the Sun Daughter ascending Mouth Endirinn and bringing Mothmar from white to green. She had begun to think of the name as something befitting a fairytale, but nothing more. Halldora cared not what gods each member of her war served. The only important distinction was who was for Erval and who wasn't. But she had not considered the loyalties such a girl could purchase. Perhaps she should reconsider.

"What if," Halldora said, "we band together—all of us. You, me, and Orson! The more the better." She would not yet reveal her work with the Crimson Chief.

The woman scoffed and shook her head.

"If it leads to victory, then we all win."

The woman stilled.

"There is victory, and there is cost, Your Majesty." She motioned to her men to release the guards. "I hope you will allow us to be of service to you."

The group released Halldora's men and retreated into the shadows. Her guards looked to her, hands going to hilts, but Halldora raised a hand to stop them; she would not chase this woman, not tonight. "What do I call you?"

The woman was already atop an elk, head and shoulders taller than Halldora's tent. Halldora tried to hide her surprise but wasn't sure if she succeeded. The creature snorted, great clouds of warm air unfurling from its nostrils.

"You can call me Maral. And I fight for the people of the Way."

TORNY'S TAVERN

PHINEAS

WITH A PROMISE TO return in the early hours to teach Solyana how to barricade her mind from Erval, Phineas headed back to the inn, accompanied only by the songs of crickets. The night was warm, almost balmy, and although the reason for his visit had been quite dire, he couldn't help the thrill that ran through his soul.

He was away from Erval for the first time in decades—perhaps centuries. A grin lit his face, and he almost skipped down the path to the main square. The tell-tale nudge of Erval's intrusions hadn't come to him since arriving in Endirinn, and the freedom was exhilarating. It wouldn't take the king long, however. Whatever his promises, he would surely intrude soon. But in the meantime, Phineas reveled in his solitude.

He had taken a wagon from Thonethren to Endirinn. A few days into the journey, Erval had begun his poking and prodding. And Phineas had allowed him, of course, though only along the paths he had curated for the man. Was Erval beginning to notice? Phineas tried to plausibly alter what he allowed his old friend to see. Aside from the predicted servitude, submission, and awe of the king and his schemes, Phineas allowed some of his true thoughts and feelings to let themselves be known: bouts of discontentment, envy of His Majesty's power.

Whatever he inwardly allowed or didn't, Erval was at least restricted from accessing Phineas's eyes. And although Phineas had a theory as to why, it was not yet clear.

Years before, when Erval had begun his experiments on children—Pallah in particular—he had recounted to Phineas how he could see what the girl was seeing. This ability didn't always convey to adults, especially ones who had never come into personal contact with him. More often than not, adults tethered by Erval went mad, and to his frustration, resigned themselves to the wider end of a noose. The finnevel was the element seemingly at fault. Although Phineas himself had crafted it, he did not yet understand why the repeated oddity took place.

Two villagers passed by him on the path, both issuing friendly nods and smiles in the moonlight. Phineas returned their greeting, his heart feeling a love for these mountain people so different from his own, far to the west. There was community here, a feeling of oneness. His people were cold, emotionally removed from one another. If they wandered at night, it was to bring tidings only dark and dangerous.

Slowing to a halt, Phineas looked over his shoulder at the couple, their hands entwined as they stopped to share a kiss beneath a lantern. A pang of loss struck deep in the furrows of Phineas's soul. How carefree could a people be?

If only he could stay to find out.

The inn came into view, a tall building that was homey, if not a bit dilapidated. Like a hearth, the ground floor of the building glowed with welcome while the second story held guttering lights set within dim windows. A group of travelers relaxed about the entrance that was open wide to let in the warm evening air. Above the door, a proud wooden sign hung to boast the name: Torny's Tavern. A realistic looking iguana was chiseled into it, wrapping the words with the bulk of its tail, the point of it forming the "T" in "tavern". An odd symbol. Phineas had yet to see an iguana anywhere near Endirinn; goats, however, were another matter entirely.

He nodded at the others as he entered, requested a drink to be sent to his quarters, and wound up the flight of stairs to his room.

It happened then, as he changed into his nightgown, the nudge of the king of Thonethren. Phineas steeled himself, cutting off the avenues of interest and knowledge he kept secured from Erval, before allowing his old friend access.

Evening, Phin. Good to see you've arrived safe and sound.

Phineas shuddered.

How are you faring?

"Fine," Phineas said as he sat at the end of his bed, hands busily moving over each other. "I've begun my hunt for the Seer. It seems he has left to travel south only recently." The lie came easily. He respected Seers, no matter their religious affiliation, and wished for Jonas to be safe from the clutches of the king.

The south? There's nothing but riff-raff in those parts.

Phineas shrugged. "Well, that's where he's gone, according to the people."

Don't believe everything you hear, dear Phineas. Your mind is growing lax. When was the last time you Took?

Cold dread seeped into Phineas. He had aged far faster than Erval, on account of his refusal to use the Taking unless his hand was forced. And when he was commanded, he would search the rabble of the streets for some old soul ready to depart from the world. Phineas cared not for the Gifts they gave him, or the years they granted. He did it only to spare whatever soul Erval would Take on his behalf. Erval, who had decided he and Phineas would stay young together forever.

When, in fact, there was nothing he desired less.

Phineas was tired. Not a simple weariness but an exhaustion in the marrow of his bones, made thicker with regret. And although he had begun on Erval's side, the desire he'd had to be part of something great had been stamped out long ago. What matter was greatness when the most important parts of him were stained with darkness?

Your silence tells me all I need to know. Erval let out the sigh of an exasperated parent. *You must take care of yourself, Phin, or you'll shrivel away to nothing! Don't worry. I will handle it.*

"No, Erval, I—"

But Erval untethered. What the man was going to do for him, Phineas wasn't certain. But he could guess, and it chilled him to the bone.

A knock sounded, accompanied by a small, muffled voice. "Your drink, sir."

Wrapping his robe tighter around him, Phineas shuffled to the door. He opened it wide to find the tavern owner's young daughter holding a tray.

Her freckled face beamed at him, her arms extending with her charge. "I like it with a bit more sugar, so I put some here." She nodded toward the small sugar bowl on the tray.

"How thoughtful," Phineas said with a nod. "Thank you, dear... And what is your name?"

"Kira." She passed the tray over.

Phineas grinned and took it just as the girl went rigid, her face dropping her smile, her eyes going blank. Then, in a voice much lower and more monotone than before, "Found one for you, Phineas. Take her quickly. Her parents are busy downstairs."

Horror clawed at Phineas's insides as he watched the girl, devoid of her will, speak Erval's words. It was a method of tethering he had only begun to employ in recent years. No mere manipulation, but total control of will and body.

A door opened from down the hall, and a woman's voice. "Just request another blanket. I don't want to catch a chill."

"Yes, dear," a man answered, stepping into the hallway.

Phineas stashed the tray and pulled the girl inside, sweat sprouting from his temples. Kira stared blankly at the wall, her body limp and malleable.

"Yes, best do it behind closed doors," Erval said through her.

"You can leave me to it." Phineas could hardly keep the shake from his voice. He hadn't performed the Taking on someone so young in decades. And even then, he'd vowed never to do it again.

"Can I, though?" The girl turned to look at him with slack and empty eyes. "You won't just release her the moment I am gone?"

"Please, Erval. I promise, I will Take someone, just not Kira. She's the owner's daughter! It will be known!"

"You gave it a name." Kira scoffed. A jarring sound coming from someone lacking all facial expression. "You've gone soft on me, Phin. But fine. Choose someone. But do it soon. You're looking...peaky."

All at once the girl blinked back to herself, her shoulders sagging, her knees buckling. Phineas reached to steady her when a second knock came at the door.

"Phineas?" A man's voice this time. Phineas felt the sweat from his palms soak into the girl's sleeves.

"Sir? How did I get in here?" Kira twisted in Phineas's grip, eyeing the door. "I need—I need to get back downstairs."

"It's Gamaliel and Rorhan. Just wanted a quick chat."

"Let me go!" Kira shook from his grip.

"I-I'm so sorry, Kira! I was just trying to keep you from falling."

"I'm not allowed in the rooms!" Kira's face filled with fear and confusion.

"Y-you looked faint! I didn't want you to hurt yourself. When I took the tray you—"

"Something is not right." The man called Rorhan. "Do not worry. I will open."

The door let out a crack and flung inward, knocking Phineas to the ground, his spectacles sliding away.

The girl screamed as Gamaliel and Rorhan entered the room. "Are you alright, child?" Rorhan dropped to a knee. "What did this man do to you?"

Phineas sat up, pressing a hand to his face, it came away bloody. He whimpered and tried to get to his feet, but a pair of leather shoes blocked his way, a staff coming to rest with a *thump* beside them. He peered up to see the blurry figure of Gamaliel in the firelight, his hair resembling a dark cloak as he stared down at him. Or at least, Phineas thought the man was staring down at him. Phineas searched the floor for his glasses.

"Don't move," Gamaliel sneered.

"He said I was fainting." The girl shook her head. "And I do feel a bit dizzy."

Rorhan led her from the room, talking quietly. Failing to find his wire frames, Phineas squinted up at Gamaliel, his hands now slick with blood. "Can I get a towel?" His voice was more nasal than usual.

Gamaliel stepped to the side of the room and threw a towel in Phineas's direction.

"Thank you," Phineas said as he picked it up from the floor and stood.

"The girl seems unharmed," Rorhan said as he entered. He closed the door behind him, but with the latch no longer attached, it slid open again. "What were you doing with a nine-year-old in your room, you—"

"She was only bringing me tea!" Phineas kept the towel pressed firmly to his nose. Gamaliel bent down, and when he straightened again, he held Phineas's eyewear out to him. "Thank you," Phineas said as he slipped them on.

Half of Phineas knew he needed to tell them the truth now, that they wouldn't trust him if he didn't. But the other half knew he had no way of proving Erval had tethered the girl. Looking at the scene as it was, he wasn't sure he'd believe himself were he in their position. "She was white as a sheet when I grabbed the tray." He motioned to the tray, where tea had spilled over the edge of the mug. "I tried to catch her before she fell. Please believe me, it was nothing nefarious. I love children."

Rorhan crossed his arms. "Do you?"

Phineas's eyes swung to Gamaliel, but the man's face was hard as stone, his knuckles white on his staff.

"Not like that!" Phineas threw his hands in the air. "I don't know what to tell you. I'm an old man who just wanted his nightly tea and some rest. Please, I have had an exhausting few weeks." Blood began to drip once more, and he pressed the towel back to his face.

Gamaliel sighed. "You show up here on the day we find Solyana. You come from the king of Thonethren who is the very same man who has penetrated the minds of both Solyana and this woman, Pallah. You claim to want to stop him, but I'm through watching Solyana get roped into other people's schemes. Jonas may trust you, but I don't. Give me a reason why any of us should act on the information you've offered."

"I only showed up at Seer Jonas's invitation. It was coincidence she appeared today. I truly had no idea."

"Hard to believe that from someone more ancient than Priestess Avi." Gamaliel scoffed. "You, Erval, Pallah...doing away with your victims just to live a few more years."

"Please believe me when I say I have put that life behind me! I am no longer acquainted with those ways."

"Yet you use the Taka Reu?" Rorhan pointed out.

"One cannot use anything but in Erval's service!"

"Do you think Solyana..." Gamaliel trailed off, gazing toward the window. "Do you think she has done the Taking?"

Phineas shook his head adamantly. "No. Giving and Taking are not the same. The name implies its very difference. When one Gives, they willingly impart their Gift to someone else. Their life leaves them, and their years are lost as honorable sacrifice. The Taking is an act of force. The Taker takes—Gifts, years, lives."

The room seemed to lose its air, sucked dry of life as the three men stared anywhere but at each other.

"There is no benefit for me coming here. This journey to find the Seer, the opportunity to speak with Solyana, it holds nothing but risk for me."

"Is Erval not staring out of those eyes right now? Is he not spying on all we do?" Gamaliel loomed over him. "I can't believe we let you in the house!"

"No!" Phineas stood once more. "I swear to you, on my life. I have found a way to keep Erval sequestered to only one part of my mind. He does not see through my eyes or enter my mind in its fullness. I keep parts from him."

Gamaliel shook his head. "And we're to believe this is all out of empathy, is it?"

Phineas clutched his robes in his hands, the deep purple fabric soaked through with tea. "No." He looked at Gamaliel. "It's self-preservation."

"You are in danger?" Rorhan asked.

"If Erval knew what I was doing, yes. But more than that, all of Mothmar is in danger. I'm here to lay bare Erval's plans, and to help you combat them."

"Why not just stop him yourself?" Gamaliel asked.

Phineas gave a dark chuckle. "One cannot stop a man made up of thousands. Erval is ancient, much like myself, but with one distinct difference: intent. He has amassed his power with the intent of being worshiped by all. Not just some, not just Thonethren... *All.* This is not simple rulership either. He desires full access to all minds, to be able to stamp out insurrection before the thought of it even fully forms."

"To control the will of all men," Rorhan stated flatly.

"Indeed." Phineas nodded. "Secondly, he wants Pallah back."

"That I don't understand." Gamaliel shook his head. "What's the point of a single person when he would have an entire country?"

"It's not who she is; it's what she is to him. A protégé, a partner, a rival...Pallah represents a version of Erval he took great pains to create. A tribute to himself that he could wield, that would do his bidding. But she betrayed him, she escaped him, she made him the fool." Phineas shook his head, memories of that day scraping across his brain. "Vengeance fuels his desires toward Pallah. He made a monster for a pet, and he hates her for having bitten his hand."

"Regardless of how powerful he is over one person, there's no possible way he can invade the minds of thousands," Gamaliel said.

Phineas hung his head. "Ah, yes...you're right. He couldn't. Not on his own. Not without a machine that could allow you to split the tether of all the souls you had stored over the centuries." He braced himself for the words he would speak next. "It started with the finnevel, which allowed him to tether over great distances. It transformed over time, from a large contraption to something resembling a single spectacle." He tapped the side of his crooked round glasses. "But then he asked me for something that would allow him to split his tether without completely severing it."

"And you made it?" Rorhan asked.

"I did."

"He has access to this now?" Gamaliel asked.

"Yes. It's called the Brextant." Phineas said. "Though it needs a final component, he may be able to use it long enough to tether every mind in Mothmar. It won't be incredibly strong, but it will allow a thin strand of consciousness to reside between him and every person for a time."

"What is this component?"

Phineas pulled his spectacles from his face and rubbed at his eyes. He hadn't wanted to give this information yet. They were not ready. "Years," he said. "He needs someone stuffed with time, built up in the soul of a person, strong enough to attach to every soul in Mothmar."

"Pallah, then?" Understanding lit behind Gamaliel's eyes. "Or you."

Phineas was silent.

"Self-preservation," Rorhan said, nodding slowly. "I see."

Gamaliel opened his mouth once more, but Rorhan put a hand to his chest. "Brother, I think it best to leave. He is not going anywhere. I take what he says as truth." The man eyed Phineas. "Besides, I must not keep my wife waiting."

"But I have more questions about the nature of his relationship with Sol—"

Rorhan clapped one hand on Gamaliel's shoulder and stretched the other to Phineas's shoulder. Phineas cowered beneath the weight. "It is late. We know where this man sleeps." He chuckled. "He has no lock on his door. And he values his life." Rorhan grinned. "Sleep sweetly, Phineas."

Phineas nodded, clutching the towel to keep from wringing his hands.

Both men turned and swept from the room. The single candle on Phineas's bedside table winked out with the *clack* of the door in its frame, leaving him in total darkness.

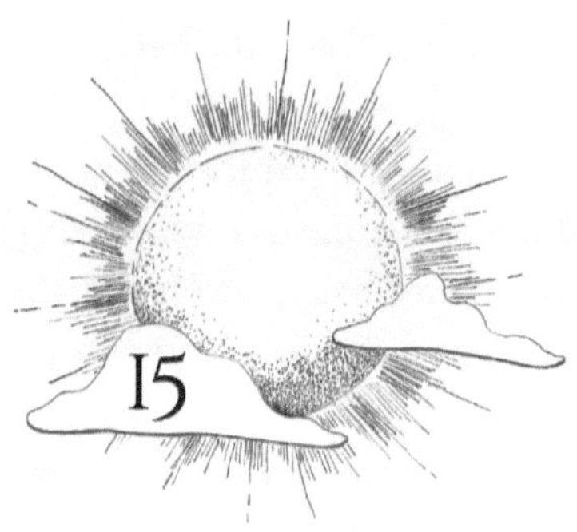

STAY

SOLYANA

AFTER JONAS REVEALED HIS alleged place in the prophecy, he had unveiled his plan.

"The day after tomorrow?" Solyana had felt something in her heart stutter. She had just returned, reunited for less than a day. Did they have to separate again already? She had missed so much. The gaps of time that had passed between them still needed to be filled. "I need to get ready," she conceded.

"No, you don't." Gamaliel had made his way to Jonas, the two almost the same height now. He had gripped the boy's shoulders to give him a playful shake. "If Erval is going to discover you any minute, you need to head to Thonethren. This one is going out on his own. Well, not entirely."

"Have you decided?" Jonas had asked, eyes on Rorhan and then Lone.

"The road is no place for Marin," Lone had said, running a hand through her cropped white hair. "I can't uproot her from all she knows. And besides—" She held up her metal leg. "I would slow you down."

"You would do no such thing." Rorhan had stepped behind his wife and kissed the top of her head. "I would carry you."

Lone had smiled sadly and shook her head. "You go, Han. Jonas needs some muscle."

Rorhan bent down and wrapped his arms around Lone, bringing his face next to hers. He kissed her cheek and then eyed Jonas. "We have already discussed. I will go."

Jonas had nodded. "Thank you, Rorhan."

Now, Solyana followed Jonas to the home he shared with Gamaliel. The moon was obscured with shifting clouds and the sky a winking map of stars. Ahren walked behind her with Vinur at his side; the wolf seemed to have taken a liking to the boy.

"So, where *are* you going?" Solyana asked, kicking a pebble from the path.

Jonas had grown sullen once they'd left. She hadn't missed the way his eyes lingered on Gamaliel and Rorhan, who had stayed around Lone's table. "I believe I have found a tribe of people, an ancient tribe, even older than Rorhan's. They live on an island in the Himmin Sea, east of here, and almost as far south as Skrim."

Solyana blinked, surprised. Skrim Sea was located south of her valley. "You're going to hike all the way back there?"

"Actually," Jonas said with a grin. "I'm going to take a boat."

"Sounds like an adventure," Solyana said. Gamaliel's quick assertion she wasn't going with them had both irked her and been a relief. "I do wish I could go."

"You could." Jonas halted. Taller than her now, he peered down at her through his round spectacles. "I don't see why Gamaliel gets to make that decision for you. We could all find the people of the Way before going to Thonethren."

"I..." Solyana chewed at her lip, weighing her options. "If I go with you, I'm risking Rhuth. If she's still with Priestess Avi—"

"Pallah," Ahren interjected. "My sister's name is Pallah."

Solyana looked at him, unsure what to make of this boy from the mountain and his association with the priestess from her home. "If they're still together, Erval will know where she is. I can't risk him getting ahold of her. Something tells me he won't make good on our deal."

"The deal where you hand me over to a king bent on tyrannical rule?" Ahren monotoned.

"I only agreed so he wouldn't hurt my sister! You would've done the same, I'm sure."

"No," Ahren said. "No, I wouldn't have. You don't know me, Solyana."

And he was right. She didn't.

"We'll figure it out, okay?" Solyana turned from him. "I thought Gamaliel would be just behind us," she said.

"He probably went into town."

Solyana blinked in surprise. "This late?"

"Torny's Tavern is open all hours." Jonas's voice held a bite Solyana hadn't heard before. "I'm old enough; he doesn't have to look after me so closely anymore."

Solyana's face burned at the detail, strangely embarrassed at this insight into his life. "How old are you now, Jonas?" she asked.

"Seventeen," Jonas said, a slight tilt in his lips. "Birthday was last week."

"Oh." Solyana wondered when the pangs of loss would abate. "Well, happy birthday, Jonas."

"Thank you." He gave her a full grin.

"How old are you, Ahren?"

"I was sixteen, last I knew."

"And by my calculations, you're approximately three hundred, give or take a few years," Jonas offered.

"Right," Ahren said. "We look to be about the same age, Solyana. So, how old are you?"

"I guess I'm...twenty-one?" Solyana shrugged.

"I'll claim that too, then."

They stared at each other a moment, dual victims of a long-forgotten curse. Jonas walked ahead with Vinur.

"I get it." Ahren's eyes sparked with intensity. "You lost years, your home, your family. And you're aching to get at least one piece of it back. What's your sister's name again?"

"Rhuth," Solyana said, unable to tear her eyes from his.

"I bet Rhuth would like nothing more than to see you again. I know Pallah has done some things. *Häfa* it all, she's as old as Phineas. She's killed for immortality. But I didn't spend hundreds of years locked away only to give up on the only person I have left. If I'm going to get her back, and you're going to get Rhuth back, we need to work together."

Solyana released a breath. "So, we go to Thonethren. For our sisters."

"For our sisters." He gave her a lopsided grin. "We'll figure it out," he echoed.

The two of them approached a small house set into a large boulder.

"And stop King Erval in the process," Jonas filled in from the stoop. "And take Gamaliel with you. I can't bring him on a boat and surround him with sailors. Too many shared hobbies."

His meaning was plain, but Solyana balked at the blatant confirmation of her suspicions.

"Is this your house?" Ahren asked, scanning the wooden door set into the stone. "It's nice work."

"It's like...your old cave!" Solyana grinned.

"Exactly why Gamaliel wanted it. He got some help from Stein and Vior Fera who could work with the stone and wood, make it weather secure." He swung the door inward. "Come on in."

Unlike Lone's home, which held the hearth on the northern wall, the fireplace here resided in the center. The stone chimney was set straight through the ceiling, and Jonas got to work right away.

"Surely we don't need a fire tonight," Solyana suggested. Though she liked the hominess of it, she didn't want the cave-home to get too warm.

"It stays surprisingly cool in here," Jonas offered. "Plus, Gamaliel usually stays up for a while after he gets home."

"There seems to be a lot I don't know about Gamaliel these days."

"He seems like a pretty upstanding guy," Ahren chimed in, grabbing a few small sticks from a basket by the edge of the hearth and passing them to Jonas.

The fire sparked to life in Jonas's hands, and he tended to it before sitting back on his heels. Solyana noticed the row of mugs and cups lining the hearth as Jonas began to collect them.

"Jonas, what happened while I was gone?"

Jonas sighed, the exasperation in it too old for his seventeen years. "You disappeared, Solyana. And quite honestly, it broke him. I don't know what happened between the two of you the night before you left, but... He seemed to think there was more than friendship."

Solyana's throat dried up.

Jonas looked at her, something like suspicion or contempt within his eyes. "Was there?"

"I'm not sure," she lied.

Their intimacy the night before she left was not a thing to be shared with anyone, least of all Jonas. But she could remember the feeling of Gamliel behind her, wrapping his arms around her in the bed they'd shared in Temple Rinn.

Jonas brought the various pottery to the sink in the corner before returning. "Well, you may not be sure, but he was. He became obsessed, searching the mountain every day for months. It wasn't until Lone and Rorhan got together that something seemed to shake him out of it. It was like he realized life was going to go on, whether or not you were there. He didn't give up, though." Jonas stoked the fire. "He returned to that mountain a few times each year. Especially on the day you left, when the Norlos is about to hit its peak brightness.

"This year, he only went once, on the anniversary you disappeared. Vinur went with him, too, for the first time. Gam had never allowed him before; he had always deemed it too dangerous. But since the snow had melted, Gamaliel thought he could handle it."

Something turned over in Solyana's mind as she thought back to the mountain's peak, the discordant meadow, and the boy before her aging faster than time. What had snapped her out of it? What had—

"I heard him!" Ahren said abruptly and Solyana nodded.

"Maybe that's what jolted me back, what made me notice something was wrong. I thought it was wind, but it wasn't. Vinur howled!"

"You should tell Gamaliel that," Jonas said. "Or maybe not. If he had brought Vinur up sooner, I wonder if you would have been back before now."

Solyana didn't want to think about that. One small decision holding the ability to change so much. "What have you been doing the last five years?" Solyana turned the conversation away from the mountain.

"I've been studying, researching, trying to find a solid answer for the prophecy I was given from Seer Brotnur. In the last few months, however, I've been putting together plans for my trip."

"And Gamaliel?"

The door slammed shut, and Solyana jumped. She hadn't even heard it open. She turned to see Gamaliel leaning his staff against the wall. Vinur trotted toward him, giving him a sniff and a sneeze. The wolf returned to Jonas, where he curled up next to the fire.

"And me?" Gamaliel inquired, his face half lit in the darkened room.

"Just catching up on what's been going on the last five years," Jonas offered. "How was Torny's?"

Gamaliel grunted as he strode past where they were seated on the floor. He poured himself a cup of water from a pitcher.

"You're surprisingly...vertical," Jonas said.

"I didn't drink," Gamaliel said, wiping his mouth with the back of his hand.

"Oh, there's something else to do at Torny's? I never knew." Jonas returned his attention to the fire.

"Let me know if you and Rorhan go again. Maybe I can come along," Ahren said.

Jonas clicked his tongue and shook his head.

"We were just making sure Phineas got home safe, is all." Gamaliel's eyes finally found Solyana's, and her face grew hot. "Jonas get you set up? Do you need anything else?"

"Well, a blanket would be nice." She gave a small smile. "And a pillow, if you have one."

"What have you been doing in here, Jonas?" Gamaliel began gathering items from a chest in the corner. "Ahren can sleep out here by the fire. Hope you don't mind."

"I think I could fall asleep standing up at this point," Ahren said as Gamaliel tossed a blanket and pillow at him.

He crossed to Solyana, handing her a soft blanket. "You can take my room."

Standing so close to him, Solyana felt her heart dip as she smelled the familiar scent of cedar and cave smoke.

Jonas paused in running his fingers through Vinur's fur to look up with a mischievous grin. "With you?"

Gamaliel's eyes slid from Solyana to the boy. "I think it's past your bedtime, isn't it, Jonas? Better get your beauty sleep before your trip."

Jonas's face fell.

"I'll sleep out here with Ahren," Gamaliel confirmed.

The group prepared their mats and beds, and before long, Solyana was left alone in the cramped space of Gamaliel's bedroom. It held nothing personal but his cot, a small table, and a basket where a shirt peeked out from under the lid. Though this cave was made to resemble his old one back in the valley, this one was nothing like it. That home had held life and love. This one held nothing but barren hopes and empty expectations.

Five years. Gamaliel must have had multiple opportunities to move on. Travel to new places, find a job he could excel at...find a woman he could have started a family with. Solyana shook her head. She wouldn't think about that, the idea that she could have been the reason he had missed out on his life, or worse, turned to drink.

Solyana lay on the cot that smelled of Gamaliel. She should sleep, but the low voices beyond the strip of hide that served as a door kept her awake and curious. She listened, hoping the rumble of Gamaliel and Ahren's voices would lull her. Yet, even after their conversation stopped and all she heard was the occasional pop of the fire, sleep evaded her.

With the intention of visiting the washroom, Solyana sneaked from the bedroom toward the door. She passed by Ahren, curled up on the floor, and Vinur pressed beside him.

"Leaving so soon?" Gamaliel's voice came from the other side of the chimney, and Solyana froze, her eyes finding him on a low stool near the fire, his mug dangling from a single finger.

Solyana's mouth opened and closed. "I was just looking for the washroom."

"Well, you know where it is." He stretched. "The outhouse just outside."

"Why didn't you have them build one inside?"

"And use it near where I sleep? No, thank you!" His words were drawn out and slurred, and Solyana realized he was drunk.

"I'll be right back," she said.

"Sure, you will." Gamaliel lifted the mug back to his lips, then realized it was empty.

Anger built up in Solyana, and she forced herself to take a breath, acknowledging the fact he had been grieving, truly grieving her loss. Then, she had reappeared. It would be jarring for anyone.

She returned inside, grabbed a waterskin from a hook on the wall and sat down beside Gamaliel, her knee close to his leg. His eyes reflected the flames as he watched her.

Solyana pointed at the mug dangling from his finger. "Is that empty?"

"Yup," he said. "Fresh out."

"Of tea?" She allowed herself a small smile.

He grit his teeth before turning it into a bitter smile. "Of tea."

She passed him the waterskin, and he took it reluctantly. "I think we should talk."

"Yeah... That's what Lone said, too."

"Is now a good time?"

"And Rorhan, he told me, too."

"Because you seem...drunk."

Gamaliel set the mug on the floor between them and leaned over it, so close she could smell the strength of the alcohol on his breath. She resisted the urge to back away. She had been responsible for enough distance already.

"And what if I am?" he said.

"Then I don't envy you come the morning."

"You want to talk about mornings?" He stood up suddenly, glaring down at her. "How about the one when I woke up and you were gone? When I thought Orson's men had returned, or the tribe's people had stolen you away? How about the mornings after that, when I trekked circles around that *häfan* mountain while the sun came up? I stood by you, Solyana! From your first steps out of the valley, all the way to Temple Rinn. And you left!"

Her heart pounding in her ears, Solyana stood and guided him toward the door, leaving Ahren and Jonas to sleep in peace.

Gamaliel let himself be led, the night air refreshing, but his temper had yet to cool. "You left." His whisper was filled with venom. Venom Solyana knew she deserved.

"I did," she admitted. "If it makes any difference, I regret it. I didn't know—"

"Yes, you did." Gamaliel's words were like knives. "You knew exactly what you were doing. You just counted on me to be here when you got back. You counted on me to forgive you." His breath came in heaves, a shuddering in his chest. "The sad part is, here I am. I looked for you, and I waited." He was crying, angry tears winking in the light of the moon. "Because I said until the end. And I meant it."

Solyana reached for him, her hand coming to rest on his arm. She moved to take a step closer, but he batted her away.

"They told me to accept you were dead." He looked at her, then dragged his feet backward until he bumped the wall of the house he'd built. He slid down it to sit. "And I tried, but I couldn't stop reaching." He grasped the empty air toward the moon, then closed it into a fist. "At least a bottle could fill my hand. Could help me swallow all the words I never got to say."

Solyana knelt beside him, the lump in her own throat too large to speak past.

"And I had to watch the seasons change." His words trembled. "I had to watch the world turn green without you."

She knew, in that moment, there was nothing she could say. There were no words that would restore or soothe his heart toward her. Her excuses, her guilt...they wouldn't be enough.

"You're right," Solyana whispered. "I let it all get to me; the prophecy, Priestess Avi, Erval, the Taka Reu..." She lifted his chin so he would meet her eyes. "You were never anything but honest and faithful. And when things got difficult, I trusted someone else. And it cost you." The pain in Gamaliel's eyes cut into her soul. "I'll live with that regret for the rest of my life. But I am alive, Gam." She pulled herself closer, wrapping her arms around his shoulders. "I got myself trapped up there, but it was you who brought me back."

"What?" His breath flashed over her cheek as he looked at her in surprise.

"I don't know the timing, but I was stuck on that mountain until I heard Vinur howl. It snapped me out of that cursed meadow."

He grabbed her then, wrapping his arms around her, pulling her as tight as he could. Stifling his sobs, his fingers slid over her back and into her hair. "I missed you so much," he said. "I'm sorry. I'm sorry I wasn't—"

"No, I'm sorry." Solyana squeezed him, her own tears welling up and over. "I'm so sorry, for everything. I shouldn't have gone alone. I shouldn't have made you go on alone. I hope you can forgive me." Solyana pressed herself further into his embrace. "I'm here, Gam. And I'm never leaving you again."

Gamaliel held her tight. "We stay together," he said.

"We stay together."

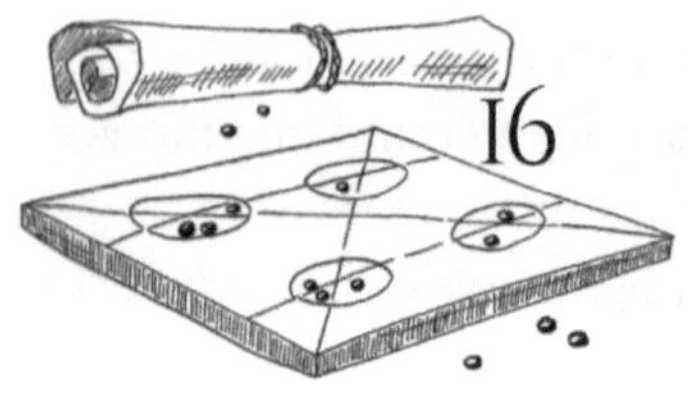

WOOL & WILL

JONAS

J ONAS SAT UPRIGHT IN his bed, covered in sweat. He'd had the dream again, filled with heat, loneliness, and a sense of loss. His hair stuck to his forehead, so he ran his fingers through it. Seer Brotnur had taught him what he could in the few months he'd had to mentor Jonas, but dreams had never been a topic of conversation. Well, nothing was a topic of conversation, as Seer Brotnur had taken the Celestial's ancient vow of silence. But he had given Jonas plenty of reading material, and between him and Rorhan, who'd assisted in tutoring ancient Mothmari, Jonas had become quite the scholar.

A scholar who knew nothing of dreams.

He sniffed, sighed, and reached for the spectacles on his bedside table. Revealing his plan to the group the night before hadn't gone exactly as he'd imagined, but it didn't bother him. They would understand, in time.

After years of research and, with the help of whatever Seer Gifts he possessed, Jonas had drawn himself a detailed map of what he hoped held his answers. Did he know for a fact if the people who worshiped the Way were on an island nestled somewhere in the Himmin Sea? Did he know how they had stayed hidden for centuries? Did he know he could hire a ship to get there? Or how he'd forage for food?

No. He didn't know the answer to any of these trivial things. Instead, he'd spent five long years tracing every line and word about them, piecing together things long forgotten in scrolls in the depths of Temple Rinn. But more than that, something deep inside him, the same thrum that overtook him when he drew out a map, told him it was true. Scant reasoning though it was, it would have to do.

Dressing in linen pants, long tunic, colorful vest, and his leather bag strapped over one shoulder, Jonas donned the amethyst necklace as a finishing touch. Then he exited his small room and entered the common area of their cave-home.

His jaw dropped.

Gamaliel was cooking.

And it smelled delicious.

He blinked, dumbfounded, as he found Ahren sitting at the table with Solyana, the two of them laughing. Gamaliel, too, joined in, pointing at them with his wooden utensil before turning back to the fire and whistling.

Whistling!

Jonas shuffled to the table and pressed his palms to the wood, eyes shifting from Gamaliel back to the two sitting before him. "What happened to Gamaliel?" he whispered roughly.

"Good morning to you, too, Jonas," Solyana said with a grin.

"What happened?" Ahren asked.

Jonas narrowed his eyes at Solyana. "You look chipper, too."

"What?" Solyana laughed and playfully pushed at his arm. "Make yourself useful and brew us some tea, will you?"

Blinking, Jonas stood up straight. "And thus, I become a servant...in my own home!" He busied himself with the kettle.

So, Gamaliel and Solyana must have talked, at least. Or done more, at most. Sprinkling tea in mugs, he tapped his fingers on his arm as he waited for the water to boil. He knew the possibility of Gamaliel accompanying him to the island was slim, but if he and Solyana had made up? There was no chance.

He had no real issue with the two of them together, and if she were able to pull him from his addiction, all the better. If only she hadn't been the one to send him there to begin with. Pouring the water, he carried the mugs on a tray back to the table and sat on one side of Solyana while Gamaliel sat on the other.

"You two make up, then?" He speared some scrambled eggs.

Ahren looked up from his plate, eyes darting between the three of them.

"You could say that." Gamaliel took a sip of his tea.

"You could do better." Jonas nudged Solyana's arm.

She grinned.

Gamaliel looked up. "What was that?"

"I said these eggs could be better." Jonas winked and Ahren smirked.

Gamaliel rolled his eyes and cleared his throat. "I expect Phineas will be back at Lone's this morning, waiting for us. For you." He raised his mug at Solyana.

"Do you trust him?" Solyana raised an eyebrow.

"Not in the slightest," Gamaliel said with a shake of his head. "Rorhan and I checked in on him last night. He had Kira, the keeper's daughter, in the room with him. She seemed to be okay, but... I'll have my eye on that man." He caught Jonas's gaze. "He told us in more detail about this machine he's called the Brextant. It's the contraption Erval intends to use to tether all of Mothmar with his Tala. And I intend to march into Thonethren and destroy it.

"If we're going to get there and get inside to find Rhuth and destroy this machine, we'll have to keep Erval out of Sol's mind while we do it. As much as I may not like it, Phineas is our best hope."

"And then back to the valley?" Ahren interjected.

The table sobered. Jonas knew they were each coming to their own conclusions on what had happened to their people in the last five years. The weather had warmed, agriculture had increased, but was it all too late? The valley was barely scraping by when they left. Had they succumbed to starvation? Jonas glanced at Solyana and wished he hadn't; nothing but hurt and confusion played across her face. He knew she wanted to go back. He would, too, if he were in her position.

Gamaliel stood. "Let's finish this conversation with Lone and Rorhan. I think they'd want to be involved."

An hour later, the group found themselves back at Lone and Rorhan's home. Mugs in their hands, Marin playing in the corner, and Phineas settled at the table—they began.

Armed with his maps, Jonas spoke first. "Phineas's claim to be able to teach Solyana the ways of protecting her mind is a bold one." He turned to see the steward's cheeks tinged pink. "But if she begins a regimen of tea…"

"He'll know," Phineas said with a somber nod. "And as of right now, Erval doesn't know of Solyana's reappearance, and until he does, we have time."

"Not much." Gamaliel raised an eyebrow. "Surely he'll come looking for you, too."

Phineas adjusted the lapels of his coat before settling again.

Jonas wondered if Erval already had.

"How long do we have?" Lone asked.

"He expects me back within one moon cycle."

"How long did it take you to travel here from Thonethren?"

"Well…" Phineas pulled his spectacles off and wiped them with a small cloth from his pocket. "It took me approximately twenty-four days. But I had a wagon pulled by two horses, and it was only me."

"Erval sent you with no protection?"

A sheen of sweat reflected off Phineas's brow. "I need none."

The group stared at him, and Jonas knew the same thought occurred between them. Phineas may appear soft and unassuming, but this man held endless Gifts and years, taken by force.

"Then we are almost out of time already," Rorhan said.

Jonas's fingers traced the map, pressure mounting in his chest. "I'd like to learn how to keep Erval out of my mind as well, but as time is not on our side, I think I'll settle for tea." He eyed Phineas. "You told your master you would be coming back with information about the Way?"

"That is the story I gave him." Phineas's voice wavered, but he spoke with decorum. "But I will stay with Solyana. Learning how to keep Erval out of her mind is of utmost importance. And once he discovers she is alive and in Endirinn, he would naturally assume I would accompany her back to Thonethren." His eyes shifted to Solyana. "That is, if you'd allow me. It will take a few weeks, during which, I will instruct you how to gird your mind."

"And when we get there?" Ahren asked. Jonas's heart sank remembering this new friend couldn't come with him, either. "I'd prefer not to be bartered like fish at the market." He gave a small, lopsided grin.

"Erval asked for a trade," Solyana said, her eyes swinging to Ahren. "Rhuth's life for Ahren. I don't intend to actually make good on that arrangement."

"So, we fool him!" Rorhan's palm slapped the table. "Pull the wool around his feet."

"Over his eyes, dear," Lone whispered.

"Yes, trip him *and* blind him."

Jonas grinned.

"To be clear," Gamaliel said with a smirk, "we won't trade you for Rhuth...unless you're a really annoying travel companion."

Ahren gave a nervous laugh. "Duly noted. But you will need me."

The room gave him their full attention.

"Pallah has been trying to find me. For years, if I'm piecing this together correctly. So, we'll let her find me, and I'll win her over to our side. She's a formidable fighter, and she'll make a great ally against Erval, surely."

Jonas's eyes darted to Solyana to find her shoulders sagging, the same thought surely running through her mind. Priestess Avi had killed countless innocent people with her blizzards and had most likely also used the Taking to increase her years. She'd held Rhuth captive, was possibly still doing so.

There was no coming back from that.

Though, Jonas weighed to himself, when were the deeds of a person stacked too high to be cleared? Solyana herself was guilty of beseeching the Mother, of utilizing the Taka Reu. Jonas pushed his spectacles up his nose. Whether or not one could be redeemed was not his decision, and he thanked the Celestials for that.

"She's fought him before," Phineas offered. "Though that was years ago. We don't know where she is now, or even if she would be willing to fight."

"Ahren comes with us," Gamaliel said with a nod before turning to Jonas. "Don't you agree?"

Jonas swallowed. He'd held a distant hope Gamaliel would go with him. They had been inseparable for so long. He was the brother, the father, Jonas never had.

"Yes. That is most logical." He stared into Gamaliel's deep brown eyes, willing him to understand what he couldn't quite say.

"Are you thinking you need more to accompany you?"

"I just—" Jonas bit his lip, already feeling the loss of his family. He looked about the room, wishing all of them would volunteer. "Solyana was gone for so long. We only just got the gang back together." He shrugged. "I know it's unrealistic, but I was hoping we'd travel together again."

A hand squeezed his own. Startled, he looked up to see Solyana smiling at him. "I wish for that, too, Jonas. But you have the most important piece of the puzzle to solve. I don't see anyone else capable enough to do it but you."

Jonas nodded and sniffed. She was right. He thought of the recurring dream he hadn't shared with any of them, and the hair on his arms raised. The loneliness he'd felt upon waking, the despondency, this seemed to be the start of it. If he told them about it now, would they change their minds? Would anyone move from this hut, or would they be content to finish out their time together in this mountain city?

He couldn't share it with them, not yet. Not until he knew what it meant.

17

TRAVEL & TRUST

RHUTH

THIS NEW PRIESTESS AVI was much kinder than the one Rhuth had grown accustomed to during her imprisonment in the Maze. She heard Fridmey's warning in the back of her mind: *You're too trusting, Rhuth. Don't be so naïve.* She wondered if she'd ever see her eldest sister again, or if her life would forever be fractured by the choices of others.

Feet crunching over snow, Rhuth kept pace with the woman guiding her, though it was growing more difficult. Her stomach growled, and Rhuth wondered if this ancient woman ever had to eat or if she was sustained through years alone.

"There's some jerky in your bag," the priestess said, as if tuning into Rhuth's thoughts. "May as well eat."

Rhuth retrieved the jerky and walked on, intent on discerning the truth of the priestess she accompanied.

"I hardly remember the first time Erval tethered to me. That life feels like it was lived by someone else. I was just a child, and Erval a grown man. He made me feel special, important. I didn't recognize the predator that lived behind his attention." She slowed, keeping step beside Rhuth, who caught a glimpse of her pained expression beneath her furred hood. "It wasn't until I was in my teens that he began making it a habit. Encouraging me to steal, to make friends with certain people, and finally..."

Rhuth glanced up at her, curious if her trailing away was because she was piecing together a lie or simply because she was remembering things better left forgotten.

"He persuaded me do things, Rhuth. Things I would never choose to do now."

"Like keeping a young girl trapped against her will?"

Avi shrugged. "The lengths I've gone to tear Erval's tendrils from my life; your injury provided my greatest chance. Keeping you gave Solyana the push she needed to leave the valley. To find my—" Avi stopped herself. "To bring back the green."

Rhuth huffed and kicked up a spray of frost. "Yeah, that worked out great."

"I said it was a chance. Chances are all I've been taking since my escape from Thonethren."

Rhuth looked behind them, at the long and winding trail of footprints in the snow.

"My original Gift is Smilodon Tala," Avi said. "Much like your fox friend here, Tinloh and I had a bond like no other." The priestess gave a sad smile. "I miss him."

"What happened to him?" Rhuth wondered with how heavy a hand Avi must have tethered such a rare creature. Had she turned the beast into a snarling menace? Had she made him kill on her behalf? Rhuth was taken aback by Avi's face, the priestess's expression sinking into what looked like true despair.

"He was taken from me. A man who wanted him for himself trapped me for two whole years—that was where I learned about the Maze. And when I got free, I got Tinloh back. Only for him to be killed by a stupid, misguided girl."

Ember was padding softly before them, leading the way. Rhuth's eyes stayed on the fox's fluffy tail, swaying with each step. The love and pain in Avi's voice was how she felt about her falcon, Halina, and she knew it would soon be how she felt about Ember.

"What happened to those people?"

"They paid the price."

Rhuth opened her mouth, then closed it again.

"I lost my entire family that night. All but my brother. There was fighting, surviving. Choices were made. Choices I wish I could change. But then Erval led me to Thonethren."

Rhuth wondered at all the details the priestess was leaving out. Were the gaps because of pain or convenience?

"It was in Thonethren where I was truly forged, in that castle, locked away like a forgotten princess." She chuckled. "Or so Erval had me believe. His aim is always for control. Control and power."

Rhuth scowled at her. "It seems you two have more in common than you'd like to admit."

Priestess Avi laughed. "What I did, Rhuth, I did for the greater good. Erval has no such desire. He's only ever cared about himself. I don't want to be the person he tried to craft me to be. I will regain what I lost. Recover the things he took."

"Your humanity?" Rhuth's tone almost turned to a snarl as she said it. She didn't want to be like this woman. "I'm not sure I'm willing to help you with that, Priestess."

"It's Pallah," the woman said hopefully. "I think if anyone can help me come back to who I'm truly meant to be, it's you."

Rhuth chewed her lower lip, trying not to cry the angry tears that pressed against her eye.

They arrived at the edge of the Pines, the Northern Mountains looming before them.

"It's been so long," Pallah said, eyes squinting against the low light of evening before the sun disappeared completely. "I'm not quite remembering how we got through the mountains so quickly the first time."

Pressure from above came over Rhuth, and she put a hand over her brow, peering upward to see two falcons coasting far above the canopy.

Find us a way through, if you would be so kind, she requested.

Immediately, they dipped in different directions, disappearing from view. Rhuth squinted until she spotted Ember a distance away.

Would you find a pass through?

Ember sniffed the ground and trotted toward the mountain's base.

Rhuth watched Ember go before meeting Pallah's eyes. "What?"

"I've told you my story," Pallah said with a glimmer of excitement. "Now share with me yours. How are you speaking so fluently with both bird and fox, without using the Taka Reu. I don't understand it, but I'd like to."

"Like I said, I don't know how to tether as 'normal' people do. This is simply how I do it. At first, I thought it was some kind of bad habit, and I tried using a tether as others understand them. But nothing ever formed. It was simply always…there for me. A connection."

"Hmm," Pallah mused. "We may as well camp here before it gets much darker. I bet there will be a useable cave along this stretch." She stomped farther out of the Pines and toward the edge of the mountain.

Soon, they found a small notch in the mountain, not quite big enough to be called a cave, but it would protect them from the elements. Once they got a fire going and Rhuth rolled out her sleeping mat, she found the courage to pry into Pallah's story a little deeper.

"Why did you go to this man, Erval?" She prodded at the fire with a stick. "He got into your mind, manipulated you, made you do terrible things…and yet, you still went to him."

Pallah was silent for a moment, her face flickering in the firelight. "Why do you follow me?"

"For Solyana," Rhuth said, but then she thought deeper. She had no way of really knowing if Pallah was leading her to her sister. A more honest answer formed. "There's nowhere else for me to go."

Nodding, Pallah said, "And thus, our lives are formed, aren't they? Like wild animals backed into corners, we can be incapable of clawing our own way out—until someone guides us. And whether it's with a whip or a word…we go."

"And you believe this man has Solyana?"

"I'm not sure what else could have happened to her," Pallah said. "There is the possibility she didn't make it at all."

Rhuth stiffened. "She's alive."

Pallah gave her a placating smile. "I'm sure she is." She pulled a few rations out of her bag. "Here, eat some more. You'll need to keep up your strength."

Every acceptance of this woman's care, no matter how small it was, felt like a betrayal to her family, to Solyana. But she took the food, regardless. What good would she be to anyone if she were too weak to move? Duplicity rolled in her gut as she ate, but ultimately her appetite overcame any angst.

"To be honest, I wasn't sure if your sister possessed the capabilities to break the curse binding my brother."

Rhuth stopped eating, the jerky halfway to her mouth. "Your brother was the one who was tethering light? And you were unsure? But you sent her!"

Pallah sighed. "Chances girl, remember? Decisions were made. They can't be changed."

"At least you had a choice." Rhuth spoke through a mouth full of meat. "You chose to run and hide. And everyone I had chose to leave me."

"They left you to save you," Pallah said with sudden fierceness that surprised Rhuth. "I spent too much of my life trying to do the right things for other people, only for them to turn around and spit in my face!" Shaking her head, Pallah rolled over on her sleeping mat, turning from Rhuth. "Go to sleep," she commanded. "We leave before dawn."

Rhuth tucked her knees into her chest as the wind whistled outside their small crevice of shelter. The fire was standing too tall, the wind buffeting the flames until they were almost horizontal. Honing her Tala toward the tallest stick of pine in the fire, Rhuth cleared her mind.

Come back to the earth, please.

For a beat, nothing happened, and then the stick shifted, sparks shooting into the air. It lowered carefully, tentatively, to the base of the fire. The flames died down, keeping her warm but steering clear of the wild wind.

Thank you.

Movement caught Rhuth's attention from the entrance of their shelter as Ember trotted in. She turned in two circles then curled up, her tail covering her face. Her ears twitched as she settled, and Rhuth searched the fox's mind for a path through the mountains. She found one. Not an ideal path, but it would do.

Thank you, Ember. Rhuth redirected her thoughts to her falcons until she felt one acknowledge her presence. *And you two? Have you found anything?*

Rhuth closed her eye and requested entrance. Suddenly she was flying high above the mountain, the cold wind blowing in her face, her wings spread wide and free. She almost laughed out loud with relief. She hadn't felt this kind of freedom since Halina. Focusing on what the bird was trying to show her, she let her eyes peer through the mountains and trees until she found a pass through two rising peaks, a perfect col to journey through in the morning.

I give you my thanks, she told the falcon and opened her eye as the girl on the ground, wingless and alone. As she drifted to sleep, her subconscious told of her elk, rabbits, even a moose beyond their cave, each settling down for the evening, seeking warmth just as she was. Even the brush, the trees, the ground beneath the snow, all of it called to her, as if she were one with them. Each of them just as alive, just as connected as she was. And as she drifted to sleep, she felt nothing but safety, cocooned in Mothmar, tied to everything.

For all was not made by separate beings, they were made by the One Above. The Way. Rhuth didn't know where she had learned it. The truth had simply always been.

And with that in mind, she fell asleep.

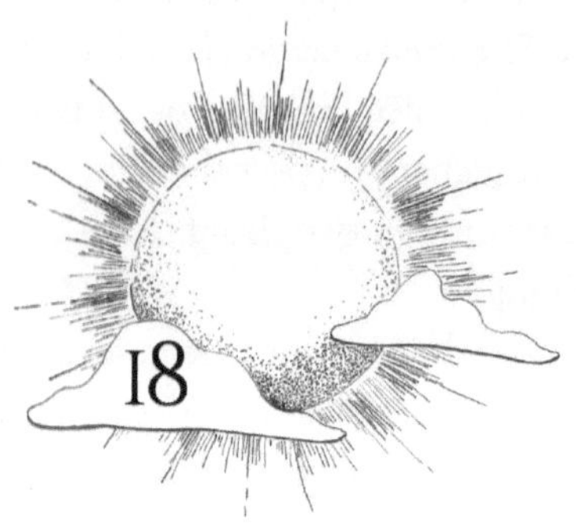

SAVIOR

SOLYANA

HIS HAND IN HER own held a rightness about it she was altogether unfamiliar with. Gamaliel's thumb rubbed the back of her hand, and she leaned into him as they wound their way along the path toward Endirinn's Main Square.

"We go in, grab supplies, and get out," she repeated.

"You know that's not how it's going to go." Gamaliel chuckled. "I don't think you understand what happened after you left, Sol. The people heralded you as a savior before, but you became a martyr—a saint—when you didn't return. There's a fountain in the Square with a statue of you at the center; people leave flowers and gifts."

Solyana groaned. "Don't remind me."

"They'll at least want a speech from the girl resurrected."

"I didn't resurrect. I never died!" Solyana worried at her braid. "We'll be quick. No one will even know it's me."

"Solyana." Gam stopped walking. "The fact they weren't outside my door when we woke this morning was a surprise. Besides," he said as he brushed a lock of her hair behind her ear. Solyana felt her entire body heat from the inside out. "Your scar is showing. There will be no denying it."

A cloud of dust erupted on the path beyond, and in its wake flew a child of about eight, leaping over rocks and tufts of weeds. Panting, she reached them, causing the two to pull up short.

"Is it true? Are you the Daughter of the Celestials? Did you bring the green?" The small girl grasped Solyana's arms and stared at her face, searching for something. "Mama said I'd see a scar!" The girl did a little twirl, her tunic billowing out around her. "We are all waiting for you!" She sped off into the city, rounding the corner of a building and disappearing from view.

"So much for going unannounced," Solyana said with a groan. "They won't stop me from leaving, will they?"

Gamaliel shook his head. "You're practically a goddess to them, Sol. You make the rules."

By the time they rounded the same corner, Solyana could hear it, the low rumble of hundreds of voices. They made their way around the last building before the market, and Solyana hoped the girl had been stretching the truth. Yet, when they came into the central square, she was greeted by the people of Endirinn in an explosion of sound.

"She's back! I told you she was back!"

"Bringer of the green!"

"Our martyr, our saint!"

"Solyana! Bless my baby!"

Gamaliel shifted from friend to protector, sliding forward to block her from view, taking point to carve a path through the crowd. Grasping her hand, he escorted her to the steps of Temple Rinn at the north end of the square. "You're going to have to talk to them," he said over the throng.

"What do I say?" Panic swelled in her throat. She couldn't admit her use of the Taka Reu to them; she couldn't explain the real reason she had been lost for five years.

Gamaliel drew her under his arm, and they walked together up to the steps. "They don't need to hear all the details," he spoke in her ear. "They just need to know you accomplished what you set out to do. You found the boy at the peak; you sated the Celestials and brought back the green. And you will now return to your home."

"But I'm not going home."

"Well, not technically. But home is where the people you love are, right?"

Solyana took heart and kissed his cheek. He released her at the top of the stairs to face the people.

The crowd fell silent.

Solyana cleared her throat and felt a wash of fear. She closed her eyes, letting the warmth of the Father of the Day soak into her skin. She asked for strength, for wisdom, hoping she had not fallen so far that her prayers would go unheard.

"People of Endirinn," she began. "My name is Solyana Marusda. Five years ago, I traveled up your holy mountain to fulfill the prophecy and bring back the green."

The doors behind her opened. Startled, Solyana took a step forward and turned to find a group of gray-clad Serviseers exiting the temple, their hands filled with fabric. The priest was behind them, his eyebrows raised in her direction.

"Excuse us, my children of Endirinn!" the priest said, his robes swishing around his legs as he stepped to Solyana's side. "I apologize for the lack of decorum. We just received word this morning our saint has returned to us!" Leaning close to Solyana, whispering for her ears alone, he spat, "If you had given me time, we could have done this properly."

Blinking in surprise, Solyana straightened away from him.

His cordial smile returned as he turned his attention to the people once more. "As the Saint of Endirinn has seen fit to address you, we shall adorn her and leave her to speak." The priest's hands appeared from cavernous sleeves, and he clapped twice.

The Serviseers scurried around Solyana like mice, draping white robes over her shoulders and adorning her head with the diadem she had left on her bed the first morning she had woken in Endirinn. Lastly, she was handed a silver scepter made in the same fashion as her crown. The base was made of two pieces of metal, interwoven like vines, and the top was a glass ball that looked as if it held an entire constellation in its depths.

Backing away with bows of respect, the Serviseers left Solyana standing there like a queen without a country. The priest's pinched mouth was turned down at the corners. He waved her on impatiently.

Solyana cleared her throat, the weight of the crown and scepter shifting her balance off-kilter. "I return to you now, the same girl that left five years ago. And though I would love to stay in your beautiful city, I must bid you goodbye and return to my home."

A wave of murmurs rumbled through the crowd, even the Serviseers turning to each other with questions written across their furrowing brows.

"Is this not your home now?" A man piped up from far within the crowd. Many around him nodded and a few gestured wildly.

Solyana's eyes followed their pointing fingers to see the stone statue looming behind them. This was how the people saw her. Not as the uncertain, Giftless teenager she had been, but as a woman, a savior, confident and mighty.

"Thank you, my people of Endirinn. I am honored and humbled by your devotion and grace. I thank you for preparing a place for me here, but I must continue on my path as it has been laid before me." She glanced at Gamaliel, and he nodded. "With gratitude for your steadfast love and kindness, I will gather what I need, and then I will be on my way."

Solyana turned to the priest who whispered hoarsely to her, "You need only supplies?"

"Yes, and a means of transportation."

Relief flooded the man's features, and for the first time, he smiled. Only then did Solyana realize he had been scared she would try to take his job. "But of course. Allow the Temple to fund your expenses. We will send you on your way. When do you leave?"

Solyana looked at Gamaliel, but he only shrugged.

"Soon."

The priest gave her a look but rubbed his hands together. "Right!" He stepped forward, arms raised to the people. "Do not hold back. The Temple will handle all expenses for the Chosen One to be sent off in splendor! Everyone, to your shops! Our saint needs supplies!"

Cringing, Solyana swung the robes from her shoulders, handing them and the scepter back to a Serviseer. She wanted nothing but the necessities and hoped the people wouldn't be too offended if she only took what she needed. When she tried to hand the diadem back, the Serviseers waved it away.

"It will adorn no other. It was crafted for you," they told her. "Please take it as a symbol of hope and victory for the people."

Solyana hesitated but nodded, deciding it best to please these people while she was still in their city. If anyone hadn't been in the Square for the speech, she could rely on the diadem to speak for her.

They descended the stairs and wove through the people who scattered to their various booths. As they wandered and purchased what they needed, Solyana talked to Gamaliel under the buzz of market chatter.

"This place is far more opulent than I remember."

"Thanks to you," Gamaliel said with a grin. "Bringing the green brought trade and travel. The whole of Mothmar is booming."

"But I did it incorrectly, and you and I suffered for it." She squeezed his hand. "I lost five whole years because of my mistakes. What if I do it again? Going to Thonethren, retrieving my sister, stopping this king...what if I mess it up?"

"Well," Gamaliel said, turning to her. "It's turned out alright so far." He brushed something from her forehead, trailed his fingers down the side of her face, and cupped her chin. "And I'm with you this time. Until the very end."

Solyana shifted away from his hand, feeling the eyes of the people on her. "But how do we even begin to take down a king bent on controlling every person in Mothmar? I don't think there will be any reasoning with him." Solyana shook her head and tossed her braid over her shoulder. "Even with our Gifts combined, I'm not sure we could ever stand up to a man who has limitless Gifts through the Taka Reu, and a limitless life to wield them."

"Then we pray Jonas's theories prove true."

The swing of the market danced around them, the shout of vendors and the chatter of children. Doubt continued to prod at Solyana's heart, but as she stared into Gamaliel's eyes, it dissolved. It was time to put faith in someone other than herself.

"Jonas, the savior of his friends," she said with a grin.

"Well, he does think he's part of the prophecy."

"Honestly, he's probably right."

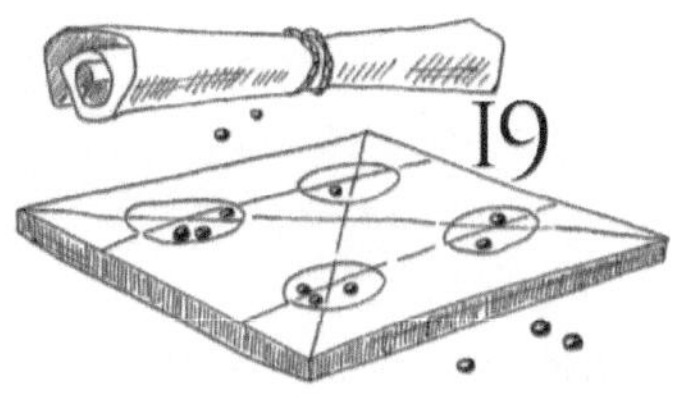

THORA & AGNAR

JONAS

THERE WAS NO WAY Jonas was part of the prophecy. At least, life would be easier if he wasn't. But that dream, that incessant dream... It haunted him.

He sat up in bed and pressed his fists to either side of his head. He tried to recover the details, but like every morning, all he could remember were hapless forms and shapes and the overall feeling he had a large role to fill. That something dark waited at the end of it, something he couldn't escape. Foreboding and loneliness: the two constants that accompanied his waking in recent mornings.

Vinur scratched at the door to be let out, and Jonas groaned. He threw on a tunic and fitted his feet into leather shoes. Ahren was asleep near the fire, and Gamaliel was back in his room, as Solyana had taken up residence in Lone's house. Vinur trotted ahead of him, ears perked as Jonas stumbled from the house, rubbing his eyes.

Mist greeted him in the cool stillness of the morning. Vinur wandered off, and Jonas trod in the direction of the outhouse.

"Good morning!" A booming voice made Jonas jump.

"Rorhan!"

The big man appeared through the mists, laughing. He was already dressed in full kit, pack on his back. "You are not ready?"

"The sun is hardly up," Jonas croaked. He edged his steps toward the outhouse.

Rorhan grunted. "Lone set me on my way already. She asked how we are traveling. Björg?"

Jonas shook his head. "It will be too hot for a mammoth. It will be even warmer down south, and he's too fluffy."

"Mm, well, it is a long way to the port if we are to catch a ship. My sister and I grew up riding horses. We will purchase a pair."

"Horses?" Jonas turned rounded eyes to the big man. "Smaller than mammoths but taller than cows and run really fast? You've ridden those things?"

Rorhan laughed again and a murder of cawing crows took flight from a bush to their right. "I rode as a child. Our tribe had no home, and horses were part of life. That winter though... By the time you found us on the ice plains, we had just eaten our last one."

"Eaten?" Jonas squeaked.

"It was a harsh time." Rorhan shook his head and waved Jonas along. "We get you a horse."

By the time they had reached the stables, the rest of the group had followed along. Solyana and Gamaliel walked together, inseparable since the first night Solyana had been back.

Jonas thought them a good match for each other, but the sight of their happiness lanced his heart with grief. Gamaliel was finally coming back to himself. He had spent the last five years pushing everyone away, Jonas included. And although Jonas had been the one to care for his brother as he'd wallowed, it hadn't been Jonas but Solyana who'd restored the man ...and was taking him away at the same time Jonas had to leave.

Perhaps they would be gone from each other forever.

Of course, he was seventeen now. A man. He pushed his spectacles up his nose a little further. He didn't need Gamaliel like he used to. Rorhan's lumbering gait drew his attention, the bear of a man carrying Marin on his shoulders, Lone at his side. Jonas realized, he had been so consumed with his own loss, he hadn't considered Rorhan's. If Rorhan could go confidently, Jonas could, too.

Rorhan spoke with the stable hand, coin was exchanged—at a steep discount, as it was for prophecy business—and Jonas found himself holding the reins of a massive dappled gray mare. He held the leather straps limply several steps away, trying to quell the shaking in his knees.

Leading a black horse just as tall, Rorhan stopped next to Jonas and grinned. "She will not bite you," he said as he gave the horse a pat on the neck. "The stable hand reassures me, these two are hardy, loyal, and have great endurance. We had this same breed when I was a child. You have no need to be scared."

"I'm not scared," Jonas said quickly.

"It's okay if you are." Solyana was at his side, her palm reaching up to the soft muzzle of his mount. "What's her name?"

"Thora." Rorhan grinned. "Thunder."

Jonas's knees shook harder.

"This one is Agnar." He patted the neck of his horse. "Warrior."

"They're named for battle," Lone said, her tone going somber.

Rorhan took Lone's hand in his own and pressed it over his heart. "We go for information, my love."

Jonas shifted his eyes back to his mare, the question of battle only sinking deeper into his soul, reminding him of his shifting dreams. It drove a sliver of fear into his stomach.

"Thora seems sweet," Solyana said, stroking the horse's mane. "I'm sure she'll take good care of you."

"I'll miss you," Jonas said quietly.

Solyana pulled him into a hug, and Jonas wrapped his arms around her. "You just find out about the Way, so you can teach me, okay? How will you contact me?"

"Ah!" Jonas held up a finger, Thora shifted, and Jonas jumped back. "She's got to stop doing that."

"Moving?" Gamaliel asked with a laugh.

Jonas shook his head. "Well, I've decided the easiest way to communicate is going to be through Phineas's Tala tether."

Solyana blinked at him. "Which one? Doesn't he have Tala with almost everything?"

"Yes, since using the Taking," Jonas said. "But the Gift you were born with has deeper roots, according to my research. It's stronger."

As if summoned, the round form of Phineas shuffled up the path toward the stables. Panting, he stopped just before them, hands on his knees. "No one told me"—he took a heaving breath—"that you two were leaving"—another breath—"so early."

"We didn't mean to keep you in the dark, Phineas," Lone said with a grin. "They've actually stuck around longer than I thought."

"What's your Gift?" Gamaliel asked the man who straightened abruptly at the question.

"The Gift you were born with," Jonas added. "It's Tala, right?"

Phineas blinked. "Why, yes. I had all but forgotten. It's been so long."

The group all stared at him. Jonas had honed the ability to sense someone's Gift, something Seer Brotnur had taught him to do, but he didn't quite know what the aptitude was.

Phineas sighed. "It's Stoat."

"What's that?" Lone whispered to Solyana, who shrugged.

"Stoat?" Gamaliel laughed. "Stoat?"

"That will do nicely," Jonas said.

"What's a stoat?" Solyana asked.

"A tiny, yet ferocious weasel." Jonas explained. "They travel well, too. They're fast, and they can swim. A perfect carrier of messages. Though..." He tapped his chin. "We will be great distances apart. How is your ability with them?"

Phineas's lips twisted in thought. "I did bring a device with me, something I've been tinkering with that might be of use." He produced a small metal headpiece from the leather satchel at his side and fitted it over his spectacles. "It's a slightly different version than the finnevel, which I crafted for Erval to tether to his aptitude over long distances. This, instead, gives the wearer the ability to connect to not only one creature, but many of the same species at once."

Much like the Brextant. Jonas couldn't help but be reminded this man was the one who'd made the terrible machine in the first place. He hoped he wasn't making a grave mistake in trusting Phineas to accompany his friends.

He stepped close to the steward, studying the mechanical piece set on his face. Though he disagreed with it being used on people, stoats on the other hand...

"Fascinating. So, if you tether to a stoat right now...it could potentially tether to multiple stoats in the area?"

"That's the idea." Phineas adjusted a gear on the side of the device before clearing his throat. "Give me a moment."

The group waited as Phineas went quiet, all eyes and ears trained on the man. All except for Jonas, whose eyes were positioned on the ground, looking by the boulders and shrubs that made up Mount Endirinn.

"There they are," Jonas said with a growing grin. A tiny white creature scuttled on top of the nearest boulder. Its long body attached to the smallest and sweetest face Jonas had ever seen. Whiskers twitching, it stayed there, as if awaiting orders.

"Should be some more..." Phineas said, his eyes staring off through the device.

Within a few more minutes, four more stoats of various coat colors bounded into the clearing. Some peeked from behind rocks, others nestled beneath bushes, and one ran right out into the open and scuttled atop Thora, a smug look on its face. The horse merely flicked at it with her tail and stomped a hoof.

"This will give me the opportunity to pass information quickly between families of stoats. They're abundant in Mothmar." Phineas paused. "But *you* have to get information to *us*...not the other way around."

"Ah, yes. Well, presumably, when we assume our Gifts through the Way, we should be able to tether to anything. Stoats should be one of countless animals and things to wield," Jonas said.

"Is it really that powerful?" Lone asked as she wiped something off Marin's face.

"Everything I've researched points to the idea we were never meant to be separated by faction. Every Gift should be available to everyone. And although we may have certain aptitudes from one to another, it was never supposed to be segregated as it is now."

"It's like using the Taking," Phineas said as he blotted his forehead with a handkerchief. "But without the...well, death."

"But that's the whole point," Jonas said, gesticulating grandly. "It's the opposite. It has nothing to do with acquisition, but with *requisition*."

"You have to ask for it?" Gamaliel cocked an eyebrow.

Jonas shrugged. "It's more than that, but I'm not entirely sure. Again, it's only been a few years of research. What I really need is to find this tribe of people who still practice it."

"You best keep this tribe a secret, Seer Jonas. Erval must not find them," Phineas warned.

"Ah, but remember"—Jonas crossed his arms and wagged a free finger—"if it's a request, it has the potential to be denied. We have to believe the Celestials wouldn't grant such power to someone with evil intent."

"If Erval cannot take the power, he will crush the people who wield it," Phineas clarified.

The group fell silent.

Agnar snorted, and it drew all eyes to Rorhan, who cleared his throat. "I agree, it is time to go."

They said their goodbyes, both Lone and Solyana sniffling, and Marin clinging to her father. Guilt gnawed at Jonas's heart, and he turned his eyes away to find Gamaliel and Vinur standing beside him.

"You ready?" Gamaliel asked.

Jonas shrugged. "Still don't want to come?"

Gamaliel grinned and looked at his feet, his hands in his pockets. "You know I've got to keep Solyana safe."

Jonas nodded his agreement, but it didn't reach his heart. "Just tell me you're done with the drinking."

Dark brown eyes snapped onto his own, and Jonas's lips twisted as he held Gamaliel's gaze. He had never addressed his brother's problem aloud. And though it had, until this moment, been harbored silently, they both knew who had taken off Gamaliel's shoes when he got home after a long night out, who had put out the fire when Gamaliel left it burning far past their bedtime.

The hard look in Gamaliel's eyes softened as he reached for Jonas and drew him into a hug. "I'm done," he said, his voice cracking down the middle. "I made you grow up too fast. I'm sorry I wasn't there for you when you needed me."

Jonas hugged him hard in return, his face buried in his brother's shoulder, his tears making their way into Gamaliel's hair. Gamaliel pulled him away and held him firm, one hand on his arm and the other on the back of his head. "You find us after you're done, you hear me?"

Jonas nodded, wiped at his eyes, and sniffed.

"Take care of yourself. And bring Rorhan home safe."

He nodded again.

"You're the best of us, you know that?"

Jonas released one choked sob. "I love you, brother."

"And I you, brother."

AFFIRMATIONS &
INVITATIONS

PALLAH

"*You're beautiful.*"

"*How could anyone have treated you so poorly?*"

"*You're home now, Pallah.*"

Erval's words to her were like a salve to old wounds as she lay in her bed in her ornate room. They had dined together; he in his cuffs and crown, she in her red satin dress that fell around her curves like water. He had spent the dinner peppering her with questions, but not the kind she had been expecting.

"*How did that make you feel?*"

"*How deeply did that hurt you?*"

"*How can I help you?*"

Answering from her heart had come easier than expected, as if the emotions she had locked away for years were finally breaking free of their cage. It was liberating, revealing her heart's desires, her soul's pains, her mind's brokenness. And he responded with the mantras that repeated in her head now, back in her down-blanketed bed.

"*You're beautiful.*"

"*You're worth all of Mothmar to me.*"

"Welcome home, Pallah."

She couldn't wipe the grin from her face if she tried.

Sweeping from her bed, she opened the balcony doors, cool air pouring in to toy with the fabric of her long black nightgown. Reveling in the goosebumps that prickled her skin, she leaned out over the edge to watch the city's nightlife in full tilt.

Mount Hekla rose far in the distance, a black silhouette amidst the velvety sky. An ache thrummed in her chest as she thought of her old friends on Eldfall. Lief and Karav had been so ready to travel to Hekla, to go to where their Taka Reu was born, where their power would be strongest.

For the first time since arriving, Pallah allowed herself to sit with those memories, knowing who else would appear.

Tinloh.

Her lip began to tremble, and she covered her mouth with her hand. How could she have left him there in the snow? What if he hadn't actually died? Had she truly checked well enough? She bit her knuckles to keep from sobbing, holding back tears that weren't supposed to have followed her into this new life. No, she had felt the tether snap like her own heart shattering into pieces. She had felt the sudden emptiness between them like a well dried up.

Erval had promised they would find her another, and though part of her found the idea distasteful, a greater part of her longed for a companion once more. When he asked for her again, she would inquire after a new smilodon.

It was growing colder. Pallah retreated to her room, closing the doors and drawing the curtains. Her bare feet padded on the wooden floor as she shuffled back to her bed to wrap herself in comfort once again.

Where was Issha?

The thought surprised her. Not because she had thought it, but because it had taken her so long to do so. Her friend hadn't been at dinner, and Pallah was only now beginning to wonder why.

A soft knock came from her door, and Pallah startled. Sliding from the bed, she tiptoed to the door and cracked it open, hoping it was Issha come to visit.

Erval's steward, Phineas, stood at the door.

"Good evening, Lady Pallah." Phineas gave a short bow. "I've come to inform you my master will accompany you for a carriage ride tomorrow morning. He'd like to show you the city."

A thrill ran through Pallah like lightning; she bit her lip and nodded. "Yes, thank you!"

"Sleep well." Phineas turned, and Pallah shut the door, turning to lean against it with a sigh.

Only after she was tucked back up in bed did the thought of Issha cross her mind again. She was probably enjoying her own time in her own room, as Pallah was. Issha could take care of herself.

WHITE AS SNOW

RHUTH

RHUTH WATCHED THE FALCONS as they danced in the wind far above them. The pass the birds had found was clear of boulders, but that didn't mean the snow between the mountains was any easier to get through. The heavy powder rose to thigh height, and Rhuth's pants, although treated with oil, were starting to lose their waterproof integrity. They had donned their snowshoes, but the snow wasn't packed enough to traverse easily.

Pallah had accepted the path Rhuth had suggested without much question. She'd given a simple nod, and after a few bites of a meal, they'd headed out.

"Your time with Erval." Rhuth broke the silence, intent on obtaining more answers. "What did he do to make you leave him?"

"You're not going to let up, are you?" Pallah asked over her shoulder, bringing her knees high to trek through the snow.

"We could always just focus on how miserable this hike is," Rhuth said, knocking more snow from her shoes.

Pallah stayed silent.

But Rhuth had played this game before; being the youngest of three had given her lots of practice in that regard. "You control the blizzards, right? Couldn't you just get rid of this snow for us?"

The woman stopped and shifted her pack. "I'm afraid it will draw too much attention. Erval is very attuned to others' use of the Taka Reu. Without the cloud cover I'd produced in the valley, he would see it clear as day in Kjarn's Eye."

"Kjarn's Eye?"

"It's…" Pallah shook her head. "How do I explain? When Erval tethers over great distances, he uses a device called a finnevel. He peers through it, like a telescope to—"

"What's a telescope?" Rhuth wasn't trying to be funny, but Pallah laughed.

"Forget it. Think of the finnevel like…an amplifier. If you use the finnevel with your Gift, your Gift can travel over long distances. That distance is not viewed like the physical world we see around us. It shows the essences of all life. Something between physical and spiritual. He calls this Kjarn's Eye."

"I see." Though Rhuth didn't. "So, you won't use your Gifts while we're traveling?"

"Not unless I really have to. It's too risky."

"But if I use mine…we should be okay?"

"Well…" Pallah turned to look at her over her shoulder. "Yes, I suppose. You don't use the Taka Reu. You can't move snow, can you?"

Rhuth shrugged. "'I've never tried before."

"I was afraid you were going to pick me apart with your falcons just a few days ago, and you had never done that before." Pallah's face held something like a grin, and Rhuth had to suppress her own.

"I wasn't really going to do that," Rhuth said. Although she did believe the woman would deserve it, the punishment wouldn't be from Rhuth's hand. Everyone wanted to do wicked things at one time or another. The difference was most people didn't act on such impulses.

"I would deserve it," Pallah said, giving voice to Rhuth's thoughts. "Don't think I'm so unaware of myself not to know that." She continued walking. "If I've had time to do anything while living in the valley, it's been to think of my past. It's hard not to when you're surrounded by it."

"So, you're going to meet this man head-on as a…" Rhuth searched for the word. "Penance?"

"Because I'll know no peace until he's gone," Pallah said quietly.

A northern wind whipped through the pass, fluttering their hair and causing them to lean against the sides of the boulders stretching high on each side.

When it passed, Rhuth straightened. "What does he want with you?" she asked.

But Pallah was silent.

Rhuth tried to find the heart of the snow to ask it to move. The ground surrounding them held a pulse, just like everything in Mothmar.

Reveal yourself to me? Rhuth asked and, within moments, the snow answered with a low thrum. *Will you clear a path for us?* she asked.

And the white listened, swirling beautifully to the sides until even the snow beneath their feet whirled away, shifting and packing itself neatly against the walls.

Pallah turned slowly, mouth agape as she watched, the two of them alone in the pass, completely surrounded by whirling snow. When it finally stopped, Rhuth caught sight of Ember looking confused far back on the path.

Rhuth grinned and turned back to Pallah, who was staring at her in wonder. "So, this is the power of the Way?"

Rhuth, who had only thought about it in those terms in her own mind, frowned and shrugged. "If that's what it's called."

"Yes," Pallah said with a solemn nod. "I believe that's what you worship. Are you tired?"

Rhuth shrugged. "Not really."

"And you're not using the Taka Reu?"

"Of course not."

Pallah shook her head, her eyes holding nothing but awe. "You asked what Erval wanted of me, and although he's never told me outright, I believe I know what it was—and probably still is."

They fell into step together as they walked the rest of the way, their path made easier now over clear ground.

"Erval has a device, much like his finnevel, in that it works with his tether. But unlike the finnevel, instead of tethering to one person at a great distance, it allows the wielder to hold a broad grip on several.

Although I'm unaware just how many he could grab hold of at once, it is my understanding this is how he plans on ruling Mothmar."

"He wants to tether to everyone?"

Pallah nodded. "He needs to be able to hold a tether long enough—and to enough people—to implant unwavering obedience to him alone. He wants complete compliance. However, he needs an energy source for this device: someone who has enough years stored up to run it for as long as he needs. You see, it siphons the life from whomever uses it."

Rhuth's eyes widened as understanding dawned.

Pallah nodded. "He never explicitly told me, but I had my suspicions, even before his steward helped me escape."

"*That's* his whole goal?" Rhuth twisted her lips in thought. "How boring."

Pallah laughed, and it echoed upward, bouncing between the mountains until it escaped out the top. "It is," she agreed. "Don't tell him that, though. He's killed for less."

"You have, too." The words slipped from Rhuth's lips before she could stop them.

Pallah just nodded, her steps unaltered. "Yes, I have."

"You killed my people." The words were coming unfiltered now, and Rhuth didn't even try to stop them. "We've suffered beneath blizzards for generations. And if you've lived this long, then you've..." The pieces clicked in Rhuth's mind as she thought of the phrase Pallah had used before they'd left the valley. *The Taking.* "You've Taken lives for your own." A shiver ran down her spine as she said it, but she knew it was true. Pallah accepted the words without argument. "People who have left the valley, people who were in darlöh before me. People you promised to heal with your Heitt and didn't make it... You took their years, their Gifts!"

Ember was at her side, growling, enforcing distance between Rhuth and Pallah. The falcons flying overhead screamed, one after another, each of them shooting down until they lighted on Rhuth's shoulders. "How dare you. How dare you!" She was screaming now, and she couldn't stop. Her breaths came quickly, her head hot inside her hood. She should have stayed back in the valley or gone with Phassa. Anything but with this woman and her blackened heart.

Pallah nodded slowly, surveying the animals that had come to Rhuth's support. "You're right," she whispered.

Rhuth sneered.

"I'm a monster." The woman lifted her chin, her hood falling from her face. She gave a smile that did not reach her eyes. "I always have been." Pallah quickly sniffed and wiped an eye, clearing any remnants of emotion from her face. "If you see fit to end my life here and now, I won't stop you." She shoved her staff into the ground where it stood vertically, then spread her hands wide in acceptance.

"I-I don't..." Rhuth suddenly found she lacked the means to shift her anger into action.

"Now is not the time for hesitation, girl." Pallah stepped closer to her, and the falcon on Rhuth's right shoulder let out a screech. "I have lived a darker life than most. Only one lives a darker one still. You could take care of him easily with all the Gifts you bear. So easily they flow through you, like the blood in your veins." Her eyes darted feverishly over Rhuth. "Like the breath in your lungs."

Pallah continued her march forward and what began as a surrender turned sinister. Ember growled.

"Save your people! Rid Mothmar of its blights!" Pallah threw herself to her knees, surprising the fox, who snapped in her direction. But Pallah simply kept her eyes on Rhuth, palms turned upward in submission. "Succeed where your precious sister failed." The false priestess closed her eyes and tilted her chin toward the sky, exposing the white pillar of her neck.

The air hung thick with silence. Rhuth was close enough she could see Pallah's face in its fullness now, the faint quiver of her chin, the wetness around her eyes. Rhuth felt at a loss as tears came to her own eye and pressure built behind the other. "Please, stop," she whispered. "Stop doing this."

Pallah took a shaky breath. "Use your fox or your falcons, I don't care how." Her tone belied no emotion. If not for her features giving way, Rhuth wouldn't have believed her.

"Stop it!" Unexpected rage filled Rhuth at this woman's cowardice. How dare she give up now? When finally, after years of hiding, she was going to take charge and act? No, Rhuth would not allow Pallah to make her the villain. "Get up," Rhuth demanded.

Pallah peered out from the bottom of her lids.

"You promised I could save my sister! You'll make good on that before you die. And your death won't be by my hand, or any innocent animal. I think you living is a more effective punishment."

Pallah hung her head, shoulders sagging toward the ground.

Rhuth stepped around her as the falcons took to the sky. Ember stuck close to her side, and Rhuth patted her between the ears before pulling her mitten back on. "We've got a ways to go, and I think we need to figure out what we plan to do when we get there."

"Are you sure you're willing to work with someone so stained?" Pallah asked sincerely.

Rhuth turned, taking in the woman, allowing compassion to take a stronger hold in her heart. "Dirty things can get cleaned, Pallah, if you wash them."

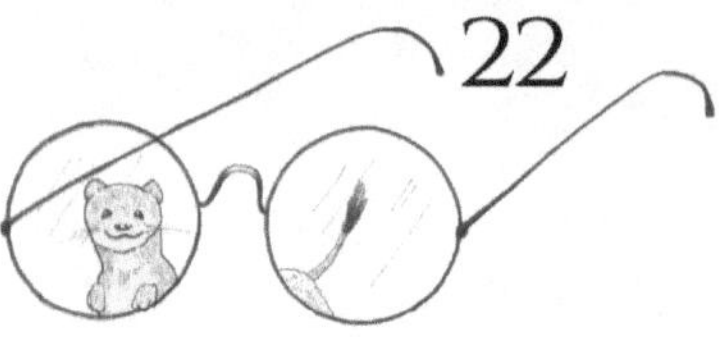

BLOCKADE

PHINEAS

SEEING OFF THE BOY and the big man a few days before had settled an itch deep inside Phineas. He missed Thonethren. Not the people or his duties, of course, but the way of life. However, with the Seer gone and no good news to bring back to Erval, he had only one other option. He had to return with Solyana, a prize for the King. Well, at least Erval would believe it to be so.

Phineas knew better.

Just the day before, he had begun teaching her how to keep Erval out of her mind. To create a blockade, as he'd called it. The sooner she grasped the practice, the safer they'd all be.

He dried the sweat from his hands with his robes as he exited the tavern, his stomach rolling. He'd had enough goat stew to last him a lifetime, or three lifetimes. The kitchens seemed to produce little else.

"Goats, such dirty creatures," he mumbled to himself. "If I never see or taste another one in my life—"

"Excuse me?"

Phineas blanched as he pulled up short. A crooked old woman and a goat stood in his path. The woman's chin lifted as she attempted to peer down her nose at him. The goat merely stared with its empty rectangular eyes.

"My apologies, ma'am," he said with a small bow. "And goat."

The woman huffed, one hand stroking the goat's side. "We may be mountain folk, but we are far from dirty." She ambled up to him, and using her walking staff as an extension of her arm, poked Phineas in the belly, where sweat stains, spilled tea, and spots of gravy marked his robes. "Best take a look at yourself before judging us, lad."

"Ma'am!" Phineas took a step backward but couldn't help peering down at himself. He'd had to do his own washing since arriving in Endirinn, and it hadn't been easy.

"With the Saint returned to us, you best tidy yourself!" she said. "Don't want her catching you so unkempt." The woman turned from him, tapping her goat gently with her staff. The both of them ambled away.

"I'll have you know—" Phineas's retort died in his throat as the woman's back stiffened, then unnaturally straightened, her crooked spine growing taller.

She swiveled around, her aged eyes bright and her mouth too wide. She strode back toward Phineas, his bowels turning to water at her approach. She leaned toward his face, their heights almost equal now. Her breath held a cloying earthy scent as Erval's words poured out.

"So...my little pet is back, is she?" And just as quick as he'd tethered her, he was gone. The goat bleated as the woman crumpled to the ground at Phineas's feet like a pile of discarded rags.

Phineas's stomach twisted, his palms growing clammy. Had Erval seen him? Did he know he had heard? His hand stretched out toward the woman but went no further, at a loss for what he could do. Nothing. He could do nothing. The adults always died, didn't they? There was no time to check. He needed to get to Solyana.

He turned in a tight circle before shouting to himself, "Celestial's Pool!"

He remembered the girl wanting to be alone for a while and Lone suggesting the place. Did she say it was through the North Gate? It was the best chance he had.

Phineas hoisted his robes and started running, his mind turning over what was set to unfold. Erval had discovered Solyana was here and had done so certainly sooner than Phineas would have liked. The girl's resurrection of sorts had incited such a stir, the king's attention was inevitable. But Phineas found himself wishing, and not for the first time, if only Erval could be just a little bit slower.

Phineas hurried through the streets as fast as his stout form would carry him.

When someone was tethered by Erval, they became subject to him. However, just like any Tala tether, a person could resist if they associated anything negative with the Tala wielder. It was how Phineas formed the blockades in his own mind. He prayed now Solyana had come to the full realization that Erval was truly evil. If any part of her saw good in him or held onto a hope he might show kindness and help her—she wouldn't be able to keep him out.

This thought made him hesitate, slowing his run to an uncomfortable jog. He had never articulated such a thought to himself.

A few skittering stoats followed in the shadows. He hadn't been able to rid himself of the creatures since he had called them two days ago.

"Hold fast, Solyana," he puffed as he scrambled up the stone pathway and out the North Gate. "Don't let him in."

RED MOON

SOLYANA

SOLYANA SAT ON A wide, flat rock, her fingers chilled by the crystal blue water of Celestial's Pool. Cold dread seeped from her head into her heart, as words dripped into her mind unbidden.

So, you are alive, Solyana. The rumors are true.

He was here, in her mind, the king of Thonethren, bent on manipulating her still. What could she say? What could she do? Phineas had talked with her briefly about something he called a blockade—but putting it into practice? She was far from ready.

"Hello," she whispered as she drew her hand out of the water. "Yes. I'm back." She would stick to the basics. Phineas had mentioned giving him only simple statements. She could do that. Even still, a chill tore through her body, and she began to shake.

I'm quite surprised, I must say! The man released something like a chuckle. *To pop up out of nowhere after five years! Quite the little trick. I should try it out myself. I'm sure you've amassed a zealous following.* He cleared his throat. *In either case, our deal still stands.*

Solyana tried to wipe her mind empty of thought. She stared at the glassy surface of the water, willing her mind to be as clear. Where was Phineas? No, she couldn't think of Phineas. She shouldn't think of anything. What if he could see?

There was a pause from Erval, and Solyana's throat began to constrict in fear.

You haven't forgotten our deal, have you? You bring me the boy... And I protect your sister.

"No," she said softly. "I haven't forgotten."

You have the boy, then?

Solyana noted the question. He would only ask it if he didn't know. Should she admit the truth? Was there benefit in lying?

Without knowing if he could see her thoughts or not, she nodded. "I do."

The man breathed out a sigh. *Your sister eagerly awaits your return.*

A knife of guilt sank deep into Solyana's belly. "You have Rhuth?"

We're partners, remember? Erval crooned. *Time is running short. The Red Moon nears.*

A scuffling noise sounded behind her, someone else coming up the path. Solyana wanted to turn and see who it was but stopped herself. What if Erval could look through her eyes? She closed them. "The Red Moon," she repeated, if only to keep her mind clear of anything else.

Make good on your promise, Earth Daughter.

"I will."

As if his fingers loosened one by one from her throat, Solyana breathed again as his presence disappeared from her mind. Eyes flying open, she turned to see Phineas heaving himself up the last few steps, a stoat skittering past to fling itself into the pool where it started swimming circles.

"Has he—" Phineas gasped for air, his hands on his knees. "Has he spoken to you?"

Solyana nodded quickly but bit her tongue. How did Phineas know? The possibility of his treachery came over her. "You led him straight to me, didn't you?"

"What?"

"You told him I came back." An icy chill ran down her spine, and she stood, heart racing.

"I promise you, Solyana, I had no idea you had even descended the mountain when I arrived. I was here for Seer Jonas—"

"Who has conveniently left," Solyana spat, keeping an eye on the stoat.

Phineas gaped at her.

The copper-colored creature slinked out onto the rock, where he turned belly up to sun himself.

"Please believe me, Solyana. I am no longer allied with Erval. His goals and methods are nothing but evil." He produced a cloth and patted at his sweat-soaked forehead. "Had I known—"

Solyana held up a hand, and Phineas stuttered to a stop. "If you really intend to teach me to guard my mind, then you'll have to do so on the road. We need to leave now."

"On that we are in agreement." Phineas pocketed his handkerchief. "What did he tell you?"

Solyana's eyes met Phineas's set behind his round spectacles. "He told me to keep my word."

They gathered at Torny's Tavern since Phineas insisted on changing into fresh robes. Gamaliel set a mug of something hot before Solyana, and she nodded in thanks. He cradled his own mug, and Solyana was thankful to see it was only tea.

He settled beside her. Ahren was next to Lone, while Marin played with Vinur, who laid by the hearth, and Phineas joined them last, smoothing his robes.

"Thanks for waiting."

Solyana stirred her tea. "I think it's important we all get on the same page."

"Agreed," Phineas said. He made himself comfortable. "Erval has begun to poke around in the minds of the people. He tethered a woman in Endirinn. That's how I knew he was coming for you, Solyana."

The anxiety in Solyana's chest loosened. "Oh. Was the woman okay?"

"I don't know." Phineas shook his head. "I was too concerned with getting to you as soon as I could. What did Erval say?"

"He wanted to be sure I was going to fulfill my half of the bargain, that I was bringing Ahren to him."

"Does he know you have Ahren?" Gamaliel asked.

Guilt spread through her. "He asked me, and I said yes."

"You did the right thing," Phineas assured. "He would have been able to tell if you'd lied."

This lessened her guilt, though it didn't absolve her completely. "He claims he has Rhuth."

Phineas sat up straighter.

"But he said she's waiting for me."

Phineas crossed his arms. "Then he's lying to you."

"You've been gone over a month now. Perhaps things have changed," Lone said.

"We've been with each other since the beginning." Phineas shook his head. "Erval doesn't keep secrets from me. He would have told me if something as important as the arrival of Solyana's sister were to occur."

"But you're keeping secrets from him," Solyana pointed out.

"And you expect us to simply believe you," Gamaliel added.

Phineas shook his head with incredulity. "How else would you like me to prove I am trustworthy?"

Ahren cleared his throat. "I think if Phineas is willing to teach Solyana how to keep Erval out of her mind, that's enough proof for me."

Lone nodded.

Something like a grunt emanated from Gamaliel's throat.

"Now," Ahren continued, straightening his shoulders. "He expects a trade. Me for your sister. And I propose we give him exactly what he expects."

Gamaliel stiffened. "Wait a min—"

"Just listen! You and I, Gamaliel, arrive in Thonethren in chains, the goods being delivered by his faithful steward and his obedient puppet." Ahren's hands almost talked for him as he continued excitedly. "Or at least that's how we'll appear! Because once we get close to the man, we'll take him by surprise and force him to tell us where Rhuth is. And then we take him out!"

Phineas flinched, and Solyana narrowed her gaze.

The steward fidgeted. "I believe we should focus on the destruction of the Brextant. We can subdue Erval afterward."

"If he survives, he'll just rebuild it," Ahren argued.

"Not without my help," Phineas countered.

"Erval will kill us if we lay a finger on the machine," Gamaliel said. "I like Ahren's plan."

"I agree," Solyana said with a firm nod.

Phineas's eyes widened. "But he's far too powerful, even for—"

"Not if you fight with them," Lone said.

A long sigh escaped Phineas's nostrils, and he clutched his arms to himself. "His strength aside, Erval is like a brother to me. I certainly disagree with his aims, but turning on him like this... It is no small thing."

Solyana sighed. "I can understand that." She reached toward Phineas with an open hand. "But can we trust you to do what needs to be done?"

His hand lifted from his lap, and he clutched her fingers in his own. "Yes, dear girl." His eyes held an earnestness she hadn't seen before. "Yes, I will."

"Anything else we should know about his plans?" Gamaliel asked.

"Well...in the name of transparency, we believe there's an overzealous warlord trying to amass an army against him. You see, Erval has used his finnevel to comb through every part of Mothmar, and he's found blank spots that shouldn't be. He's been able to tether people in surrounding areas, and they speak of soldiers, an army gathering somewhere in the south." Phineas shrugged. "He believes whoever it is, they've gotten ahold of the tea, and have been drinking it en masse."

"So, you're saying we could have a war on our hands?" Gamaliel's eyebrows rose.

"Possibly. His attempts at stamping out this tea have only worked as far as Thonethren and some surrounding towns, but any farther, and he'd have to send in ground troops."

"Why doesn't he?" Lone asked.

"Erval is a man of subtleties. He's had Mann Tala his whole life, and he is determined to make it the most prized aptitude. He finds outright war distasteful. Subterfuge is much more his style."

Marin, bored of playing with Vinur, ran to Lone and clambered into her lap. "War can't come here," Lone said, smoothing her daughter's downy hair. "It can't." She hugged Marin closer. "Mama will make you some special tea at home. Okay, Little *Elskan*?"

"No tea," Marin said with a pout. "Yucky."

"He said something else to me," Solyana continued. "About a Red Moon drawing near. What did he mean?"

Phineas massaged his brow. "Ah yes. A full lunar eclipse. Erval always feels closest to the Mother Below during these astrological events, particularly when the sky turns red. He usually has some kind of experiment he wants to try, village he wants to cull, or new dark Gift he wants to wield. A sign of his impending arrival, of sorts." Phineas shook his head. "My theory is it will be during the Red Moon when he uses the Brextant."

"How long until then?" Solyana asked.

"A few weeks, at most." Phineas pushed his spectacles up his nose. "I left all my celestial charts in Thonethren."

"But who would he use to sit on the Brextant?"

"Pallah, if he has her." Phineas paused a moment. "Or me."

"Could he force you?"

"Ah." Phineas raised a finger. "I built a simple contingency into the Brextant. It would not work fully unless the one who sat upon it was *willing* in some way. They cannot be fully forced against their will."

"But if he plans on using it at the Red Moon, he must have someone in mind. Someone he is sure he can persuade," Ahren said. "He would have had to raise up another, cultivating years in them much as he did my sister."

Fear lanced through Solyana so abruptly she almost fell off her chair. Her hands began to shake, and she pressed her palms together. "If you were to guess," Solyana began, her mind working in too many directions, "how many years would it take him to form a disciple with enough souls and adequate trust to run this device?"

Phineas removed his spectacles to wipe at his eyes with the cuff of his sleeve. "At least a decade, if not more."

"He couldn't do it in less?" Solyana asked, her theory ringing with terrible truth.

"What are you getting at?" Phineas cocked an eyebrow.

"Rhuth." Solyana's voice shook. "He told me he would protect Rhuth. What if this is what he has in mind?" She didn't want to believe it, but it was a possibility she had to face. If Erval had retrieved Rhuth and had been holding her captive, could he have been grooming her for this very purpose?

Phineas's lips twisted in thought. "Someone forced upon the machine would not be viable, unless a small part of their soul was willing." He waved his hand in dismissal. "They cannot be coerced. It would have to be someone that held a love for him."

But who knew what Erval could accomplish, given the time?

Solyana wondered if their success against him was probable, or even possible. For who could stop a man who could enter the minds of others at will? Her eyes flicked to Phineas, and she thought of his blockade. With his help, perhaps she could. She would have to trust him.

"Alright, then." Gamaliel folded his arms. "Next stop: Thonethren.

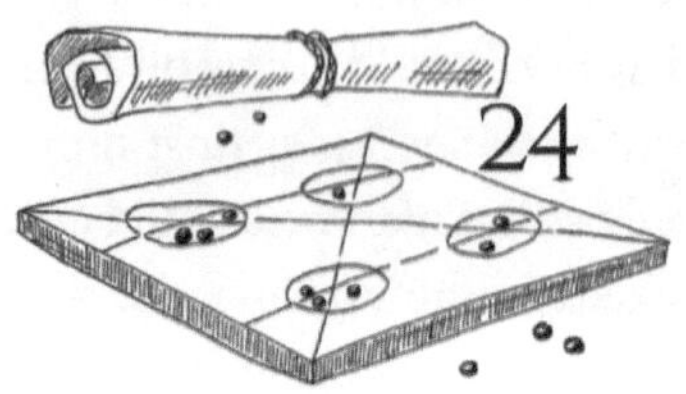

MOTIVES & MEANS

JONAS

THE FREEDOM OF A horse was unlike anything Jonas had ever felt before. Sure, he'd ridden a mammoth across Mothmar, but those lumbering beasts were nothing compared to the speed and dexterity of riding on horseback. At first, Jonas thought he would be thrown at every step, but Rorhan taught him how to hold tight with his thighs rather than his hands, to breathe deeply into his belly, so Thora would not sense or replicate any tension. He still had yet to figure out how to manage that.

"I don't have Tala," Jonas had whined as he balanced in his saddle.

"You don't need Tala to have a tether with a horse," Rorhan had said with a chuckle. "They're a creature that latches to your soul and doesn't let go. Trust her, but more importantly, prove to her that *you* can be trusted."

And with that, they were off, trotting down the precarious rock-ridden paths out of Endirinn. Soon, Jonas learned to move with Thora, not against her, imitating Rorhan's up and down movements with every step. When they reached the strait, the city high and behind them, Rorhan kicked Agnar into a canter and Thora followed, almost leaving Jonas behind.

Once he got his yelling and cursing under control, Jonas lifted his wind-whipped face and peered through watery eyes to see the landscape of Mothmar in new form: beautiful and green, lush and filled with color and light. This was the Mothmar of his imagination, the land he had painted since he was a child. His tears brought by wind turned into tears of joy as he took it in, overwhelmed by the sheer beauty he had missed his entire life because of the cold that had taken his country.

But they had done it; they had brought the green. And here it was. He wished he could have been with Solyana when she saw it in its totality from the mountaintop, when she experienced it in full as he was right now. While the snow and ice had been dissipating slowly over the last few years, watching it from the back of the gray-dappled beauty he rode now filled him with such emotion, he had to hold it back so he could see where he was going.

"This land is beautiful!" Rorhan shouted from Agnar just ahead.

"It is!" Jonas choked through a laugh and wiped his nose on his sleeve, his cloak billowing out behind him.

When they got to the end of the strait, Rorhan slowed to a stop, and Jonas pulled Thora up beside him. Jonas was unsurprised to find his friend's face holding a smile as big as Jonas's own.

"Well, my map-making friend. Where to now?"

Jonas shifted his knapsack to his front and slid a folded map from a side pocket. Tracing a finger over the path he had mapped out, he landed on a port city southeast of Endirinn. "After speaking with a few leirman at the last festival, this is our best bet for getting a ship out of here."

"Will we bring the horses?"

Jonas hadn't thought of that. "Could we?"

Rorhan's face brightened. "So, you like them?"

"They might be my new favorite."

Rorhan grinned.

They continued at speed for the rest of the day, taking breaks as the horses needed them. Jonas quickly realized the longer they rode, the more sore he became. By the end of the first evening, he was walking as if his legs were in a permanent curve, one hand on his back for support.

"I don't know how you're not sore," he told Rorhan as he sat down gingerly on the ground by the fire. "I can hardly move."

"Your muscles will get used to it," the man said with a smile. "You will be alright in a day or two."

Rorhan handed Jonas a stick that had a few chunks of meat on the end. "Dinner tonight is rabbit."

"Thanks, Han. I don't quite know what I would've done without your help. I was prepared to go alone, but...I was just going to forage."

"And that is a fast way to move slow. We will need more than just meat, but it is known: a man without meat is a man without stamina. And we cannot have that."

Jonas nodded and finished his meal.

"You really believe this group of people is on an island out there? There is no one closer who knows of the Way?"

Jonas shrugged. "I mean, there could be. But without knowing for sure, all we can do is press on. You've helped me translate a lot of the texts these last five years. If what we've translated is true, the Way would provide access to every Tala, Fera, and Heitt aptitude there is. It's the ultimate weapon. King Erval wouldn't stand a chance against us."

Rorhan poked the fire with a stick. "Is that what it is for?"

"What do you mean?"

"This whole journey, your desire to find this people, is just for a new weapon?"

Something like guilt bloomed inside of Jonas, but it confused him. "Defending ourselves against an evil ruler isn't wrong, Han. It's necessary."

"I do not disagree." He took a breath, considering. "From what I helped you translate, it seemed to me the Way is a relationship of the heart." He pressed a meaty hand to his chest. "A connection to the Celestials, so close there is only room for light, no darkness."

"What does it matter *why* it's given or used? If we can gain access to it, it's ours to wield."

Rorhan shook his head and clucked his tongue. "I think the why is important."

Jonas quieted.

Whatever his motives might be, he was determined to find the answers to help Solyana. He had seen her walk through too many things to not be equipped to take down the man that was trying to trap them all.

THE LADY OF THONETHREN

PALLAH

B OUNCING DOWN THE COBBLESTONED streets of Thonethren in a carriage built for two, Pallah kept a hand pressed to her chest. Her heart hammered beneath her plunging neckline. When Erval had asked her to accompany him, she'd never imagined they'd be *alone*, in his carriage *together*, for *hours*. It was like a dream. From the winding spires of the city proper to the low canopied hovels of the districts surrounding, Pallah couldn't get enough. He showed her the entire city, taking the time to observe everything from steam pools to mud pits, from mansions to the bardagi fighting rings.

Thonethren was a city of opposites. Luxury mingled with austerity with no middle ground. The people that walked the streets were just as recognized for their jewels as they were for their rags.

Now, they wound their way through a market square that held the city's best fiflas—according to the king who sat across from her.

Pallah had mentioned they were her favorite, and he had laughed. "Mine too!" he'd exclaimed. "If we hurry, we can get a few for our midday meal before they run out."

The carriage pulled to a stop, and the footman opened the door for Erval to hop down the steps where he waited for her, hand outstretched.

"Why, thank you," she said demurely.

"Only the best for you, m'lady."

She bit her lip to hold back a giggle and adjusted her dress. She would not be caught acting a foolish girl, not here. The courtyard was made of wide stone, much larger than the cobbles used for roads. Vendors lined the perimeter, each calling for their wares to be bought, waving down patrons and pushing samples into empty hands.

Though the air was cold, the ground itself held an indescribable heat that caused most of the people of Thonethren to forgo any outer layers. King Erval walked beside her, and she couldn't help but glance at him every chance she got. Everything about him oozed authority and power. From the diadem set in his dark brown hair to the tasteful dusting of gray by his ears, from the cape that flowed out behind him to the rings that glittered on his fingers. He was wealth; he was prestige. He was everything Pallah's father had wanted to be, and more.

Pallah spotted the guards who had ridden alongside their carriage; they spread out, mingling with the crowd. She felt protected, worthy, almost feared, and she drank it in.

They approached a bustling booth whose line disintegrated at their arrival. Erval's boots clacked against the stone one final time before he clicked his heels together.

"Good morning, Yarna!" he said brightly. "What flavors do we have today?"

The old woman behind the booth turned quickly, fingers caked in dried dough. "King Erval!" she squeaked. She offered three jerky bows in succession before feverishly dusting her hands on her apron. "What brings my king to my humble stand?"

"My new apprentice is in need of a meal," he said with an open palm toward Pallah. Was she supposed to wave? Curtsy? She settled for a half bow, cheeks burning. "Do we have goat today? Ewe lamb? Oh, perhaps ostrich?" He gave Pallah a half smile and wiggled his eyebrows. "You'll never have meat so tender as ostrich."

Pallah nodded. She'd heard the term in a scroll somewhere but had no idea what kind of animal an ostrich was. Eyes coming back to the woman behind the booth, Pallah was taken aback to find her face clammy and pale. Her lips trembled and there were tears already pooling in her eyes.

"I'm so sorry, my liege. Please forgive your servant. I have no fiflas left today. I just sold my last." She gave a strange chuckle. "Business has been booming under your wonderful leadership!"

Erval stared at the woman, the warm smile he had held turning to ice.

"You have none left?" he clarified.

Yarna bustled around her counter and fell to her knees. "Oh, King, show me mercy! I am making more dough now. It will take but thirty minutes! And you need not pay."

"I need not pay, anyway," Erval said stonily. "Is this not my kingdom? Every booth, every stone upon which they rest belongs to me. How dare you." He turned in a slow circle, eyes darkening further. "How dare you *all*."

The bustle of the market disappeared, the people crypt-silent. A few patrons, food still in their mouths, appeared afraid to even chew. Pallah could taste the fear in the air.

A crow cawed from high above, the only sound apart from Yarna's sniffling. She was prostrate on the ground, her entire body shaking.

Pallah's mind flashed back to her father, pinned against the wall of what had been her home, the cracking of that wall behind him, the pressure of Erval's tether pumping through her until the life was squeezed out of him. This man standing before her, head cocked to the side, cape billowing out behind him, was the same man who'd poured power into her enough to kill her own father.

"Erval," she whispered.

His head snapped in her direction, his eyes holding nothing but darkness, and Pallah's insides turned to water.

"Erval," she repeated. "I'm not very hungry. Why don't we eat at the castle?"

He turned slowly toward her, eyes narrowed to slits. "You're...not...hungry," he said haltingly, his features lupine, his skin stretched back over an angry smile. "What does that matter?"

Pallah opened her mouth to answer, but no sound escaped.

"All that matters is..." The king of Thonethren took a step in her direction, and the fifla vendor behind him went quiet. Then, her back arched, lifting her chest unnaturally up toward the sun. Erval sneered. "Obedience."

Mouth open in a silent scream, the woman's body cracked, each bone snapping with pops that made Pallah flinch. She tried to cover her face but couldn't move her eyes from the woman dying before her.

Swinging his hand out to the side, the woman was flung backward into her booth, her body slamming into her supplies, crushing everything in its wake.

The power. What had siphoned through Pallah against her father had been nothing in comparison to what she witnessed now. The sight filled her with horror. And adoration.

A few screams and cries erupted from the courtyard, but before they could increase, the king turned on his heel, and silence once again gripped the crowd. His hand still outstretched toward Yarna, Erval curled his fingers into a fist as he closed his eyes, breathing in. Dark tendrils of thick smoke Pallah recognized as *aska* rose from the woman. Her soul and her Gift, borne along a river of black, traveled through the air and shot straight for Erval.

Wrapping his arm and snaking into his face, the inky substance filled every orifice, until finally, it was consumed. Erval released a sigh as his chin slowly lowered until he was staring down his nose at Pallah. "There's another vendor in the next courtyard. It's a short walk." He held out his elbow and grinned as if it were a simple stroll in the park. "Walk with me?"

He had to do it, Pallah told herself. How would the people continue to follow him if he didn't put them in their place? If he didn't establish his authority? Pallah reached for his arm with a steady hand, the fear she had felt moments before transformed to awed curiosity. Could she learn to wield such power? Could she become this type of leader, bending any and all to her will?

With all four guards flanking them, the horse-drawn carriage trundling steadily behind, Pallah felt an overwhelming sense of purpose. For too many years, her life had been spent trying to bend over backward for the whims of others—but no longer. She would stand at this man's side and do what he asked of her, for he could make her more than she ever could be without him. With him was power, and power deserved. She saw it in the eyes of the people as they passed, the need to please him, to know him.

They longed for what Pallah had earned, what she had given her life for.

A smug smile fell over her lips as they walked arm in arm. She was the Lady of Thonethren, and she would do what she must to retain the title.

REGRET

RHUTH

RHUTH PEERED UPWARD, SHIELDING her eye with a mittened hand. "Do you remember what comes after this range?"

The pass between the mountains ended just ahead.

"Ah, yes. First, a large plain, and then the geysers."

Frowning, Rhuth tried to posit what the word 'geyser' could mean. Exiting from the high walls of the mountains, they picked their way down the rocks into a snowy landscape spotted with clumps of trees and brush.

Beyond the tundra, she could barely see lithe streams of steam rose from the ground. They dissipated quickly, and Rhuth could almost fool herself they were merely low clouds. Curiosity got the better of her. She requested to connect with the falcons that were still keeping pace with them overhead, and one allowed her entrance.

She closed her eye and opened two healthy ones set in the feathered head of a falcon far above. Grinning, she urged the bird forward, and it shot like a fletched arrow, intent on escaping the snowy landscape that surrounded them now.

It wasn't the first time Rhuth had wished herself to be anything but human. Animals had many advantages she did not. She was in awe of her bird as it approached the geyser field. After a few more flaps, she looked down.

Just beneath her sprawled a wide flat range, all but cleared of snow. Crater-like holes marred the ground in various spots where steam rose lazily from the earth.

Rhuth gasped. "I've never seen anything like this before." But in speaking, she was brought back to her body, opening her good eye to Pallah who was stepping up beside her.

"You've never seen what before?" Pallah asked, eyeing her curiously.

"The geysers you spoke of. They're magnificent."

The woman arched an eyebrow. "Did you just do it?" She released something between a bark of disbelief and a laugh. "The thing you used to do with that bird of yours? You tethered, er...connected to it? Are you looking through its eyes?"

Rhuth nodded slowly, watching the falcon make its way back. It was probably annoyed she had abandoned it so quickly.

"That's...amazing. I've never heard of connecting without, well...losing your animal, eventually. What happened to that falcon you used to have?"

"Halina?"

"The one with the missing talon."

Sorrow and anger suffused Rhuth at the thought of her lost friend. She wondered where Halina was now, what had become of her. She cleared her throat. "I released her, so you wouldn't get your hands on her."

"I wouldn't have harmed her," Pallah said.

"But you wouldn't have let me continue working with her."

"I won't deny that. But I don't kill innocent creatures."

"You just trap them in Mazes," Rhuth spat. "And let them freeze to death in blizzards."

Pallah huffed, but whether it was with amusement or derision, Rhuth couldn't tell.

"How did you know Solyana needed help the last day you were connected to your bird?"

Rhuth felt secrets unfurling between them like strategic moves on a stökk board. "I didn't, not really." Rhuth shrugged. "I was—" She hadn't admitted to Pallah she had in fact spoken to Solyana through her Tala connection with Halina, or what had happened during that conversation. It wasn't a moment she was particularly proud of. "I was hoping I could get someone to connect to Halina using Tala and then enter the Maze alongside me. Warn them about you."

Pallah's eyes widened. "Did it work?"

Rhuth blinked, and she stamped down the pride she felt at Pallah's awe. "It did, actually."

Shaking her head, Pallah turned back to the steam field. "Did Solyana do it? Did she gain Tala?"

Before she could stop herself, Rhuth's head was nodding in confirmation. She bit the inside of her cheek; she didn't need to give away all her secrets.

"Your warning didn't bring her back, then."

"No. I think I scared her...or she thought I wasn't real. I don't know. My eye..." She motioned to it, forever encrusted in scar tissue. "It was whole in the Maze. I think it was enough to cause my sister to doubt if it was truly me."

"It did the same to me," Pallah admitted, and Rhuth's ears perked up. "I grew up messing with axes and hatchets. I had all sorts of scars on my hands and arms at the time, little things. But they were clean and clear in the Maze." Pallah felt for the metal staff strapped across her back, as if reassuring herself it was still there. "I believe whatever the Maze is, it shows our truest selves."

Rhuth bit back a retort, that it would have shown Pallah a monster. The woman would have probably just agreed with her. They continued to pick their way down the cliffside and into the snowy expanse before them.

Ember hopped into the snow like a rabbit, digging tunnels and disappearing before popping back up in a new place. The sun was bright in the sky, and Rhuth marveled at it though taking care not to stare at it directly. She hadn't realized until now, but she had never truly seen the Father of the Day; her valley, being perpetually clouded, kept Him hidden.

"You asked what Erval did to make me leave him." Pallah seemed to be in the mood to share her past, and Rhuth paid attention. "The answer is quite simple. He'd made a promise to me, but it became clear he had no intention of keeping it." The woman used her staff like a walking stick. "My brother was the victim of a Taka Reu curse. It displaced him in both time and space, and all I wanted was to find him again. Erval promised to help me, but he really isn't the type to help anyone, especially if it doesn't directly benefit him. I did my own digging, my own research, and found that every curse has a sister prophecy with which it is associated. I'd found the prophecy; I just needed to find the person who fit to fulfill it—the one who would bring the green. I couldn't do that in Thonethren. So, I left. As you can imagine, Erval had not been thrilled at my...disobedience." She looked out toward the horizon, though it was obscured with steam. "My guess is he got his hands on Solyana, and possibly Ahren, too. And he knows I will come for my brother. But I have no intention of powering his little machine for him."

Rhuth eyed the woman beside her: the squaring of her shoulders, the set of her brow, the twist of her mouth, all of it convinced Rhuth that Pallah already knew what she would have to do, and persuasion had little to do with it.

"All that time you were with Erval, were you alone? Did you have anyone but him and his steward?"

Such loneliness was something Rhuth could understand.

"I wasn't." Pallah's gaze grew distant. "And she's one of my biggest regrets."

DECEPTION

SOLYANA

WAGON LOADED, CLOTHES LAUNDERED, and goodbyes said, Solyana sat in the back of the wagon, eager, yet terrified, to leave. The farewell song of her people rang in her mind, reminded of the time she had been packed into Gamaliel's sled, wolves at the ready. They were but foolish children then, sent on a wild goose chase.

In the two days it took to gather enough supplies, the people had grown ready for a grand departure of their Chosen One. There was a mass of them at the southern gate, ready to bid farewell to the Saint of Endirinn, no expense spared.

Music erupted from the group for people to dance and sing. Food, clothes, and coins were tossed into the wagon, and before long, Solyana found herself walking to shake hands and give thanks where she could. Gamaliel was ever-present beside her, keeping a watchful eye on those all around.

Ahren stayed in the wagon with Vinur, organizing the gifts and tools as they were passed over.

Lone stood at the gate, Marin in her arms. "Send word when you can, please." She wiped a tear.

"Why are you crying, Mama?" Marin pushed her face into Lone's neck.

Lone pressed a hand to her daughter's cheek, blue eyes boring into Solyana's. "Go save Mothmar again, okay?"

Solyana pulled them in for a hug, and Gamaliel wrapped his arms around them, too. How different their dynamic was now, Lone so loving and caring with her daughter on her hip.

"Take care of your mama, okay?" Solyana said to the three-year-old.

Marin gave a coy smile and hugged Lone tighter.

"And please"—Lone grasped Solyana's arm tightly—"if you do run into Jonas and Rorhan, make sure my husband returns to me." She released her to press the hand firmly over her womb. "He needs to meet this next little one."

Solyana's eyes widened in surprise. "You didn't tell him before he left?" She hugged Lone again, and Marin began to protest.

"He would never leave if he knew." Lone gave a wilted shrug. "And Jonas needs him."

"He *will* come back. We all will."

They caught up to the wagon amidst the sound of pounding drums and tinkling bells.

"You promise?" Lone shouted before their wagon trundled clear of the gate.

"I promise!" Solyana yelled back to her, imbued now with new energy. She would emerge victorious; she had to.

"Hop in!" Phineas called from the driver's seat, reins in his hands as he steered the horses.

Scrambling into the back, Solyana and Gamaliel stowed their gifts and hung on as they rocked back and forth in time with the wagon.

"You ready, Solyana?" Phineas's voice came through the leather canvas. Solyana ducked her head to see through the circular viewing space that looked out the front of the wagon.

"Are we starting?"

"The sooner the better."

"I'll be up with Phineas, then," Solyana said to Gamaliel.

He reached forward and tucked a stray curl behind her ear. "I'll be here when you need me."

Grinning, Solyana settled herself beside Phineas.

The steward was dressed in his usual cream and deep purple robes, a tailored belt around his middle. His feet, donned in matching leather moccasins, were kicked up on the buckboard of the wagon. Reins held loosely in his hands, Phineas whistled a tune.

Though she still held reservations about the man, the whistling reminded her of someone else, a dear friend of similar build who'd enjoyed carrying a tune while he traversed over the countryside of Mothmar. Thinking of Odie stirred compassion in her heart, and Solyana folded her hands, ready to get to know this new guide a bit more.

"What are the horses' names?" she asked him as she watched the dual set of rumps swing this way and that over Endirinn's rocky countryside.

Phineas's whistling halted mid-melody, and he blinked beneath his spectacles. "Bran and Barley."

"Cute. They look very different from the horses Jonas and Rorhan took. They're huge."

"Ah yes, well, a perfectly reasonable explanation to that." Phineas settled back into his seat, appearing more comfortable now that he had a topic of discussion. "Jonas and Rorhan needed horses built for speed and endurance, these on the other hand, are farm horses. Drafts."

"Which one is which? They're both brown with blonde tails."

Phineas pointed to the horse on the left. "That one's Bran; he's got a short tail. This one's Barley." He pointed to the one on the right, whose tail was three times the other's length. "Bran is a bit of a bully. You won't get them confused, once you see him nip Barley."

"I'll admit, I'm a bit surprised."

Phineas raised his eyebrows in her direction.

"I would expect a member of the royal household of Thonethren to be above all this." Solyana motioned at the reins and the wagon behind them.

"I grew up on a farm." He grinned at the horses swaying before him. "But that life feels like a distant dream."

From atop the bench of the wagon, Solyana felt she was finally seeing the green of Mothmar for the first time. Sure, she had seen bits and pieces coming down the mountain, but here, when she didn't have to focus on her feet or her situation, she could take it all in anew.

Awe filled her heart, and tears came to her eyes at the rolling hills, the waving verdant grass, and the trees covered with lush foliage—broad thin leaves that would never withstand cold. The burble of small streams and whistling of the wind brought music to her ears. It was as if their world had awakened after so long asleep. Flowers dotted the hillsides, just like the ones Jonas had drawn on his maps.

Skittering in the long grass beside the wagon, Solyana noticed tiny black eyes and shuffling claws. She grinned at the stoats, who clearly had not yet released Phineas, even as they traveled away from Endirinn.

"I'd like to make it clear before we begin," Phineas started, his eyes shifting from her to the path ahead. "I don't expect you to trust me fully right away. But know I am on your side, Solyana. I told Erval I was coming out here to research the Way and to find the Seer to help alleviate his fears of the future. And while both are true, I *was* hoping to find you."

Solyana shifted in her seat, her unease deepening.

"When he first lost his connection to you, Erval believed you had simply begun drinking the blocking tea. But after prodding around, he realized the tea had not yet been fully discovered in Endirinn. So Erval assumed you had died. I chalked it up to another deluded hero trying to bring the green and failing to do so. You see," he said kindly, "there have been many who thought they would be the one to do it. But once the world began to thaw, and the green returned, I knew you had succeeded.

"For the last decade—well, to be honest, it's been longer than that—I have felt the darkness of Thonethren like a tangible thing. I no longer wanted anything to do with it. What's the point of power and prestige if it only brings death and suffering? But I had to keep up my act with the man, or I would surely be next on his list of people to Take. I knew if you truly had brought the green, that you of all people would be worth saving from Erval."

"I may have brought the green," Solyana said. "But I don't know if I have a place in this new prophecy...the *true* prophecy. Sometimes I wonder if I was just in the right place at the right time. Or maybe the wrong place at the wrong time."

"Regardless, if you're a foretold piece to this puzzle, then you *are* a piece of it. And I say this to emphasize it is important Erval gleans as little from you as possible."

"What if he discovers your deception?"

"Then I expect to sit on the machine." Phineas's eyes seemed to stare out into the past.

They spent the next three hours of the trip talking it over. Now that Solyana had Tala, it would be far easier for her to understand, according to Phineas. Just like how beasts take on a resistance if they associate negative feelings with the person casting the tether, so could Solyana. And not just a natural callousness that Erval would fall flat against, no. Instead, it would be a path, a road along which she could guide him and keep him. He could step in no deeper than she allowed, no wider than she bid, as long as she kept those pieces of herself compartmentalized.

"Long ago," he continued. "Back when Pallah was young, before she came to us in Thonethren, she had been trapped in a Maze. Her explanation of that place, and how to erect it in an animal *or* human's mind, is what gave me the idea to formulate a similar structure in my own. It was tricky at first. I had to be sure whatever path or maze I created—only *I* could hold the key to escape. And it couldn't look like a maze either, unlike the ones we could erect in others' minds. Erval would notice, surely. Instead, it must mimic everything about your unadulterated mind, but with new direction."

Solyana's mind spun at the onslaught of information. Rhuth was held in a Maze much like Phineas was describing, his information made sense in that regard. But Solyana had no idea how to pursue such a thing.

"I know it's a lot." He glanced in her direction. "I know what I'm suggesting is near impossible. I'm asking you to hone, in days, a skill that took me decades to perfect." He smiled softly. "But you're a smart kid. And if you can pull it off, I believe we can do this with minimal casualties."

Eyeing him, Solyana felt that compassion again. If Erval was truly like family to him, their plan to kill him wouldn't be an easy one to swallow.

"If we could do it in a way that led to no casualties at all, what would you do?"

His lips twisted in thought. "Total circulation of the blocking tea would be enough to temporarily subdue him. But since it requires regular dosing, it would be difficult to maintain. And then, of course, there's the issue of supply. Erval's soldiers are always bringing smugglers into the cells, and their punishment is almost always to be Taken. By either his hand or the person he's trying to stuff full of years."

"Like you?" Solyana asked.

Phineas blinked once as he studied the mountains in the distance. "Like me."

"When was the last time?"

He emitted a nervous huff. "Erval tried to get me to Take a young girl just days ago, while I was in Endirinn."

Solyana remembered Gamaliel telling her about finding the keeper's daughter in Phineas's room and gasped.

"I didn't," he admitted. "Thankfully, Gamaliel and Rorhan burst into my room that night." He grinned. "They're good men, those two. I'm thankful they came when they did. I've never liked Taking." Something dark came over Phineas's expression and his knuckles turned white on the reins. "I hate it, actually, since the very first time."

"Does Erval know?"

"My feelings matter little to him. It became a task I gave up fighting against in his presence. Apart from him, however, I am my own man and can make my own choices."

Solyana raised her eyebrows. "And Pallah? I doubt she put up much resistance."

"I think you'd be surprised about her." Phineas's eyes swung up to look at the clouds. "She has a rebellious strength I quite envy, if I'm honest. But I had known Erval for longer and had given him more than she did. The king will not use me to power the Brextant; I'm too valuable to him. I've made sure of it." He gazed ahead, his countenance turned cold. "If he were to use me to power the machine, it would work, but he would have to rule Mothmar alone. And deep down, he's still just a young boy, ousted from his throne and stripped of his title, looking to carve a home for himself."

Solyana couldn't imagine what it would be like, living and working with a man for centuries of time, only to betray him in the end, even if the reasoning for such a betrayal were sound.

"You *will* help us defeat him..." Her eyes bore into Phineas, willing him to speak the truth.

Phineas kept a hard stare on Bran and Barley. "You all underestimate him."

Solyana opened her mouth to argue but closed it again. "Perhaps," she said.

Phineas nodded. "In any case... Your first lesson."

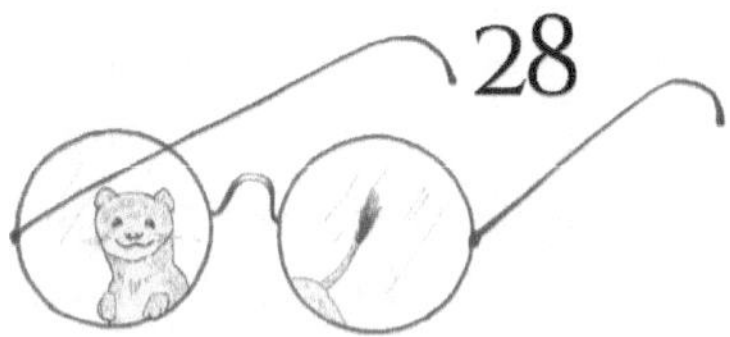

A MAN AND HIS STOAT

PHINEAS

THE WAY BACK TO Thonethren would be far more pleasant than his journey to Endirinn. With the group's extra hands, ready and willing to help, he was able to delegate the horses' needs to those with a bit more energy. Phineas couldn't deny he was growing weaker, and he knew he would draw Erval's ire when it was discovered how little he'd been Taking.

How long had it been since he had taken his last soul? Two years? Five?

Erval trusted him enough to allow him free reign in this area of his life, but his imposition back at Torny's Tavern was proof the man's trust was waning.

They made camp just southwest of Endirinn, the three children—for that's what they were to Phineas—slept peacefully around the fire. It surprised him really, the way in which they so readily believed him. Sure, Gamaliel gave him a hard time at first, but now? Phineas scanned each one of them, their faces serene, peaceful. So untouched, as they were, by the cares and worries of the world.

He shook his head and prodded the fire with a stick. No, they did have worries, worries enough. They understood as well as could be expected that they were walking into a kingdom that boasted a man who had lived for centuries with his will uncontested. But did they truly know what that meant?

"I see you there," Phineas crooned to the copper-colored stoat that had been watching him with glossy eyes. "You are not hidden from me." He gave a sly grin. "Not much is." The creature took a tentative step forward, eyes flashing in the firelight, before its body came into view. It was a pretty thing, its neck and underbelly white as the moon.

He didn't need to tether it, but he was curious about its power. Latching on, he commanded the stoat to come, and it did, quite compliantly. Phineas sat with his legs crossed at the fire and the creature hopped onto his knee. "You seem content to follow us."

The stoat blinked.

"You have a pretty coat. May I call you Kopar?" He reached out to pet the thing, and it nuzzled into his hand. "It means copper in the old tongue, though I'm sure you knew that." Phineas was growing far too sentimental in his old age. He raised a finger to wipe at a rebellious tear. "This life is precious, isn't it?"

The creature curled into his lap and promptly fell asleep. The tears wouldn't be stopped then, and he allowed them, his bleary vision passing from Kopar to Solyana. They both reminded him there were greater things in this world than success or power. Their innocence, their softness, had been so foreign to him for so long.

And just like the stoat, who would surely live no longer than a handful of years, Solyana's days were numbered as well. Both these innocents would be used to quell things beyond their control. The thought stilled his tears. Solyana knew not the horrors awaiting her at the hands of the king of Thonethren. He had not told her because she would have fled. Any sane person would.

In creating the device, Phineas had been sure to install a gap in the machine's defenses. Hidden beneath the guise of science, Erval would not discover it, but Phineas knew. If Erval were ever to truly find someone willing to sacrifice their gathered years to allow the king to dominate all of Mothmar, he would have to be stopped. And since Erval himself was too powerful to kill, the Brextant then must come to destruction.

For this, Phineas crafted a fail-safe.

Ages ago, formed from information found in the depths of Temple Rinn, before the Green Prophecy had yet to be fulfilled, he built it, weaving the means of the Brextant's destruction into the heart of the machine itself. If his theories were true, Erval was the *one who was all dark*, and for some time he'd believed he himself a part of the second line: *of which there will be two*. Thus, Phineas had crafted the key to the Brextant's ruin into a shape he himself could fill.

To destroy the Brextant, truly and wholly—one had to be a part of the Green Prophecy.

But now? With his heart growing ever colder to the Taka Reu, Phineas no longer believed himself to be part of any prophecy. Solyana, however... She had brought the green. There was viable proof. Should Solyana sit upon the Brextant, she could slip through the machine's defenses. She could destroy it from the inside out, and Erval's plot along with it.

The night breeze wound its way through their makeshift camp, and Phineas listened to Bran and Barley snorting in their sleep. He watched the girl who held the world in her hands and his heart twisted in his chest.

He could only pray she would forgive him, even as her life would be taken from her on that wretched device. He wasn't deserving of it, of course, but he selfishly longed for that forgiveness all the same.

"Kopar," he asked the stoat in a shaky voice. "Do you forgive me? For what I have yet to do?"

The stoat sighed in his sleep.

BEASTS

HALLDORA

Erval may have taken the throne, but Halldora had managed to employ tailors far superior than those working in the castle of Thonethren, and their work was simply magnificent. When they had dressed her before dawn, she hadn't been able to properly appreciate the full scope of their design. But now, with the sun at its height, sitting upon the throne that took four Stein Fera and one Malmur Fera to craft in just as many hours, she was pleased. Her tunic and pants were soft dyed leather, tied tight and fitted to her form. Layered over that were individual pieces of plated metal, quenched in oil before burnished with beeswax. Each piece was interlocking, allowing her fluid and graceful movement. Erval would never be seen in armor, with his unnecessary capes and glittering knuckles. He knew not how to truly lead, her big brother.

Her hair was pulled back, piled high on her head. Though a few untamable dark strands came down on either side of her face, her maid had told her it was the picture of regality. And Halldora couldn't help but agree. She envisioned how she must look now, perched upon the hill, her guard flanking her royal person, her army setting out in rows down below. Let the procession coming look upon her and tremble. They would swear their allegiance to a warrior queen.

He was here now, with his men. They lumbered up the pathway, the chief at their head riding atop a polar bear. She had to admit, it struck a terrifying picture; she should get herself such a beast. She glared over the ranks of her men, a few of them quivering and shying away, and she scowled. They had better not embarrass her. Behind the chief, three more of his men strode atop a different beast: a mountain lion, a moose, and a boar. Each animal was far too large to be natural, and the state of them... Fur grew in ragged tufts, scars ran the lengths of them. These animals had seen battle. By the looks of them, more than one.

Halldora reminded herself her men outnumbered Chief Orson's five-to-one. He would be a fool to incite any conflict here. But she knew he was not pleased with the missive she had sent a week ago. Although his feelings were of no real import, she could indulge his pride and withstand his ire, so long as he bent his knee.

Chief Orson's bald head glinted in the afternoon light, his eyes shadowed in tattoos. His body, only covered by a pelt below the waist, was heaped with corded muscle. Halldora sat up straighter and crossed one leg over the other, the plates of her immaculate armor shifting and clanking together. He would find her relaxed, unaffected by his appearance here.

"Halldora," he crooned as his bear lumbered halfway up the hill before her soldiers halted him, bravely standing in the way. "You are even more beautiful than the whispers say."

"You flatter me, Orson." If he wouldn't use her title, she would pay him the same courtesy. "You are as bold as I've heard, coming to my camp, dressed for war."

"I see I am not the only one in my battle leathers." He nodded toward her, a lecherous smile creeping over his face. "Word reached my ears of your plans to accept aid from that *tik*."

"We will have no disparagement of any loyal faction in our presence. You will address this court and those who support it with decorum and courtesy." She rested her hands in her lap.

Darkness descended over Orson's face. His polar bear shook its mighty head and spittle whipped out, enough for her to hear the slap of it hitting her soldier's armor. Orson's hand rested on the handle of a massive meat cleaver he kept strapped against his thigh.

"My Beast Riders, do they not meet your expectations?" He glanced at his men to his left and right. "That you must enlist lesser, weaker beasts? I thought we had a deal," he snarled.

Halldora fought hard to keep her body relaxed against her seat. "I desire no ill-will between us, Orson. I said nothing in my missive of your army being dismissed from my service." Though Halldora knew Orson and Maral's Beast Riders were just as likely to fight each other on the battlefield as their common enemy, she would cross that bridge when she came to it. "We have the same goals, Orson. Tear down my brother from his false throne and bring about a more prosperous Mothmar—a large section of that prosperity given to you of course, once it is mine to give. The more men we acquire the better; surely you can see the strategy in that." She extended an open hand toward him. "You are a military man, after all."

Orson's nostrils flared, and he drummed his fingertips over the handle of the cleaver. "One cannot warm two beds and expect each man to welcome you back home. Maral has nothing to offer but disruption to what is otherwise certain victory."

"They are swords in hands, offered to eradicate our mutual enemy."

The polar bear shifted and the soldiers nearest the beast cringed away. Halldora uncrossed her legs and sat forward.

Orson's lip curled. "I never said Erval was an enemy, Dora. You simply gave me a better offer."

He used the nickname only her family knew—only Erval knew. She kept her face blank.

"He promised land, you promised more land—and women," he added with a leer. "You both allow worship of the Mother Below. The three of us have more in alignment than Maral and her people of the Way." He scoffed, and the men sitting atop the beasts behind him chuckled. "They will not join us in battle as much as they will stab us in the back."

"They will do as they are paid to do, just as you will, should you see simple reas—"

"You make it clear you have chosen Maral and the Way. You have no loyalty to us—or the Mother."

Halldora stood. "You can worship whatever you want on your vast lands, once I have my crown."

"I care not for your paltry promises. You have made your choice." He turned his bear in a great circle, the other riders following in kind. "Perhaps we will meet again, one day. Though, I doubt our next encounter would be so cordial." And his force cantered away.

Fuming, Halldora considered launching an attack right then. Her men could best them...though not without casualties. And numbers, as she had argued, were now even more paramount. She had made her decision, and now she would live with it. Maral and her Riders, with their numbers and stores of blocking tea, was a necessary alignment.

Clad in armor and the green cape that signified his position, her general approached and took a knee, tucking his helm beneath one arm. "M'lady, I beg of you to rethink how you ally yourself. Chief Orson's men and beasts are invaluable to our cause."

Halldora peered down at him. "Which is better, General Ivan? The fox behind you or the fox beside you?"

The general was silent before clearing his throat. "The fox beside you, my Queen." Halldora could hear the waver in his voice.

Halldora turned from him and surveyed her army. "The answer is neither." She would make do with her men, Maral's Beast Riders, and the Crimson Chief. "A fox, whether beside or behind, will always bite you in the end. The only good fox is a dead one."

He glanced up at her. "M'lady, I worry for you," he whispered.

She trailed two fingers over his face, and he leaned into her touch, closing his eyes against her palm as she rested it against his beard. "Come to my tent tonight," she said.

Halldora clasped her hands behind her back and left her general, descending the hill through the sea of glinting metal beneath the beating sun.

Row by row, the soldier's fists curled to beat their chests before going still at Halldora's presence. She strode before them, her mind turning with renewed vigor. If Orson ran back to his master, tail between his legs, would Erval strike him down for defection? Or raise him up for information of her incoming army? Regardless, time was no longer on her side. Her brother would know they were coming, and it was time she showed him who was truly fit to rule.

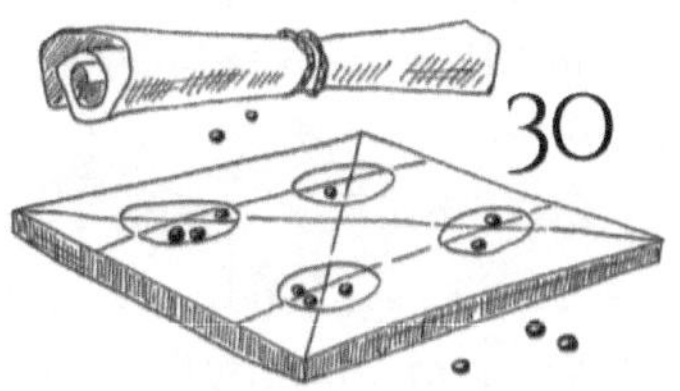

CAPTAIN VIGGO

Jonas

Two days of riding brought the duo to the peninsula. Endirinn was far behind them, but the mountain was still visible, though barely. Riding south, passing small cities and smaller villages, Jonas was reminded how grand Endirinn truly was. A structural marvel, especially coming from his modest home in the valley. Jonas stood up straight in his stirrups, catching glimpses of the ocean beyond.

Back in the valley, his parents had promised him a trip to Kana Ocean, but they had been lost to him before making good on it. After arriving in Endirinn, he had wanted to go to the Himmin Sea with Gamaliel, but the city was so high above sea level, the most they had accomplished was a visit to the cliffs. Jonas's hair had been tousled by the far-off sea air as he had watched the seagulls surfing on the winds and tasted the brine of the sea in the mists.

Now, as he found himself trailing behind Rorhan on a well-traveled road, he couldn't help his jaw from dropping as he took in the sights and smells, excited for a closer look at the water.

The horses' hooves clopped from dirt path to stone-bordered road, signaling their turn from rural countryside to a more affluent area. A bustling hub had bloomed in this place steeped in sea salt and fish.

Reining their horses to a stop, the pair craned their necks upward. A sign hung above them, held up by two large poles, tied on with rope.

"'East End,'" Jonas read. "'Most are Welcome.'"

"Honest people," Rorhan said with a grin.

"Keep moving!" a voice that sounded like a frog caught mid-croak called from behind them.

Jonas looked over his shoulder to find a parchment-thin man hunched over the leads in his hands. He sat with his feet propped up on the buckboard of his wagon, his mouth chewing on something the color of mud. "Some of us have goods to sell and don't have time for dawdling."

Jonas followed Rorhan off the path, where the two horses swished their tails against the flies.

The driver raised his hand as he passed, in what Jonas could only assume was a crude gesture, as the man's face held nothing but contempt. The plaza was lively, and Jonas couldn't help but feel very much in the way.

"We should dismount and lead them from here," Rorhan suggested as he swung his leg over his saddle. "These are a busy people."

Jonas followed his lead, although walking in front of Thora scared him more than riding her. He held his head high, praying the horse wouldn't forget he was there and step on him.

"We need to find someone willing to take us on board." Jonas looked toward the piers, wondering how he was to decipher who was seafaring and who wasn't. Seagulls screeched overhead, hecklers shouted from the row of booths, and Jonas could, very faintly, hear the sea. "Should we make our way to the dockyard?"

Rorhan nodded firmly once and seemed to take it upon himself to lead the way. Jonas breathed a sigh of relief and followed, taking in every detail he could of East End. From children dressed in ragged tunics, to merchants decorated in the finest gold, the port city seemed to hold every kind of person. Most were selling goods, their shops open-air and their voices loud and cajoling. But it was the quiet ones that gave Jonas pause. They blended in with the buildings, or sprawled out on the ground like lichen, bowls in their hands, begging for coin or bread.

Jonas wished he had something he could give them.

There were others who were quiet, tucked carefully into the alleyways and eaves, their beady eyes watching each traveler, assessing who they were, why they were there, weighing what might be gleaned from them. Before these men were sets of women, boisterous and jaunty. Their whistles and calls persuaded more than one man walking ahead of Jonas. They would disappear with these women into a tall building on the corner, a rich purple fabric serving as the door.

Jonas had no idea what to make of it.

"Rorhan," he asked as they walked. "What is that building there? Why would so many men want fabric?"

Jonas had never seen his large friend's face go such a shade of pink, but it was as deep a hue as sunset on a clear evening. He opened his mouth as if to answer but then closed it again, tried once more, then snapped his mouth shut.

"Just keep walking, young friend. Pay them no mind. If you have to be turned toward a darkened corner to purchase something, then perhaps it is best to remain on the road."

Keeping their horses moving, the two made their way farther east until the path petered out. Jonas took a deep breath as a gust of wind rode off the sea and filled his lungs with freedom. Before him lay an expanse of water, so wide his eyes refused to take it all in. And it was not the simple deep blue of the Vatino Sea. This water was a bright and clear cerulean that let him see all the way to the bottom. Various docks poked out from the port, each lined with vessels bobbing in the waves.

How had he lived his life up until this point, so tied to the shore? How had he not known about the great world beyond? It was unfathomable, as was the breadth and depth of the water he stood before now.

Scanning the docks, Jonas suddenly felt ill prepared. In all his study the last five years, he had focused solely on understanding the Way and how to grasp it. He had painted a few maps, one of which they were using for navigation. But he had failed to truly plan ahead, believing—naïvely, he now realized—his Seer abilities would lead him one step at a time. Now, standing at the precipice of adventure, he had no idea what to do.

A small hut sat perched before the ramp that led down to the water's edge, a sign nailed to it: Mariners and Travelers. Below it, there was a board with the word "vacancy" burned into it, and to the left of that, a small, empty slot.

Jonas clicked his tongue to encourage Thora along and began to make their way to the awning below the sign, when suddenly a side door on the hut slammed open. Thora stopped and flung her head to the side, nearly yanking the reins from Jonas's hands.

"Hush, girl, it's okay," Jonas soothed as a plump woman ambled out of the wooden building. She slid a small wooden tile into that empty slot with the word "No" burned into it.

"No vacancy?" Jonas said, taking a few steps closer. "Ma'am, excuse me, no vacancy? Does that mean there's no ships?"

The woman gave no notice that she'd even heard Jonas and waddled back toward the door, her wide berth barely leaving any room for her to squeeze through. She slammed it shut behind her.

Jonas and Rorhan exchanged a glance, and the bigger man shrugged. "I will hold the horses; you go speak with her."

Jonas handed over his reins, pushed a lock of curls from his eyes, and approached the front of the hut.

"Good afternoon, ma'am. Your eyes be upward," Jonas said politely to the woman across from him. She sat atop a high stool, her elbows leaning lazily on the front desk. While her face held no true wrinkles, something told Jonas she was not exactly young. Her eyes were huge, hazel, and Jonas almost jumped when they snapped up from the scroll she was reading.

"And be filled with flotsam." Her voice was unexpectedly girlish. Her owl-eyes shifted back to her reading. "If you'll excuse me, Jon just proclaimed his love for Kara, and I think they're about to kiss!"

"Who?" Jonas peered around the woman, but she held up a hand and made a shooing motion.

"Quit bothering me! Can't you read the sign?"

Jonas blinked, completely astounded. Was this woman sick? She was speaking nonsense. "Perhaps I've come to the wrong place. I'm looking for safe passage from here to Skrim."

The woman leaned forward, her heavy bosom sliding on top of the desk. Jonas stumbled back. She reached a hand out of the window and pointed to the side. "No vacancy!" she said impatiently before sliding back, her scroll rumpling beneath her breasts. "Jon! No!" She fished it out and smoothed the parchment. "There you are. Now, where were we?" She laid it flat against the countertop once more and leaned on a fist, eyes roving over the text.

"Shelly won't be much use to you today, now will she?" A rich voice came from behind Jonas's right shoulder.

"Captain Viggo!" The woman within the hut—Shelly, as she appeared to be named—turned as bright a red as a tomato and immediately began fanning herself with her scroll. "You caught me unawares," she said, lowering her lashes and blinking them furiously toward the man now stepping before Jonas.

A pair of brown strapped boots wrapped his feet, his pants were so tight Jonas thought perhaps that's why the man seemed to sway as he walked, and his shirt was a flowing cream-colored linen tucked into a doublet that remained open at the top, his red chest hair spilling out like moss over a boulder.

"What number is that this week?" he asked as he sauntered forward, pointing a finger to the scroll in her hands.

"The seventh." She tittered and swatted at his finger with the scroll. "Long days here in the hut and the heat, as you know. What is a girl to do but read?"

"You never cease to amaze me, Shelly." The man leaned on the counter, the feather festooning his massive hat brushing the top of the window. "Truly, a rare catch. A hidden pearl." Another scroll materialized in his right hand, and he slid it onto the desk. "I stopped by Hugo's to get you another."

The woman fanned herself harder, the deep chasm between her breasts rising and falling as her breath accelerated. She snatched up the scroll and sampled the softness of the maroon ribbon it was tied with. She smiled so hard Jonas feared her cheeks would cover her eyes like moons eclipsing two suns.

"Now," Captain Viggo drawled, "I hate to talk business with you, darling, but is Coletta ready?"

Shelly's smile disappeared and she leaned on her fist once more. "I knew it." She pouted. "You're leaving East End."

"It pains me," he said before turning to the side where Jonas finally got a good look at him. His bright orange hair was matched by a mustache that was twirled up into a second grin. "But yes, Shelly. Now as to my ship? My crew?"

Shelly sighed. "Everything is ready to go, as you requested."

"Thank you, love. I'll bring you something new from West End." The Captain lifted Shelly's small, pudgy hand, kissed the back of it, and winked. "Read that"—he pointed at the rolled parchment—"and think of Captain Viggo."

Shelly gave a soft moan as she handed the Captain a rope fitted with a skeleton key at the end. He tipped his broad hat and turned to face Jonas.

If any man could embody the true spirit of a seafaring captain, it was this man, of that Jonas was sure.

He winked at Jonas, who was entirely unsure how to feel about the gesture, and swaggered away, the curved sword at his side swishing.

Jonas turned to Rorhan, who was staring at the Captain with something like amused disgust. "Rorhan?"

"Hm?" The man grunted, eyes not leaving their mark.

"I think I found us a ship."

A MIDNIGHT DISCOVERY

PALLAH

HAD IT TRULY BEEN a month? A full moon cycle since arriving in this affluent city of darkness? Pallah's sheer black cover-up draped over her body, nothing but her sleeping clothes beneath. It was late, though that meant little to those living in Thonethren. Pallah watched them from her balcony, the lights and laughter that danced below.

She could join them. The thought thrilled her. Erval had given her free reign of the castle; surely the city was included. She was wise enough to know, however, going by herself would be foolish. The king was not a loved man, but a feared one, and Erval had done little to hide her presence. Quite the opposite. He flaunted her in the streets, taking strolls no less than twice a week, during which it had become a bit of a habit to find someone for her to Take. Erval had made it clear she was to do this regularly. That he needed her to become a force to be reckoned with, someone the people would look to with the same fear with which they looked upon him. It brought her little pleasure to kill, but ever since the battle that had waged in her valley, Pallah found the act becoming significantly easier.

And the way Erval looked at her once it was accomplished made it worth every death.

However, Pallah knew if she were to venture out alone, she might very well be more of a target of the peoples' ire than their praise. But the truth was, she was bored. She would never admit that to Erval, of course. But two walks through the city a week was not enough. She couldn't help but feel like she was trapped once more, just in a different kind of Maze.

The wind picked up, and goosebumps rose on her skin. Thinking of the Maze brought back a host of memories and sent her mind in directions she wished it not to go. She stepped back into her rooms and shut the balcony doors, the fire in her hearth keeping her room too warm. Her eyes found the flame and trailed upward to the mantle, where her hatchet lay on display. It sat there, yet to be touched or relocated by the attendants. Surprising, since the attendants were charged with keeping the room to a strict standard and tended to relocate her things against her will.

Pallah's eyes went to the corner of the room in search of her double-headed axe, the one she had stolen from Dahvid's smithy. The corner was empty. She crossed the room, searched the washroom, looked under the bed, but the staff was gone.

Could the servants have taken it to be cleaned? Unlikely, since Pallah had taken care to clean it on the road to Thonethren. But then why would it be missing? She didn't like the idea of being left with nothing but her hatchet to protect herself.

She flung open her wardrobe, donned a deep red cloak, crossed to her door, but froze with the knob in her fist. Even after a whole month here, she was still too nervous to leave her rooms without an invitation or escort. Whether it was dinner with Erval, strolls through the city, or garden walks with Phineas, she had yet to explore the castle herself.

The burning coals of annoyance in her belly flared with anger. If they'd preferred for her to stay in her room, then they shouldn't have stolen her staff. She boldly exited into the hallway. It was somehow easier to breathe out here. She smiled to herself, and for the first time since their first week in Thonethren, she thought of Issha.

Guilt gnawed at her. How had it taken her this long to even consider reuniting with her friend? Too little time, too busy, too exhausted; all paltry excuses in place of the truth. Pallah had simply forgotten about her. Whether Issha had simply slipped her mind, or it was a deeper, more subconscious disconnection from Pallah's life in the valley, she didn't want to know.

She would rectify this oversight tonight.

Standing alone in the wide stone hall, Pallah thought back to their first night here, when Phineas had led Issha to her rooms. Where had it been? One floor down? Two? Were they even in the same wing, or would she have to cross to the western side of the castle?

Left, she'd go left.

She began to stride down the hall, attempting to imbue her steps with a confidence she didn't feel. The hall was lit by lanterns nestled in alcoves lining the walls. The magnitude of work that must go into keeping their oil filled, to lighting and dousing them every night, Pallah could only imagine. Heavy draperies, all made from a similar crimson color as her robe, hung from ceiling to the floor between each light.

A stairwell appeared from the darkness at the end of the hall, half of it ascending, the other descending. Pallah went down. After a few rotations, she reached the bottom and spotted a second hallway slightly wider than the one she'd come from. There were no drapes here, the walls plain with simple torches hanging from pegs. They were spread farther apart along the wall, creating pools of shadow in between.

To her surprise, Pallah had run into no one. She had expected a few servants, perhaps even Phineas. But the halls were silent and devoid of movement, save the miniscule flickering of the torches' flames.

Wooden doors lined the hall on both sides, and Pallah twisted her lips trying to remember which her friend had been led to. Approaching the first door, she gave a knock, so quiet she hardly heard it herself. Nothing happened. It was dark beneath the door. Nervous she would wake up the wrong person, she moved on.

The next door had a faint light flickering beneath it, shadows dancing in the hall by her feet. She knocked, louder this time.

The light went out.

Pallah knocked again. "Issha?" she whispered. "It's me."

The door opened, a hand whipping out to wrap around Pallah's wrist. She was tugged into the room. Pallah pulled her arm away. "Hey!"

"What took you so long?" Issha's voice came before pulling Pallah in for a hug.

"Issha! I'm so sorry! I've been meaning to find you," Pallah lied. "I've just been so busy with Erval and this new city, I just...got caught up."

"You've been to the city?" The whites of Issha's eyes almost glowed in the darkness. She fumbled with something in her hands before a small flame came to life at the end of a long matchstick. She inserted it into a lantern, and it bloomed to life, bringing the room and Issha herself into view.

Pallah's breath caught in her throat. Issha looked different. Haggard. Before Pallah could ask any questions, Issha was pulling Pallah further into the room. She curled her legs atop a small bed in the corner. Pallah sat, too, thinking of her own opulent bed a floor above.

"I've stored a bit of food back here," Issha whispered as she reached behind her mattress to reveal a cloth napkin bundle. "I'm trying to save enough to leave. Have you done the same?"

Nothing came from Pallah's mouth. What could she say? While she had been living in luxury, her friend had been starving just one floor beneath her. Issha's eyes slid over Pallah for the first time, and realization seemed to dawn. "That looks...warm." Issha's fingers trailed along the collar of Pallah's cloak before she drew her hand back to herself.

"Issha," Pallah began, her stomach squeezing and turning over. "I had no idea you were living like this. It's unacceptable! Why haven't you told someone? Why didn't you come find me?"

"They told me if I left, they would kill you." Issha blinked. "I see that was a lie. Did they tell you the same about me?"

Pallah bit her lip, ignoring the question. "I'm sure there is a reasonable explanation for this."

"Reasonable explanation?" Issha stood, her linen tunic and pants a far cry from the warmth needed in this fire-less room. "They feed me once a day, Pallah. And I'm never to leave. Every day they send—" Issha began to shake. Something about her behavior sent unbidden memories through Pallah, the Maze and her wishing for death. "They send someone who tries to harm me. I have to use my Fera."

Horror coursed through Pallah, her eyes finally adjusting. She took note of the trail of multiple dark stains dragging across the stone floor.

"The first time, I protected myself only enough to send my assailant into unconsciousness. But that's when the soldiers came in. They ordered me to finish the job and to say...say the words." Issha held a hand up, staring at it as if it were a parasite latched to her body. "I've practiced the Taking twenty-eight times."

Pallah pulled Issha close, almost frantically. How could they ask this of her? Sure, Pallah had performed it, too; Erval expected it of her at least once a week. But she had been able to perform it on her own terms, with beggars and nobodies lining the alleyways of Thonethren. This...this was barbaric. And calculating.

Issha shook in her arms.

"Why?" Pallah asked in her ear.

"I ask that every time." Issha's lips trembled in the lantern light, tears leaving tracks of pain down her cheeks.

Pallah wanted to reassure her friend she would speak to Erval on her behalf, but something told her such a sentiment would be dangerous territory. If Issha was being asked to do this, who else would mandate it other than the king himself?

"Well, if we are going to escape, we're going to need my staff." Pallah had no intention of leaving for good, but perhaps she could get Issha outside the city. "Once we find it, we can get to the city's edge."

Issha wiped her eyes. "Why take the risk? Let's just go."

"No." Frustration flared deep in Pallah, and it confused her. "I mean, I don't have much to my name. And it was my father's, after all." Another lie. It came too easy.

Issha nodded, though Pallah could tell she was reluctant. They left the room in darkness as they carried the lantern between them, and as Issha stayed pressed to Pallah like a lost pet, the rage that had flared at Issha transformed into rage for her. Issha, who had taken down a grizzly bear, who had stood against the Taka Reu Rebellion, *that* Issha was now cowering, shrinking into a version of herself nearly unrecognizable.

"I have Malmur Fera now," Issha said quietly as they shuffled along. "I've been practicing with it. There's not much else to do." They stopped, and the older girl closed her eyes, reached out a hand, her fingers dancing in the dark. "There's something downstairs made of mostly metal."

"I didn't know Fera worked like that," Pallah said, thinking of finding Tinloh as a cub in the same way so long ago. She held Fera as well, of course, but hadn't really thought of practicing. Perhaps she should start.

"It helps if I'm familiar with an object. I've used my Blou Fera to find people I know well."

Pallah shuddered at the thought but followed Issha's lead. They wound their way down a set of stairs that ended in a locked door. The padlock was made of metal, and Issha made quick work of it. They entered a dank room, holding the lantern high.

The room was circular, layers of bricks making up the floor and walls. Along those walls were wooden tables fitted with all kinds of scientific tools. From beakers to tubing, copper wire to vials, they littered the tables like a madman's workshop. Pallah walked forward, her lantern outstretched, coming upon a simple wooden chair fitted with tubes, metal wires, coils, and something like a cap attached to a wire coming from the ceiling.

"What is this?" Issha asked, awed, setting the lantern on the table.

"I don't know, but it looks...awful."

"Is someone supposed to sit there?"

"Looks like it." Pallah fingered the headpiece. "Do you sense my staff down here?"

"It's in the corner," Issha said, making her way across the room and picking it up. "It's so light."

The sound of the door creaking made Pallah crouch and reach for her staff. Issha handed it over as she stepped next to Pallah.

A pair of feet shuffled into the room, a face coming into view above the light of a flickering candle.

"You girls shouldn't be here," the stout man said, his upper lip shining with sweat even in the frigid basement.

"Phineas," Pallah said as she stood straighter. "You're up late."

"I'm up *always*," Phineas said, pushing his rounded spectacles up his nose. "You girls should have let yourselves out of the castle to descend upon the city for a night of fun rather than creep around my workrooms."

"You knew?" Issha asked.

"Of course, I knew," drawled Phineas. "I know everything that goes on in this castle. The real question is what Erval knows. And he needn't receive word of your little foray down here if you head back up to your rooms."

Pallah wasn't intimidated by this man. In fact, she'd almost come to see him as a friend. But she didn't appreciate the tone he was taking. She was the lady of this city. She was Erval's favorite.

"Why have you been treating Issha so poorly?"

Pallah didn't meet her friend's eyes as Issha's head swiveled in her direction, her lips parting in surprise.

Phineas merely shook his head and tutted at them, circling around the two as if herding sheep. "Time to get to bed."

"No," Pallah said, and she pumped the staff in her hand, dual axe heads shooting out from either end, sharp as the day they were first forged. "Issha is my friend, and you've been treating her like a prisoner. She deserves three meals a day, and I want you to stop forcing her to perform the Taking."

Phineas chuckled unnervingly, the mirthful gesture not matching the dead look in his eyes. "We can freshen up her room, bring her more food, but I cannot stop the tide of Takings."

"You've been living well, haven't you?" Issha bit out and Pallah met her gaze. "You left me to rot while stuffing yourself with food and Gifts."

"It's not the Gifts he needs." Phineas crossed to the machine and dusted it with a hand. "It's the years."

"I promise you, Issha, I was coming to find you. I'd just assumed you were doing what I was—"

"And what was that?" Issha stood rigid, the softness she had held for Pallah all but evaporated.

"Well...healing, eating, taking walks through the city. I just—"

Issha threw her hands up and stalked away from both Pallah and Phineas.

"Stop fighting, girls. All will be revealed, in time," the steward reassured. "Now, please. If King Erval finds out where the three of us are, there will be no promise of new rooms and no food to be had—for any of us."

Pallah's hands tightened on her staff. A strange need to protect Issha came over her, a pulsing violence she couldn't ignore. And this steward was standing in her way. One slice and Phineas would be gone. How long would his body rot down here before someone found it? Issha could escape, and Pallah could claim she had no idea.

"Consider carefully, child," Phineas said, stepping close to Pallah, his eye line slightly lower than her own. "If you think you could do away with me right here, think again. I'll have you bound and tied before you can take your next breath if you make me."

Pallah scoffed. "You're nothing but a small man. A steward doing other people's biddings. And now, you can do mine."

Phineas's eyes grew feverish behind his spectacles. He continued to step toward Pallah, as if he hadn't heard her declaration. "Do you know how many people I have Taken since coming alongside Erval?" He let the silence stand between them. "You've had, what, a dozen? Two dozen?" His eyes darkened. "I could fill this entire castle, all of Thonethren, and the cities beyond at least twice over: the bodies with all their years and their Gifts sucked dry, stacked up over the walls like a reeking monument."

Pallah stepped backward until she was pressed flat against the wall.

Phineas continued toward her. "Still think you could best me? Try it." He waited, long enough for Pallah to break eye contact. The steward released a sigh and turned to his tables with their materials and tools. "Back to your beds, the both of you. And see to it I never find you down here again."

Pallah marched obediently back to her room, and Issha spared not even a glance her way.

That night was the first night Pallah cried herself to sleep.

THE QUEEN OF CAVES

SOLYANA

SOLYANA HAD CROSSED ALL of Mothmar on sleds and mammoths; she had escaped a madman chief and his burning city; she'd chanced the ice plains of Greater Mothmar, and wandered for days in underground caves...but this practice with Phineas? It was taxing on a whole new level.

Southwest of Endirinn, high on a hill overlooking a small river where her team refilled their waterskins, Solyana, Ahren, and Phineas sat in tall grass. Stubborn patches of snow clung to the boulders around them, but with the sun rising, the land looked nothing short of heaven.

They had traveled for six days, and on the third, Phineas had begun to train her in earnest. On the fourth, Ahren insisted on joining, and by the fifth, they'd tried to convince Gamaliel. He'd refused with a grunt, stating, "Someone has to work around here. I'll stick with the tea."

Cracking an eye open and peering over at the man beside her, Solyana watched her teacher, his usual fidgetiness and shifting of weight replaced by a serene stillness. Like the Celestial Pool with its wind-pushed ripples, his only movement was the rise and fall of his breath.

"I hear you staring." Phineas's mouth quirked in a smile.

Solyana squeezed her eyes shut. "No, you do not."

"She was staring," Ahren said with a grin, and Solyana widened her eyes at him.

"Deny if you wish, but I haven't grown this old without learning a thing or two." His scant hair danced in the early morning breeze. "Do you think you have a path in place?" Finally opening his eyes, he peered at the both of them.

"I think so," Ahren said with a shrug. "Hard to know without someone coming into my mind, though."

"You must have a clear picture of the path, a distinct separation from the rest of your mind." He nodded and turned to Solyana. "And you?"

"I feel the same as Ahren."

"Then only time will tell." Phineas got to his feet, though a bit laboriously; his knees cracked. "It's a new day! Let's get to it." He ambled down the hill, a tiny copper-colored creature flinging itself after him, joyously bounding through the weeds.

"How are you handling all of this?" Solyana asked Ahren beside her. "It's harder than I thought, sectioning off memories and motives and locking them up. It's got me thinking a lot about the time I lost." A lump formed in Solyana's throat. She could feel the conversation tipping out of her though she tried to hold it back. "Like all I've managed to do is lose five years and fail to keep a lot of promises."

The depth of her loss began to envelop her then, and as her chest began to heave. She suddenly wished she were alone to cry.

Instead, she felt Ahren shift closer to her, the length of his arm pressing against her side. "Five years is a long time," he agreed.

"I don't know how you stay so strong," she said to him. "I feel overwhelmed by five years, while you've had centuries taken from you."

"The time wasn't mine to begin with." He took a breath, his gaze distant. "I shouldn't have survived that night. It should have been me, not my sister." He shook his head. "I should have saved her."

"Pallah?"

"Vámae. Pallah. The both of them," he said quietly.

"What happened?"

"Pallah..." Ahren's face paled, and he grit his teeth hard. "Pallah killed Vámae, right before sending me to the mountain. She killed her."

The memory of finding Ahren on the mountain, his hands and clothes splattered with blood, came to the forefront of her mind. "I'm so sorry, Ahren."

Ahren shook his head and inhaled, squaring his shoulders toward her. "You saved me, Solyana. Without you, I would still be stuck on that mountain. I owe you." He looked into her eyes, his own such a deep blue Solyana felt transfixed by them.

Solyana looked away. "You don't owe me anything."

"We'll find your sister. And then I'll find mine. We'll find them together." He reached around her shoulder and drew her back into another hug.

"Am I interrupting something?" Gamaliel's voice jolted Solyana out of Ahren's arms, her face growing warm.

"Nope!" Ahren threw his hands up over his head. "No, sir. You just..." He grabbed Gamaliel's hand and tugged him forward until he was face to face with Solyana. He pulled her hand up to meet his until their fingers were entwined. "There, much better. I'm going to go help Phineas with the horses."

Ahren strolled down the mountain toward the wagon below. Solyana grinned after him before turning to look at Gamaliel.

"What?" she asked as his face held no emotion.

"Like the older men, do you?"

Solyana rolled her eyes. Vinur nuzzled into their clasped hands and Solyana let go to pet him. "He was telling me a bit about his time before he was trapped on the mountain. All the memories are coming up again since training with Phineas."

"Ah," Gamaliel said as he tied his hair back in a knot. "Another reason I'll stick to drinking the tea."

"I don't blame you." Solyana stood up on her toes to plant a kiss on his cheek. "Ready to go?"

"Should be. If Phineas's map is up to date, it should only take us another ten days or so." He turned to look over his shoulder and shielded his eyes from the sun. "You really think he'll go through with our plan?"

Solyana watched the man tend to the horses with Ahren. "It's hard for me to imagine the guy hurting anyone, least of all the man he's served for hundreds of years. What do you think?"

But Gamaliel's eyes held her own, a fresh fire in them that hadn't been there before. "I think I'd rather spend my time on this hill doing something other than speculating about Phineas."

A smile crept onto Solyana's lips. "Oh yeah? And what's that?"

His eyes swooped down, and he grinned. "Certainly something with less talking..."

Solyana leaned in close, happy to be halfway hidden in the tall grass.

He brought his lips closer, and Solyana bridged the gap, leaning forward until she melted into him, their mouths moving together in a rare moment alone. His hands wove into her hair, holding her in place, and a thrill ran up her spine.

This moment felt right. It felt safe.

Then there was a quick whistle, a thump, and Gamaliel's body weight slammed into her. Solyana shuffled back a few steps, her eyes wide. "Gam!"

His face was a pallid shade of gray, his mouth open and eyes wide. "Gam, what happened?"

Vinur barked and circled, then barked again. But Gamaliel just stood there, as if—

He twisted and fell to his knees, and that's when Solyana saw the arrow protruding from his back. His lips curved to form a word, but no sound escaped as he fell, face-first, onto the ground. The fletching of the arrow stood stiffly amidst the waving grass.

"Gamaliel!" Solyana dropped to her knees, heart hammering in her chest. He wasn't moving, even as Vinur nudged him with his nose, whimpering, licking, and whining. Solyana peered over the grass with wild eyes, trying to catch a glimpse of their assailant, only to find Phineas atop Bran, and Ahren cowering behind the wagon.

Movement, back east. A group of three pounded forward on horseback, arrows nocked and ready. Solyana rolled Gamaliel to his side and pressed two fingers to his neck. There was a pulse—he was alive. That would have to be enough for now.

"Stay with him, Vinur!"

And she took off down the hill, intent on reaching Ahren and the other draft horse, who was already hitched to the wagon.

Legs pounding, leaping down the hillside, another arrow whizzed past her, stealing the breath from her lungs. Her face began to burn, the familiar ache of her scar coming to the surface. A sensation she had not felt since Endirinn.

Her mind reeled but shoved one word before all other thoughts: *Run.*

"Ahren!" she screamed. Where had he gone?

His head popped up from behind a wagon wheel, his blue eyes wide with terror.

"Unhitch Barley!"

He crawled to the front of the wagon as Solyana slid at the base of the hill. Another arrow flew above her head, barely missing her.

"You're an Eldur, aren't you?" Ahren yelled back as he got to work on the hitch.

Pressed against the side of the wagon, Solyana blinked and nodded, more to herself than to Ahren. She hadn't used her Gifts, not since she had lost connection to the Celestials. She wouldn't dare use them with the Taka Reu, not again.

"Please!" The cry released from her unexpectedly, drifting to the heavens above. Surely, the Celestials would show her mercy. Surely, they would not leave her to die after all this time. She opened her palms, but nothing happened. No warmth, not a flicker or even a spark. She released another cry and looked around for Phineas. Had he abandoned them?

A thundering of hooves drew her attention as Phineas and Bran came charging from behind a boulder. The steward's hand was raised, two large rocks extended from his palm, balanced with nothing but his Gift. He launched them forward as all three riders came near. One of them was struck directly and thrown from his mount. The second rock rolled in front of another speeding horse, causing it to trip and tumble with its rider still attached.

"Halt!" Phineas commanded the last horseman as he slowed. The steward's free hand lifted, a massive section of earth tearing from the ground in response. It hovered in the air between them. "Come to us willingly, or I'll end you here."

"They shot Gam!" Solyana informed him. She hadn't been sure how they'd have fared in his absence, but Phineas's show of strength surprised her. If he was capable of what she'd just witnessed, and the steward feared the king of Thonethren as he did, what did that say of Erval's power?

The rider that had been thrown dragged himself from the dirt, half his face awash with blood. He grabbed Ahren by the hair, bringing a knife against his throat.

The one still on horseback smiled.

Prayers whispered through Solyana's mind.

Phineas's eyes narrowed.

"We'll take the horses," the rider barked. "And your blocking tea."

"And your food!" The man pulled Ahren's head further back, his armor glinting in the sun.

"Everything's in the wagon." Solyana stepped forward. "It's all yours."

"Solyana!" Phineas hissed. "Stay back!"

"Solyana?" The man still atop his horse pulled off his helm to get a better look at her. He was older than Solyana expected, clean shaven with salt-and-pepper hair. "What luck!" he said. "Good thing you're a bad shot, Piehter."

"Hey, she was running." The man holding Ahren shrugged, causing the knife to draw a small line of blood. "Oi, Jon!" he shouted to the man on the ground, or what remained of him, tangled up as he was beneath his horse. "Jon?"

There was no reply.

Piehter's face contorted with anger.

"That's fine armor for a bandit," Phineas said to the horseman. "Who do you work for?"

"We serve the true queen," the mounted soldier proclaimed, straightening his shoulders. "The queen of Thonethren."

Even from where Solyana stood, she could see Phineas's face go as white as the clouds.

"You can call me General Ivan." His eyes found Solyana's, and fear wrapped her bones, freezing her in place. "And Her Majesty has been anxious to meet you, Solyana."

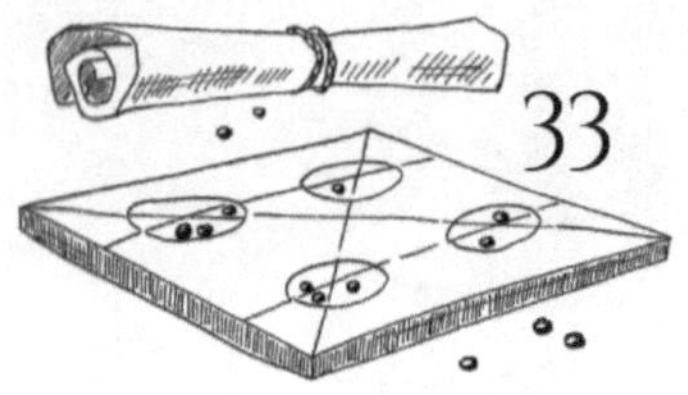

THE SEER AT SEA

JONAS

A HAND GRIPPED THE back of Jonas's tunic as he leaned too far over the edge of the wooden rail of *Coletta's* main deck for the third time.

"If I have to pull you back one more—" Rorhan's lecture was cut short by his own retching. He threw his head into a bucket. "How many days of this? I cannot..." He groaned.

"Captain Viggo suggested going below deck," Jonas said, giving his friend a conciliatory pat on the shoulder. "At least you can throw up wherever you are, now that they gave you a bucket."

"They told me I needed to stop painting the ship."

"Sorry, Han."

"I miss Lone." Rorhan sniffed. "And Marin." Hair tied back in a braid, the man stumbled away from Jonas and through a small door leading to the decks below. Jonas watched him go, his gut twisting with guilt. It was his fault Rorhan was away from his family.

They had been sailing for two days now, and Jonas had all but convinced himself he was destined to be on the sea. How had he never explored the oceans before? His world was now open in a way he could never have imagined.

But even with that thought, his dream flashed in the back of his mind. His dream, which had always instilled a convoluted feeling, had now clarified and sharpened like a weapon, taking his mind hostage. Without Seer Brotnur for guidance, Jonas had little to research when it came to his fears. He didn't allow himself to dwell on it for long. Instead, he looked out over the water to watch a cormorant dip and glide over the waves.

He was a Seer, or at least had Seer blood in his veins, enough to give him the ability to understand some futures. He could prophesy one day. The ramifications of that truth hit him like an ice pick to the brain. When a person's Gift was lost, their soul went with it. But Jonas had gone through that before, atop Eldfall Mountain all that time ago. He hadn't died then, and he wasn't ready to die now. There was too much to see, too much to experience. The world had only just turned green. And not only that, but what of his history? He had hardly dipped a toe into his heritage and wanted to know more.

It would have to be saved for another day. One that wasn't so pressed for time. He wished he had a way to communicate with Solyana. Not knowing how her journey to find Rhuth was faring plagued him most.

"Jondar!" The Captain's voice boomed behind Jonas, pulling his eyes from the waves.

"Captain Viggo!" he answered to his false name. Jonas wasn't so naïve to believe his fame as Seer of Endirinn had gone unnoticed by the rest of Mothmar, especially at a port city so close to Endirinn itself. Not everyone would be sympathetic to his Gift or his mission.

"Has your friend finally taken himself below decks?" The captain twisted one side of his mustache as he approached. "It should let up in another day or so. Hasn't bothered you one bit, I see. You've sailed before?"

"No," Jonas admitted. "This is new for me, too, I'm afraid. How long have you been at it?"

"I can't remember a time when I wasn't. My father was a merchant, and I was his only son. I have a lot of sisters, or so I've been told." Viggo winked and smiled. "But I've spent more time on the waves than on land. Though you'll hear no complaints from me. It's a profitable life I lead." He turned his full attention to Jonas, putting a callused hand on the

Seer's shoulder. "You, Jondar, come at an opportune time. Where's that map you had?"

Teeth together in something like a smile, Jonas pointed with his thumb. "In my cabin. I'm still working on it, though. Most of it is up here." He tapped his temple.

"Where'd you say you were from again?" The hand on Jonas's shoulder squeezed.

"My friend and I are travelers. We aim to explore all of Greater Mothmar."

"So you said." He released Jonas, who stumbled a step away and adjusted his spectacles. "We'll keep on this heading toward West End, and you let us know when we're close to this new land you speak of. Just keep an eye out for the red sails of the Crimson Chief, yeah?"

Jonas blinked, unsure what to make of that.

Then with a final clap on Jonas's shoulder, the captain swaggered away, his boots clacking on the wooden slats beneath them. A few sailors flagged him down near the helm, and Jonas turned back to the waves.

Though they had offered funds from Temple Rinn, the Captain had been far more interested in Jonas's ability to show him new lands. Jonas had painted a rough map at East End, thanking the Celestials for the abilities they gave him. It had revealed a new island or two, according to the captain's understanding of the waters Jonas had drawn. And while the promise of discovery had been enough for Viggo, Jonas believed the islands would reveal the truth of the Way.

Captain Viggo had made his disinterest in any sort of religion clear, but he was happy to oblige Jonas as he believed him only to be a scholar. He was even willing to take Agnar and Thora, though under the contingency that in the case of any onboard emergency, they would be first to be taken for meat. The captain had laughed and said, "Better them than you, right?" And clapped Jonas on the shoulders again.

Jonas stretched his neck, beginning to wonder if he was developing a bruise.

His thoughts landed on his dream again, bringing a singular question to the forefront of his mind. With his Seeing ability, was he able to see the future as it *would* happen? Or as it *could* happen? His gut twisted, and he wondered if he would be seasick, but when he took a breath, it stilled. He had to believe there was a different end toward which they strove. One that didn't involve the death he foresaw.

One that included him.

PATH OF STARS

RHUTH

I T WAS NIGHT, THE third day. Pallah lay asleep on the other side of the fire, and Ember was curled next to Rhuth, their bond growing with each moment they traveled together. She wondered if Ember would allow her behind her eyes as the falcons did. Falcons were a bit simpler in mind, and they allowed her in without much persuasion. A simple request and she saw through their eyes as if they were her own.

The fire was before her, flickering light onto the soft docile face of the fox. Studying the whiskers that lined her red muzzle, peppering it with white, Rhuth made her request.

May I see?

Ember's eyes cracked open, and she lifted her head, ears coming forward, curious. Then she lowered her chin back to resting on her front paws, settling into a light sleep. Rhuth gave her soft ears a few pets before returning her hands into her cloak. Ember wasn't ready yet. Rhuth wouldn't push.

Breathing out, billowing puffs of white into the cold night air, Rhuth tipped her head up to see the stars. Scattered across the night sky like a blizzard hung in stasis, they shone. She couldn't help the smile that came to her lips as she traced the different shapes with her eyes. She had always felt, of the three Celestials her people worshiped, the Children of the Sky were the least discussed. Even at a young age, Rhuth had felt the need to get to know them more.

She couldn't remember when it had started. If she were being honest with herself, the need to see them was always there. As if her very soul longed to be awake at night to catch a glimpse of the patterns and connections they formed.

Rhuth thought about the last morning her family was all together at the house, getting ready for Solyana's Stada. Mama, Fridmey, and Sol had all been talking about the hours Rhuth had spent squawking as a baby. Perhaps even as a newborn, Rhuth's soul had been called to the stars, pushing her to remain awake while others slept.

Little Fyug—that's what Sol had nicknamed her. Little bird. Rhuth felt for her connection to her falcons and found them roosting in a copse of trees farther back near the mountains. They didn't want to leave their valley; she could sense it in them.

Was it selfish of her to pull them out? To take this journey with her simply because she felt more comfortable knowing they were there? She hugged her knees into her chest and tucked her mitten-less fingers into the tops of her mukluks. Perhaps it was time to relinquish them.

Even the thought sent warmth through her body, and she realized intuitively it wasn't her keeping them with her. They could leave anytime they wanted.

Thank you, she told them with her mind. *I appreciate the time you are with me.*

Her eyes fell back to Ember, and she wove a hand through her fur. "Did you know?" she asked the fox. "The stars speak to me. Well, not out loud, but I hear them in my mind. They ask me to connect as they connect. To make peace as they make peace. That they simply want me to do my part."

Ember's eyes slid open again, her brow twitching as if to ask why this human was so insistent on waking her.

"Well," Rhuth continued. "Pallah is asleep, and I figured one of us should stand guard."

The fox cocked her head to the side.

Rhuth shrugged. "I don't know. I've never been out of the valley. I saw through Halina what happened in the city Solyana went to, people riding beasts, wreaking destruction and fire. What if those people come here?"

Ember chuffed.

"You're not wrong. We are far from there," agreed Rhuth. "But what about wild animals?" Hand snaking through thick fox fur, she felt the animal relax. "I would feel them coming, wouldn't I? Why do I seem to be the only one with this ability?"

The fox unfurled herself, stood, stretched, and shook out her coat, eyes bright on Rhuth.

Deep within her, Ember conveyed something to Rhuth as clear as the stars above. It wasn't that Rhuth could connect to everything more clearly than everyone else—everyone else just had it slightly *wrong*. Ember looked up at the star-laden sky and sat back down, fluffy tail twitching. The stars spoke to the animals too, keeping them on the path they were meant to take, guiding them, protecting them. It was the humans who skewed it.

Understanding dawned over Rhuth like a soft morning snow, wrapping her in a blanket of knowing.

"How do I tell others about this Gift? How do I explain it?" Rhuth whispered to the fox.

Ember bowed her head, curled up, and wrapped her tail tight around herself to go back to sleep.

"They must watch...and learn," she whispered to the Children of the Sky. The stars seemed to twinkle in response.

Rhuth smiled and decided it was time to sleep.

THE MOTHER

PALLAH

PALLAH REVISITED PHINEAS REGARDING Issha's accommodations, but Phineas had merely nodded and bustled away. She would check in again, she told herself, but part of her—deep down—refuted the idea.

She was still steeped in dark memories of home, and Issha was a reminder of them. It made her remember Tinloh, and once the image of him filled her mind, she felt nothing but pangs of grief and emptiness.

Now, six months living in Thonethren, she felt the ache for her beast more than the day she'd arrived. Bringing up her desire for a new smilodon only brought a *hmm* from Erval. She'd assumed he was thinking it over, but now she was beginning to wonder if he was putting her off.

She was also anxious about Ahren. From the research she had done about the Stasis curse she had used, she knew wherever he was, he was safe. But how to get to him? She had been scared to ask Erval about it. He had begun to show flashes of jealousy whenever she spoke of others, and she did not wish to incite him again. Not about Ahren.

But she was lonely. Besides her visits with Erval, and occasionally Phineas, she saw very little of anyone else. The servants of the castle seemed to avoid her, even in the moments when she offered conversation.

Tonight was the night, then. She would bring up both issues. Erval had sent a missive, informing Pallah to don hiking gear. They would be going out adventuring, he claimed. Perhaps the physical activity would help the conversation go more smoothly, give the man something to distract his mind from directly settling on offense.

A knock on her door came as the sun began its descent, and Pallah straightened her cloak before opening the door.

"Hello there," Erval said with a half-smile.

Pallah almost stumbled backward. He had never come to her room before. She knew without needing a mirror her face was flaming red. "My king!" She curtsied, thankful to Phineas, for once, for tutoring her on the ways of a lady of Thonethren.

"Oh, none of that here." He swatted at her and strode into her room, looking more like a thief than a king. He wore closely tailored leather pants, a layered shirt covered by a light hooded coat, and fingerless gloves on each hand. "You ready?" He grinned at her from over his shoulder and a thrill ran from her lips to her toes.

"Ready." She matched his smile.

Shoving open the doors to her balcony, he stepped out into what should have been spring air but had warmed only minimally in the last few months. Phineas had been sputtering about the change of weather, his brow always furrowed with worry. Pallah shoved all thoughts of the stout man from her mind. Erval was here, standing on her balcony, his hair tousling in the breeze.

"You just try to keep up. I'll tether you if you need a bit of help and keep the both of us from sustaining any injuries."

The thought sent waves of discordance through her. She only saw him tether to those he intended to Take. But he had proven he cared for her... Surely, he wouldn't hurt her.

Stepping beside him in the light of the setting sun, she glanced up to find his hand outstretched.

"Would you do me the honor, m'lady?"

She took his hand. "The honor is all mine, m'lord."

The two of them leapt off the balcony and into the deepening eve.

Sweat snaked down Pallah's back as she followed Erval over the rooftops. She had known Erval had spent several of his younger years creeping around the roofs of Thonethren. But watching him in practice was an entirely different ordeal.

Like a shadow, he coasted over the stuccoed shingles, hardly making a sound. Pallah felt like a clumsy new lamb as she followed behind. He was patient, even if she wasn't patient with herself, always stopping and checking to make sure she wasn't too far behind.

Thonethren was set up in such a way that the closer one got to Mount Hekla, the more impoverished the communities became. This kept the wealthiest near the castle in the center, and in circles spiraling outward were communities in descending degrees of wealth. Pallah hadn't spent much time far from the castle, but now, as they ran across rooftops toward the dormant volcano, she couldn't help but think of her time with Vil and the Taka Reu.

There was a time, just a few years ago, when Pallah had considered herself part of the group of friends that gathered around the fire on Eld Plateau. They had announced grand plans for a quest to Hekla, to return to where the Mother herself was said to have been born. Now, as Pallah jumped from one rooftop to the next, scrabbling feet and fingers on the stucco, she wondered what she had gotten herself into.

"My king," she panted, wiping at her brow. "What are we doing?"

Erval was perched at the very tip of the roof, his back to her. "When it's just the two of us, call me Erval," he said so quietly Pallah almost didn't catch it.

She squatted beside him, then slipped. She flailed as she slid down the side of the roof, catching herself on Erval, who offered his arm with a lopsided grin.

"Alright, Erval." She pushed her hair out of her eyes with her free hand. "Did you just decide I needed some exercise?"

Wrinkles appeared at the corners of his eyes as he chuckled. "Though I'm sure it's good for anyone, no, m'lady. That's not why you're here. I simply thought it time for you to see where I was raised, to see the Mother in all her glory."

Pallah blinked at him. "Are we climbing up the mountain?" Neck craning to see the top of it, Pallah was sure of one thing, there was no way she was climbing all that way tonight. After two years of being trapped in Dahvid's mind Maze, and then six months spent eating rich foods and laying around in her rooms, she was in no shape to hike such an incline.

Erval stood, his long coat rippling behind him in the wind, his shirt and pants clinging tight to his lean body. He raised an eyebrow at her and crossed his arms. "Too much for you?"

"Yes!" Pallah found a flat section and sat hard on the roof, tucking her knees into her chest. "I might have extra years, but I don't have the energy of dozens."

"Ah." Erval sat beside her, pressing himself close, his body warming her, causing goosebumps to spread over every inch of skin.

Pallah couldn't bring herself to look up at him, her nerves on fire. Instead, she kept her eyes on the lights and nightlife below. The people had no idea their king was high above them, exploring the rooftops. It made her grin.

"That is one of the reasons I have encouraged you to keep practicing the Taking, so you can keep up with me. Scouring these rooftops is one of my favorite pastimes. I'd like you to accompany me on them more often."

A question tickled at the back of her throat, threatening to burst through. It had often been there, but now, after living in Thonethren for half a year, she couldn't keep it in any longer.

"Why me, Erval?" Pallah tried to think of a better way to ask her question that wouldn't reveal her suspicion that she was being used. Her past wouldn't let her accept his doting at face value. "What do you want with a girl from Sodur?"

He leaned back on one hand, his shoulder dropping, and Pallah could feel his gaze burning into her like a brand. Swallowing her nerves, Pallah met his eyes, and a thrill ran through her entire being. He was looking deep into her, as if nothing else in the world mattered, as if there were only the two of them—*häfan* it all. She didn't care why anymore. She was wanted. And that was enough.

"You've been used before; I saw it myself," Erval began, as if reading her deepest thoughts. "But it's not like that here, Pallah. You have your own will. You are free to learn, to grow, to gain insight and knowledge." He pressed two hands to his chest. "I'm not here to hold you back! I'm here to foster a sapling into a mighty tree. You're special, Pallah," he said, cupping her face with one hand, his thumb caressing her cheek. "And with you by my side, we'll be unstoppable."

His words were like a match to her soul, igniting a flame inside of her, making her feel like the regal woman he saw her to be.

"Now," he said, clearing his throat, "shall we meet the Mother?"

Exhausted, Pallah gave a half-hearted hop along the face of the mountain. The last of the housing had trickled away, leaving only a few farms and hovels. Surely dawn would be upon them soon. Erval grinned back at her, his hair whipping over his forehead, his smile drawing her in like the moon to the tide.

"Well?" Pallah caught her breath, hands on her knees. "You promised me ease, sir," she said playfully. "I have yet to find it."

He chuckled and motioned her forward to where he stood on a black rock, so shiny it reflected moonlight. She stepped up, and he pulled her close, toe to toe. He pulled his hood up over his face and pulled Pallah's hood up as well. Then, with hands outstretched, he closed his eyes and deep within the mountain something shifted.

Pallah's eyes shot open, all prior tiredness gone. "What was that?"

"Shh." Erval's grin lay crooked on his face. "Hold on to me."

Pallah didn't know where to put her hands, both of Erval's arms were outstretched and the closest thing to her was—the rock they were standing on broke off from the mountain. Pallah flung herself around Erval's waist and clung there, her eyes squeezed shut. She felt the rumble of his chuckle.

"Don't let go now," he said, and Pallah pried her eyes open to see him raise his arms, and with the motion went the rock, them atop it.

They shot high, the rock arching up the side of the mountain like an arrow at speed. The wind whistled around them, threatening to tear the hood from her head, the breath from her lungs, her feet from the rock.

"If you keep your eyes closed, you'll miss the view."

She hadn't even noticed she'd shut them.

Prying them open, she couldn't help the curse that ran over her lips. "*Häfan* to Hekla."

The beginnings of dawn began to creep from the farthest portions of the sky, the moon fading. Mothmar, her country that had done nothing but take and take, finally gave her something to see. And it was beautiful. Rolling hills green with grass and trees, white capped mountains rising in the distance, and beyond—though closer than she had assumed—an ocean.

"I thought you'd like it," Erval crooned, and Pallah felt the vibrations of his voice in her chest as she kept tight to him. "But this isn't even the best part."

Then they were soaring downward, toward the gaping maw that was the peak of Mount Hekla.

"It's dormant, right?" Pallah asked over the whistle of wind and flapping of fabric. It was what she had been taught her whole life, but Erval had turned her world upside down; the confirmation couldn't hurt.

"Like a hibernating bear," Erval said, which was not much comfort to Pallah. Bears could wake.

They came to rest at the peak, the stone finding purchase altogether too close to the edge.

"You can let go now," Erval said.

She pulled her arms away and sought the best way to step off the rock.

"I feel her so strongly here, can't you?" Erval pulled his hood down and took a few steps to the very edge of the rim.

Reluctantly, Pallah came closer, an intrusive fear wriggling its way into her mind that Erval had brought her this whole way only to shove her into the mountain. She pushed the fear aside. Erval had looked at her like she hung the stars. Erval treated her like nothing less than a queen. She mattered to him.

Leaning over the lip of the volcano, a gasp released from Pallah's lips. Far below, unfathomably far, there was red. A gust of hot air blew out as if in welcome. Deep in Pallah's chest she felt a tug—the tug of Taka Reu—pulling her, wooing her to *jump*.

"Beautiful, isn't she?" he asked.

Pallah straightened. "The Mother?"

"Yes. She is in and beneath, both around and below." He crouched and plucked a hair from his head. He kissed it and dropped it into the yawning mouth. "Remember me, your servant. The one who keeps you, cares for you, tempers you." He motioned for Pallah to kneel as well.

She plucked a hair, pressed it to her lips, and released it as he had—though without his words. Nothing miraculous happened. Erval smiled grandly.

"She is pleased," Erval said. He gripped her shoulder and gave it a quick shake of approval. "As am I!" He stood, hands on his hips as the sun began to wake in the east.

He was the happiest and most at ease Pallah had ever seen him. Perhaps now would be a good time to ask of her brother.

"My king—"

"Erval," he corrected, and Pallah could have kicked herself for the mistake.

"Yes, Erval." She gave a partial bow, and he turned his full attention to her. "The night I left for Thonethren, the night of the Rebellion, I performed a charm on my brother."

The king folded his arms across his chest and moved one hand in a circular motion as if to say, *go on*.

"It was called Stasis. I'd found it in one of Dahvid's old scrolls. And when I performed it, my brother disappeared from my arms."

"And where did you set him to stay?"

"To stay?" The scroll had said nothing about a location. Fear coiled around her heart and squeezed. "What do you mean?"

"Charms, my dear, are simply trussed up curses. And as with all curses, you must be specific! Without specificity...he could be anywhere." He gave a halfhearted sigh, his eyes swooping to the mountain's mouth and back to Pallah again. "What were your thoughts set on when you performed it?" he asked lazily.

"I-I…" It had only been six months, but it felt an eternity. Pallah had killed her sister, had allowed herself to be filled with rage, and had pillaged her own village. "There was so much darkness and evil. I just wanted him to be safe. I remember thinking I wanted him sent to the safest place."

Erval turned from her and clasped his hands behind his back as he stared down into the deep fire. The quiet of the morning hummed loudly in Pallah's ears.

"Erval? I'd like to find my brother. Please. I did this to him, and I—"

He grabbed her. So forcefully and quickly, Pallah didn't have time to react. One minute, she was standing beside the maw of the mountain, and the next, she was hanging over it. Pallah gripped the rocky edge with her toes as Erval held her in the air, his hands fisting her cloak by her neck, his eyes filled with nothing but blackness.

"Do not speak to me of family," he said.

Pallah's hands carefully sought for purchase around his clenched fists.

"I brought you into my city, welcomed you into my home. Is that not enough? You ungrateful *tik*." His lips snarled around the word, and he gave her a shake. "I've clothed you, fed you, and lavished you with life and Gifts, but it's not enough. You dare to demand more. But you don't deserve another moment of my mercy."

He released her, and she dropped.

Pallah screamed.

But her body came to an abrupt stop, suspended in the empty air, cloak flapping in the wind, powerless. He had a hold of her somehow, whether through his Mann Tala or some other kind of Fera, she didn't know. Her eyes kept falling to her feet, dangling over nothing. Fear choked her, and she gasped.

"You deserve your past! After all I've sacrificed and saved you from, you *long* for it. You want to go back. Why did you even come here?"

"No!" Pallah finally found her voice, though it shook. "Please, Erval! I am so sorry. Please, forgive me. I simply wanted my brother back. He's—"

"ENOUGH ABOUT YOUR BROTHER!"

Pallah fell, far enough for her to scream, to soak her pants, to think she was dead. She stared up through the massive hole at the peak, her breath coming quickly and uncontrolled.

"Perhaps I chose the wrong one," Erval said, devoid of any emotion at all.

"Choose me! Please!" she called to him, desperate to live. Though now it was not only death that scared her, but this man. He was more than she could handle. How had she not seen it before? "I promise," she pled. "No more about Ahren. He is nothing to me! You're right! I've been ungrateful!" The words poured out of her. Words that had been a mask her whole life with her father, words she had begun to use with Vil, words she was sure came out of her during her time in the Maze, though she couldn't remember those dark days in detail. Tears soaked her face, and her nose ran; she didn't bother wiping any of it away. "Forgive me, my king! Please! I will do what you ask! I want to serve you!"

Erval's silhouette stood at the top, still and stoic as the rock itself. Just when Pallah was imagining herself dropping toward a fiery death, he jerked his chin upward, and she followed as if attached by a rope.

Her body floated to his side, and he brought her into his arms, wrapping her in his coat as she shivered with shock.

"There, there," he crooned, as if he hadn't just been holding her over a pit. "I never would have dropped you. I've got you, my darling. Looks like we learned a valuable lesson here today, haven't we?"

"Y-y-yes," Pallah agreed, body quaking.

And there on Mount Hekla, in Erval's arms, Pallah lied to herself.

She was safe.

She was wanted.

She was cherished.

SAINTS AND QUEENS

SOLYANA

"**H**E'S ALIVE. HE'LL BE okay. He's alive," Solyana repeated to herself as she gripped Gamaliel's hand, though it had only grown more clammy, and he no longer squeezed back. It struck fear into her core, chilling her faster than any blizzard.

"Gamaliel," she whispered over the clink of armor and the rumble of wagon wheels. "Please, stay awake."

With Phineas's help, they had been able to remove the arrow, and he used Blou Fera to staunch the blood. But Gamaliel had waited too long on the side of the hill while the rest of them had talked with the soldiers. Solyana prodded with her fingertips, trying to assess how badly the wound had become. But with the sack over her head and her wrists tied tight, there was little she could do.

The wagon suddenly rocked back and forth hard, and Solyana clung to Gamaliel, afraid he would be flung from it.

"Halt!" the voice of the General sounded, but from where, Solyana couldn't tell. The command bounced and echoed off cavernous rock. Solyana heard the crackling of fire, the shuffling of boots over loose dirt, and the clacks and clanks of moving armor.

Suddenly voices were everywhere.

"Check and see if the queen is ready for an audience."

"These horses are hearty, but they're no war horses."

"Who are these people? The queen asked only for supplies, no prisoners."

"Did they have any tea?"

"There's a wounded one in the back!"

Solyana clutched Gamaliel tighter. Seeing nothing but black, she was terrified someone would reach in and take him.

"The girl is from Endirinn. She's the one that brought the green."

Someone laughed. "Stop kidding around. We have little time before the eclipse."

"Do I look like I'm kidding?"

There was a pause.

"I honestly can't tell."

"Oh, shut up, Kairn. Is the queen ready or not?"

"She said to bring the girl with you, if it truly is Solyana."

"She has the scar." General Ivan's voice again. "If she's not the saint, I'll eat my scabbard."

Solyana's hood was ripped from her head, revealing a cup of steaming tea beneath her nose.

"Drink this," the General said.

There wasn't a whole lot of light in the cave, making it easy for Solyana's eyes to adjust from the dark. But when they did, she was awed by the space—not just a cave, but a massive one. An enclosed expanse as vast as if the entire ice plains themselves had been hollowed out.

"What is it?" Solyana asked, sniffing the mug before her.

"I don't see any scar." Kairn stood above her, his immaculate armor glinting in even the low light.

Ivan gave his compatriot a look of annoyance before making his way to a fire that rippled nearby. "If you would be so kind, Kairn, to tell Her Majesty we are on our way now."

"If you say so." Kairn turned, the same half-cape that adorned General Ivan swaying behind him. "Personally, I don't want to go from riding the beasts to becoming one."

Ivan snorted. "You're enough of a beast already." He turned to Solyana who still held the mug in her hands. "Drink it."

"Is this blocking tea?" she asked.

"You know of it," he said, squaring her up. "You've been drinking it, then?"

Solyana blinked up at him and then down at her drink. She couldn't drink this; Erval would know.

"Yes," she lied.

"Good." The general took the cup from her. "We need every drop we can get. Can you confirm your sainthood?"

"Yes." Best to tell the truth in this regard. "I am Solyana Marusda. I brought the green."

"Fantastic." He ticked his head to the side, motioning for her to follow. But Solyana shook her head, her hands coming to rest on Gamaliel.

General Ivan blinked once. "We have healers. He will be seen to."

Solyana's fingers twitched. She was Heitt, but she still had no idea how to connect with the Celestials since tethering through the Taka Reu. The General's hand hung in the air, waiting for hers to help her off the wagon. Unease wound its way around Solyana, and she shook her head, her grip on Gamaliel tightening.

"Let me rephrase." General Ivan's manner shifted, his eyes going dark like cave smoke. "You can come down and walk, or I can pull you from that wagon and drag you, saint or not."

Solyana stood and, disregarding his offer of help, jumped down and clutched her cloak tighter about herself.

The General looked her over, his hard gaze making Solyana want to shrink.

"Shame you don't have time to freshen up," he said. "You'll have to see the queen as is."

Winding through a narrow passage, Solyana found herself entering what looked like a makeshift throne room. A chair rested upon large, stacked stones, the space lit extensively with braziers and lamps. Upon the chair sat a woman Solyana had certainly never seen before because, had she, she would have remembered.

With dark hair meticulously arranged above striking eyes, a chin held high, and clothes tailored to perfection, this woman not only exuded regality but she was absolutely stunning. Solyana couldn't tear her eyes away if she wanted to.

"Welcome, Solyana, Saint of Endirinn. I am honored to be in your presence." Even her voice dripped with royalty. "You, who have brought the green! A feat none before you even came close to accomplishing. You have my gratitude." She rose from her throne, stepped down the stones, and knelt before Solyana with her head bowed.

Solyana's face burned hot, disarmed at the sight of this powerful woman humbling herself before her. She recalled the image of Gamaliel getting shot, remembered the dark of the sack thrown over her head and the rough tug of her hands being restrained, and any kindling of awe between them was quickly doused.

"No need to kneel..." Solyana paused, trying to remember if she had caught the woman's name. Her mind failing to produce anything, she finished with, "Your Majesty."

The woman stood and gave a soft smile. "It's lonely being at the top, isn't it?"

"I would hardly say I'm at the top." Solyana noted the soldiers standing at each side of the makeshift throne dressed in full armor, their helms covering their faces. She would play the part of saint here, if only to leave unharmed and with her friends.

"And so humble." The woman's smile dissolved. "I'm Halldora, true queen of Thonethren, ousted from my throne. We are currently in the process of taking it back."

Phineas had mentioned this woman when he had detailed Erval's past. A sister, chosen over the brother. Could this be her? Phineas had also revealed their theories of a warlord amassing an army... Solyana wondered if they were one and the same.

"You're Erval's sister," Solyana said softly.

"Ah, good, good. You've heard of me." The woman grinned, her perfectly straight teeth outlined with smooth pink lips. "It's been too long since I've paid my pretender brother a visit." She turned, swaying back up the stones to sit.

Erval's sister. Solyana's brow furrowed. A pot and a kettle, both black as pitch. Solyana wondered how many people Halldora had Taken to look the way she did now.

"Our forces are finally of substantial size and strength. And with the eclipse, we know Erval will be distracted. In less than a fortnight, we will overturn his plans."

So, Phineas's theory was true.

Solyana's eyes flicked from Halldora to the guards beside her. "A sound strategy," she said. She would play along, at least until Gamaliel was healed. "Although, I am uncertain as to why Your Majesty has need of me."

"I would offer you a position on my council, of course! You are the Chosen, the Saint of Endirinn, the Bringer of Green—beloved by both the Celestials and the people. Your voice is the one Thonethren needs to bind her together, to guide her through this time of violent and bloody transition." She seemed to relish the last few words.

But Solyana had no intention of doing any such thing. All she wanted was for Gamaliel to be healed and for her sister to be returned to her. All she wanted was for Thonethren, Erval, and their threats to be behind her. "Your Majesty is gracious and generous, but I am entirely unsuited to s—"

Halldora tutted. "When my throne is returned to me, you will want for nothing. And the new legends will reflect it was I who snatched you from the serpent's jaws and delivered you to safety, as you delivered Mothmar. That you were lifted to the good queen's right hand, just as you ascended Mount Endirinn to bring the green. The Celestials will see their Chosen cherished, and Thonethren will thrive." Too much white showed in Halldora's eyes, her smile just a touch too wide.

"I..." Solyana looked at the guards again, their faces an array of stony concern.

"Now, the men with you are a different matter." The queen's expression changed in an instant. "The steward is quite a prize. I don't know what he told you or promised you that you followed him of your own accord, but let's put it behind us." She smiled, and a sliver of chill ran through Solyana. "He is no longer any concern of yours; I have my own plans for him."

Solyana kept her reactions in check. So far, Halldora didn't seem too different from the brother she sought to replace. The information Phineas had divulged and the work they were doing was perhaps best kept to herself.

"Now, the guard," Halldora continued. "The one that was unfortunately injured during your rescue."

"Gamaliel." Solyana tried to keep the bitterness from her voice. "His name is Gamaliel, and your men shot him."

"Yes, well, we couldn't be sure he wasn't working for Phineas, now, could we? Captor or companion, it's always better to be safe than sorry. And the other one, with the shorter hair. He's offered to enlist, and I see no reason to dissuade him. Unless you oppose?"

Solyana postured herself as the saint she was told she was. Whatever it took to get her people out safely. "I do oppose. I would like him returned to my service as soon as possible. And for Gamaliel to be healed, at Your Majesty's earliest convenience, of course."

Halldora truly smiled now. "Please avail yourself of the amenities, and we shall more formally reconvene after dinner. Ivan, if you'd be so kind as to escort our Lady Solyana where she needs to go."

The general sidled up beside her, and he bowed to his queen before leading Solyana away, the large hand above her elbow gripping uncomfortably tight.

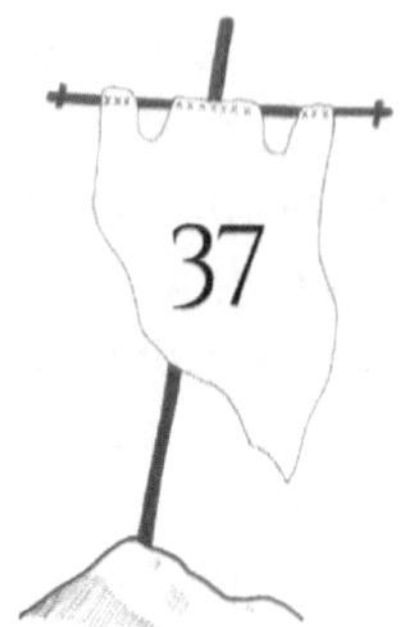

AN OLD FRIEND

HALLDORA

THE SAINT OF ENDIRINN and Erval's steward traveling together.

Halldora drummed her fingertips on the end of the detailed armrest before rising to stand and sweeping from the room, her guard wordlessly trailing behind.

When Erval had gone into hiding, back when she was but a girl, she had searched for him. It had taken spies, their twitchy little ears against the ground for months, to find where he had squirreled himself away. Dug in throughout the network of caves in and around Hekla. Surprisingly close to home. That's when she first heard the name Phineas.

A young, nervous man with little confidence to speak of. A mouse, though an exceedingly smart one. Just the assistant Erval needed to help him accomplish his plans.

At the time, she had foolishly attempted contact with Phineas. But what the man lacked in confidence, he made up in shrewdness, and Halldora determined never to underestimate him again.

She wove her way through the ill-lit passageways, ignoring the bows and platitudes from those she passed. She arrived at the outskirts of her army, where enemies were kept, where interrogations were performed. There were rumors of torture Halldora knew to be true. She had ordered it on more than one occasion. And there Phineas sat, sack firmly over his head, hands tied behind him, his round belly stretching his shirt to its limit.

Erval's treachery, she was certain, Phineas had connived. She had wanted her brother to return, to support her as their father and the Celestials had ordained. Phineas had assured her Erval's blood would cool, that his young pride was but temporary. So, she'd answered the mouse's questions and did not seek to retrieve Erval from within Hekla.

She was answered with an army at her door.

Trusting Phineas had come at great cost, and her people had paid the price.

She would not underestimate this sniveling man, not again.

Her steps were silent as she observed his manner up close. She was noting the sour wetness of his clothes when something scuttled inside one of his wide sleeves.

Halldora jumped back. "You appear to be infested," she told the man.

Phineas jumped and squeaked at the same time. "Halldora?" The man spoke through his nose, his tongue clicking against the dry roof of his mouth. "Please, take off this hood. Let me have a look at you."

She gave a short nod of her head and stepped back, one of her guards leaning in to pull the material from his head. The tea was in her system. She would be protected from any type of bodily Fera he might attempt to use.

At the sight of his face, Halldora found herself able to do little more than sneer. She was tempted to borrow a dagger and cut the man's throat herself, though all the information trapped inside that balding, perspiring head would be lost.

Phineas lifted his bound hands to adjust his spectacles. "It is you." His beady eyes took in her royal presence. "Your renown precedes you, Halldora of Thonethren. I've heard whispers of your growing army, but I must say, a sizeable force has flocked to you. Keeping this many topped up with tea must be taxing."

She fit a small smile onto her face.

"And this cave... My legs are weary from being prodded through it. It must have taken several Stein Fera to create a hollow this vast. Or did Her Majesty see fit to craft it herself?"

All his words, she would have to sift through them, and the anger rising from her belly to her throat made her head swim. She took a cleansing breath, refusing to allow her hatred to cloud her judgment.

"For all it can do," Phineas mused, "the finnevel can't quite penetrate rock."

Halldora had no idea what a finnevel was, but she would not take this man's bait. "How many of the militia does Erval keep at home?" she asked. "How many roam the outlands, desperately trying to maintain his slipping grip on my people?"

Phineas grit his teeth, a bead of sweat falling from the top of his head to his jaw.

"You can tell me, steward, or I can have my men pluck the knowledge from your fingernails." She stifled the smile that came at the thought of his screams.

"I cannot tell Her Ladyship what I do not know."

She drew herself closer, the smell of his fear rising in her nostrils. "You will address me by the title my father, the king, bestowed upon me. And you know plenty. Unless..." Halldora pouted. "You've fallen out of favor? That would be a shame because then you'd be useless to me." She extended a hand over her shoulder and her guard filled it with a long dagger. "Is he looking through your eyes right now? Are his words filling your mouth?"

Phineas tore his gaze from the blade, failing in his attempts to keep his breathing steady. "Neither. I have created my own methods for keeping him out."

"Is that so?" The gears in Halldora's mind turned. Perhaps this mouse had more than numbers and screams to be wrung from him. The ability to neutralize Erval's Mann Tala without having to search for and consume rare herbs would be a devastating advantage. She eyed him.

"What are you doing with the saint of Endirinn? Am I to believe you've converted?"

Phineas gave her a pained look, his lips in a grim line.

Halldora waited for him to answer her, but when the silence stretched, she sighed. She looked at the dagger in her hands, releasing the blade to let it hover in the air between them. It began to spin, slow circles that rotated faster and faster, until the handle and the blade blurred together. It crept through the air toward Phineas.

Phineas's eyes, which should have been filled with fear, narrowed instead. The dagger halted and dropped to the floor, narrowly missing Halldora's booted foot. The man tilted his head and said nonchalantly, "She plans to stop him."

Halldora kicked the weapon aside. This man was on similar ground in terms of Gifts and abilities; she wasn't going to give him an opening again.

"From doing what? Ruling? She and I are aligned in that. Or..." Halldora's manicured fingernail tapped her chin. "Are you leading a crafty little lamb to her own slaughter?"

"Erval, he's..." Phineas's face contorted with what appeared to be genuine remorse. "He's going too far," he continued. "And if Solyana were to stand a chance, she needs to be able to keep Erval from her mind. I was..." He squirmed. "Yes, I was escorting her. And I was teaching her my methods. No tea, just protection from his Tala."

Halldora smiled, full and true, for the first time in decades. She pointed at him. "You will teach my men this method."

Phineas stammered, some bubbling excuse Halldora didn't bother to hear.

"You will teach them, or I will make an example of you. A long and vivid example of what will become of my brother's followers. And that thieving pretender's visits into your mind will be the very last of your worries."

Halldora felt her heart swell and wondered if it were the Celestials or the Mother Below she was to thank for their providence. Perhaps neither. It was her scraping and planning, her tenacity and will, that had brought her to this moment as the key to Erval's downfall dropped into her grateful hands. She would charge into Thonethren untouchable. She would strike with both sword and shield. The Red Moon would reflect the color of her brother's blood as it covered the marble of the throne room's floor.

The Red Moon was fast approaching.

"You have less than a fortnight, Phineas." Halldora turned, striding away. "I suggest you get started."

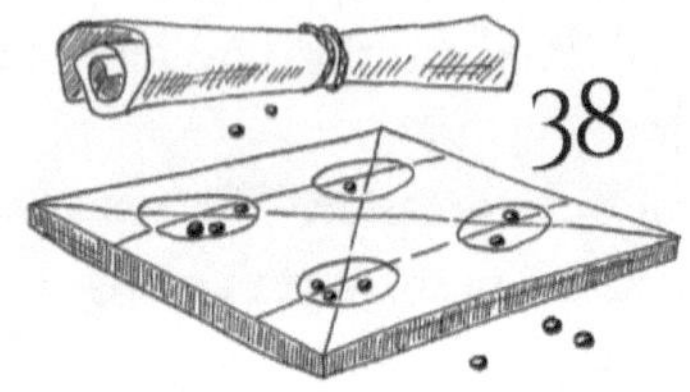

EYE IN THE DARK

JONAS

T HE MOON WAS RED. Red like an apple; red like clay. The sounds of war were all about him; the clash of sword and mace, the whistle of arrows, and the screams of dying men. Jonas stood in the middle of the mêlée. He tried to run, but his feet wouldn't move. He screamed, but no sound came from his throat.

He stood there, uselessly turning in circles, watching allies get cut down, slaughtered in the name of freedom. Then the tide shifted, and the battle seemed to switch victors. Jonas's heart felt lighter—hope had arrived.

But this was always the worst part of the dream.

A rumble, a shake, as if the earth itself was awakening from slumber.

Then choking ash.

Raging fire.

And he was alone.

He was alone, and all had been lost.

Gasping awake, Jonas clawed at the hands gripping his shoulders.

"Wake up!" Rorhan's ice-blue eyes were too close and filled with fear. "Something is attacking the ship!"

"What?" Jonas squirmed out of his hammock only to be upturned onto the floor.

A sharp whistle followed by a deafening crash rang in the air as Rorhan jumped on top of Jonas, covering him with his body. The ship shuddered and creaked. Jonas could hear the hiss of invading water.

Rorhan rolled off, grabbed his throwing knives, and shoved on his boots.

Jonas followed suit, though with no weapons to his name he gathered all his belongings and stuffed them into his bag.

Shouts and cries rang throughout the three-story ship, men screaming—so similar to his dream—Jonas could have fooled himself into believing he was still asleep. But then the planks beneath his feet shook so violently, he was certain his current experience was reality.

"The Crimson Chief?" he asked Rorhan as the two ran up the companionway to the upper deck.

"The ship is hit but no sound of cannons."

A massive red length of sinew burst through the wall and plunged deep into the space where Jonas and Rorhan cowered. The tentacle's pink underbelly was covered with massive suction cups that pulsed as if they were breathing. Salt water and seaweed washed over them as they ducked and cowered beneath it. It tore back and forth in two quick strikes before Rorhan stood and threw one of his knives, the blade sinking in up to the hilt. The tentacle retracted back out of the gap, its puckered skin scraping over broken wood.

"A kraken." Rorhan stared as they huddled under what remained of the handrail, his breathing rapid and out of control. *"Hine skur blessi okur."* He shut his eyes tight, his body shaking. *"Hine skur blessi okur."*

"Rorhan! We need to get off the ship!" Jonas wiped the water from his face and shook the man. "The Celestials *will* help us," he said. "But we need to move! Now!"

The ship lurched again, and Jonas heard a deep crack that could only be the mast snapping in two. There was water pouring in from the upper deck, threatening to push Jonas back down the ladder. A few sailors bolted past, their arms loaded with large metal balls.

"Get up!" Jonas tried again to bring Rorhan to his feet and finally succeeded, though the man shook like a leaf at autumn's turn. They stumbled up the steps together, keeping each other standing through the sloshing water and the rocking and lurching of the ship.

Another blast rang off, and Jonas's hands flew to his ears. Emerging onto the upper deck, he received a full view of the carnage. Men were jumping into the sea; a few were huddled around a large metal contraption, into which they were feeding metal balls. Two Eldurs stood against the gunwale, shooting fireball after fireball at the creature.

"It will break the ship in half!" Rorhan cried, and Jonas's jaw dropped open.

He craned his neck upward to see five tentacles high above them, two of them fishing for men within the ship, two holding the ship at each end, and one coming down like a cleaver onto a slab of meat.

He had not foreseen this. This had not been in his dreams or his maps or his thoughts. Jonas could not die here. He would not—he knew better, though that didn't stop his knees from shaking.

The wind from the tentacle falling blew past him, and he heard the impact, felt the shockwaves as he ran. Another crash filled the air, so deafening Jonas thought his ears would break. His knees buckled, and his feet were swept out from under him. The floor of the ship rippled like a wave, and Jonas smacked the decking as it tilted, each side of the ship folding inward like a piece of parchment. Fingers scrambling for a hold, eyes searching for Rorhan, Jonas began to hear the screams of horses atop the cries of dying men. Jonas only caught a glimpse of where Thora and Agnar had been kept before the entire section of deck dropped from view. Jonas's heart sank with them. He could only pray they would escape and swim to safety.

Then everything shifted. The side of the ship Jonas clung to rose quickly into the air, and he slid down its slope. Squeezing the broken vessel like a piece of ripened fruit, the massive beast began tugging it wholly downward.

"Rorhan!" Jonas called after his friend as he slid down the almost vertical deck, grasping for purchase and finding none. His satchel, Celestials be praised, snagged on a peg, and he gripped the bag, looking up to find a rope near the straining strap. Kicking his legs, he prayed it would hold as he used it to reach and grab the rope.

"Rorhan!" he screamed over the cracks and groans of the dying ship. "Rorhan!"

"Here!"

Relief flooded through Jonas as he found the man hanging from a shroud.

Jonas threw the rope out as far as he could, but it fell short. He gathered it and tried once more with the same result. Panicked, he looked at his friend from across the ship, and Rorhan was shaking his head.

"We can't die!" Jonas cried. "Lone will kill us!"

Rorhan let out a single laugh as the ship sank further toward the massive beast at its middle. He searched the churning dark water lit only by the moon and stars. "We have to jump!"

"I can't swim!" Saying it out loud transformed Jonas's fear into stone-cold terror. He couldn't swim. Perhaps his foresight had been false, and every path he had chosen had led him here to his death. "I can't swim!" he sobbed at the roiling sea. When he looked back up, Rorhan was gone, the shroud he was hanging from snapped, flapping in the wind.

Bursting from the darkness, a tentacle rose from the pitch and clinging to it was Captain Viggo, his cutlass coming down again and again. Jonas admired the man's fighting spirit, though he doubted it would save him.

He shimmied out of his satchel and fell, his every limb flailing until his body struck the waves. The wind was knocked from him, and his skin burned as he slipped beneath the frothing surface of the sea.

Kicking frantically, clawing his way upward, he came up for air once, his arms flying out to the sides, before gravity and the pull of the waves dragged him under again.

He opened his eyes in the salty murk, a flash of fire blooming above him as the last of the Eldurs released a ball of flame. It gave enough light to see the beast in full view, one giant eyeball swiveling to focus onto Jonas as he began to sink, his lungs screaming for air.

Jonas wished he was Tala so he could reach out and tether such a beast. Instead, the broken pieces of *Coletta,* and her men, sank and drifted into the black depths of the ocean around him. He regretted having brought Rorhan as the edges of his vision began to blur.

He couldn't refuse his need for air any longer. He sucked in a breath—but there was no air to be found.

He choked.

And the darkness devoured him.

PRACTICE

RHUTH

"WE'LL REACH THONETHREN'S BORDER within three days," Pallah said as the two of them picked their way across the wide expanse of snow. "More, if we run into trouble."

"Animals?"

"Worse. People," the woman said with a smirk. "Animals, we can handle."

Images of Pallah cutting down hapless creatures flashed through Rhuth's mind, and she cringed. "I'll handle the animals. You handle the people."

Pallah stopped and stretched, eyeing Rhuth over her shoulder. "If we're going to make sure I get to Erval and handle him cleanly... I will need to know all you can do."

"I told you," Rhuth said. "I'm not sure what I do. It's impossible to explain."

"Then don't tell me." Pallah shook her head. "Show me." She stopped walking and lowered her pack to the ground, staff standing vertically in the snow. "If I do something like this..." Pallah brought her palms together before pulling them apart, a flame spawning in the air between them. "What would you do to stop me?"

Rhuth's eyes widened, and she dropped her pack into the snow. Her steps were made clumsy by her snowshoes as she back-pedaled. "What do you mean stop you? I can't—"

The fire shot out at Rhuth like a whip, and she only just dove out of the way, keeping her clothes from being singed.

"What are you doing?" she shouted, scrambling out of her snowshoes and dusting white powder from her coat. "I'm not going to fight you!"

Pallah laughed, and with one quick movement of her hands, brought the fire into a ring around her that pulsed and turned. "You think we're going to just walk into Thonethren and demand Erval stop what he's doing?"

"I mean—"

"Wake up, girl! This man is bent on complete domination of Mothmar! You are something he'll scrape off his shoe!"

Rhuth stood. "I thought you were going to reason with him."

The words had hardly come out of her mouth before Pallah took three quick steps, the ground shaking and breaking beneath her feet, snow exploding in all directions, blinding Rhuth. She ran backward, a shout escaping her lips. Gaping holes had sunk deep into the ground, and the snow poured into them, threatening to take Rhuth with it. She scrambled back and finally saw through the powdery white to where Pallah stood on a circular island formed from the earth itself.

Pallah's arms were outstretched, her expression somewhere between focused rage and insanity. "This world is at my disposal, Rhuth. It bows to my whims. I twitch a finger, and it is *mine*. I brought the clouds to your valley; I kept the sun from touching your people's skin for hundreds of years." Stepping forward, she placed one foot after the other onto blocks of hardened snow, creating stairs out of nothing but the elements. Pallah's dirty-blonde hair whirled in all directions, her clothes rippling and waving in the wind.

"I've killed countless, I've Taken and Taken—I could stop now, and I would still live for centuries with how much I've accrued. And you think Erval, a master of the Taka Reu who has practiced far longer, and Taken from far more than I, will be swayed by reason?" Pallah shook her head and gave a humorless laugh. "I wield a fraction of the power that man is capable of. If we want to get our families back from him, we'll have to be strong enough to take them."

Wind whipped around the two of them, the ground shaking as if the earth itself quaked with fear. Rhuth crouched, everything inside her warring between peaceability and violence.

"Protect yourself!" Pallah drew her staff, allowing the double axes on each side to protrude. She twirled it, slicing through the blocks of snow and ice she had formed. She landed on the ground, a wave of snow coming up like a wave from the sea, ready to consume Rhuth. "Stop me, or die!"

Rhuth crumpled to the ground, arms covering her face from the onslaught of icy cold that assaulted her skin, unable to stop the scream that then became a sob. The earth stopped shaking, and something stilled in Rhuth, a quiet peace that snuffed out her fear. She blinked, then peered out from her fetal position on the ground.

Pallah was standing far from her now, her eyes wide and mouth hanging open. She was much farther than she had been just before, and Rhuth's brow furrowed. How had that happened? She stood, looking down to find the earth itself open around her feet. One wrong step, and she would plummet to her death. Somehow, in her terror, Rhuth had created a chasm around her.

Hardly wide enough for even her small frame, Rhuth stood on the tiny platform. And in front of her, like a line of warriors, were every kind of creature. Ember stood at the center, and to her left and right were boar, rabbit, elk, and wolves. The falcons screamed from above.

"How did you do that?" Pallah whispered with disbelief from beyond the animal perimeter.

Thank you for your protection, she told them. *You may go.* The animals dispersed in different directions through the disrupted snow. Rhuth shook her head. "I don't know. I've never done that before."

"Well, do it again."

Rhuth's snowshoes slipped, and she threw her arms out for balance.

Pallah took a few strides forward and held out a hand for Rhuth, who grasped it and jumped to safety. "If you can learn how to control that...you could defeat Erval without my help."

"I'm not going to defeat anyone," Rhuth said, and she fought the urge to yawn. "I'm only coming to help Solyana."

"And if defeating Erval is a part of that?"

Rhuth shook her head. "I can't control how nature fights for me. And I don't want to." She grabbed her knapsack, slung it over her back, and began a pointed march to a row of trees far on the other side.

Rage licked deep within her at what Pallah had forced her to do. She never wanted to hurt anyone, never wanted to disrupt lives. Even calling those animals, she had felt their willingness and their weakness. No one needed to die for her, especially the innocent who walked on four legs.

"Rhuth, you need to learn to protect yourself. I can't be responsible for you when we get to Thonethren. There's too much at stake. I—"

"Leave me be!"

Rhuth's heart grew callous, content to make the rest of the journey toward her sister alone.

TENUOUS DEALS

SOLYANA

AFTER A MEAGER DINNER of meats and flatbread and a warm bath, Solyana and Ahren were brought before the Queen of the Cave once more. Their conversation, led by the queen, revolved around her future duties as council member until Solyana found an opening in the conversation and finally broached the subject that coiled tightly around her heart.

"And what of Gamaliel?"

"The injured one? I am told his wound has turned grievous." Halldora folded her hands in her lap.

Solyana released a slow breath, barely keeping the scream of grief from crawling up her throat. Instead, she said, "With all due respect, has everything been done?"

"My own Healer has seen to him! His skill is unmatched, but he cannot work miracles."

Ahren looked to Solyana. "I can find him other help."

Halldora turned her attention. "Surely you would not imply our care is insufficient. Men get injured. Men die. It is a sad truth we all must face."

"Respectfully, Your Grace"—Solyana gave a small bow, anger flashing over her skin—"my men and I are grateful for the generous hospitality we have been shown. And we would not seek to stretch your camp's resources any further than we have. If Her Majesty would permit—"

"I do not permit. You may be chosen by the Celestials, but you belong to my court now. And the crown sees fit to keep you close, safe from my brother's creeping fingers." Halldora's smile turned dark. "And from the battle that will reclaim our throne."

Solyana's mind worked. Halldora's men had stripped them of their horses and their goods. She had already been pressed into service, and Ahren's position was tenuous at best. What could Solyana offer that hadn't already been stolen? How could she convince this queen whose mind was set?

"I have information," she said. "Regarding your brother." Solyana watched the woman's face change. "It may be of use to you."

Halldora pointed a finger at Solyana and gave it a gentle wag. "You...are more clever than I thought." She smiled. "We are going to make an excellent team. Have the boy wait outside until we've concluded things, Ivan. And you, my dear..." Her smile at Solyana turned predatory. "You and I are due a very interesting conversation."

Locking eyes with Ahren, Solyana wished, more than anything, she could confer with him one last time but knew better than to request it. He gave her a firm nod and was escorted from the room.

"Now," Halldora began, crossing one leg over the other and leaning back against her makeshift throne, "you were saying?"

"As you know, Erval is a man of subtlety, a man confident in his Gift. He knows you're coming?"

"I expect so, by now." Halldora eyed her, swirling the contents of her glass.

Sweat broke across the small of Solyana's back. Discussions with Phineas over the last few days fit together like a puzzle in her brain. There was something Halldora didn't know, and Solyana would use it to stay with Gamaliel. "Then you'll need every distraction at your disposal. We have a plan to infiltrate the castle."

"I am no queen of shadows. I will reclaim what is mine."

"And how do you plan on keeping all these men supplied with tea? Your men are loyal, but they do seem to talk...I fear there may not be enough to go around."

Halldora's lip quirked. "Phineas trains my men as we speak. The tea grows redundant by the minute."

"As I have been under Phineas's tutelage this last week, I know it is a difficult and tedious skill to learn." Solyana paused, stomach squirming in knots. "The Red Moon approaches soon." She locked eyes with the queen and was glad to see understanding dawn in the woman's eyes.

"So, I run out of tea...or I run out of time," Halldora summarized. "My most recent alliance has guaranteed us stock of the former. And between the tea and the steward, the latter is of little consequence. Though he may have fooled you into believing he is omnipotent, the man can only tether to so many people at once."

Solyana cleared her throat, ready now to reveal the final point. "With the Brextant, he can tether to everyone."

The queen's smile remained, but her eyes hardened. "Brextant?"

"A machine crafted for the singular purpose of arresting control of every soul in Mothmar." Goosebumps peppered Solyana's arms. "And he only needs one person stuffed with years strapped to the machine to do it."

Halldora stilled.

"If you allow, Your Grace, I will join my men, slip into Thonethren, destroy the machine, and leave you to your brother. Then I will be free to serve on your council as you wish." Solyana added the last line hoping she could iron out the details later, as joining the queen's council was the last thing she desired.

"How self-sacrificial of you. Though, I fail to see how you are required for this mission." The Queen's eyes flicked to the guard at the back of the cave. "General, a wagon and provisions for Solyana's two guards. You," she said, her attention back on Solyana, "will aid me in persuading the Celestial worshipers that allowing them their Temple is better than a king bent on having them destroyed."

The queen stood and Solyana took a step backward, bowing as the woman strode past her, mind racing at what was to be done. For the Queen of Caves would not simply allow her friends to go, not when they held such influence over Solyana's actions—she didn't have to be fluent in politics to know this.

No. Halldora would tie them up like the loose ends they were.

"We'll do great things together when this war is won, Saint. Now, get some rest. General Ivan will come for you in the morning."

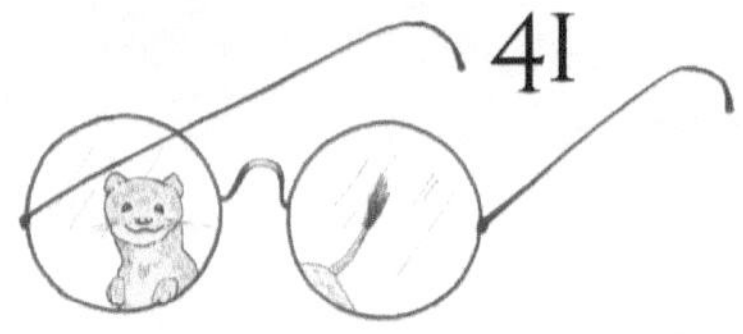

41

CRUMBS & FEASTS

PHINEAS

PHINEAS WAS BEING WORKED to the bone. Held in a corner of the cave, stalactites dripping to the floor, he shivered beneath a guttering torch. Without knowing how deep they had taken him, he had no way of navigating himself out. He had escaped Erval only to fall into the hands of his sister. Phineas would laugh if he weren't so tired. A staunch man of science, and yet politics would forever claim his life.

Groups of soldiers had come and gone, all intent on learning how to gird their minds. All leaving as clueless as they had come. Despite his efforts, there was simply no time. It took quiet, peace, and hours alone to truly formulate a path for Erval to tread. This dank cave and rush to leave stole any semblance of serenity.

He hadn't given Halldora the truth in its entirety, of course. She wished to bar Erval from her mind completely. The blocking tea did that trick. Phineas's mental blockade, however, wasn't all encompassing.

Phineas had weighed the results of Erval finding it was his sister who was bringing war to his walls. He surmised the revelation would do nothing but help his cause. If Erval was distracted, fighting no mere rebellion but his sister for the throne, Phineas was less likely to be discovered. He could destroy the Brextant without notice. There would be no need for any extraneous confrontation with his old friend. Phineas found he could not bring himself to wish ill upon Erval, no matter his grievances with the man. Erval's desires for power were something Phineas could understand, even if they had grown to too large a proportion.

A commotion drew his eyes.

"Ma'am, we received no word you would be coming here."

The queen? Phineas hefted himself from the floor and straightened his shoulders.

"As a member of Queen Halldora's council and Saint of Endirinn, I am allowed entrance wherever it pleases me."

Phineas sucked in a breath.

The guards stepped to the side, and Solyana walked to him in a stately manner. She had adapted quickly, or so it would seem. Kopar skittered out from his sleeve and perched upon his shoulder.

"Tell me, how fares your teaching, Phineas?" Solyana enunciated carefully.

"Slow-going," Phineas began, eyes flitting over her shoulder to the guards at the entrance. "These men possess little peace to receive my instruction."

The guards at the front stepped away from the entrance, talking between themselves.

He gave Solyana a quick nod, affixing a small smile to his face. She dropped her voice to a low whisper. "I told Halldora of the Brextant and our plan to destroy it. Though I explained we all needed to go, she refuses to release either myself or you but is allowing Gamaliel and Ahren a horse and wagon."

Sweat prickled his forehead. Halldora was sending the boys to their graves. But it would simplify things if—

"I can't let them go without me. I think she plans to kill them!"

When had she gotten so shrewd? "And you with them, girl." And him, though he left that out. Perhaps Halldora was the only one, aside from Erval himself, that held the Gifts to do it.

"A good portion of her men seem to worship the Celestials, as they have shown me more deference than I would think from men following the Taka Reu. I don't think she would risk doing away with me."

"Maybe not in front of her men, but if she found you on a wagon in the middle of nowhere..." He took an exasperated breath. "You're safest by the queen's side. Stay with her—with me—when we arrive in Thonethren we'll escape together."

A deeper fear blossomed in Solyana's eyes. "I can't let Gamaliel die, Phineas."

Fool girl.

"Has your power returned?" He searched her face for hope but found none as she gave a tiny shake of her head. "You better beseech your gods, girl." Already he was running over the list of possible outcomes, searching for another path or even another person that could fill her place.

"I think she means to kill you," Solyana said.

"Of course she means to kill me," he agreed, still with that faux smile on his face. "But she can't." He took a breath, eyes darting to the guards and back. "I believe these caves are somewhere beneath the plains of central Mothmar. Just northwest of here there's a small fishing village I stopped at on my way to Endirinn. Go there if you must get Gamaliel help before going to Thonethren." What he offered was a trade, and he waited patiently for a return of information.

"The queen is on her way," one of the soldiers said from the door.

Phineas leaned around Solyana and nodded. "Quite right."

"Time to leave, Saint," a soldier called from the entrance.

"I'll just say goodnight," Solyana called back with a small smile as she grasped Phineas's hands in her own. A small, folded parchment rested in her palm. He held onto her for a few moments, unsaid words passing between them as the parchment slipped into the folds of his robes.

He gave her shoulder a squeeze, more warning than comfort. If only she would forget about Gamaliel and stay put. "Goodnight, Solyana."

"Goodnight, Phineas."

Then she was gone, saying something to the guards about finding her own way to her cot. Much like he would find his own way out. He sat in the corner, back to the cave's entrance, and extracted the parchment. His eyes scoured the map he knew he'd find. A small dotted line traced the steps he would take to leave when the time came. He was only as useful to Halldora as her patience was long, and he did not wish to test it.

Killing the queen did not align with his aims. Alternatively, he could stay safely tucked beneath Halldora's wing before arriving in

Thonethren. But to what end? The king beneath the mighty mountain, more powerful than he and the queen put together, would sniff out his deception as fast as his head would fly from his shoulders.

And then where would that leave Mothmar?

Or Solyana?

Something twinged in his belly, and he furrowed his brow. Kopar hopped down from his shoulder to perch on his knee. Standing up on his hind legs, he blinked at Phineas.

"I'm not sure what to do, boy," Phineas said. "I am...worried." He stroked the creature's head. "I'm afraid I've grown fond of her."

Watching Solyana these past days had brought Phineas to the conclusion that he wasn't so cold-hearted as he thought himself to be. Intertwined with these thoughts, questions choked his understanding of the world, queries he had not posed these last few lifetimes. If he so staunchly disagreed with Erval, master of the Taka Reu, did he not also disagree with this kind of worship? With the use of Gifts in such a manner?

Turning to the Celestials was more than inconvenient at this time; it was dangerous. He was skilled in the Taka Reu. His victory from any battle was almost guaranteed. But with the Celestials? He would be like a colt on new legs, learning to navigate uneven ground.

Had Phineas and Erval not proven they could stamp out any Celestial power? Instead, he would wait for Jonas's discoveries. The Way, as Jonas called it, was something to be gleaned. With it, perhaps he would be strong enough to subdue Erval so that his old friend may yet survive. And until Phineas received word about it, he would bide his time with the Mother Below.

He stared at the parchment another moment, committing it to memory before commanding Kopar to eat it.

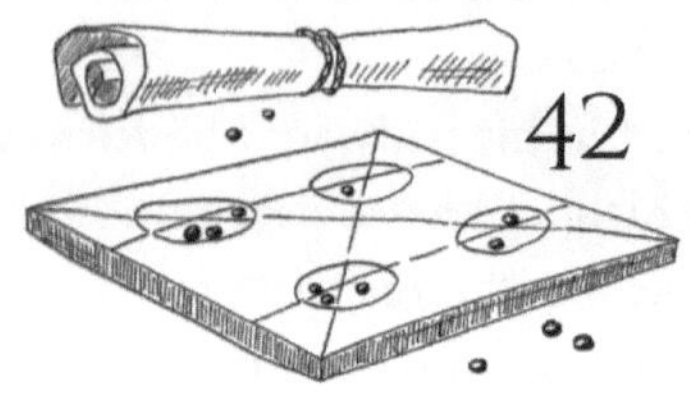

42

THREE AS ONE

JONAS

THE ASH COVERED EVERYTHING, leaving nothing clean. Like a disease, it took over the land, as if the blizzards were black instead of white, the evil of it threatening to drown Jonas where he stood.

The ash was in his mouth, stuffing itself down his throat. Jonas coughed and coughed and tore at his throat, but nothing would free him.

Water spewed from his lungs as he turned onto his side, gasping for breath. Air! Sweet air. And where ash had covered him, he found drenched clothing sticking to his skin.

"Jonas!"

Covering his eyes from the sun, Jonas peered through his fingers to see Rorhan's face much too close to his own.

Jonas shoved the man limply away, coughs racking his chest. "Space," he choked, struggling to get on all fours, his lungs clearing.

Rorhan sat back on his heels and released a chuckle, wiping at his mouth. "We were much closer a few seconds ago."

Jonas coughed up more water, tasting the brine of the sea. Peering up at Rorhan, his long stringy hair pulled back over his shoulder, Jonas wiped at his mouth. Anything was better than Rorhan's lips.

Sand coated his back, covered his arms, and crunched between his teeth. "Where..." He sat back on his haunches, eyes adjusting to the bright white of the beach. Long tubular trees swayed in the hot breeze, crystal clear water lapping near his feet, and Jonas saw nothing but water, water, and more water.

Dread landed hard in his gut.

How could he ever have thought the ocean beautiful?

"Where are we?" He licked his lips, tasting more salt and grit. He needed to drink.

"I was hoping you would tell me." Rorhan flopped to the ground and began massaging his shoulder. "I swam with you mumbling nonsense on my back all night. Then just when I spotted land, a squall came over the waters. I almost drowned." The man's sad eyes found Jonas's. "I thought I had lost you."

Jonas blinked. He hadn't remembered any of that. "What star patterns were you headed toward?"

Rorhan looked at the young Seer. "Most do not worry about the stars while swimming for their lives."

Jonas took in a full breath. "You're right, Han. I'm sorry. Thank you for saving me."

Rorhan nodded solemnly and moved onto his legs. "You would do the same for me."

"I would *want* to." Jonas grinned sheepishly. "But we would've died had it been up to me."

"I know."

Jonas gave his friend a sidelong glance before surveying the beach. "We're going to need some water." He sighed. "All my work. My research..."

"I am sorry, Jonas." Rorhan heaved a mighty sigh.

Five years of work...left to sink to the bottom of the ocean. The fate of the crew, the horses, and Captain Viggo, who Jonas had last seen... Jonas blinked as the memory came back to him. Had they all truly been cut short by one ill-fated trip?

"I managed to save these!" Rorhan held out something that glinted in the sun.

"My spectacles!" he said as if greeting an old friend. "Thank you, Rorhan!"

The two rose and dusted off the sand before scouring the landscape for necessary supplies. Wreckage, debris, and other evidence of the shipwreck was being dragged in by the waves. Soon they had found a cloth Jonas was able to fashion into a bag, a waterskin, a small barrel of food, a rope, and a long knife.

Then they ventured inward, in search of fresh water. But the sun began to lower, and Jonas knew if they didn't start on a shelter soon, they would be stuck out in the open after dark—and that was usually never a good idea.

"I hear a stream!" Rorhan's voice boomed in the low light, and Jonas fought the urge to shush him; they didn't know who or what inhabited this island.

He followed his friend through the trees and vines until, sure enough, a brook tumbled from the side of a rock. It was a good indicator the island was more than a simple land mass, but something that held a bit more elevation. Tomorrow, Jonas would climb higher.

They washed up in the small stream, rinsing and squeezing the salt from their skin and hair, drinking the fresh water, and filling the waterskin. They ended up on a small hill devoid of trees. The grass cover would provide a good spot to sleep. At least from up here, they would be able to see if anything were to approach.

They cracked open the barrel and ate a few of the fruits found inside. Then, exhausted, the two laid down in the grass, content to watch the sky as it burst with new stars.

Rorhan was snoring within seconds, and Jonas wondered if he should stay awake to keep guard through the night. Perhaps he would take first watch and wake Rorhan in a few hours. Jonas's eyelids drooped, and he shook himself, staying awake already proving to be a challenge.

He focused instead on the stars once more, scattered across the night like spilled snowflakes—shining, rippling with color, winking with movement. Jonas brought his research to the forefront of his mind.

When he had received that final prophecy from Seer Brotnur five years ago, he had set his mind on a few choice words from the script.

One who must follow the paths of the sky.

Unaided by this world's Gifts, filled with the one—the way that connects one to all.

The studies he'd conducted in Endirinn had reflected minimal findings, if he was being honest with himself. But one thing was clear: it was in the *stars*. The Children of the Sky were much more important than any of them realized. And he had begun to think perhaps the words 'one who possesses the three as one' was a way of saying the Father of the Day, Mother of the Night, and Children of the Sky were never supposed to be split.

They were one Celestial body: the Way.

But even with his understanding, how was Jonas supposed to put his knowledge into action? Into practice? It was as if his eyes had been blinded, and he needed someone to heal them.

He took off his spectacles and stared at the stars without them. They became a blurry haze of light and dark. He squinted, spotting the moon among them, trying to make out if there was some pattern he could see better without the aid of his glasses. But alas, nothing emerged.

He curled up on the ground and whispered through dry lips, "Please help me to see. I want to know. Not just to *know,* but to see." He heaved a sigh and felt himself going so quickly. "How much more of Your worth could we know, if we knew the true You?"

He wasn't sure who specifically he was talking to—the Children of the Sky? The Celestials as a whole? Regardless, he felt heard. And he fell asleep.

A VOICE IN THE DARK

RHUTH

ALONE IN THE DARK, regret wormed its way into Rhuth's heart. She knew she should stop and make camp, but getting herself as far from Pallah as she could pushed every step she took. No matter what kind of reasoning the priestess gave, Rhuth knew it was only to achieve her own ends.

"I know you're tired, girl," Rhuth said to Ember. "You already follow me during the day when you should be sleeping. The least I should do is give you a good night's rest."

The fox trotted beside her with far less enthusiasm than she had displayed an hour or two before.

Rhuth directed her thoughts on the ground around her, swiftly clearing the snow away. Almost subconsciously, she asked the earth for wood so she could build a fire, and within moments, she knew where it was. Before long, she had a comfortable space and a warm fire, and her eyelids began to droop.

"Just some advice..." A voice cut through the dark. "Don't start a fire when you're trying to hide from someone."

Rhuth ground her teeth, but didn't bother sitting up. She had known Pallah would catch up eventually. It wasn't like she had a different destination.

"I'm sorry I pushed you," Pallah said. "We only have a few more days until we're face to face with the most destructive man either of us will ever know. And if we stand a chance at getting our families back, we have to be prepared."

"You're not trying to prepare me; you're trying to use me," Rhuth said, finally giving voice to her thoughts. "I'm still trying to figure out what my Gifts are, how or why they even work!" She shuddered as a chill wound its way through her. "I need time!"

Rhuth rolled over to find Pallah sitting, staring at the flames, her gloved hands wrapped around the straps of her knapsack.

"I understand. It took decades to learn my Gifts and to hone my skills. But time is the one thing we don't have. I should have trained you from the start."

"You're really trying to stop Erval to protect all of us?"

Pallah's eyes shifted in the light of the fire. "I'm no saint," she admitted. "But yes. I'm tired of hiding. And I won't be safe—all of Mothmar is under threat—until he's gone." She looked at Rhuth. "Do you want to draw in dinner, or shall I?"

Rhuth sat up. "I'll do it." And she reached out to the rabbits in the area, requesting a willing sacrifice.

Three came within the next few minutes, and Pallah dealt with two of them swiftly before shooing the third away.

"Amazing," she whispered under her breath. "You couldn't call a smilodon here, could you?" She shook her head. "Never mind; forget I asked."

"What happened to the one you had follow me? When I brought Halina to that city?"

Cutting and pulling the fur from one of the rabbits, Pallah wiped at her nose with the back of her hand. "When I use a beast like that...it's not like a normal tether. Or..." She waved her knife in Rhuth's direction. "Whatever it is you do. I was using an old body for that. That particular smilodon had not been alive for some time."

"Wait, and you...can control it?"

"I'm able to enter it. It's almost like a Maze. I locked my doors at the Temple Celestial, laid down on my bed, and siphoned my soul into the taxidermied cat. It's not pleasant. And I can only do it for so long. But I haven't found a smilodon since that one."

Rhuth didn't know if she should be nauseated or intrigued. "Was that the one you raised from a baby?"

"No," the woman whispered. "Not him. I would never do that to him." Rhuth thought she heard a catch in the woman's voice.

"I've been thinking," Rhuth said as the rabbits crackled and hissed over the spit. "If you truly want to learn what I do, I think you'll need to renounce all use of the Taka Reu. Whatever I'm doing, however I'm connecting...I know it has to do with the Children of the Sky."

"Fera?" Pallah blinked at her. "But you're using Tala."

"I think I'm using all of them. But I think the Children of the Sky control more than we have been led to believe. And to gain true connection to their power, you'll need to give up the Taka Reu."

"Simple as that?" Pallah asked, her voice small in the darkness.

"Simple as that."

It was quiet, only the pop and hiss of the fire between them. "Let's make a deal," the woman said plainly. "I'll try to change my methods, but you..." She pointed a stick in Rhuth's direction. "You need to practice your Gifts without throwing a fit."

Rhuth smirked. "I'll try."

"That's all any of us can do."

Pallah wasn't perfect, and although Rhuth wasn't close to trusting her...she felt her heart soften. She watched the woman prepare supper for the two of them, and Rhuth felt through her connections. The hunt had been made easier under the light of the Children of the Sky. And somewhere far in the distance, there was a smilodon.

Rhuth asked it to come join them, if it wished.

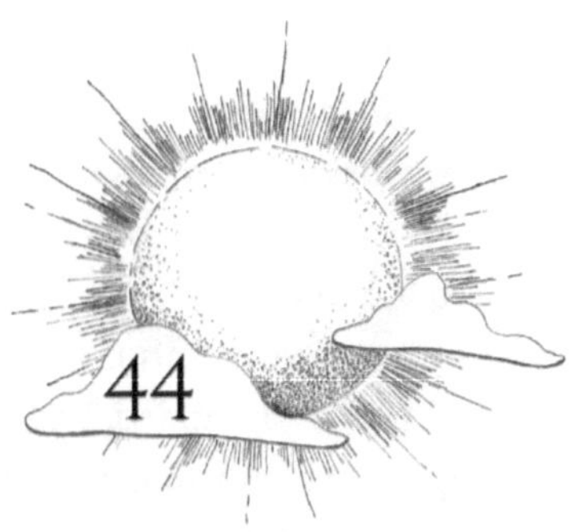

ESCAPE

Solyana

WITHOUT THE OPEN SKY, Solyana had no idea the hour, but she knew it was late. Soldiers turned to their cots, small fires sprouting in cleared rooms. She kept her shoulders square, returning the bows and affirmations sent her way by the devout. Many more ignored her, either steeped in the Taka Reu or uncaring for this newcomer.

This part was key, being recognized. For when the soldiers were undoubtedly asked about her whereabouts, they would all have seen her turning in for the night.

Feet marched to her side, the slight whoosh of wind blowing her hair as her guard slowed to match her meandering walk.

"Saint Solyana," he said, "where have you been? I've been searching for you these last twenty minutes."

"Oh, just bestowing my blessings on those who believe." A soldier to her right took a knee at her presence. She walked to him and pressed a palm to his head, hoping this would pass as whatever blessing she had promised.

"I am honored, Saint," the man said in a whisper.

Solyana nodded solemnly before turning back in the direction of her cot. The guard at her side fidgeted, apparently unsure what to do with her. He was the main hindrance to her escape, and Halldora knew it. Though, she wondered how much the soldier himself knew.

"I wish to retire," she told him as the cave narrowed. "Do you desire a blessing as well?" She faced him, a man not much older than she.

He blinked at her, his jaw working until his face broke into a sheepish grin.

"By the stars, yes!" He took a knee.

Solyana repeated the same gesture to this man whose brow was slick with sweat. "Your eyes be upward," she added, and meant it, praying the Celestials would not disapprove of her using her title to escape.

"And be filled with…light?" the man asked, raising his head.

"Indeed." A new convert, perhaps even in the past few seconds. "Oh…Saint Solyana, where is the map I gave you?"

Making a show of checking her sleeves and pants, Solyana sighed in exasperation, one hand on her forehead. "It must have fallen out of my pocket. I'm so sorry."

The man gave a stiff nod, feet already turning away from her. "If you're settled then, I'll find that and…"

"Please, go," she reassured. "I will sleep well here."

"I'll come back when I find it and make sure no one bothers you."

Solyana pressed a hand to her breast. "Very thoughtful, thank you."

The soldier bowed again and left.

Solyana retrieved her cloak from inside the cave.

Having memorized the map before handing it off to Phineas, Solyana made it to the mouth of the cave, where a wagon sat just outside, Bran and Barley already hitched. With most of the soldiers asleep, only a few stood watch as Ahren climbed onto the wagon's seat, reigns in hand.

Keeping pressed against the cave wall, Solyana watched the wheels begin to turn. She scanned for General Ivan and breathed a sigh of relief not to see him. There were two options before her now, and she was hoping she wouldn't have to resort to the second.

She prayed, asking the Celestials to return her power. But instead of Heitt, she pushed her Tala tether to form. Eyes squeezed shut, she petitioned the Mother of the Night, so different from the Mother Below.

A flicker of life extended from her, and she almost gasped. There again! Finally, she launched her Tala tether out to who she knew was inside the covered wagon and found him as she latched securely onto Vinur.

The wolf jumped from the wagon and headed straight for the only cookfire left burning inside the cave. Exclamations from soldiers peppered the air as Vinur did as he was bid, grabbing the meat from the spit and loping around the room. It was important that he acted playful, not territorial. She didn't want him to get hurt and was trusting these men to lean into some much-needed camaraderie.

Vinur played it perfectly. He skittered to the left, bolted to the right, and even laid the half-roasted meat before one soldier before playfully growling and pulling it back.

The wagon halted.

Solyana took her chance. With the attention on Gamaliel's wolf, Solyana crept quietly as a shadow into the rear of the wagon.

"Vinur! Come here, boy!" Ahren's voice came from the other side of the canvas.

Solyana encouraged the wolf to obey.

The soldiers, laughing and chatting, gave a few whistles to the small wolf before he leaped into the back of the wagon once more. Once he was inside, the wagon lurched to a start once again.

Solyana's eyes fell on Gamaliel, who was wrapped in blankets. She reached for her Heitt, hoping it would respond as well as her Tala.

It worked! But her elation was tempered as heat washed over her. Gamaliel was far too warm, the tether revealing a deep infection. Vinur curled up beside him, his ears twitching in her direction, though he kept his chin resting on his paws. She gave his soft ears a few scratches, thankful to be near those she loved once again.

The wagon trundled neatly out of the cave, and Solyana breathed deeply as night air cooled her skin. She stayed crouched near Gamaliel, afraid to relax, so filled with fear that Halldora's men would come running out any minute to take her—

"Oh!" Ahren exclaimed, and Solyana crouched lower, listening. "Are you to join us?"

Eyes wide, Solyana glanced around until dread pooled deep inside of her at the sound of a voice.

"Only so far as to get you on your way." There was a shift in the wagon and Solyana peered through a flap in the canvas to see two soldiers mounting the wagon's seat, squeezing Ahren between them.

"Never know what kind of unsavory folk are out here," the female soldier added. "Why don't you hop in the back?"

Ahren's shoulders tensed, and Solyana hoped what was passing through her mind was going through his as well. These soldiers were sent to kill him and Gamaliel, loose ends who knew of Halldora and her charge. Her suspicions were confirmed—the queen had never intended to keep her word to Solyana.

Ahren climbed through the canvas flap, and Solyana pulled down her hood, pressing a finger to her lips.

His mouth dropped open, eyes wild. "What are you doing here?" he whispered beneath the roll and rock of the wheels.

"Halldora would have forced me to serve her the rest of my life." She shook her head. "And I think she means to kill the both of you." She pulled Gamaliel's clammy hand into her own. "Did you know these two were joining you?"

"No." Fear was etched into every part of Ahren's face.

"Maybe if I make myself known now, they'll stand down if I—"

"I don't think your presence is enough to stop the inevitable," Ahren warned. "It's a bad look to kill friends of the saint either way. We have a few minutes before we're far enough from the cave." Ahren ran his fingers through his hair. "Solyana, I think we need to—"

Solyana pressed her hand on his arm, quieting him before he got any louder. "Kill them first," she mouthed.

Ahren nodded firmly, mouth set in a grim line.

"But then she'd be on us like wildfire," Solyana whispered.

"I'll watch your back if you watch mine." Ahren maneuvered himself between Solyana and the flap in the canvas. Solyana kept her eyes on the rear. She felt again for her Heitt. It hummed expectantly at her fingertips.

Minutes passed at an excruciating rate, and the chill of the night air did nothing to dispel the sweat snaking down Solyana's back. Perhaps they were wrong? The soldiers were quiet. Maybe they did just intend to escort them, keep them safe.

The wagon came to a halt.

She shifted to Vinur with Tala, ordering him to stay at Gamaliel's side, to keep guard and attack anyone who would do him harm. He placed a firm paw on Gamaliel's arm.

Switching back to Heitt, fire sparked beneath Solyana's fingertips, and her eyes found Ahren's once more. He gave a firm nod, palms open, surely tethering to the wagon itself with his Vior Fera.

A column of flame shot through the canvas and straight at Ahren who dropped to the ground, screaming. Solyana lunged forward as he rolled away, dousing the fire on his clothes. She returned her flame through the flap and the horses shrieked as the canvas caught fire, but no sounds came from the soldiers. Solyana poked her head through the gap to find the wagon's front seat empty. She stepped through, untouched by her own fire, and crouched low as the horses picked up speed.

Leaning around the side of the canvas, Solyana caught sight of the back of one of the soldiers as they gripped the cloth and swung themselves into the rear. The canvas was catching quickly, flames licking up the sides, smoke choking the air. Ahren released a shout from inside the wagon, and Solyana burst back through the burning gap, siphoning the fire back from the wagon, drawing it into herself like she did in Takanah.

The female soldier crouched over Gamaliel, her shortsword poised to strike. Vinur shot like an arrow, launching into her chest, throwing her to the floor of the careening wagon. Her sword flew out the back. Sliding across the wooden boards, she screamed as the wolf tore into the joints of her armor. Her body knocked the second guard off balance, who had Ahren in his grip, tossing them both to the floor where they slid together out the back of the wagon in a tangle of limbs, dropping them from view.

The fire winked out, the last of it eddying into Solyana's palms, and a wave of heat pulsed through her. She grit her teeth through the firesickness, pushing it down, trying to reign in her power, uncertain how to wield it in this tight space without burning all in the process. Vinur cried out, and Solyana tethered him, commanding him to escape while nausea rolled in her gut. She was going to lose control. The wolf leapt from the careening wagon, leaving Solyana, Gamaliel, and the final soldier inside.

The woman got to her feet, clutching one arm tight to her chest, face mangled and bleeding. A flicker of confusion came across her face before resolution took its place. She roared and lifted her hand until her crooked fingers held her Fera, tethering to Solyana's linen clothes, dragging her to herself.

Scrabbling over the floor, desperate to get Gamaliel out of the wagon, she grabbed his ankle, and the two were bumped toward the edge. His body dangled over it, the ground racing beneath them.

Stored fire rose up inside of Solyana, threatening to burst from her body. The woman grabbed hold of Solyana's braid, lifting it before slamming her head into the floor. Stars popped in her vision, her control waning. She was about to burst, but she still had a hold on Gamaliel. With a desperate scream, Solyana shoved him over the side where he rolled into the darkness. The woman was over her, stale breath in Solyana's face.

"You're no saint," she bit, her hand pressing down on Solyana's throat.

Solyana felt her scar rise to the surface as darkness rushed to the edges of her vision. Her eyes rolled back in her head, and her body gave into the firesickness, a wash of flame erupting over her skin before an explosion rocked the wagon.

The pressure on her neck disappeared, and Solyana gasped for air as the wagon flipped, tossing her through the charred and torn canvas. She rolled to a stop, tufts of grass and dirt beneath her fingernails. Peering up, she saw the wagon go up in flames, both horses running madly away, kicking as they went.

Stumbling to her feet, Solyana looked wildly around.

"Ahren!" she screamed, but little noise came from her damaged throat.

A howl rang from behind a small hill, and Solyana stumbled in that direction, her way guided by the wagon's fire. Bits and pieces of smoldering supplies and dark shapes Solyana tried to ignore passed underfoot. She set her jaw until she rounded the hill to find Gamaliel face down, his limbs askew. Solyana rolled him over and tethered him with her Heitt. She pushed healing into him, feeling his body relax under her touch. Relief coursed through her, allowing her a chance to breathe.

Vinur was curled up beside him, whimpering, eyes focused on his master.

"He'll be okay, boy," she reassured the wolf and herself. "Ahren!" she tried again.

"Here!" he called, and relief shot through every part of her. He was limping, his face splattered with blood, but he was alive.

Solyana ran and embraced him, grateful to not be alone. "What happened to the soldier? Are you hurt?"

"I'm fine. Him?" He glanced back at the direction he came. "Smacked his head on a rock when he fell off the wagon. It was quick," he said, pushing her gently away to look her over. "What about you? I saw that explosion. Where's Gamaliel?"

"I'm okay, Gam is with Vinur back there."

"Where's the other guard?"

"Gone." The woman had been directly overtop Solyana, and she was glad the darkness hid the parts of her that were now scattered over the ground.

"I tried to unhitch the horses with my Fera, but I don't think I was able to get them fully clear before we fell out of the wagon."

"I can find them." Solyana reached out with her Tala, finding Barley first. She drew him to herself, hoping Bran would follow.

Within minutes, the two draft horses were trotting back to them, their eyes wild. Solyana sent calm and peace into them as she rubbed her hand down their necks. Ahren fashioned a sled out of remaining untouched pieces of wood, easily crafting it with his Vior Fera. Solyana helped him drag Gamaliel onto it, affixing him with cloth and wrapping him up again until he was secure.

Ahren hitched the sled to Bran, deftly fixing the wooden boards with a strong Fera Solyana wasn't aware he had. Barley's harness had come off completely, but he waited patiently, still tethered to Solyana.

"They'll hunt us now," Ahren said gruffly as he wiped at his brow. "We need to go."

"Phineas told me of a place we can go." She looked up at the stars and pointed northwest. "A small fishing village."

Ahren's lips twisted in thought. "The smaller it is, the easier we'll be found."

"We have no choice, Ahren. Gamaliel is going to die if we don't find help now."

He raked his fingers through his hair and groaned, hoisting her atop Barley. Solyana began to shake, whether from the cold night air or shock, she wasn't sure.

Ahren scrambled on top of Bran, Vinur on the ground beside them. He looked back at Gamaliel. "I'll keep him stable, don't worry." Then he gave Bran's side a firm kick and led the way.

Sitting bareback on Barley, Vinur trotting beside her, Solyana left the burning pile of wreckage behind. Her fingertips traced the scar on her cheek, feeling its familiar form. The Celestials had accepted her back, it seemed, yet she couldn't help but wonder at the path before her and its inevitable descent into war.

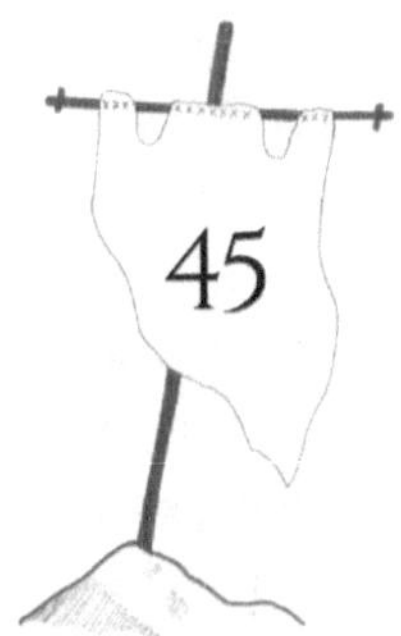

45

CONTINGENCY

HALLDORA

WITH ONE MISSIVE ALREADY crumpled on the floor, Halldora held the second, this one from the Crimson Chief. She stared at the sealed scroll, the slavering wax, and the imprint smashed into it. Alone in the tent her soldiers had erected for her deep within the cave, Halldora ripped it open in the light of a flickering candle.

Halldora of Thonethren,

Rightful queen. He always seemed to forget that bit, though Halldora knew better than to believe it was accidental.

The paths of the Way have led us to Skrim Sea. I am aware this is farther than the point of contact we agreed upon, but when the Way draws a connection, we must listen.

We will meet you when we can along the fjord outside of Thonethren to aid you in retaking your throne and washing your kingdom clean.

As followers of the Way, may nothing be concealed between us, lest we falter in our stewardship and our guidance become marred.

Your eyes be upward,

The Crimson Chief

Halldora sat back, skimming the letter again. He had the gall to doubt her credibility. What's more, he had purposefully sailed away from a perfectly advantageous position to follow some hair-brained notion they needed to go south!

She dropped the letter, not caring where it fell. The Crimson Chief, distracted like a maiden along a high street, and then there was Maral, the leader of the Beast Riders who also seemed to be taken with this "Way." Halldora had been promised war-worthy men—plus their ample tea supply. It was altogether a better deal than what Orson had offered. But, with her procurement of Phineas and the skills being taught to her men, Halldora was beginning to regret her decision.

Phineas. Her dear brother's steward, his closest confidant for centuries. She would not dismiss the possibility he had been sent to her as a spy, but if so, he would be a dead one. In either case, she would not relinquish him just yet. Not until she had wrung from him every ounce of usefulness.

And then there was the unfortunate loss of Solyana. Halldora leaned back in her chair, two front legs coming off the ground as she balanced and mused. She had already doled out appropriate punishments to the guard tasked to the girl. But where had she gone? None of the soldiers seemed to know. All claimed they had seen her go back to her cot. But Halldora knew better. She had seen the flicker of fear behind the girl's eyes when she sent her men away. Stowing away on the wagon, if that was what she had done, had unwittingly volunteered Solyana to be killed.

But the girl had teeth, it seemed.

Halldora's chair came down with a solid *thunk,* and she shook her head. Leveraging Solyana's sainthood was a surefire way to gain not only her men's loyalty, but the city in which Halldora would raze and rule. Thonethren was steeped in the Taka Reu, as was Halldora. Under her brother's tyrannical leadership surely the people were ready for change and be apt to follow the Celestial's saint. The Mother Below or the Celestials above, Halldora had no qualms about what was required of her. She would worship whomever she needed to be seated on her ancestral throne.

A saint, killed in the line of duty...there was a ring to that. Perhaps she could use it. Though, it was more likely the girl was alive, as they had only found the bodies of her two soldiers at the site. That made up her mind. She would send out a man to find them.

She snatched the letter from the floor and held it over the candle until it caught flame. The fire bloomed bright at first, before dissipating into a trickle of smoke, pieces of parchment breaking away until it crumbled to ash smoldering on stone.

Was this a reflection of her rule? A flaming spot in a darkened sky doomed to be snuffed out? A flash of glory only destined to fall to dust?

Her eyes flitted to the other crumpled letter, the one she had opened first. Her spies had informed her of Orson's return to Thonethren and subsequent execution. A smile touched her lips. Her brother wouldn't stand for any loss of loyalty; in this they were aligned. Halldora had been careful not to reveal details to Orson during their brief time allied. But he had seen her, talked with her. Erval would know she was coming.

She shook her head with refusal. He would never believe a man such as Orson at face value. He would send spies to verify, and she would be ready. Besides, she had not waited so long to simply be put out by—

The second missive caught her attention. It had sprung back to life, an orange and red glow that reminded her so very much of the mountain near which she spent her childhood. Something wormed tight around her heart, a recollection she hadn't felt in some time. It took a hold and squeezed tight, causing her breath to catch in her throat.

Fear. She felt fear.

For the first time, her strategist's mind locked onto that fiery mountain and wondered if Erval knew just what he had at his disposal. If he knew of the contingency that ran beneath his feet. Even thinking it put the intelligence at risk. She had to get her hands on more tea...or time with the steward.

She stood and crossed to where her guard waited outside.

"I need to speak with Phineas," she whispered into the cave's eternal night.

STRÖNDBAR

SOLYANA

THE FISHING VILLAGE PHINEAS suggested would have been easy to miss if Solyana hadn't been searching for it. From a distance it looked nothing more than a few boulders bordering a cliff face. But Solyana, exhausted and terrified though she was, heard the call of vendors at the market right as she was beginning to lose hope at finding anything at all. They wound their way through the boulders until the village came into view.

Two large poles carried a wooden sign hung between them boasting the script: *Ströndbar, People of Sand and Sea.* Seagulls coasted on brine-laced wind, shouts echoing from the market. A few half-dressed young people dove from the cliff into the clear waters far below.

Ströndbar sat tucked inside a channel that fed into the Kaldur Ocean. Similar to Takanah, the houses were colorful and bright. They stuck out like fields of flowers along the bank, inlaid into the steep and rocky ground that descended to the water.

Solyana looked back at Gamaliel, gut twisting. They needed to find a Healer, and quickly.

"There's no way to get the horses down there," Ahren said from beside her. "But I can use my Fera, and we can carry Gamaliel ourselves."

Eyes trailing the steep steps that wound their way down into the village, Solyana bit at her lip. "You've been going all night, Ahren. Maybe we can find someone to—"

"And risk us all getting killed?" he snapped and then took a steadying breath. "Never mind; I'll do it myself." He slid from Bran and made quick work of unlatching Gamaliel's makeshift sled. "They must have a stable somewhere near the top here... Hey!" he called to a sopping wet boy climbing up the stairs. "Where's the stables?"

"Over there!" The boy pointed to a large barn-like building, only accessible by two different swaying bridges.

"And a Healer?" Solyana asked.

"The witch is down by the rocks."

"The witch?"

"Follow the green stones along the sea!" He scrambled up the last bit of stairs as a group of boys came up behind him. "Just don't let her curse you!" Then, as a pack, they ran off the cliff's face, whooping and laughing as they fell.

"Wait here, I'll be right back," she told Ahren as a knife of fear twisted inside her.

Solyana tethered to Barley, leading him across the swaying bridge. Vinur tried to follow, but she shook her head.

"No, boy. Stay with Gamaliel."

The wolf whined but circled back to Gamaliel's side and placed his chin on his master.

The bridge felt precarious as a strong wind buffeted them. Barley stiffened through her tether, but with some coaxing, she got him to the other side. She did the same for Bran until she had both horses outside the stable.

"Hello?" she called out, and a head poked out of the last stall.

"Hi!" A woman about Solyana's age, carrying a pitchfork at her side, jogged out with a grin on her face. "My name's Tarin. Welcome to Ströndbar!" She extended her arm in a traditional greeting, and Solyana took it.

"Thank you. We just need two stalls."

"Beautiful horses." The girl circled Bran and Barley, a hand running down the length of them. "How long are you staying?"

"Not quite sure…" Solyana debated asking about the witch Healer but decided the less people knew the better.

"Well, the inn is cozy. We don't get many visitors, so they usually have vacancy."

"Thank you," Solyana said with a nod.

"Under what name shall I place the horses?"

Solyana's fingers brushed over her cheek; her scar was hidden—praise be. "Rhuth," she lied.

"What brings you to Ströndbar, Rhuth?"

Solyana swallowed past a dry throat. "Just enjoying traveling now that we have the green," she said.

The woman narrowed her eyes briefly before a smile returned to her face. "Aren't we all?"

Solyana thanked the woman and left before she could ask any more questions. Thunder rolled from somewhere off-shore as she made her way back across the swaying bridges, where Ahren waited with Gamaliel.

"All settled?" he asked, hoisting one side of Gamaliel's stretcher off the ground.

Solyana bent down to lift the other side, which was made significantly lighter by the help of his Fera. They began their descent.

"The stable hand was asking a lot of questions. I'm Rhuth now, by the way."

"I guess I'll be…Jon." He shrugged.

The moss-covered stairs branched like a spider's web, leading to different groupings of huts and buildings set into the cliff. A small inn was set in the center of the cliff side, looking dilapidated and unused. Though the town was small in number based on the amount of homes, the expanse of stairways made it feel larger than it was. Ahren led the way, keeping them on whichever path seemed to take them closest to the water's edge.

Delicious smells wafted through the streets, though they didn't quite mask the constant smell of fish.

Solyana's whole body was aching as they continued their descent, and she felt Ahren's Fera diminish as well. Though every muscle screamed for rest, her mind wouldn't slow for a second, her eyes constantly scanning the faces of passersby. Vinur picked along the way behind them. How long would it take Halldora to find out about what happened to her men? How fast would she deploy more soldiers to hunt them?

They had to get Gamaliel help and then leave without discovery, but the truth rang in the back of her mind: Gamaliel would need time to heal. He would be in no condition to continue their race toward Thonethren. She stuffed the thought down and gripped the wood tighter. He would heal quick enough. They would find the healer, and she would be able to mend his injuries in a matter of days.

They didn't have days.

She pushed that thought away, too.

A heavy mist descended on the cliff side, and Solyana had to take extra care on the stairs, eyes straining to see. Shadows passed through the mist along various steps and bridges that connected the cliffs of Ströndbar. The people seemed to be returning to their homes above the sea. All except for one shadow, a figure she couldn't bring herself to ignore completely. Vinur's ears twitched beside her, and she connected to him with her tether, feeling a wariness in him.

"The stones!" Ahren exclaimed as they came to a set of steps that ran along the surf.

Solyana, drawn from her thoughts, looked ahead. The sea-sprayed path was a beautiful turquoise. Dark clouds peppered their steps as they began across the slippery surface, balancing Gamaliel all the way.

"It's starting to rain," Ahren warned, the first few drops plopping onto the stones around them.

"I've never seen rain before!" Solyana exclaimed, feeling a mix of terror and excitement.

How odd, falling water that wasn't snow. Then the heavens unloaded their waters, rain pouring down in a deluge that almost blocked their vision entirely and soaked them to the bone.

"Is it always this heavy?" She was shouting over the thunderous rush, peering around Ahren to catch a glimpse of yellow at the end of the path.

"No! Keep steady! I think I see her house!" Ahren called back, and the two of them plodded on.

Teeth gritted, body aching, Solyana took one step at a time, slipping and sliding on the slick ground. Vinur kept tight behind her, trying to shield himself from the rain.

With lightning cracking overhead, the woman's hut stood squat before them at the end of the lane. A small window near the door glowed softly, promising warmth. The water, so bright and blue just before, was now like black and turbulent ink, threatening to pull them into its depths. Ahren pounded on the door.

It opened quickly, as if the woman had been standing guard, waiting on them to arrive. "What do you want?"

She was younger than Solyana had expected. Perhaps her own mother's age, with a long rope of hair that almost reached the floor. Small in frame with deep-set eyes, the witch by the water watched them keenly over an upturned nose.

"We have a man with a severe arrow wound," Ahren said over the rush of rain. "He needs help!"

The witch's eyes squinted, scanning Gamaliel from the doorway. "I'm not in the business anymore." She slammed the door.

Solyana locked eyes with Ahren, then turned to Gamaliel, soaked through on the stretcher. She dropped her end and pounded on the door.

The door remained shut.

"Please!" Solyana pounded again. "He'll die!"

A strangled cry came from behind her, and Solyana whirled to find Ahren grappling with a figure in the rain. Vinur had a hold of the person's pant leg and was jerking him closer to the edge. Solyana's heart leapt to her throat. The figure raised a hand above his head as if to strike Ahren, but instead a shadow shot from his hand and shot through the rain and into the night. She tethered Vinur, calling him back to the stones, afraid he would fall headlong into the waves.

"Help me!" she begged the Father of the Day as she released her Tala and readied her Heitt. Then, with her palms facing the scuffle, she shouted, "Ahren! Get down!"

Ahren dropped, and Solyana shot a burst of sputtering fire from her palms into what she could clearly see was a man dressed in dark clothes, all but his eyes covered. He screamed, and his short sword clattered to the stones. The flame dissipated quickly in the rain and Solyana rushed him, keeping her palms trained at his face.

"She's found us!" Ahren's voice barely reached her over the pound of rain.

"She'll have to try again." Holding her Heitt inside her palms, Solyana pooled it there until it formed a ball so hot, the soldier wouldn't feel his death—a small mercy. The rain hissed into steam as the fire grew, the soldier's eyes widening.

"Your days here are numbered. You betrayed the queen, *Saint*." He spat out the last word like it was poison before he turned to run.

Solyana shot the ball of fire in between his shoulder blades. He flew forward, collapsing before sliding off the green stones into the sea, where the waves hungrily carried him away.

Blinking against the rain, Solyana closed her fists and pulled them shakily to her sides.

The creak of hinges drew her attention back to the small hut. "Saint?" the woman from the doorway asked, eyebrows raised.

Soaked to the bone, Solyana nodded wearily.

"Bring the boy in. I'll fix him, and then you will leave this town as soon as he's able to walk."

In less than ten minutes, Solyana and Ahren were toweling off in the witch's dimly lit hut. After putting a kettle to boil, her dark fingers pulled back the crude bandage on Gamaliel's shoulder, and she hissed. "I'm going to guess this was no hunting accident."

"No," Solyana admitted, preparing to tell the woman all. "It's an arrow wound, but one inflicted by the nomad queen who has gathered a force intent on taking Thonethren." She hesitated. "You know of the king there?"

"I live on a rock, not under one." The witch began to mix different herbs in a mortar, and the room filled with an earthy aroma. "From what I've heard, the man doesn't deal with bows and arrows but in far more terrifying means."

"You've heard well, then," Ahren said. "His sister, Halldora, prefers more brash methods."

The witch, hunched over Gamaliel, worked in earnest. Solyana took a few steps forward to peer over her shoulder, nausea cramping her stomach. Not only was the wound bright red, but white pus seeped out the sides, and it smelled putrid.

Something like ice wrapped Solyana's body, similar to the *aska* that had kept a hold on her in the Cave of Red, but internal—in her very veins.

She gasped. "You're Blou Fera."

"Interesting..." The witch spoke softly, eyes still on her work. "I can't tether the boy."

Ahren shifted, eyes darting between them. "She's tethered to you?"

Solyana nodded, wishing she could drink her tea as the feeling of ice slid into her veins.

"Couldn't tether your assailant, either." Deft fingers prodded at Gamaliel's wound.

The ice disappeared, and Solyana released her breath.

"How long has he been like this?"

Solyana's eyes met Ahren's.

He shrugged. "Two days."

The witch's lips twisted. "Odd." She looked up from her work and folded her arms. "What are your names?"

"Jon," Ahren said quickly.

"Rhuth."

The woman narrowed her eyes but then turned from them, hands going to her mortar and pestle once more. "I'm Marnie. And I'll treat him as best I can...Rhuth, out of respect for a saint."

Solyana liked this woman already. "How long does he need?" Neither the Red Moon nor Halldora's forces would wait for them. They had to get to Thonethren.

Marnie straightened and blinked at her, lips pulling into a thin line. "Based on the severity and rapid progression of this wound, two to three weeks." She folded a small towel into a bowl of piping hot water and squeezed the water out of it. "Assuming, of course, he survives the night."

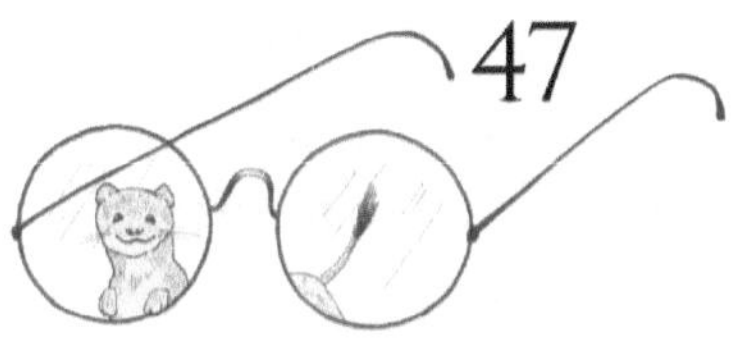

GAMES

PHINEAS

P HINEAS'S FOREHEAD HADN'T BEEN dry in days. He dabbed at it again with his soiled handkerchief and removed his spectacles to give his whole face a once over. Living alongside Erval had never been easy, but living beneath Halldora's hand was more than his nerves could take. He wondered if Solyana had wriggled through Halldora's net, if she had escaped the falling of the royal axe. Phineas wondered if he would be able to do the same.

Today, he would find out.

He hoped the girl lived, although his well wishes did not extend to Gamaliel. He thought of the two of them, sneaking kisses and whispered conversations throughout their trip.

Young love.

Phineas had no interest in such things, as they accomplished little more than clouding the mind and muddying one's judgment. Solyana was less pliable with Gamaliel around. So, Phineas had accelerated the boy's infection with his Blou Fera, if only slightly. His timely death was supposed to have left Solyana in need of comfort and guidance. It was supposed to have encouraged her to seek him out, to escape together. And there would have been no Gamaliel to stop Solyana from doing what Phineas would ask of her.

He sighed. Blaming himself for his stranded solitude was a waste of time and energy. Having spent so much of this trip running from connection, it was an odd feeling wishing for it. The caves in which Halldora had taken up residence lacked magma or any other line to the Mother Below. Without it, Erval's finnevel couldn't reach him so deep inside the rock.

These facts, he couldn't change. He had information to acquire, an escape to make. He peered through the dim light at the guard standing solidly at the entrance to his alcove.

Phineas cleared his throat.

The guard ignored him.

He tried again. "Excuse me?"

With obvious annoyance, the man turned and sneered. "I just changed your bucket last night."

"And for that, I thank you." Phineas gave a small smile. "But I was simply wondering at how many days have passed since my arrival?"

The guard snorted and turned away, ignoring him again.

By his own calculations, Phineas believed the Red Moon would arrive in roughly one week. It simply came down to who could overtake whom in a game of stökk. In the end, it would have to be Phineas with all the pieces. And to do that, he would have to make his opponent believe they were winning before he toppled them off the board. And where once he was playing this simple game with Erval, now a third player, Halldora, was added to the mix.

"Up." General Ivan's voice jolted Phineas from his cot.

Was he to be brought before the Queen? Was she unsatisfied with his teaching? Perhaps she would extract what else he held tightly to and do away with him. Or was she simply wanting another lesson for herself? His mind wouldn't stop its racing.

"We're leaving." Ivan's brusque tone brooked no argument as he urged the guard by his side to unlock Phineas's chains.

"To Thonethren?" Phineas inquired.

General Ivan grunted and strode out, leaving Phineas scuttling behind him in the dark. He wouldn't be given any information, of course. He could continue on with Halldora; march on Thonethren at her side. But once the battle was won, his use to her would surely run out. No, he would approach his home on his own terms, or not at all.

He tethered to the stoat in his sleeve, calming him in one swift latch.

"Come on, little beastie," he whispered. "It's time to find Solyana."

ACCEPTANCE

PALLAH

PALLAH RAN TO FIND Issha. Her trip to Hekla with Erval had fed her fears until they were a roaring monster in her mind. But when she burst into her friend's room, she was answered with a dark and silent space, the furniture coated with dust.

Pallah was left to stew over her friend's whereabouts, perpetually sick to her stomach with worry. It took a week before she was willing to brave the question.

"Where is Issha?"

Phineas stopped eating, his eyes on his plate. The few servants who lined the wall shifted, their hands clasped before them.

Erval continued chewing as if nothing had been said.

"My lord?" Pallah cleared her throat and wiped her mouth with her embroidered napkin. "If I could—"

Erval's fist slammed into the table, plates and cutlery clattering in tandem.

Phineas let out a squeak.

Pallah sat up straighter, almost knocking over her wine.

"We leave the past behind, Pallah." Erval speared a piece of steak. He slid it into his mouth. "First your brother, now your friend. Are you still discontented?"

"No, no." Pallah shook her head firmly, her elegantly pinned hair loosening. A strand of it released, cupping her face. "I just visited her room, and..."

Phineas's eyes caught her own, and he widened them with warning. Sympathy, perhaps? Guilt? Pallah doubted either could be true.

"It was empty," she finished, reaching for her wine and staring into it to avoid Erval's steely gaze. "I'm not discontent, only curious."

Erval seemed to relax. "I think it's time you knew the truth, Pallah." He glanced at his advisor. "Phineas, do you think it's time?"

Phineas's eyes darted between Pallah and Erval, the man just as subject to Erval's mercurial manner. "Yes, sire."

Erval turned back to Pallah. "As you *requested,*" he said, gesturing with his cutlery, "I ceased her Taka Reu instruction and gave her more comfortable accommodations. She was so grateful, she insisted she begin performing the Taking again!"

Pallah's eyes narrowed, finding the information impossible to believe, but equally finding no cause for him to lie.

"Issha—smart girl. She saw the true benefits of the Taka Reu. She thanked me for having opened her eyes. I had to stop her from groveling at my feet, right, Phineas?"

"Right, sire." Phineas's voice held no inflection.

"She begged me to allow her to use the Brextant. I explained the risks, but she assured me she was ready. That it was her utmost desire to use the years she had accrued for the Mother's glory." Erval pressed a hand to his chest, apparently overcome with emotion. "I wish she had survived; I truly do." He gave Pallah a sorrowful smile. "A martyr for the cause, our Issha. You know how to choose good friends, that's for certain."

The wine glass in Pallah's fingers slipped, spilling its contents onto the table, her dress, and the carpeted floor. She made no move to rise, hardly felt the liquid as it seeped through her clothes and spread over her skin, turning it wet and cold. Realization and pain bloomed onto Pallah's face like a wilting rose, a slow grimace she couldn't choke down.

"She..." Pallah's throat wouldn't say it. Her heart wrestled her words away and shoved them into her mouth. "You killed her."

Erval's eyes bored into Pallah, his grip on his cutlery tightening. Then it softened, and his shoulders relaxed. "I've killed many people, Pallah, but not your friend. She sacrificed herself," he clarified. "I'm sorry you couldn't say goodbye. She didn't want to boast of her achievements. Truly, a humble servant." He sighed. "But science must soldier on. I tried it myself you know, the Brextant. I wouldn't allow just anyone on that machine. But it's impossible to utilize it while sitting upon it. It took quite a few years from me—left me with these little beauties." He motioned to the gray at his temples. "Only in my thirties, and I get this badge of honor."

Pallah squeezed her eyes shut and grit her teeth at his lies. She got to her feet, the chair behind her raking over the stained carpet, and she stumbled out the doors leading to the balcony.

Under the full moon she examined her dress, the stain spreading, her fingers sticky. Did Issha's blood coat the Brextant now? Had it been a violent death? Her mind conjured up images of Issha strapped to the device, her head held back as Erval somehow connected through the machine. Tears dripped to the balcony railing around her white knuckled grip.

What did the machine even do? She had yet to find out and wasn't sure she was ready to discover the answer. Regardless of its purpose, the means by which it was used was pure evil. Darker than Vil, darker than her father, perhaps even darker than Dahvid and his warped Maze. Erval had instilled his influence over Pallah since she was a small girl; how had she not seen the true darkness of his intent?

Even so.

In spite of seeing it now, she could not leave. Wind rippled through her hair and dried the tears on her cheeks. Ahren was still missing, and where else would she find the means and resources to find him? How else could she avenge Issha and bring this king to his knees? She bolstered her resolve, shoring up her heart with layer upon layer of grief and rage. She would make do with what she had been given.

Pallah had been nothing. But now? She had a position here, a purpose: the Lady of Thonethren who ruled at Erval's side.

Squaring her shoulders, Pallah walked boldly back into the dining room. She would not ask of Issha. She would not bother the king with questions of her brother. She would not request another smilodon. She was the Lady of Thonethren, and she would grow her own network of people willing to help her, to do her bidding.

All it would take was a bit of pressure pointed in the right place. And though such a thing would take time, with the Taka Reu, time was the one thing she had an endless supply of. She would make Thonethren a home for herself. No matter how long it took.

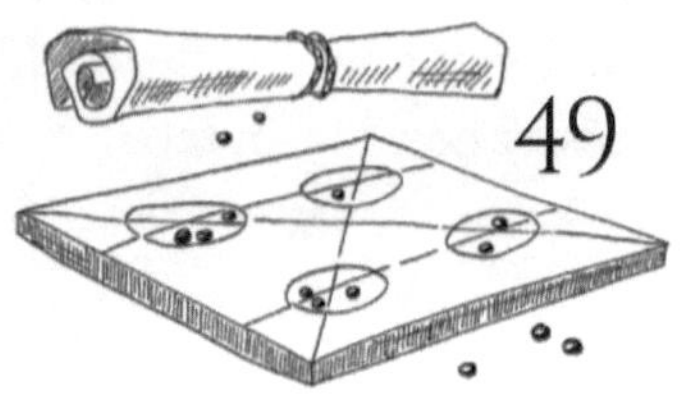

THE WAY

JONAS

BRIGHT LIGHT ACCOSTED JONAS through his eyelids, and he rolled over to escape from it.

"Time to wake up, friend." He did not recognize the voice.

Jonas scrambled to his feet, finding himself surrounded by people, all dressed like...vagabonds? Yet their attire was littered with weapons of all shapes and sizes, cured leather satchels, fitted vests... No. Not stranded islanders. These were—

"Pirates?" Jonas asked, his heart pounding.

The group chuckled, and one of them prodded Rorhan, who woke with a start. He sat up, spotted Jonas, and relaxed a bit, though Jonas watched the big man's fingers scour the sand—presumably for a weapon.

"And where did you hear that term?" One of the strangers stepped forward. "From a scroll of stories?"

The group laughed again, a good-natured sound.

Jonas's heart calmed, and he grinned along with them. "Actually, yes. Until I met Captain Viggo."

"Jonas." Rorhan's tone held a warning, and Jonas clamped his lips shut.

The group around them parted, and a woman stepped through, her attire decidedly more clean. A large hat sheltered glimpses of her freckled face, and curly red hair spilled out from beneath it. The color starkly contrasted against the cream of her shirt, which was held in place with a bright purple corset.

"Captain Viggo?" She placed a hand on the scabbard at her thigh. "Is he here? That man owes me a ship."

"I'm afraid he was lost in the attack," Jonas said quietly. His stomach growled, and he tried to swallow against the dryness in his throat. "Do you have any water?"

"Attack?" the woman asked, and Jonas's ears perked. He knew that voice. But it couldn't be her.

Rorhan stepped up beside him. "A kraken. It took the whole ship."

Standing beside each other, Jonas and Rorhan took in the group of pirates, and the woman before him removed her hat, revealing the face that lay beneath. Jonas's eyes widened as he stumbled backward—shocked. He'd been so young, it was hard to remember. But she had come enough times to the Temple Celestial to be seared into his memory.

"Fridmey?" Jonas said in an almost whisper.

Her eyes locked onto him, bright blue but shaped like her sister's, her mouth opening as she gasped. "How do you know my—" She blinked rapidly, as if taking in his appearance for the first time. "Jonas? Jonas?!" She covered her mouth with her hand.

Jonas nodded, already feeling pressure build behind his eyes. Never in a million years had he imagined meeting anyone from back home out at sea—and Solyana's sister, of all people!

Fridmey ran to hug him, leaving the men and women behind her dumbstruck.

"Uh, Chief?" someone behind their embrace called.

Fridmey wiped at her kohl-lined eyes and took a step away from Jonas, holding him at arm's length. "You were wondering why I brought you all here," she said to her crew, though she still held Jonas in her pale blue gaze. "I followed the Way."

"The Way?" Jonas's lips formed the words of what he'd been searching for. The reason he was away from his family; the reason he had been able to cheat death through a shipwreck. "You follow the Way?"

Fridmey grinned, fist on her hip. "You seek it?"

"I do. As does your sister."

Fridmey's smile faded slightly. "Solyana."

"Yes."

"We have much to discuss."

"Yes." Jonas nodded but then covered his growling stomach with his palm. "But first, can we eat?"

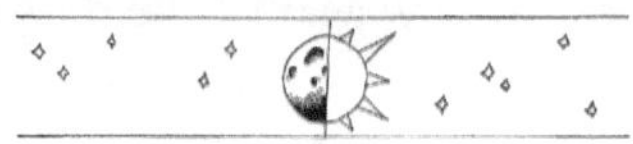

A fire crackled and popped in the balmy sea air. The moon hung low, and the stars were scattered beyond it like sea foam. Never before had they been so bright and alluring to Jonas; never had they held so much mystery. Ever since researching the Way, the *one* Way, he knew the Children of the Sky held much more to them than he'd ever thought or dreamed.

Now, sitting cross-legged in the sand across from Fridmey, he finally felt his years of searching were coming to an end. She followed the Way. She held the answers he'd been looking for.

"So, tell me of my sister, of your adventures. What's been happening?" Fridmey asked as she held her tea mug close.

Jonas held another containing the blocking tea, thankful Fridmey had some, as all of Jonas and Rorhan's supply had been lost. "After we left the valley, Solyana was able to acquire Heitt and Tala, but we quickly realized the sacrifice to do so was too great."

"She didn't use the Way, then?"

"This was five years ago. We didn't know anything about it."

Fridmey nodded and blew away the steam rising over her mug.

"We were attacked in a city called Takanah, chased out of the ice plains in central Mothmar, and lost Solyana and Odie in a cave leading to Endirinn for a time."

"Odie?"

"He was the keeper of the mammoths. Great guy. I miss him."

"Mammoths?" Fridmey's eyes widened, and a grin touched her face. "Sounds like it was quite the adventure."

Rorhan's bellowing laugh rang out from over the fire on the next sand hill, and Jonas's attention was drawn toward the man.

He smiled. "We found Rorhan through all of it, too. He was part of the tribe who sacrificed one of their own for Solyana's Tala. He and Lone are married; they have a daughter named Marin."

Fridmey's curls blew softly over her shoulders. "And what about Gamaliel and Solyana?"

Jonas rolled his eyes. "After they reunited, no one could separate them, that's for sure."

"After the cave?"

"No, after she returned from Mount Endirinn. She was up there for five years."

"What?" Fridmey lowered her mug. "That's not possible."

"I have my theories," Jonas said. "A few months after she disappeared, I was given the *real* Green Prophecy. And it became strikingly clear Solyana had gone about fulfilling it the wrong way. She was still able to break the curse that kept Ahren up on the mountain, and thus, the eternal cold; she is still part of the prophecy. But, because it had been done in a way not prescribed, it forced the curse and the prophecy to war with each other, keeping Solyana and Ahren in place for five years."

"I don't understand," Fridmey said over the lapping of waves on the shore.

"It's taken me five years to wrap my head around it." Jonas grinned up at a darkened shape of a palm tree. "To them, it was only a few moments in time. To us, it was half a decade. I believe it was for going about the prophecy the wrong way." He shrugged. "But we weren't reunited long before we had to split up again."

"Why's that?"

"I needed to find out about the Way." He motioned to Fridmey with an open palm, pleased to have accomplished just that. "And she needed to deliver Ahren to Thonethren to make good on a deal to recover Rhuth."

Fridmey's hand flew to her mouth. "Rhuth? What's happened to her? *Häfa* it all." She massaged her temple. "Mama was right! We shouldn't have left her there. But...she's with Priestess Avi, isn't she?"

Jonas winced. "We don't know. What we *do* know is Avi was no priestess. Her name is Pallah, and she was an imposter."

"What?"

Jonas explained the rest quickly. Trying to make sense of the twists and turns he didn't quite understand himself. To her credit, Fridmey kept up, her eyes tracking with Jonas's as the story poured from his mouth.

"And that's why we split," Jonas concluded. "I had five years of research; I felt ready to find and implement the Way as the one weapon we truly have against Erval and his overpowered Taka Reu. Well, that is, before we were shipwrecked. Now the only research I have is up here." He tapped his temple. "But I'm sure you can help me...right?"

Fridmey looked down, twisting her mug into the sand by her side. "I've been at sea for four years, Jonas. I left our valley believing I would never meet another person from there again. And when the green came? We were overjoyed, obviously. Solyana had done it! But there was also this ache for not knowing where she was, or Rhuth, for that matter."

"How are you here?" Jonas finally asked, the question having been burning on his tongue. "We were stranded just yesterday. If it had been much longer, we would be nothing but corpses."

"The Way," Fridmey said, as if it explained everything. "I was preparing for the upcoming battle against Erval, working with a few others. There's a nomadic self-named queen who is intent on taking the throne from him. She's going to be livid when she receives my missive that we've gone south, away from Thonethren. But we'll get back. The winds will favor us."

Jonas thought back to conversations with Phineas. "What's her name?"

"Halldora," Fridmey offered.

"Ah, I've heard of her."

"You and all of Greater Mothmar." Fridmey gave a soft chuckle. "If someone must rule, I'd much rather it be her than her brother, that's for sure."

Jonas's cheeks warmed. "The stars... They told you to come here?"

"In a way, yes. They created a clear path in this direction. I knew however we were to win, we had to do it going south instead of north."

"Solyana is on her way to Thonethren now. If we can impart information of the Way to her quickly, she'll be ready to meet the king."

"He's no king," Fridmey said with a shake of her head. "A king is a servant to his people, a ruler that upholds justice and truth. Erval is not that. The man is a tyrant, bent on wielding every person in Mothmar as a weapon for his personal use. We knew nothing of kings and grand cities when we left the valley. It's been a hard five years."

"Why did you leave?"

"Food." She shrugged. "The valley was barren. Papa had already left by then, intent on finding Solyana. The longer he was away, the faster hope dwindled. Mama stepped up to lead the valley in his place, and between the two of us, we were able to convince everyone of the need to leave. We tasked the Vior Fera to gather wood, build ships, and we set sail."

Eyebrows raised, Jonas studied the freckled woman across from him. "Impressive."

"Oh, the designs were awful, at first. We kept taking on water." Fridmey grinned. "But we adapted and survived."

Jonas sat up straighter. "How did you discover the Way?"

"When I first started sailing, we followed the stars and came across an island. I was intent on trading and leaving, but my mother befriended them, asking about their customs and their culture. She felt something different in them that I hadn't stopped long enough to consider."

"They taught you?"

"They did. It was the first time I had heard anything of the sort. I had grown up like you, believing the Celestials were three separate bodies. Each to be worshiped for something different, each giving us access to a different piece of the heavens." She pulled up a handful of sand before releasing it slowly back to the ground below. "The Celestials are not three; they are *one*. They are the heavens as a whole, and the stars themselves are what guide us. When you learn to read them, they show you what to do. My biggest regret is that we didn't find out sooner, that we didn't know about this when we were in the valley."

Jonas nodded, grateful for all of Fridmey's confirmations. "We couldn't have known," he said. "There was no one to teach us."

"The people we learned from—they claimed you didn't need a teacher. Simply the knowledge and love for the Celestials, the understanding they had your best at heart—it should have been enough. Sometimes I wonder..." Fridmey shook her head.

"Wonder what?"

"If Rhuth had it right all along." Fridmey caught his eyes in her own. "She always spoke of the animals as if she bore a relationship with them instead of a tether of manipulation. If I had only opened my eyes a bit sooner."

"You had no way of knowing." Jonas tried to phrase his next question delicately but wasn't quite sure how. "Why did you leave her behind?"

"Priestess Avi had all but convinced us Rhuth required her constant care. After Solyana didn't return, I thought she was simply too scared of my father. She stayed holed up in the Temple much of the time." Her eyes darkened. "Had I known who the woman actually was, I never would have..." she trailed off, biting at her lip and crunching a fistful of sand. "I pray Rhuth is still alive. And that she'll forgive me."

"I would forgive you," Jonas said before he could stop himself, cheeks growing warm. He blinked rapidly and looked away, grateful for the dark of night.

"Well, we have only a few more days before we need to be back up by Thonethren—to stop Erval, once and for all. Are you two with us?"

Jonas found Rorhan across the sand once more, the man silent now, staring up at the night sky. He would get him back to Lone and Marin if it was the last thing he did.

A flash of his dream, his recurring nightmare, caused him to squeeze his eyes shut.

No, nothing was set in stone. He could change things...if only he could figure them out.

"We're with you," Jonas said with a firm nod. "Now, teach me the Way."

A PROMISE

RHUTH

HEKLA ROSE IN THE distance. Rhuth could see it poking from out of clouds like an arrowhead. Rhuth had grown up at the base of Eldfall and had always thought it massive. But Eldfall was miniscule in comparison to the looming volcano, even at this distance. She and Pallah had crossed the snowy fields and now stood before something altogether new.

A field of geysers lay before them, the steam having melted the snow, leaving dry, cracked land. Across the field, if Rhuth squinted her single eye, she could see the beginnings of buildings—the edge of Thonethren itself.

"We're so close," Rhuth said to Pallah, who was crouched on the ground, unstrapping her snowshoes.

"Ready to make good on our deal?" Pallah stood and clipped her shoes to her knapsack. "I'll go easy on you," she reassured.

There was a man who lived beneath the mountain, and he was intent on ruling her land with a tyrannical fist. Was Solyana with him? Would he keep her like bait until they arrived? Rhuth gave a firm nod. "Let's practice. Have you been staying away from the Taka Reu?"

Pallah released something in between a laugh and a groan. "I said I'd try." The priestess motioned for Rhuth to follow. "Let's get down. It'll be easier to practice without the snow."

Walking amongst the geysers felt other worldly, as if Rhuth had found her way onto the Mother of the Night with all its craters and holes. She walked near a geyser as it released steam into the air, narrowly avoiding getting burned.

"Alright, you stand there." Pallah pointed to a spot within a triangle shape of geysers. "I'll be over here. I want you to practice connecting to what you have control over, one thing at a time."

Rhuth squared her body over the section and took a breath. How had she drawn all those creatures to herself? It hadn't been a conscious decision, really; it had just happened. She had been in peril, and nature had responded to her need.

Ember? The fox was keeping herself far from the unpredictable bursts of steam that rose from the ground. She felt the animal pause. *Would you bring your friends?* Even in thinking it, Rhuth felt foolish. Without true urgency, there was no real need to displace creatures who were happily about their own business.

"You drew them last time," Pallah said from a distance. "Why don't you try using your Fera this time?"

Staring at the ground beneath her feet, fear crawled up Rhuth's limbs. In the snow, she had rent the earth and almost lost herself to its depths.

"I don't know how to do it, Pallah. I don't know if it's safe to—"

"I will catch you if you fall," Pallah said. "Trust me."

Trying to conjure the determination within herself, Rhuth closed her eyes. She felt for the ground, the air around her, even the water in the air. And she did feel it. Not like the tether she had been taught by her family and then in Lóthkol, but a connection that was an extension of herself. One that began in her own blood and was one with the earth all around.

"When you feel you have a hold, I want you to attack me!" Pallah shouted, and Rhuth only then realized a mighty wind had begun to whip around her, tugging at her hair and clothes.

Eyes shooting open, Rhuth watched in awe as whatever connection she had made began to work. The pebbles and dirt around her feet shook; the geyser steam rose and coalesced into swirling suspended clouds, the cracked ground beneath her rumbled, and with a thought, a small platform lifted her into the air.

Keeping her mind on her task, fearful of falling from her new height, Rhuth crouched slightly, keeping her weight planted. She didn't doubt Pallah could catch her, but she wasn't ready to try it willingly.

Stretching her arms, Rhuth called on Ember, the falcons, and even the smilodon that had begun making its way from its home far off. She could feel them so clearly now and felt a pull from the sabertoothed beast to join it. A small grin lit her face as she tried it, allowing herself to enter into the beast as it ran.

Rhuth closed her eyes atop her hovering plateau, and opened them as a smilodon, running on all fours with dizzying dexterity as it tore through the snow on its way to the field. A laugh escaped her as she saw herself from the cat's eyes, high in the air, her hands outstretched.

To her left and right were several other animals, many of them familiar as they answered her call once more. The beast began to close off its mind, and Rhuth pulled herself from it, opening her eye as a girl again. Her scarred eye throbbed as if it ached to work. She looked down to see Pallah's face as the sabertooth came onto the geyser field.

Rhuth released her hold on the earth, requesting it lower her. With a terrifying swoop of inertia, the plateau descended until Rhuth was safely on the ground again, animals of all types stepping forward as if in ranks around her. Ember was again at the lead, but this time the smilodon was beside her.

Covering her mouth with a trembling hand, Pallah watched the procession with wide and wet eyes. "Did you do this?" Pallah asked. "For me?"

Rhuth stared at the mighty creature, its coat a dusty brown, close to the color of the ground around them, black stripes running over its face and body.

"I requested he come, and he did."

Pallah took a step forward, but Rhuth held up a hand.

"Wait, Pallah. Don't tether it with the Taka Reu. Try doing what I'm doing."

"But I don't know—"

Rhuth requested the animals stand down, and each of them near her relaxed, stopping Pallah in her tracks. "Just try."

Pallah nodded, bringing her emotions under submission as her face turned stoic and her body straightened with focus. "Where do I draw my energy from?"

"Instead of pulling energy from somewhere else, simply accept that the energy is already there. It's your job to request of it, not command it. You must leave room for its will, and perhaps it will leave room for yours in return."

"That makes no sense."

Rhuth chuckled. "Just try!"

Pallah puffed out her cheeks and looked up at the bright morning sky.

"Close your eyes," Rhuth encouraged. "Now, erase all thoughts of control, manipulation, and coercion from your mind."

Peering out of one eye, Pallah twisted her lips. "Only the three things I've been doing the last few centuries."

"It's never too late to change," Rhuth said with a grin.

Closing her eyes again, taking a deep breath, Pallah stilled herself.

Rhuth could feel the shift, like something solidifying in the air. She couldn't help the smile that came over her. *Please, help her understand*, she prayed to the Children high in the sky, only invisible as the sun was the greater light. *Give her this peace.*

Pallah's brow, wrinkled in concentration, began to loosen, and Rhuth could feel understanding dawn over her.

"Now," Rhuth said quickly, softly. "Remember the goodness of the Celestials. Think on them, the paths and roads that connect us all through life and through death. Remember that you are but a mere stepping stone. You are nothing without the greater work."

Rhuth was unsure if the woman was truly believing what she was saying, but the shift continued in her heart and in her mind. Then Rhuth felt it, the release of the smilodon from Rhuth's company as it took a few steps toward Pallah on its own.

Soon, the animal sat beside Pallah, staring up at her as if awaiting her lead.

"Pallah, open your eyes." Rhuth beamed.

The priestess jumped at the closeness of the sabertooth at her feet. "It worked!" She gasped. "Did I really use the Way?"

Rhuth shrugged. "You did what I always do. Doesn't it feel better to treat him like an equal?"

"It's...scary," Pallah said, reaching out a tentative hand to the beast. "To know he still has his full mind, that he could turn on me at any moment."

"But why would he, if you offer nothing but a chance to come alongside you?"

Pallah nodded, hand still hovering in the air. The beast reached up and pushed against it with its massive head, leaning into her and almost knocking her over. Pallah made a sound that was both laugh and choked sob. "I haven't had a smilodon in so long. I thought maybe... I thought Erval had eradicated them all. He was so bent on my full submission, my full loyalty... Even the thought I could love something else was impossible for him to live with."

"Well," Rhuth said, a new fire of hatred burning in her for the man. "He didn't get all of them." She focused on the smilodon once more and asked his name.

"Thank you, Rhuth." Pallah's eyes latched onto Rhuth's. "You've given me so much, and after all I've done. I don't know how to thank you."

"Just promise me you won't turn back to the Taka Reu."

Pallah blinked at her, twisting her lips. "I can't promise—"

"You can. You've said no to it once now, you can do it again. Also, his name is Magnus."

"Magnus." A slow nod bobbed Pallah's head as her fingers wove through the smilodon's fur. "I promise."

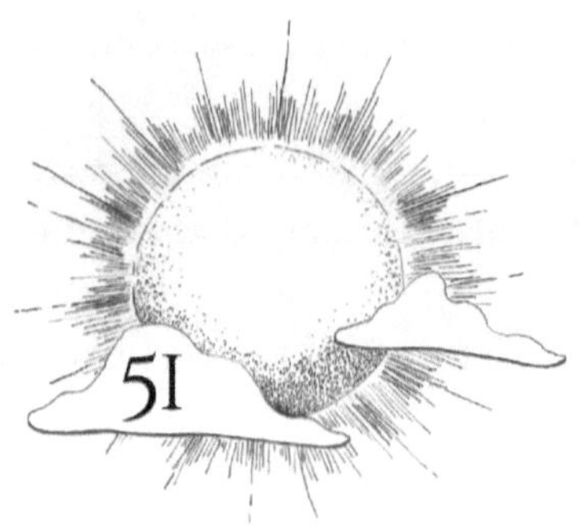

THE WITCH BY THE WATER

SOLYANA

"WE CAN'T WAIT HERE any longer," Ahren whispered as he and Solyana peered through dusty drapes.

Her palms squeezed her upper arms, each finger pressing one at a time against her skin. "I'm not leaving him."

She turned back to see the edge of Gamaliel's cot through the narrow doorway. Dust floated lazily through a solid beam of sun. Marnie was in there with him, humming while she worked.

"How many times do we need to have this conversation, Sol?" Ahren grumbled. "There's nothing we can do for him here. We're just wasting time." He stood up and began to pace, as he had done every morning.

"So we just leave him here?" She motioned wildly to the next room. "He'll become perfect collateral when Halldora finds him!"

"It's not like I *want* to leave him behind!" Ahren spat. "But I think we have more important things we have to focus on. Stop thinking with your heart for one *häfan* second and use your head! There will be no Gamaliel to come back to if Erval succeeds!"

Solyana opened her mouth to rebuke him, but her voice caught in her throat. She shook her head. "I left him once. I won't do it again."

Ahren's lips pressed to a straight line.

"Besides, we don't have Phineas. And I don't know the first thing about infiltrating the castle, do you?"

"You could find out," he suggested, his tone going dark. "The next time Erval tethers you, you can needle information out of him."

Solyana gave an incredulous laugh. "You overestimate my abilities."

He jabbed a finger in her direction. "You underestimate you." He walked pointedly from the room, hands jammed in his pockets as he took the stairs two at a time. She heard a door click shut.

Hanging her head, Solyana took a few deep breaths. She wondered if Ahren was still drinking tea every day, if he had asked Marnie for a supply. Or, if he had stopped, would he try to do what he was asking her to do?

Living with the incessant anxiety of discovery coupled with Gamaliel's health, she found her stomach was bound in a constant knot. Marnie worked all through the day, keeping Gamaliel on a strict regimen of tinctures, medicines, and rounds of Blou Fera healing.

It was difficult to find out more about Marnie, as she kept mostly to herself and preferred to work in silence. Solyana thought she had seen her use Vatin Fera but had pushed the prospect from her mind. If she were using the Taka Reu, if she had gained other Gifts by Taking them...but no. Solyana had been keeping watch overnight and was exhausted. Perhaps she had been seeing things. Tethered to Gamaliel with Heitt, she was careful to notify the Healer of any changes. He had woken in fits, but never enough to hold a conversation, never enough to reassure her when everything inside of her was screaming.

He *was* improving, though only just.

She rubbed her eyes, her body longing for rest. Ahren hadn't been sleeping either, his endless pacing making the floorboards creak and groan in the night. His argument hadn't been wrong. They were running out of time.

She exited the small home, finding her way to a jutted outcropping of rock close to the sea and practiced implementing what she'd learned from Phineas. It had been difficult at first, but she thought she was getting the hang of it. In fact, she was finding peace in the meditation it required. However, she wouldn't know if she was successful until he tried again. The thought of him stepping into her mind, even on the path she had created, sent fear coiling her muscles and drying her throat.

The ease at which she had allowed him before, during her journey through the caves below Mothmar, terrified her now. Had she really so readily accepted his voice, as if he had belonged there?

She had learned her lesson. She would never welcome the king of Thonethren again.

A window pushed open from the side of Marnie's house, and Solyana turned to see the Healer herself. "I think it's time you told me who you really are...Solyana," she said, her lips in a grim line.

Solyana stuttered over her words, fear rolling over her skin. "How did you—"

The woman displayed a scroll, extending it with one long-fingered hand.

Solyana gasped. A depiction of her—scar and all—was drawn across the page, with script running beneath.

Solyana Marusda, false Saint of Endirinn, is wanted for crimes against the crown.

Any information leading to her capture will be richly rewarded.

Harboring her or her two companions will be considered high treason.

Your eyes be upward.

All hail the Queen of the North, True Queen of Thonethren

Her Majesty Halldora Mikkaelson

Dread pooled in Solyana's belly, and she kicked herself for not listening to Ahren sooner. Would this Healer turn them in? Would she have to leave Gamaliel to flee? Would they catch and kill him? Would they find her?

Perhaps she could overpower this Healer. But even as she thought it, Solyana knew it was false. She could not contend against Blou Fera. Neither of them could.

"I didn't bring this to hand you over. I came to warn you."

Solyana leveled her eyes on Marnie, searching for any hint of a lie, of betrayal, but found none.

Emotion wound its way up her throat, and she choked back a cry. "What do we do?"

"We don't make it easy for them, that's what. Did anyone see you before you came to my home?"

"Yes," Solyana said miserably. "The stable hand and a group of boys who were cliff jumping."

Marnie waved them away. "Tarin won't tell a soul; she may even help us. The boys? It'll be easy to keep them quiet."

"How much longer must we wait until we can leave?" Solyana's mind was on Gamaliel. She had told him she wouldn't leave him. She had *promised*.

"I can hide one sick man better than I can hide three known fugitives. Her soldiers are staying at the tavern." The woman leaned her forearms on the windowsill. "You've got to leave in the next day or two."

"And why would you help us?" Ahren's voice cut through the crash of waves as he rounded the corner of the home, his eyes hard as chips of dark rock. "You risk your life for ours."

Marnie straightened. "I am Blou Fera. Do you know what that means, boy?"

"You can manipulate blood," Ahren answered simply.

"It means I'm hunted." She spat the last word. "There were many Blou Fera in my family. Each of us were hunted down by those who practice the Taka Reu. The king of Thonethren? He would Take from me in an instant. This queen? She masquerades as a ruler of the people. She rejects her brother's Taka Reu rule and yet expects us to believe she is as young as she portrays herself to be." The woman's face grew slack, sorrow leeching into her skin. "At least with the king you know what you're getting. The queen? Well, she's nothing but a wolf in sheep's clothes.

"I don't want either Mikkaelson getting what they want." Marnie stood taller, releasing the sill and smoothing her dress. "And besides," she continued with a small smile. "What good is this Gift without the chance to use it?" She took a breath and leaned forward to close the window. "I'll give the two of you some privacy."

With the window closed, Ahren turned to her. "We leave tonight."

Solyana's heart sank. "They don't know for sure we're here, or they'd be beating down doors. No one but a few kids have come by Marnie's, and no one has seen us."

Ahren's brow furrowed. "Solyana—"

"Gamaliel is improving! I can feel it in my tether. He's doing better. A few more days and he'll walk out of here with us. I promise he—"

"Solyana."

"He can come with us! He can ride with me! I'll make sure he doesn't slow us down! Vinur can help! We need them both! We—"

"Solyana." Ahren's rough hands pressed either side of her face, focusing her erratic gaze on his own. A sob broke through, and then another, her eyes filling with tears.

"I can't leave him again, Ahren." Her shoulders shook with sobs.

He brought his forehead against her own, eyes closed, breathing deep until she calmed, matching his breaths.

"I can't force you to come with me. But I am going." He pulled away from her, finding her eyes once more. "If there's a chance Pallah is in Thonethren and needs my help, I'm going to find her. And I think...I think you should, too, for your sister."

Solyana didn't stop the tears as they fell from her cheeks, the lump in her throat refusing to dissipate. No matter how she wished the circumstance to be, Ahren was right. A war was coming, and her little sister could be caught up in it. Who would protect her, if not Solyana? She would have to do exactly what she had promised not to do. Again.

She had to leave Gamaliel.

They spent the rest of the day peering out of windows and planning what little they could. Without Phineas, they would have to get to Thonethren as early as possible to search out a way to infiltrate the castle before the Red Moon. It wasn't impossible, but it was close enough to it.

Ahren turned in for the night, and Solyana promised to wake him in the wee hours.

Finally alone, she wove her fingers with Gamaliel's. "I have to break my promise," she told him softly. The fire crackled and popped, filling the room with things she couldn't quite voice. "I love you, Gamaliel." She leaned forward and pressed her lips to his forehead, remaining there a moment longer than it warranted, breathing him in.

A scratching noise drew her attention to the window near the hearth. Vinur growled but Solyana patted his head, and he quieted. Solyana released Gamaliel's hand and stepped up to it. Two tiny black eyes stared at her from the darkness, and it took a second for Solyana's eyes to adjust when she realized it was Phineas's copper colored stoat.

"Kopar?" She opened the glass pane, and the tiny creature slid into the room.

He ran up her leg, sniffed her neck, her hair, then gave her hand a tiny nibble before springing off. With a mighty leap, he flew from the window ledge, back into the darkness of the evening.

His touch twinged something in her Tala tether. She latched onto the fleeing stoat, and her mouth went slack as information flooded her mind. Phineas was on his way, mounted on horseback, running for his life—for hers. She pictured the direction they'd gone to arrive at Ströndbar, the small hut at the base of the cliffs, and the stable at the top.

She had never experienced information inferred via Tala before, but it was so natural, she wondered why she hadn't done it before. She hoped the stoat would make it back to Phineas, that he would latch onto it quickly and receive her instructions.

"What was that?" Marnie's voice came from behind her, and Solyana turned to see the woman clutching her nightrobe, a flickering candle in her hand.

Though she had been confident in her decision just a moment before, now apprehension flooded Solyana instead. What if Halldora had made him find her? But no, she was not so subtle as that.

Solyana set her shoulders. "We'll leave tonight. Is there a way to notify Tarin to ready our horses?"

Marnie nodded slowly. "Leave it to me."

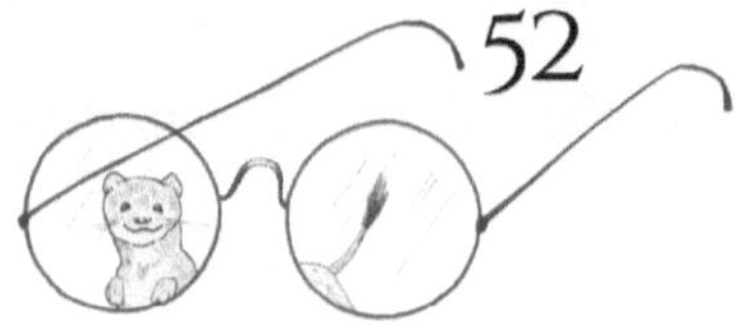

THE COST OF ONE

PHINEAS

THEY HAD GROWN LAX.

Phineas crouched over the withers of his stolen horse, reaching up for his spectacles and pocketing them before they could be stolen away by the wind. He would have to trust his horse's eyes. Phineas had once again used his rotund appearance and bumbling manner to get those around to underestimate him. Halldora, on the other hand... She had known better. She had almost seen through him.

Word would get back to her of his escape once they found the bodies. Ivan had left him with a few guards as the rest of them sorted themselves, readying to leave, to catch up to Halldora and her personal retinue marching in the fore. He admired that about her, the willingness to lead from the front. They had taken his finnevel upon arrival, but Phineas was nothing if not persuasive.

"Surely Queen Halldora would never deprive even her prisoners of the ability to see," he had whispered to the soldier responsible for it as they made their way to the mouth of the cave. "These spectacles give me nothing but clear short distance." He motioned to the glasses resting on his face. "If you expect me to ride, then I'll need the whole set."

The soldier had only hesitated briefly before tossing them in his di-rection. Phineas had slipped the device over one side of his glasses and the moment they exited the cave, tethered each man surrounding him at once.

With one quick strike, his Blou Fera halted the blood flow to their brains, and they dropped within silent seconds. While they were on the ground, he held their blood a few moments longer, until their hearts stopped altogether.

There had been no time to Take them.

Now, on the back of a galloping horse, he knew what had to be done.

Kopar had found Solyana, though later than Phineas had hoped. Though he'd been to Ströndbar before, he was unfamiliar with his current location and was at the mercy of his stoats.

He needed to retrieve Solyana and get to Thonethren before the lunar eclipse. War was coming, whether he liked it or not. He had seen it now with his own two eyes.

Did Erval know Halldora was coming for him? Phineas didn't think so. The king had grown too arrogant for his own safety. Too cocky for his own good. But Phineas had seen Halldora's army—the entirety of it. He had heard the talk amongst the soldiers of two separate factions coming to join her men: some kind of beast riders who were not led by Orson of Takanah and a fleet of ships captained by someone called the Crimson Chief.

Phineas dug his heels into soft flesh, pushing his horse harder. Stopping the battle before it began was Mothmar's best chance of survival. Only Phineas knew of Erval's truest intentions, his back-up plan, should all else fail. He remembered the young forsaken prince back when he had first been ousted from his throne, so many centuries ago.

"Why establish your kingdom in Thonethren?" Phineas had asked the young prince, wiping at his spectacles. "There are other, more beautiful, places to rule. Step out and create your own kingdom. Earn the respect of your father and sister."

"How could you even suggest such a thing?" Erval had responded while juggling three small stones in the low light of the torch lamps. "I could never leave my mountain."

"Hekla?"

"My mountain," he'd repeated, catching the stones. "My weapon."

Phineas had blinked at him. "Weapon?"

Erval had chuckled. "You're quite slow for an inventor, Phineas." The stones took back to the air, rising and falling and rising again. "When my father rejected me, I felt powerless. They drank a horrible tea that prevented my Mann Tala from affecting them. Never again will I feel that weak. I want to hone my skills to a point where I can control the Mother herself. The mountain, in all its glory, with all its bubbling and boiling possibilities—at my disposal."

"But it's dormant," Phineas pointed out.

"Incorrect! It has erupted. It's in the scrolls. Some priest was up there at the time; they say he toppled in."

Phineas had rolled his eyes.

"Regardless..." Erval ceased his juggling, the stones clacking against the ground. "What if there were a way to tether the mountain itself? To access the power of the Mother Below, the red flow beneath the earth? What if I could control her as she is? What if she herself fought for me?"

"I doubt a god would bow to the whims of a man," Phineas had said.

Erval had smiled. "I think I could convince her."

Phineas had grinned himself. "You're mad."

That was the last they had spoken of the mountain and controlling its fires below. But he knew Erval too well to think the king had forgotten of such an endeavor.

They had both been so young, and with so much potential. Erval, with his talk of valor and reform; Phineas, with a future of innovation ahead of him. If only he had stayed at his father's farm instead of trying to make it as an inventor in the big city.

His back began to ache as he moved with his horse, intent on keeping up the speed as long as possible. Phineas would atone for his mistakes; he would make good on his promises. And if one girl was the cost to save so many?

So be it.

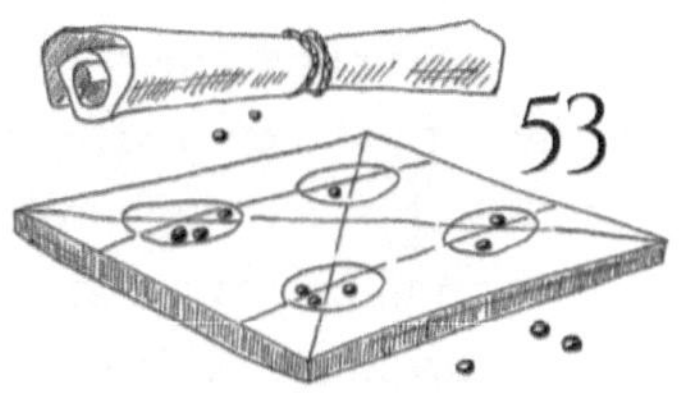

SEA OF STARS

JONAS

"The Children of the Sky?" Jonas asked for what felt like the hundredth time.

"Yes!" Fridmey laughed as she paced the sand, hand outstretched toward the stars above them. "You see this constellation right here?"

"The Hjötur?" Jonas peered up at it again, wishing he had the telescope he'd crafted back in Endirinn. "It's...incomplete. So, not the Hjötur?"

Fridmey shook her head, her curls dancing in the moonlight, her face lit by the light of the fire burning at their feet. "To the left of the Hjötur. Do you see where the stag is missing the points of its antlers?"

Squinting, Jonas spotted what she was talking about. "Yes." Though he didn't understand the significance.

"I've spent the last five years sailing all around Mothmar, exploring every ocean and sea. When we first left our valley, no one knew where to go, so I suggested we follow the constellations. That's what led us to the island where we were shown the secrets of the Way."

"That's exactly what I've been looking for!"

"They've since abandoned that island, so it's a good thing I found you here." Fridmey grinned and ruffled his hair. Jonas swatted at her, heat burning in his cheeks. It was hard to remember this was Solyana's sister; she was so different, both in appearance and personality. And she'd grown up, just as he had.

"Right about the time we'd made landfall on their island, they were heading out as missionaries into Greater Mothmar."

He had heard her mention the term earlier. "Greater Mothmar?"

"Everything on the mainland. All the islands off the coast are known as Lesser Mothmar to them. It's a bit of a joke, considering the population of Lesser Mothmar makes up more than that of Greater Mothmar." Fridmey tilted her face back up to the sky then shook her head. "I can only hope my father discovered the truth." She straightened and gave a sad smile. "I have hope I'll find him again one day. But you're no stranger to losing people you love, too, I know."

Jonas blinked. "I was only three when they died. I don't really remember them." Though he had dreams of them, and quite recently, too. "You said your mother sails with you?"

Fridmey rolled her eyes. "Yes. And I love her, though she does get on my nerves sometimes. I see why Papa had a hard time being chief with her by his side. When she agrees with me, it's not so bad—though it tends to be a rare occurrence. She's on the flagship right now." Fridmey motioned toward the sea, but Jonas saw nothing in the darkness. "The whole armada is there, waiting for my return. It's made up of about a hundred from our valley, but a few thousand have been added to our number during the last five years."

Jonas's mouth dropped open, only now understanding the true scope of Fridmey's force. The commanding woman standing before him was a far cry from the valley girl she had been.

"I only brought a few to shore to explore with me." She cleared her throat and motioned toward the people in the distance who were with Rorhan. "We went back to the valley to check up on Rhuth and Priestess Avi. And a few of my people didn't take to sea life, and others were old and wanting to return to our homeland. But the valley was abandoned." She waved her hands in front of her. "Ah! You keep distracting me with your questions. Here's the big reveal! When we constructed our ships and left, we quickly discovered that every island off the coast of Greater Mothmar held no semblance of cold. They were balmy, warm, and it became truly clear our land had been unnaturally cursed."

Jonas's mouth dropped open. "All of the islands were...warm?"

"Yes!" Fridmey clapped her hands, shaking her head. "I knew then, a life at sea was for me. I've been sailing, exploring, and discovering new places ever since."

"So, the Way," Jonas prodded, knowing his time to get this information to Solyana was growing short. "How did you discover your worship of the Celestials was faulty?"

"I wouldn't say faulty; more like incomplete. We've spent our whole lives worshiping the Celestials as three different beings: the Father of the Day, Mother of the Night, and the Children of the Sky, right?"

Jonas nodded, running his fingers through the sand.

"While there's evidence Gifts do still come from these entities, they were never meant to be worshiped separately. In fact, we were never meant to only get one Gift or another. We were created to have access to all Gifts. I met a group of monks living on an island on the northeast side of the continent, and they had the oldest scrolls I've been able to find. They had no idea we had shifted our worship to individual Celestials instead of revering them as a whole.

"They were aghast and called us heretical! I explained it was how we had been taught, that it was what the world had been brought up believing. And according to them, it turns out, there had been some faction of the Taka Reu, back in its inception, before it had its name, that decided the best way to cause dissent within Celestial worship was to simply inject slight falsities into what Celestial worship actually was and how it worked. This seeped into tradition over time, and pretty soon, we had fractured." Fridmey held up her hands, forming a circle in one spot, then another, then a last. "Three factions: Heitt, Fera, and Tala." She drew her hands outward encompassing all three circles. "When we were always supposed to be following one and gaining the powers of three. The Way. Well, more accurately, the Leídín. It's what these monks called it, the most ancient name."

Jonas stood, clasping his hands behind his back, beginning to pace. "So, you're saying we could access the powers of all Gifts without any type of transfer—death or Taking?" His research had proven as much, but hearing it straight from Fridmey, who had actually met these monks, only strengthened his resolve.

"Right." Fridmey nodded. "Although, I would add, this is more than just knowledge of constellations and theory. You must believe in your heart and truly surrender to the will of the Celestials. Without that, it's just awareness with no true power." Fridmey sat down and wrapped her arms around her knees. "I'm not sure if you've heard from my people, but I'm known out here on the water as the Crimson Chief."

Jonas stopped pacing, turning on her. "You're the Crimson Chief?" A laugh bubbled from his throat. "Captain Viggo was terrified of you! He said you were the fiercest pirate to ever sail the four seas." He raised an eyebrow in appraisal. "How can you be both a staunch believer in the Way while also a chief named for shedding blood?"

"Crimson." She pointed at her locks. "My hair. People hear the name and assume I'm violent." She shrugged with a sly smile. "I simply haven't dispelled the rumor—it comes in handy when people see my flags in the distance. We have never really had to harm anyone; others tend to give us provisions willingly."

Jonas shook his head with a grin and resumed his pacing. "How very clever of you."

Fridmey nodded, eyes closed. "That doesn't mean I haven't done my fair share of protecting my people. I'm not out to pillage and plunder, but I'll fight for my own."

"I feel much the same," Jonas agreed and caught her up on everything that had happened after Solyana's descent.

"Once I established who was part of the true prophecy," he concluded. "I knew I had to set out to fulfill my role."

"Which brought you here?"

"Well," Jonas said with a sigh. "Yes, I suppose. Though a shipwreck was never part of the plan."

"The Way holds its own intentions, higher than our own," Fridmey said wisely. "And this new prophecy?"

Jonas cleared his throat and repeated the prophecy that was now forever sealed in his heart. When he was done, he opened his eyes to find Fridmey smirking.

"Sounds like the old one."

"It's not," Jonas said modestly. "But I believe I'm the one who must follow the paths of the sky."

"But I'm the one who just taught you—what if it's me?" Fridmey grinned and pushed Jonas's knee playfully. "But what do I know? I'm just an uneducated pirate."

Jonas smiled but looked down at his hands. After all his research, he had reason to believe the prophecy was the thread of commonality that brought all the people involved together. A spider web of interconnecting truths and pathways that drew them all in before dispersing them apart. Could that mean Fridmey was the path follower? What would that make Jonas? Fear and doubt slithered along his spine, but only for a moment.

His dream. He couldn't deny his dream.

"Regardless of who it is," Jonas said slowly. "I think it's time I know the Way, wouldn't you say?"

"I would." Fridmey grinned. "And if you're determined to figure it out tonight—"

"Which I am," Jonas said eagerly.

"Then you'll need to stay up all night."

Jonas's eyes found Rorhan, who was now sleeping soundly far down the beach. His fire matched Jonas's own as it all but burnt to embers. "I can't rest at all?"

"When does Solyana need this information?"

"Yesterday."

Fridmey nodded and raised a hand, accompanied by a high and quick whistle.

A man rose from the low fire, jogged over, his ears heavy with golden jewelry. "Chief?"

"Get my friend here the Map of Leídín and my spyglass."

With a firm nod, the man jogged away.

"Dearest Jonas," Fridmey said with sudden fervor. Her hand was on his cheek, and it grew hot beneath her touch. "Do not be tempted by sleep this night. For if you falter, even a little, our enemy is given a chance at victory."

It was already late, and Jonas knew he was going to have a hard enough time staying awake. "Will you stay up with me?" The man Fridmey had sent off returned, the two items requested in his hand. He passed them to Jonas, who took them as if they were sacred.

"This vigil, you must do alone." Fridmey stood and dusted the sand from her trousers. "I will see you rise a changed man with the sun." She turned on her heel and walked away with her companion, leaving Jonas alone beneath the vast sea of stars.

SPIES

PALLAH

PALLAH HAD ARRIVED IN Thonethren a fool, a lovesick teenager. Now, fifty years later, she had fallen in step with the man that captained this darkened ship.

Her memories of her time before were trivial, useless. Even the thought of her brother, which was the only thing that incessantly plagued her, was nothing but a buzzing gnat in her ear.

Side by side, she and Erval ruled Thonethren with little opposition. Skirmishes would arise now and again, but crushing them was child's play. Nothing could stand in their way now that their supply of years and Gifts had grown to insurmountable heights. With the stamina and strength of hundreds of people, Pallah felt invincible.

Phineas still tinkered with the machine in the basement. Pallah had asked Erval of his plans with it. Who was he planning on placing in the seat next? But he remained vague on the subject, obtuse even. It only served to deepen her impatience. Were they not supposed to be partners in this? Co-rulers of Mothmar?

Her life had become a monotonous turn. Meals with Erval and Phineas, strolls through the market, the occasional sit-in on meetings of strategy with Erval's generals. All driving toward what? In the little village of Sodur, most people found someone to share their life with, settled down, and had a family. But Erval had made it unjustly clear he would never be that for her. His desire remained in fleeting affairs with women from the brothels or courtesans from the northern districts.

Pallah never thought she would find herself envious of those working women. Yet, here she was, watching them exit his room escorted by servants as if they were royalty themselves. False royalty, more like. The dross of the earth. Pallah watched from her balcony as another set left the castle, one appearing to walk with a limp.

She held up her perfectly manicured hand and examined the work her servants had done just that morning. They had come up with a new polishing system that caused her nails to gleam in the moonlight, as if a light glowed behind them that glittered and shone.

Pampering herself hadn't been her sole responsibility these last few decades, however. She had been doing what she had promised herself, forming her network of spies. They crawled all over Thonethren and beyond. A group of three of them, in fact, were the closest she had ever been to finding Ahren.

Standing on her balcony now, snow falling lightly around her, coating her hair and dress, she awaited word from these spies. It was well into the summer season, but the snows hadn't stopped. As if winter was a guest overstaying their welcome, the cold simply refused to leave. Phineas was in a tizzy about this development, and although it also worried Pallah, she chose to poke fun at his concern.

A flash of dark wings drew her eyes in the deepening dusk. The crow was an unlikely creature to carry her missives, but she found she had a fondness for them. Already they were in abundance in Thonethren, and Pallah assumed they would draw less attention than a more exotic bird. And now that she had any Gift at her fingertips, it made manipulating creatures second-nature, no matter what the species.

The crow flew silently to her balcony, where it came to a stop on the rail, flapping its wings twice before folding them gently behind it. Pallah bent, untied the scroll, and held her palm open for the nut the crow was undoubtedly waiting for.

"Your payment, Princess Falej," she whispered as the crow's eye flashed in the firelight coming from Pallah's room.

Falej gobbled the nut and then pecked at Pallah's hand. "Hey! Do you have more than one missive?"

The crow shook her head, ruffling her feathers. "One," the bird repeated. "Missive."

"One note, one treat. Don't get greedy." She would never get used to them talking, the crows. Phineas said they merely repeated phrases and sounds, but Pallah had worked with Falej long enough to believe there was more to it. There was intelligence behind those eyes, far more than any of them gave the creatures credit for.

The crow's blue-black feathers flashed in the firelight, and she cocked her head in Pallah's direction. "Wax moon," she said with a click before launching into the night.

Finding the celestial being among the clouds, Pallah noted it was in fact waxing. She shook her head as she unraveled the tiny scroll.

Vai,

The very top of Mount Endirinn holds something of a supernatural bent. We have yet to penetrate the way in and have lost Ulrist to the storms. Our interrogations lead us to believe the curse must be broken by someone of prophecy. We request leave to return home to find someone who fits the job.

Your loyal servants,

Pathren and Jöst

Pallah wandered back into her room and warmed herself by the fire as she read. She balled the note and dropped it into the flames. No one else need know, not that this missive would have truly informed them. Guesswork and hearsay, and she'd lost a spy in the process. She shook her head, fingernails clicking against the polished stone. Perhaps she would go herself, find out what had become of Ahren.

He was alive.

She was sure of it.

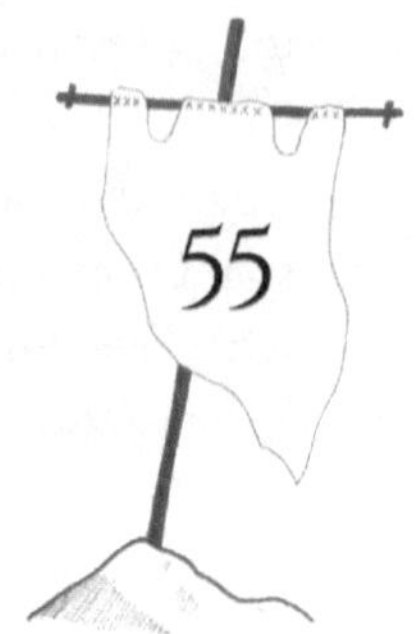

DEEP FJORD

HALLDORA

FOUR DAYS OF TRAVEL and Halldora's anticipation of arriving at Erval's doorstep still fluttered within her chest. She had planned this march for years—decades, she could argue—and still uncertainty crawled through her like a venomous spider. She cracked a few of her knuckles, then made quick work of the rest until they were all even, stretched.

Her army stood on one side of a fjord, stoic beneath her banners snapping in the breeze. Halldora paced before them, inspecting her soldiers. It wasn't that she mistrusted them, but the speed at which her support had accrued undoubtedly left holes for potential deception.

General Ivan marched beside her, his hand ever ready on the hilt of his sword. "Still no sign of Solyana or the men who were traveling with her, Your Majesty. But I bet we'll have usable information by end of day. It's not a large town, just a fishing village. If she's there, the people will turn her in with the right pressure. It's only a matter of time."

Halldora nodded, keeping all emotion from her face as she surveyed her men. "Merely a bump in the road, Ivan. Though I prefer to keep any information of our movements from my dear brother."

"Of course, my Queen," Ivan agreed.

"Speaking of, where is that bumbling steward of his?" She squinted, hand shielding her eyes. "I'm curious if that overripe melon of a man might finally divulge something useful."

Ivan raised a hand, motioning for a soldier to approach.

A boy in armor clanked forward with a nod, a black feather at the peak of his helm bobbing. "Sir!"

"Where is our prisoner?"

The boy went pale, drawing Halldora's attention in full.

"Well?" she asked.

His young eyes cut from Ivan to Halldora before he bowed his head and spoke to the ground. "The prisoner has been lost. And after a roll call, five men and a horse are missing."

Halldora went stone still, eyes boring into the boy before shifting to Ivan. She had few advantages over her brother—Solyana had been one. But Phineas she had prized.

Ivan took a knee beside the soldier on the ground, removed and tucked his helm under his arm, and bowed his head. "Forgive me, my Queen." His eyes stayed locked on her feet.

A sneer formed on Halldora's lips, and she tempered the desire to drive her foot upward into his nose. The soldiers shifted, and she reminded herself of the eyes watching—measuring her worth.

"The Red Moon draws near," she said, putting a gloved hand on his armored shoulder. "The underestimation of our foes ends here. From now on, we assume the strengths of others, not their weaknesses."

General Ivan gave a firm nod and rose to his feet. He fell into step as she strode ahead, assessing the landscape. "Does Her Majesty wish to go over this fjord or around?"

"Enough foolishness, General. We have no time for anything but through."

Halldora motioned her general out of her way and began to climb stairs as she formed them from rock. Soldiers standing before her stumbled backward, falling out of rank as they watched stone after stone press upward to meet her feet.

She formed them as easily as breathing, creating a spiral staircase that ascended until she was over her men, each of them craning their necks to watch the woman clad in black float in the air.

She shielded her eyes as she looked to the opposite side of the fjord, noting a line of movement coming into view, lumbering and slow. Halldora smiled at Maral and her Beast Riders.

The wind was stronger up here, buffeting her hair in every direction. She caught Ivan's eye and felt his tether connect to the stones spiraled beneath her feet. This allowed her to shift her Fera to Vindur, the wind itself at her control. Immediately, the air surrounding her ceased to blow, while the flags below her billowed and cracked.

"Men and women of the New Kingdom!" Her voice rang clear as she used her Fera to push the sound with the wind. The soldiers below snapped straighter to attention. "We ride on toward Thonethren! Each of you is equipped with your Tala, Fera, or Heitt. And now our Beast Riders come to strengthen our arm against the pretender! We cross, my faithful, toward victory!"

The ground rumbled, and the soldiers shuffled and shifted with concern. But their worry gave way to awe as Halldora broke apart the ground. Like cracking a nut, she brought the pieces up to make a bridge of sorts, one that hung suspended over the chasm.

With a sound like the birthing pains of a mountain, the last piece of land fell into place, and Halldora began walking down her spiral steps.

"To Thonethren!" she called out to them without the aid of Vindur Fera, for she could not release the bridge. Then, once her feet touched down on the tall grasses of the fjord, she marched her way to the suspended rocks, her mind focused completely on keeping them locked in place.

General Ivan strode proudly at her side, and this time, Halldora was grateful. With his own Stein Fera, if he felt the bridge begin to slip, he could tether to reinforce it. Between the two of them, no soldiers or morale would be lost today.

She could hear the wind howling over the chasm and knew it would be worse on the rocks. Looking back at her men and the array of their expressions, she grinned. Squaring her shoulders, she directed her eyes back to the opposite side of the chasm, where Maral and her Beast Riders had come into full view.

"My Fera must remain true, or the bridge will fall," she reminded General Ivan. "You have your tether ready?"

"I am ever at Her Majesty's will."

The two of them picked their way carefully across, stopping once in the middle as a few pieces of rock broke off and tumbled from the edge beneath Ivan's feet. A chill ran through her at the thought of Ivan falling to his doom, but before the gasp could fill her lungs, he righted himself and gave her a stalwart nod.

Her men were watching. She must not show fear.

Crossing over to grassy land once more, Halldora was flooded with relief and pride. She turned back to them with shoulders square and amplified her voice again. "The pretender yet sits upon our throne with a hand around the necks of our people. We march upon this sacred land to free it from the yoke of his tyranny. Let the ground shake with our sure steps toward Thonethren, that the tyrant may hear and know his false reign ends with us!" She drew her sword, pulling it cleanly to lift it high. "I fight with you! For your families! For our land! Nevermore will we be nomads without a home! We return to take what has always been rightfully ours!"

The soldiers on the opposing side burst into howls and barks of approval. Hundreds of them struck their shields with their spear or sword, thousands beat their chests with their metal armored fists.

Then, like a massive eel lured from its cave, the line of soldiers funneled over the bridge. Halldora found a boulder on the west side of Deep Fjord, and with the assistance of Ivan, climbed atop it—keeping an eye on her men's progress. They worked quickly, but it still took hours for every groundman to cross safely.

Halldora ground her teeth, the truly difficult part approaching: getting the cavalry to cross. She knew it would be a miracle if she didn't lose any horses to the slick rock, but the time they would save would be worth it.

The first of them began, the echoing click of hooves on stone like hammers striking in coffin nails. Almost all riders had dismounted, opting to lead their steeds across rather than ride—a wise decision. However, as the horses continued their way across, she spotted a team of about sixty mounted men who seemed intent on crossing atop horseback.

"Ivan, get those men to dismount."

He dropped his Fera to obey, and she shored up her strength in the stones, feeling them shift and scrape. The general had only taken three sprinting strides before the riders took off to cross the bridge, intent on speed over caution. Halldora held her breath, concentrating all her efforts as the weight of so many pounded across the boulders.

Ivan skidded to a halt, his boots spraying gravel as he fought to return to his queen, the charge of cavalry thundering behind him. To Halldora's surprise, it seemed they might just make it across, when one of the horses slipped, and it sent the rest of them skittering. Hooves lost traction on the surface of the rock, and Halldora couldn't help the gasp that escaped her. Ivan leapt to safety as the boulders shifted downward, Halldora's loss of control minimal but enough to throw the rest of those crossing off balance. A shrill cry rose as every horse remaining on the stone bridge lost their footing.

Eyes wide, shaking hand extended toward the bridge, Halldora found Ivan below her perch on the boulder. "Ivan!" She felt his tether then, strong and secure. He latched to the sections of the bridge she was struggling to hold, but it wasn't enough to prevent the horses from falling.

The first slid off the side, its rider's cries desperate as he attempted tethering to whatever he could—whatever his Gift was, it wasn't going to help him today. The horse released a piercing whinny as hooves pounded against the rock and then silence as they struck out at air, and the two dropped—running on nothing—falling for what seemed like forever.

She had expected a splash when they hit the water of the fjord, but it sounded far less forgiving. A loud smack echoed from below before it was lost to the wind. Her eyes shot back up to the bridge to find half of the horses still struggling, and the other half sliding from the stone as surely as the first.

"No!" It would be too many lost. Her eyes scanned, counting as fast as she could. Twenty. There were twenty horses scrambling, their riders uselessly shouting in dismay.

From the corner of her eye, she watched something on four legs come barreling toward the western edge of the fjord. One of Maral's men? Catching him in full view, it was a man, his long dark hair streaming behind him, riding atop an enormous wolf—a direwolf? One hand clutched reins, the other reached out to... *Häfa*! He was tethering the horses!

Halldora's eyes cut back to the bridge to find each horse that had been sliding toward its demise halt abruptly. Her heart thudded hard against her chest. This man was tethering *twenty*. Hope surged through her, and she redoubled her efforts on the rocks, keeping them whole and secure; she could feel Ivan doing the same. Even from her distant vantage point, she could see the sweat on the forehead of the man on the direwolf. His arm shook, muscles twitching, and after agonizing minutes, all horses came to their feet and began their march across the ravine.

They'd lost an entire day and a half, waiting on her army to cross. Longer than she'd wished, but shorter still than it would have been if they had gone south around the fjord. Her men fell into obedient formation, grouping and positioning themselves as they had been trained.

Once the bridge was no longer needed, she and Ivan released the boulders from their grip. With the sound of ancient stone scraping, like a roar of the earth itself, they crumbled into the ravine, burying the fallen men.

Halldora allowed them a few hours respite and a meal. She walked amongst her men, congratulating them, mingling and allowing herself to relax—if only a bit.

She made her way to the direwolf rider, a man wearing little more than a few choice furs. He sat before a fire, surrounded by the men he had saved. They sipped from husk cups of tea.

"That was an impressive feat, sir." She waved away their standing to attention.

The dark-haired man looked up quickly before averting his gaze, bowing his head slightly. "I only did my duty, ma'am."

The men around the fire stilled, but Halldora gave a gracious smile. "Well, the Queen of the New Kingdom thanks you. What is your name, Beast Rider?"

"Reynir, m'lady."

He still forwent her title. Halldora bristled but would not let it show. Now was not the time to make enemies. "Well, Reynir, direwolf rider, you have my appreciation. When my throne is returned to me, I will see you properly rewarded for your valiant deed. Good evening to you all."

She left him, ready for a night of sleep before they would continue on to meet her brother in battle. Weaving through her army, she noticed Maral's men had found seats among them, and she was glad for it. Morale would be boosted after this trial together—though it had cost them more dearly than she'd have liked.

Making it back to her tent, she found Ivan at her door. He bowed his head in her direction. "Well done, my Queen. These men owe you their lives."

"No more than they did yesterday." Though Halldora could still hear the screams of the horses as they fell. "Until tomorrow, Ivan." She entered her tent and let the flap close behind her. Ivan was still for a full minute before she finally heard him step away. Only then did Halldora release her breath and collapse in a heap of exhaustion on her cot.

TREASURE TROVE

SOLYANA

"**P**HINEAS IS ON HIS way?" Ahren asked as he packed a few things into a knapsack. "With or without an army behind him?"

Solyana threw her hands in the air, shaking her head in exasperation. "I don't know. I only have what Kopar showed me."

"And you trust it?"

"I can't think of a reason he would lie."

Ahren slung the sack onto his shoulder. "Unless Halldora is making him."

Solyana paused. "It doesn't matter. Thonethren is our goal. I'm packed and ready; I just need to say goodbye." Whether Phineas had stayed true or not, tethering to the stoat and imbuing it with information had given her an idea.

Using Tala, Solyana tethered Vinur in the room below. The latch happened quickly, and the grief that filled her was immense, the wolf aching for his master. Solyana imparted words of farewell to Vinur, trusting when Gamaliel woke, he would tether him and learn the truth of their absence. That she longed to stay, that she loved him, but they'd had no choice. That not just her promises, but all of Mothmar, would be broken if Erval were to succeed come the Red Moon.

Then her eyes were back on Ahren. "Gamaliel is in good hands. I trust Marnie."

"Well, I would hope so." The woman's voice came from the door, her long braid almost sweeping the floor.

Ahren's face hardened. "Who is this?"

"Tarin," Marnie said as Solyana turned to face the two women. "She works at the stables."

She was as Solyana remembered, tiny yet muscled, and she looked up at them with bright eyes even in the dimly lit room.

"Your eyes be upward," Tarin whispered with awe.

Solyana felt her scar burn to the surface of her skin. "And be filled with light," she said.

"Now, I'll warn you," Marnie began. "This may sound mad, but Tarin, like many of the young people here, grew up diving off the cliffs. She knows these waters better than anyone." Marnie motioned Tarin forward.

"If you show your face in town, the soldiers will spot you. There are no places to hide on the stairways here."

"Then what do we do?" Ahren asked.

Marnie held up two loose, dark tunics. "We swim."

Dark water lapped the sides of the small boat as Tarin paddled them out into the deep waters, a single lantern swinging from a post extending from the front of the boat. A fishing line trailed behind, slicing the waves.

Solyana and Ahren had tucked themselves against the sides of the boat, their dark tunics keeping them well hidden. Solyana's neck ached, but she kept still, anxiety tumbling inside her with the bob of every wave. When Tarin had explained her plan, it became a glaring problem that Solyana had never learned to swim; not well, anyway. Breaking through the ice of the Vatino Sea years ago was the closest she'd ever come to learning. Thinking back to that time the massive cyclone of snow and ice ravaged her valley, she shuddered.

After changing clothes and packing their things into waterproofed leather skins, Solyana had taken a minute to say her last goodbye to Gamaliel. His chest had moved solidly up and down, his shoulder appearing to be well on its way to healing. Solyana had allowed her tears to leak onto his shirt as she clutched it to her face, praying to the Celestials to heal him, to keep him hidden from the soldiers.

Now, as her body moved in much the same rhythm of Gamaliel's breath, she steeled herself for what was to come.

"You there!" a voice barked from the shore.

Solyana froze.

"Mornin'!" Tarin called back.

"It's the middle of the night; why are you out here?"

Tarin leaned over to pluck the fishing pole off the back. "It is, in fact, morning, soldier," she said sweetly. "And I'm afraid all your shouting is going to scare off my catch."

"I see no one else on these waters," the soldier continued, unwavering. "Come to shore; I need to check your vessel."

Solyana watched as Tarin's shoulders tensed. "Oh, you'll have to wait for your fish at the market like everyone else," Tarin said with a wave and a nod of her head.

"That's an order by edict of Queen Halldora," the man's voice echoed over the waters.

"Tarin," Ahren whispered, eyes wild.

Images of the three of them being hauled away, back to the Queen of Caves, flashed in Solyana's mind.

"Of course." Tarin's voice had grown strained. "But these rocks are sharp, and as I'm sure you don't want to fall into the sea, I'll pull up to the corner there." She pointed with her fishing rod.

"Hurry it up."

Solyana could hear the clink of his armor over the waves and gathered her pack to herself. Tarin cast her line back out behind the boat, settled the rod, then sat back down to the oars.

A tense few minutes passed as the boat languidly floated closer to the rock-lined shore. They were running out of time. Though the morning held a chill, sweat broke out on Solyana's temple.

"Get ready," Tarin whispered to them before jumping to her feet. "I've got one!" She lunged for the pole and the entire boat shifted, the sides dipping close to the water.

Understanding dawning, Solyana began to shift her weight, rocking the boat back and forth. Ahren joined her until Tarin was flailing at the rear.

"Hold your breath," Ahren said, and Solyana took a great gulp of air.

The boat bobbed one last time before capsizing away from the rocky bank, dousing the lantern, and spilling the three of them overboard.

The warm water pulled Solyana down, and she released air until her feet touched sand. Ahren's hand wrapped around her arm and tugged at her to move. Eyes squeezed shut against dark, salty water, Solyana followed. Though Tarin had explained swimming, without practice Solyana felt only like she was clawing at nothing, her lungs screaming for air.

Prying her eyes open, she spotted Ahren's feet kicking away from her, and she followed. When she could go no further, she kicked her way to the surface, pumping her legs and windmilling her arms.

Breaking the surface, she pulled sweet air into her lungs before falling beneath the waves again. Her hand caught on coral encrusted rock, and she pulled herself up, blinking with relief as the rock blocked her from view of the shore. Ahren was a distance ahead, hand on the side of the cliff where she was meant to be. He motioned her to continue. She adjusted her pack to her back and set off underwater, kicking and hoping she was deep enough not to be spotted.

When finally she broke the surface a second time, she heard Ahren whisper loudly, "Get down!"

With only half a breath in her lungs, Ahren's hand pressed solidly on her head, shoving her back beneath the water. Struggling beneath his weight, she heard Tarin's garbled shout before Solyana broke free and burst upward again.

"Hands off me!" Tarin shouted.

"Shut up!" the soldier barked as Solyana clung to rock.

Ahren surfaced as Tarin released another cry. "What's happening?"

"I don't know!" Solyana blinked the water from her eyes, but it was too dark to see. "If we go to shore, we can help—"

"Solyana, look at me." Ahren's hand was on her cheek, redirecting her gaze to his own. "We talked about this possibility. Tarin went over this; Marnie is going to help her."

Nodding quickly, Solyana tried to put Tarin's cries out of her mind.

"Are you ready?" Ahren asked and Solyana found his eyes again. "I found it."

She nodded.

"Remember, release all your air or you'll be fighting the water."

"I know."

"Stay with me."

Solyana and Ahren took a simultaneous breath before slipping beneath the waves once more. This time, Solyana released all her air. Bubbles tickled her face as she fell in slow motion, hand entwined with Ahren's to keep them together. He used his free hand to push them down faster, and Solyana closed her eyes, focused on keeping her body from breathing in water.

Her eyes flew open as she touched sand. Ahren released her and felt the rock of the cliff, hands crawling all over in the dark. Panic rose as the seconds passed. Where was the cave? She didn't want to risk rising to the surface again, but a few more seconds would force her up for air.

Ahren found it, the lip of a wall, and he grabbed it, dragging himself and her forward in a rushing lurch.

Solyana kicked, her body slowing, her lungs aching, begging, screaming at her to take in a breath.

A bubble burst out of her, and she sucked in water.

Ahren kept pulling her deeper into the dark before their bodies began to rise.

Solyana sucked in a second gulp, white hot terror searing through her mind. Was this how she was going to die? The water pried another gasp from her lungs as they quickly filled with fluid.

Ahren's arms lifted her as he kicked hard.

They burst from the water, and Solyana began to cough, great hacking heaves that pushed the water from her lungs. Shakily she pulled herself up the inlet, sand digging under her fingernails. She doubled over, vomiting the sea water that clung to her throat.

It was darker than pitch in the cave, and Ahren's voice was closer than she expected. "You okay?"

She took in a breath. "Yeah." Her voice came out like a croak.

"Can you give us some light?"

Solyana lifted her palm and produced a flame. It wasn't much, her body exhausted and spent as it was, but it was enough to see the small cave.

Tarin had called it the Treasure Trove. A cave common enough to the children of Ströndbar and distant enough in the memory of the adults that they were allowed to squirrel away their treasures.

The pool which they had emerged from flowed up to a small sandbar that met the walls of the cave. Littered in the coves and pockets of the walls were countless shells, driftwood, coral—cliff diving rewards. Solyana spotted a small black iridescent pearl buried in a pile of cream ones. Plucking it from its place, she was reminded of the last time she was surrounded by beautiful things in a cave. She had taken a stone for Jonas then, too.

The water-resistant leather bags Marnie had given them had held up well, their clothes and shoes dry as they took them out. They took a few minutes to change, turning away from each other as they did so. The pearl found its home in her pocket; she would give it to Jonas when they reunited.

"She said the stairs are back this way." Ahren ran his hands along the wall, finding the gap in the stones easily. "Ready?"

Solyana squeezed the excess water from her hair. "Let's go."

"The stairs come through a narrow crevice between a boulder and the ground near the stable," Tarin had told them a few hours before. "It's a tight fit coming out the other side, but you'll both fit...I think." She had pointedly eyed Ahren.

Solyana understood now, peering out into the quiet early morning.

The stable lay across the swaying bridge, a squat man in a cloak sitting behind the main building. A familiar-looking creature rode atop his shoulder, the sheen of its coat glistening in the moonlight.

"It's Phineas!" Solyana whispered to Ahren behind her.

"Let's hope we're not walking into Halldora's men," Ahren said with a grunt.

The two extricated themselves from the narrow cavern and into the night. Phineas jumped at the sight of them. The stoat skittered away.

"Heavens to Hekla! Where did you two come from?"

"We could ask you the same," Ahren said as the three of them shuffled across the bridge.

"We don't have the time to bicker regarding my loyalties or allegiances any longer," Phineas strained. "We need to leave now." The horses were tacked and ready, and Solyana wondered how long he had waited for them. He tossed a pair of reins toward Ahren and another to Solyana.

Ahren wordlessly hefted his bag, stuck a toe in the stirrup, and mounted the horse.

Solyana eyed Phineas, the reins in her hand, and for a moment, the temptation to stay with Gamaliel overwhelmed her. All the times he had protected her, the years he had spent waiting, and she was leaving him defenseless. If Halldora didn't kill him, he would never forgive her. And he shouldn't, she thought.

If she got on this horse, she was saying goodbye to him forever. But if she stayed...

"Solyana," Phineas said from atop his horse. "We must hurry. The fate of Mothmar rests in our ability to reach Thonethren before Halldora and her army. I need you. We all need you." His eyes shifted to Ahren beneath his spectacles. "You, too, Ahren."

"My sister..." was all Solyana could say, the lump in her throat and the aches in her heart cutting off her speech.

"Halldora will have made it to Deep Fjord by now. Our only advantage is that we can travel faster." A flash of red fur drew Solyana's attention as a tiny stoat flung itself at the tail of Phineas's horse, scrambled up its length, and crossed to the man's shoulder. "Hi, Kopar. Great job, my friend." He gave the stoat a scratch beneath its chin.

His blue eyes landed on Solyana, and she was surprised to see genuine fear within them.

"If you have any love for your land," Phineas said to her. "Any love for your people, for that boy you dragged here—you will mount that horse, Solyana. Before it's too late." Then he pulled the reins, turning his horse around, and gave the animal a solid kick, sending them speeding off into the dark of night.

Ahren followed suit, leaving Solyana and her horse alone. She shoved her leather boot into her stirrup and hoisted herself up, her knapsack heavy on her back. She settled into the saddle, gathering the reins as she surveyed the village behind her.

"I'm coming back for you, Gamaliel," she whispered. "Don't give up. Please, don't give up." With slight pressure from her legs, she turned her horse toward the bridge to leave.

Halldora at her back and Erval ahead, she forced her mind on the task before them. Jonas had yet to make contact, and Solyana was beginning to worry her friend wouldn't deliver, and that they would confront the king of Thonethren and all his plans without the power of the Way, without control of all Gifts. She grit her teeth as the horse thundered beneath her, catching up to her companions. If her sister was in Thonethren, Solyana would find her first.

The three shot off, their speed growing from trot to gallop as they wound their way out of Ströndbar and to the west. The scar on Solyana's face pulsed, as if signaling she was on the right path. Or the wrong one. She sniffed and wiped at the tears that slid over her face—tears from the wind and the speed at which she flew, surely.

IF ONLY

GAMALIEL

THE BLANKET DUG ROUGH fibers into his skin. The fire blazed too hot, while something cold and wet prodded his hand that dangled from the bed. Soft fur pushed its way beneath his fingers.

His wolf. His Vinur.

Flashes of memory accosted him: a wind-tossed meadow, a frigid cave, water hitting his face like spikes.

Solyana.

The Red Moon.

Sleep pulled him backward, though he strained against it, reaching for the urgency that had been dormant for too long. He needed to be with her, to protect her, to stand by her side while she... Vinur prodded him again.

Somewhere in the distance, he heard voices and a door shutting closed.

Sleep dragged him beneath its surface, into its dark and silent depths.

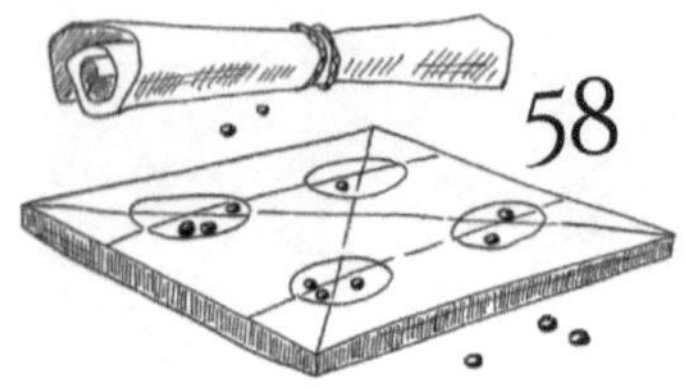

BE FILLED WITH LIGHT

JONAS

A LONE ON A SMALL island, awaiting understanding of some ancient truth, Jonas felt much like the scribes of old. He had read only a few accounts of those young boys who had assisted seers deep within the spired mountains of Endirinn. And now, here he sat, staving off sleep for the chance to learn greater truth from beings far above him.

He held the Map of Leídín before him, spread open between two piles of sand. If he was interpreting it correctly, he was supposed to find the constellation of Leídín. He searched exactly where Fridmey had pointed, his spyglass pressed firmly to his eye, yet it seemed ever changing. After hours of searching and studying, he was left with nothing but a bruise on his cheekbone.

"One who must follow the paths of the sky..." He clicked his tongue. He had been at it for hours, and sleep tempted him. "Stay awake, Jonas," he told himself. "You've come this far. Take this one night, learn it, and relay the information to Solyana." He looked up at the moon, growing closer to full every day.

There was but little time. The Red Moon was coming, and with any significant celestial event was great opportunity...and great fear. Jonas had more than theories that pertained to the upcoming eclipse.

The Red Moon was a significant part of his dreams.

He squeezed his eyes shut and shook his head. If he was to believe his dream, then not only did he have to discover the secrets of the Way tonight, but he needed to somehow make it all the way to Thonethren in only a few days.

His eyes shot open. Closing them had been a bad idea. He rolled onto his back, arms and legs spread out like one of the stars he was desperately trying to find.

Then something sparkled. Way out in the distant blackness, like a piece of quartz among mountainside rock, it shone. He sat up and scrambled to stand, his feet sending sand flying in every direction. The sparkle disappeared, leaving him staring at countless stars spread across the sky once more.

"*Häfa!*" he cried.

He was close, really close. He could feel it. Training his eyes on the spot, he thought back to what Fridmey had told him. Knowing all the secrets of the Way would do nothing for him if the information did not sink into his heart.

"What do I call you? You still are technically Celestials, but should it be singular? Plural?" Jonas stood and began to pace, kicking sand against his linen pants.

An idea struck him. He grabbed the map, shook loose the sand, and held it above his head, lining it up as best as he could to where the singular star had sparkled so brightly, right at the tip of the Leídín.

It glowed *through* the map.

Not just the star, the entire constellation, glowing across the leather map. Jonas froze, afraid even the simplest movement would dismiss the effect. His mouth went dry as it hung open in wonder, the design of the constellation seeming to hop off the map and dance before him. He dared not blink.

"You're real." He spoke to it and somehow didn't feel insane for doing so. His entire body thrummed. "You're real, and we have been wrong for generations. Now, you trust us with the truth once more."

The image pulsed, glowing brighter as if in response.

Jonas's heart ached, and he couldn't help the tears that ran salty tracks down his cheeks. He was really here, finding the secrets he had worked for half a decade to realize. Understanding mysteries his parents had searched for, that they had never found.

"Forgive our wayward hearts. Forgive our need to control and manipulate. Help me to simply let go and exist in truth. I submit to you." He didn't know if it was the right thing to say, but it felt right. The connections displayed on the map looked to be a combination of the three symbols of Tala, Fera, and Heitt, all somehow cohesive, all connected as one. There weren't enough stars to make it as full as the traditional symbols, but Jonas could fill it in.

He could see it.

"Forgive me," he said, his voice catching as the sky lightened a shade.

Morning was coming.

With a final pulse of light from the map, Jonas felt his entire body lighten. As if he had been weighed down his entire life by some invisible anchor, now lifting in this moment of surrender.

He dropped the map to his side and closed his eyes, basking in the final moments with the Leídín before the night sky disappeared. Jonas remained there, face turned upward toward the sky, his body limp as the sun ascended.

He could hear the sounds of footsteps moving across the sand, but he remained still, feeling none of the urgency he had known before. Though Solyana was still at the back of his mind, he knew it would all work out; it would be okay.

Even if he wasn't a part of it.

Profound peace filled him.

"Jonas?" Rorhan's voice intoned. "What have you done to him?"

"I think he's found it," Fridmey answered, and Jonas could hear the smile in her voice. "The Leídín."

"Is that what I feel? That serenity?" Rorhan sounded awed, and Jonas finally opened his eyes to see his friend staring at him in wonder. "I want it, too."

"I can teach you," Jonas said with a calmness that felt both foreign to him and as if it had belonged to him for a long while.

"I do not need to wait a night, as you did?"

"No." Jonas shook his head. "Though I'm glad she made me." He rolled the map up into a scroll and motioned with it toward Fridmey.

"I understand now how to teach it, how to make it palatable for those who cannot see it for themselves."

"You truly do understand," Fridmey said, eyes growing wide. "It took me a long time to wrap my mind around it. I thought everyone *had* to see the constellation if they were to be brought into the fold."

Jonas smiled. "It's a privilege, not a right.'"

"Indeed." Fridmey gave a firm nod. "But I believe we are both expected somewhere in just a few passings of the moon. We must go now and pray for swift winds."

"I think they'll heed us," Jonas said, letting his fingers dance in the breeze that blew past. The sand beneath his toes, the fishy brine in the air, the taste of salt on his tongue—all of it held a vibrancy that hadn't been there before. It was all more than just a means to an end, more than items to be directed.

Where Fera, Tala, and Heitt demanded, Leídín *requested*. This was the core of it. There was no control, only respect.

"Solyana needs to know," Jonas said, but a plan to communicate the information via a stoat felt ridiculously foolhardy. How could he imbue such truths into a tiny creature? The doubt darkened his heart, and he felt a slight fissure in his connection with the stars above.

He shook his head and called for one, anyway.

Within the hour, a stoat the color of midnight swam onto shore, its tiny body soaked to the bone. Jonas knelt, and through something like a tether, whispered all it needed to know. Then he released it, hoping it would find them in time. Hoping he wasn't too late.

The creature scampered away and launched itself back out into the sea. Jonas turned to Fridmey, who had gathered everyone back at the dinghy. "To Thonethren, then?" he asked with a yawn.

"To war, Jonas." Fridmey motioned for Rorhan, Jonas, and the others of her crew to clamor aboard the tiny boat. One of them pushed it into the water before hopping in. They began to cross toward her fleet, anchored and waiting in more open water. "We go to defeat a madman."

"We have the Leídín. We will not fail," Jonas said with absolute confidence.

"Evil still maintains a tight grip." Fridmey secured her hat over her hair. "It can still overwhelm the greater good if we aren't careful."

"Then we'll teach those we can what we know."

Fridmey turned back, grinning at him—though it held a sadness Jonas hadn't seen before. "I like your spirit, Jonas. We must pray they listen. While my people know, not all have accepted. Teach Rorhan to start. Then, the more that know the truth, the better off we'll be."

Jonas bit at his lip, deep in thought. People still had to be willing to listen. The Way had become so obvious to him once he'd seen it. Would others be swayed as wholly? Perhaps he had been naïve. The Red Moon was coming, and although it seemed to be the moment Erval himself was waiting for, Jonas wondered if this singular event could help them, as well. With the moon so dark, the stars would be even more visible against the black of night.

He prayed it would be then that people would turn their eyes upward and be filled with light.

TIME

PALLAH

SIXTY YEARS HAD COME and gone. Pallah should be feeling the pull of gravity on her skin and the creak of age in her bones, but her body remained exactly as she wanted it. Having always been someone passed over easily, unrecognizable in a group of two—she had quickly learned how to manipulate her skin and bone structure using both Bein and Lakimi Fera.

And not only structural manipulation, but her body itself had seemed to stop aging wherever she desired it. Taking so many lives had imbued her with the strength, youth, and stamina of those she Took from. She was seventy-eight, but her body was that of a twenty-five-year-old.

The Taking had become routine, a craving she had to sate almost every day. Erval was right: the desire to live forever was formidable, all-encompassing, and powerful. She would rule Mothmar by his side. And she wasn't sure how much longer they would have to wait.

Erval regaled them at the dinner table of his latest conquests and plans for strategic takeover. But to what end? It all always came down to the Brextant. Though they tried person after person on the thing, it still wouldn't work as Erval hoped. Pallah wondered when Erval's ire would turn from the machine to its maker. Phineas's constant tinkering was beginning to arouse Pallah's suspicions.

But Pallah occupied herself with other things.

One activity, in particular, she had been planning for some time.

She packed the last of her knapsack. Erval didn't often leave the castle, so she had to be careful when she chose to go. Now that he was away on a diplomatic visit to some islands off the coast...

She would find her brother and come right back.

Then maybe, just maybe, she'd be whole again. After decades serving the king of Thonethren, she'd come to realize, when she lay awake at night, it wasn't romance she dreamed about. It wasn't fame, or power, or glory... It was her brother. Again and again, the unfilled need that pulled at the seams of her heart. It was Ahren.

In the dark cover of night, Pallah escaped the castle grounds and traveled east toward Endirinn.

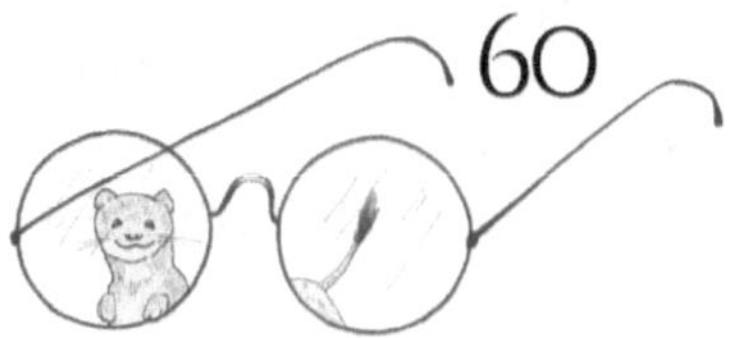

CONNECTION

PHINEAS

P HINEAS'S GAZE SLID FROM the moon back to the path lit by the celestial being. The eclipse was due to happen that very night, and although they had taken little rest and pushed their horses to breaking, he wasn't sure they would make it in time.

Circling Deep Fjord had been time consuming. He still wondered if they should have attempted to cross it, but Phineas's analytical mind had run through every possibility and found it wasn't worth the risk. Horses over some handmade bridge? He wondered if Halldora had attempted it. But without Taking to the extent Erval urged him, he was weak and growing more so.

Turned earth, discarded encampments, animal carcasses, and the occasional horseshoe were signs of Halldora's army. They had been here, as Phineas had predicted. They were too late.

Erval had not attempted to step into his mind again, which worried him even more. He looked over at Solyana. If anyone could be described as bone-weary, it would be her. And yet she rushed dutifully on, at Phineas's urging, toward her doom. Sympathy tugged at him, and for the hundredth time, he shoved it down. He would gladly stand in her place, if only he'd been part of the gods-forsaken prophecy. But he wasn't. There was simply no other choice.

He signaled with his hand, and all three horses slowed to walking. His horse fell into step beside Solyana's. "Has he attempted to enter your mind?"

"Yes," she admitted, and Phineas blinked in surprise.

"You didn't tell me?" he squeaked.

"Four days ago, just after Deep Fjord. You were tracking something in the sky." She looked up at the wash of warm evening colors. "I think what you taught me worked."

"You were able to keep him on the path?" A thrill wound through Phineas. He had never truly taken the time to raise an apprentice, and hearing his work being passed along was nothing short of amazing. "What did you show him?"

"That we're doing what we told him we'd do. Traveling now, to bring him Ahren."

"Do you still believe he has Rhuth?" Phineas asked.

Solyana nodded. "He won't tell me outright, but I believe he does. Why won't he just admit it?"

"Information is a valuable currency. When you live as long as we have, coin has very little persuasion compared to knowledge."

"But you never saw her? You never heard that she or Pallah were there?"

Phineas grimaced. "I was his closest confidant. I'd like to think I still am, but..." He remembered Erval's comments toward him over the past few years, his intentions seeming to drift further from the friendship Phineas thought they had. The king becoming more calculated, more cold. Phineas still wondered if Erval planned on seating him in the Brextant at the end of it all. Phineas had Taken enough; he could probably handle it. He might not even die.

But he would want to.

"I would have known if they were there. But I never saw them. I never even heard he'd found them. Knowing Erval as I do, I'm not sure it would be possible for him not to brag about such a thing."

"And no word from Jonas?" Ahren trotted up beside them. "We're due to arrive tonight, and having every Gift on our side would greatly increase our chances of surviving this."

Phineas nodded gravely. This was the hitch in his plan over which he had no control. If the information of the Way didn't reach them in time, all his planning would be for nothing.

Solyana's horse stopped. Phineas plodded on a few steps before reining his to a halt as well.

"What is it?" he asked her, keeping an eye on the descending sun. "We're almost there. Halldora and her men must be somewhere, hiding in these mountains."

"When was the last time you tethered to your stoats?" she asked with a glint in her eye.

He always thought she was a bright girl. "Good idea." Phineas pulled the small metal device from his knapsack, securing it over his spectacles and reaching out with his tether. Kopar was there, of course, riding on the back of his horse, but he extended himself further, calling to multiple stoats. Each one felt like normal connections, nothing new or noteworthy. "I'm not feeling anything different. I hope nothing happened to—"

A tether formed to a new stoat. It felt so entirely different, it stopped Phineas's mouth and even his horse slowed.

"What is it?" Ahren asked, glancing around.

"I think I found it," whispered Phineas. "This one is new, and it bears something of import."

"Bring it here!" Solyana's eyes were wide, and he gave a quick nod.

He called the creature to himself, and it obeyed, though sluggishly. The poor thing was exhausted, close to death, if Phineas was any judge of it.

Phineas slid from his horse and met the creature halfway. It crawled, tiny legs moving through willpower alone. "Come here, little traveler." Phineas picked up the black stoat, which collapsed in his palms, closed its eyes, and slept.

He tucked the creature between his neck and shoulder and mounted his horse once again.

"Well? Is it Jonas's?" Solyana asked.

"Yes, his presence is known." He shook his head.

"Oh, praise the Celestials! Jonas is well."

There was no guarantee of that, but Phineas kept his thoughts to himself. "Let's give the stoat some time to recuperate before we tether it again. We must continue west."

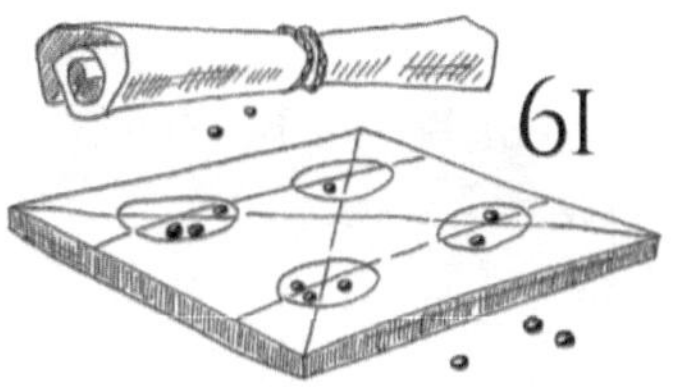

IMPENDING MOON

JONAS

WITH THE WINDS AT their call and the sea at their bidding, the Crimson Chief and her crew made headway faster than Jonas had ever thought possible. Fridmey ran her ship with a strong hand, and Jonas couldn't help but admire her leadership. Behind them, sixteen other ships of varying sizes and differing speeds followed. Fridmey had truly accrued an armada that was a force to be reckoned with.

Solyana's mother, Koláme, had kept Jonas in an embrace so long he thought he would lose the ability to expand his lungs, but he couldn't fault her. He, too, felt like he had come home when she'd pulled him into her arms. She had answered Jonas's prying questions, fiercely proud of her eldest daughter and her leadership. After two years at sea, Fridmey's reputation had spread like fire, ship after ship flying white flags upon their appearance, either giving up or seeking to join her outright. The sailors and soldiers who came under her command quickly found themselves under a far kinder captain than they had expected.

Before long, her force matched the rumors, and the Crimson Chief was born.

Speaking to Koláme made him think of home, the valley, and Gamaliel. And in doing so, a pit of sorrow opened in his soul that he had yet to find the will to close. He missed his best friend, his brother, the man who had only been a boy himself when he'd raised him.

Departing the island in Skrim Sea, they now sped through Kana Ocean toward Thonethren. Jonas fell into the routine of the ship as he and Rorhan were given duties to attend to. Jonas had trouble focusing on the more menial tasks, but Rorhan leaned into them, as they helped with his sea sickness.

Jonas found him below deck, the yawn of homesickness open wide within him. "Rorhan?"

"Over here!" The man coiled rope and checked knots below deck.

"Here, let me help." Jonas tried to pick up a section but could hardly make it budge.

"I think not," Rorhan said with a chuckle. He hefted the thick rope as if it were nothing but a pair of horses' reins. "What is on your mind?"

"I didn't say there was anything—"

"I have not traveled with you so far to not know what happens in that brain of yours." He grinned at Jonas, and for a boyish moment, Jonas wanted to cry.

"Do you miss Lone? And Marin?" Jonas huffed at himself, running his fingers through his sandy hair. "What am I saying? Of course you do!"

Rorhan shifted the ropes to a peg and sat down on a wooden box with a sigh. He patted the small space beside him. Jonas eyed it, then shrugged and sat down, feeling the warmth of his friend and grateful for it.

Wrapping a large arm around Jonas's slender shoulders, Rorhan pulled him into his armpit and held him there. "I miss them very much, little brother."

Jonas's eyes prickled with tears, and he tried hard not to sniff.

"There has not been a day I do not think of my beautiful wife and my sweet *elskan*. But we go to protect them, do we not? To save them. To bring to pass something greater than ourselves." He squeezed Jonas hard. "You are strong, Jonas. Not your body, of course—you are a slender branch of a boy. But your mind..." Rorhan reached over and tapped Jonas's temple. "That is where your strength lies."

Jonas twisted in his seat and hugged the woolly mammoth of a man. So concentrated on stifling his own tears, Jonas failed to hear the footsteps descending the wooden steps.

"Well, isn't this just the sweetest?" Fridmey's rich voice was underlined with laughter.

Jonas's eyes shot open, and he tried to scramble away, but Rorhan held him tighter. "Join us, Fridmey. We are missing our people."

Jonas finally extricated himself and gave Rorhan's arm a shove for good measure.

"Do not worry—women love to see sensitive men. It is beautiful quality."

Jonas's face burned red as he stood, keeping his eyes from Fridmey's. "What can we do for you?" he asked the Chief.

"I just thought you'd like to try your hand at wielding the Gifts now that you have access to all of them."

Jonas straightened and raised an eyebrow. "I've been practicing since we left the island." To prove his point, he raised a hand and tossed some of Fridmey's hair to the side.

Her eyes widened, and an amused grin grew on her freckled face. "Cute. But I want to show you what happens when we do it together."

Jonas blushed.

Fridmey laughed. "Come on, I'll show you."

Both Rorhan and Jonas followed Fridmey up the steps to find her crew standing in a line. Koláme was on the end and waved at them.

"Alright. As you can see, we have two people at the stern." She pointed toward the back of the ship. "And two at the masts." Her hand shifted to the two just a few paces from where Jonas stood. "Those at the stern are using Vatin Fera; they're asking the water to help propel us forward. Those at the masts are using Vindur Fera, requesting the wind continue to push us."

"Do the waves and wind ever refuse?" Jonas was amazed at the simplicity and ease, so contrary to all the training and practice their old methods required.

"At times." Fridmey clasped her hands behind her back and began pacing the deck. "But we believe it is simply the Celestials making our path clear. We go where the Leídín guides us. It's how I found you. But not why I brought you up here." The Crimson Chief grinned and spun on her booted heel. "People of Mothmar!"

The two lines of crew bellowed together, "Raise the tide!"

Jonas could feel his mouth drop open and didn't bother trying to close it as he watched them move together. Were these truly the people of his valley? He had been young when he left and struggled now to match faces with names. But seeing them together like this made him emotional all over again. He wished he could be a part of them but knew he never would be.

Fire, ash, and the earth's rumble flashed again in his mind, but he quickly stuffed it away, intent on being in the present moment. He would not dwell on his dream now, not during something so pivotal.

Fearlessly, Fridmey jumped atop the bulwark, arms outstretched as she prayed out loud for all to hear. "Oh, Leídín, bend the water to our will. And give us the strength to wield it!" She gripped a rope to balance herself, looked over her shoulder, and winked at Jonas.

Jonas's face, which would usually burn at that sort of behavior, simply remained slack with shock.

The people moved as one, their arms outstretched and turning as they pressed all energy toward the water itself. Then, out of the water, a safe distance from the ship, rose a wave ten times the size of their massive vessel. At the crest formed the face of what Jonas could only imagine would be what a dragon would look like, created by the water itself. It released a crashing roar before moving with supernatural speed away from the ship and dissipating back into the ocean.

Just before it completely disappeared, a mighty tail of water rose from the blue depths and slapped near the ship, sending salty spray to cover all aboard.

Fridmey laughed, jumped from the rail, and swaggered back to Jonas, her hands on her hips and joy singing in her eyes. "You see now? Following the true Way is not only beneficial for each individual, but as a whole, it serves a greater purpose. And not just for fancy tricks." She motioned toward the sea. "I wanted to show you exactly why I'm not concerned to face someone so small as the king of Thonethren. He doesn't worship the Leídín. He doesn't know the truth. And for that reason, we haven't any reason to fear."

"But what if we aren't facing just a simple man?" The question surprised Jonas, himself. "What if we fight the Mother Below?"

Fridmey's smile lost a bit of its glow as she thought on this, twisting her pink lips to the side. "Well, I've had my doubts as to whether she is real or just a figment of the imagination of those who use the Taka Reu. What say you?"

"They use their Gifts through *some* kind of energy source. And it's proven that it brings about earthly change. All signs point to yes."

"I still believe if we follow the Leídín, we will come out victorious. Though that may be a biased opinion."

"I suppose." Jonas took off his spectacles to wipe them on his tunic. He returned them to his face. "If Erval is using the Taka Reu, and the earth itself is at his beck and call... If we use the Leídín...would it then be a battle of gods? Would we find ourselves decimated between mightier powers?"

Fridmey ruffled Jonas's hair. "You worry too much. I suppose you've really grown up, haven't you?"

Jonas rolled his eyes and folded his arms across his chest.

"You're right, though." Squinting up at the sky, she shielded her eyes. "Tonight is the night isn't it? The Red Moon?"

There was nothing to see at this hour. Jonas kept his gaze leveled on the chief. "It is. And we won't be there until tomorrow. Halldora expects you to be in position when the eclipse happens, right?"

Fridmey waved a noncommittal hand. "We're going as fast as we can. Besides, her people will be far more experienced on land than ours. We will fight as she needs us, though we have many families staying out at sea and away from the battle. You're to stay with them, Jonas."

"Thank you," Jonas said quietly. "But I'll need to go ashore, one way or another. I belong beside Gamaliel."

"Do you think we'll have a wedding when this is all over?"

Jonas blinked at her, his mouth gasping like a landed fish.

"Gamaliel and Solyana!"

"Oh!" His face and neck grew hot. "Probably." Jonas felt a gaping maw of fear open up in his chest. The recurring truth that visited him every single night for the last few weeks only coming into more clarity. Yet, it was still missing an important part.

If his dream was to be believed—and Jonas did believe it—there would be no 'when this is all over' for Jonas. He would be present at the battle of Thonethren, and he would be surrounded by fire for the second time in his short life. But the heat would not be coming from his own hands; the ash would not be of his doing.

"Jonas?" Fridmey's voice tore him from his thoughts. "Are you okay?"

"Yes," he answered quickly, a small placating smile passing over his lips. "Yes, Frid. I'm fine."

NOT ONCE

PALLAH

EVERYTHING IN PALLAH'S LIFE seemed destined to fail by her hand. No matter what choices she made, no matter whom she trusted—it was all for nothing. Even after years of meticulous planning, after the excruciatingly long and cold journey to Endirinn, after all the whispers of a supernatural feeling at the peak of its mountain, she had left empty-handed.

Pallah sat on the edge of her balcony overlooking Thonethren. Her eyes were dry; there was nothing left to cry about. Instead, she seethed, every bit of her aching to shift her weight forward, to feel the coveted weightlessness before death itself.

Erval wouldn't allow such a thing, of course. He would sense what she was thinking, what she was feeling—no thought truly her own—and he would catch her before she hit the ground.

She had been so close. She had interrogated the locals and scoured the impassable mountain. She had climbed and searched, certain she had sensed her brother's presence. But whether by some supernatural guard or her own inability to find him on that spire-filled rock, she was left desolate.

There was something about the mountain that was crushing, suffocating. As if the Celestials themselves knew of her worship of the

Mother Below and were attempting to squeeze it out of her. Perhaps there was something to what her spies had claimed, that the curse needed a prophecy to combat it. But where could she find such a prophecy? Who could she find that would be so ingrained in one that their presence alone would free her brother?

And if she couldn't... Would the rest of her eternal life be filled with regret? She had no answer for that. What she did know was, of all the mistakes she had made, the people she had betrayed, all the circumstances she had manipulated—Ahren was the only one she wished to rectify.

But her ultimate failure was when Erval had finally stepped into her mind. She had been at a tavern in Endirinn, nursing her second cup of mead.

Are you done throwing your tantrum?

Pallah hadn't even reacted, simply sipped her drink, content to ignore his crooning.

I told you to forget about him, that brother of yours. He's long gone, Pallah. And even if you were to retrieve him—why would he ever forgive you?

Pallah froze. "Forgive me?"

For trapping him there. You are the reason he has been held against his will for the last hundred years, Pallah. You are the reason he wastes away. If you were seeking his forgiveness before, he has even less of it to offer you now.

A tear rolled down her cheek.

"Are you going to tell me to come back?"

That's up to you, m'lady. We have nothing but time, and it's been far too long since you've explored anywhere besides this city. You're welcome to have your fun. But don't be gone too long. I may get bored and find someone new.

Pallah had left the very next morning.

Now, sitting precariously on her balcony, Pallah realized her thoughts then and now were the same. Erval was a master puppeteer, and she the willing little puppet.

He knew it, too. He knew the hold he had over her, pretending to give her the space to feel like she was still in control.

But she was far, far from it.

She edged closer, feeling her heart dip toward her toes. One more shift and—

There was a knock at her door.

Pallah gripped the banister, her eyes on the dizzying distance to the ground below.

Unfolding herself from the rail, she moved back through her room to open the door. But there was no one there. Only an empty hallway. She peered one way and then the other before her eyes found a small burlap sack of something on the ground, a scroll secured to it.

Retrieving it, she unrolled the parchment to find Phineas's familiar scrawl.

Drink a bit of this every day to keep him from entering your mind.

Pallah pried open the small satchel to find a pile of herbs. She sniffed it. Saxifrage and rosebay. Wrinkling her nose, she stepped back into her room and found herself placing a kettle of water on the metal stand in the hearth. She used her Heitt to make a quick fire, pushing the heat to its limit so the kettle boiled almost instantly.

She dumped a bit of the herbs into her tea kettle and set the lid back on, giving it a few minutes to steep. While she waited, her mind turned and her heart began to race.

What consequences would she incur with this small act? No, she corrected herself, it was not small. Erval would know, and it would not be small to him. And then what? Her hands began to shake, and she pressed them against her thighs, worrying her lip between her teeth.

She pulled the note back out and realized there was something written on the back.

And then leave, Pallah. Hide yourself well and never come back.

Emotion choked her. Phineas had been nothing but indifferent to her over all these years.

Hadn't he?

She searched her memories, bringing to mind every interaction she could recall. When she had first arrived, he'd stared down his nose at her, but now? Had he become some kind of secret friend? Was he, too, partaking in this tea? Or was he trying to get her in trouble?

Maybe he was trying to be rid of her.

Eyeing the kettle from the corner of her eye, Pallah drummed her fingers on her knee. Then, before she could change her mind, she poured a cup of it and downed it in one swallow, eyes squeezed shut against the heat and her sin.

Nothing happened.

She had thought maybe some kind of feeling of protection might come over her. But all she felt was the burn of the liquid in her belly.

And now, she was to run away without a word? Leave her home of more than a lifetime to live as an outcast and a nomad?

But this was no home. It never had been. Her desire to be wanted and loved had never been fulfilled with Erval, for he had nothing to give but cold fury and control. She had escaped one father, abusive and biting, to enter the home of a second father, who had trapped and threatened her.

She had killed them both.

Pallah felt fury and rage pour through her, hotter than the tea.

She should kill this man, too.

The thought sent her heart pounding furiously against her chest.

But even now, living the lives and wielding the Gifts of hundreds of others, she was still no match for the man. He had honed his skills to even further precision than her own. And he would not take her leaving kindly. Did she really want to live the rest of her years waiting to be caught? How could she effectively hide herself from a man who could step into the mind of any unsuspecting victim at will? It was impossible.

Or was it?

If she was able to get her hands on the tea and not only drink it but actively give it to others, she could surround herself with what was effectively a human barrier. With her stored up Fera Gifts, she had the ability to control any type of water. Weather would be easy to create and manipulate.

If the properties of the tea worked through infusion, could it also work to cloak an area from prying eyes? If she could infuse the tea into the mists, the clouds, the snow...how long could she hide herself?

Another knock on her door sounded, and Pallah jumped. She scurried over to the satchel and hid it in one of her shoes before throwing Phineas's note into the flames.

Answering the door, she bit back a gasp.

"Hello, m'lady," Erval said as he walked into her room, hands clasped behind his back. "I thought it best we have a chat."

"I'm actually feeling a bit ill. Perhaps we could talk at breakfast in the morning." Pallah's forehead was slick with sweat.

Erval turned toward her, eyebrow raised. "Ill?"

"Yes." Pallah's eyes searched him. Did he know of the tea? Why else would he be here?

"You have unlimited Fera and Heitt at your disposal, and you're feeling...ill?" He crossed his arms and leaned against the wall. "Sounds like you're trying to get rid of me." His lips turned upward in a smirk. "I kind of like it. It's refreshing. And makes me want to stay all the more." He traveled around her room, stopping before the hearth and the tea kettle at rest beside it, a bit of the tea still inside.

Panic clawed at Pallah's insides, but she took a deep breath, attempting to quell it. "Let me take care of this; it's old." She whisked the kettle from the table, intent on dumping its contents into the fire, but quicker than she thought possible, Erval was behind her, arms wrapping her, his hands covering her own to slowly pry the kettle from her fingers.

He chuckled. "You will always be too slow."

"Let go of me," Pallah growled and tried to shake him off.

"I like this woman," he said. "Where has she been this whole time?" His lips caressed her ear. "The Pallah I knew was always so docile, so submissive—all these years, rolling over at my will."

Pallah couldn't breathe. He had never held her like this, had never spoken to her so intimately. Part of her wanted to turn, to press into him, but the better part of her wanted to light him on fire. Her body betrayed her, shaking in his hold.

"I thought I was training a warrior, someone ready to fight. Have I made it too difficult for you? Did you not have the strength to combat me?" He *tsk*ed, and rage boiled in Pallah's veins. "I'm quite disappointed."

He wanted a warrior, did he?

Fine.

Bein Fera first. She tethered to his hands, popping the bones backward until she could feel them about to break. But just at the point of snapping, Pallah heard wood rather than bone as her four-poster bed splintered apart, a piece of it flying toward her face. Twisting away from him, she switched to Vior Fera, catching the thick beam. Each of them fought to control it, and the ragged wood shook in the air.

He chuckled behind her, and she glanced over her shoulder to see him throwing a punch. Ducking away, she lost control of the beam, and it shot into the wall before clattering to the ground. The air in the room began to swirl, her hair and clothes whipping against her skin.

Pallah realized the tea must be working. He hadn't struck out with his Mann Tala, or any type of bodily Fera, for that matter. Phineas had potentially saved her life. Or he had doomed her; time would tell.

Scrambling away, Erval kicked her in the side before she could stand, sending her sprawling across the wooden floorboards. Using Blou Fera, she tethered to the blood in Erval's veins, constricting and twisting, attempting to clot what she could.

He grimaced and stumbled backward, clutching at his chest as the wind died down. His eyes locked on hers as she stood, one hand on the ribs he'd broken with his foot. Without even blinking, Erval ducked, a wingback chair flying from the corner of the room behind him, the leg clipping her in the temple, tossing her back down to the floor.

The interruption disconnected her tether, and she scrambled on all fours, the sound of his boots running at her raising fear and desperation from deep within. Using Malmur Fera this time, she extended her hand toward her broken bed, her double-headed axe sliding from beneath it, fitting firmly in her grasp.

She tried to roll, but he was on top of her, hands grabbing around her throat, wrapping and squeezing. Her eyes bulged, threatening to explode from her face, and her heart began to slow. Everything in her told her to go limp, but she couldn't; there had to be—Lakimi Fera. Tethering to the muscles in his arms, she shoved them away from her, his grip loosening. It was enough to let her blood through, fresh oxygen fueling her brain, her clarity returning as she swung the staff at his skull. He moved to dodge it but was too slow, throwing him off balance. Pallah knocked him back, leaping to her feet.

She twirled her staff, the axe heads protruding from each end, her chest heaving.

Pressing a hand to the side of his head, blood dripping down his temple, Erval faced her, a smile stretching across his face. Perhaps the first genuine one she'd ever seen.

"How have we gone this long without some honest combat training? Delightful!" He held his other hand to the side, an iron fire poker bounding into his ready grip. He swung, arcing it high over his head.

Her weapon raised in both hands, she blocked his descending blow, dropping her left hand as the iron raked the length of the metal before catching on the axe head. Without a pause, Erval's boot slammed into her chest, and she flew backward, barely holding onto her staff as her body smacked into the floor.

"You toy with me," Pallah said between coughs.

"Well, it would be no fun to just kill you." Erval twirled the iron poker in his hands. "You seem to have prepared yourself for this. Leveled the playing field, if only slightly."

"What are you talking about?" Her ribs screamed, her head spun, and her throat pulsed with bruising.

"The tea. I could smell it before I even entered the room." He pulled his ascot from around his neck and wiped the blood trickling from his head with it. "This is merely a squabble, Pallah. A little spat. We'll be right as rain tomorrow." His smile darkened. "You'll see."

Pallah screamed, lunging forward with her axe, striking down hard once, twice—and on the third blow, his hold loosened on the iron poker. Using her Malmur Fera, she flung it away from him, and thought she caught a flicker of worry on his face.

Shifting her stance, she brought the axe around, intent on slicing from the side. She would let the blade meet skin, meet bone. She would free herself from the prison of Erval's twisted control. Pallah braced herself for the rending of his body. She would pour the remnants of the tea down his throat; no amount of Heitt would save him then.

He launched backward, his Vindur Fera stronger than before. Wind filled the room once again, her slippered feet sliding over the wooden floor, her hair snapping and stinging her face.

"Enough, Pallah. I don't want to kill you." The neck of his shirt snapped in the wind revealing a quick flash of sparkling gold.

"That makes one of us." Pallah tethered to the brick in the fireplace behind Erval, pulling it down to crush him. He brought up a hand, not bothering to look back, and the wind died down as he stilled the hearth. But then Pallah connected to the floor, commanding the wood to splinter and break. Erval's face registered surprise as his feet fell through, the jagged ends of the wood catching his knees. He let out a cry of pain.

Pallah took two steps forward, the axe swinging. The blade sank into his side and came to an abrupt halt.

The break in momentum threw Pallah off balance, and the bricks behind them fell. She raised a hand, now in the path of the crumbling hearth herself, and steadied it with her Fera. Erval's eyes found hers beside him, all his concentration on the axe in his side, though Pallah still held it in her grip.

He shoved the weapon away, and Pallah's body slid with it until she collided with the opposite wall, a cough and blood rushing from her mouth.

The bricks fell, but before they could crush him, Erval took hold, suspending them in the air. He rose from the floor, releasing a grunt of pain as the jagged wood ripped at his legs. A shift came over the room, and Pallah knew she had drawn his wrath. His rage poured off him like smoke. She tried to get to her feet, but her body refused, every ounce of her worn through, exhausted.

Erval suspended his body in the air, using Vindur Fera or some other Gift Pallah wasn't aware of. He brought himself back to the floor as the bricks stayed in place—using multiple Gifts at once. That wasn't possible. Pallah gaped, a stream of blood still dribbling from the side of her mouth.

She caught his eyes then, dark as pitch, black as night. She had seen this look only when he performed the Taking. Fear froze her in place. Could he perform it on her with the tea in her system? Would he kill her?

Hands pulsing forward, he tethered to her clothes, drawing her to him roughly, where she felt a new sharp lance of pain.

Shaking, afraid to look down, Pallah glimpsed the iron rod protruding from her belly.

Her hands grasped at it as her mouth opened wordlessly.

He would kill her now and then Take everything from her. The countless years she had stored, the thousands of Gifts.

She'd avoided using Heitt this whole time, afraid she would lose herself to the flames. But what did it matter now? Drawing on the Gift stolen from her sister so long ago, Pallah brought forth her fire. Wild and untamed, her flames shot out like a horizontal tornado, consuming the man intent on taking her life.

Erval screamed, stumbling backward from her, his arms attempting to shield his body. Pallah stumbled away, steeling herself as she yanked the rod from her middle, her blood pooling over the ground. The fire was catching, consuming drapes, bedding, even the floor itself.

Steadying herself with her staff in hand, Pallah grabbed her shoes and fled.

Behind her, she left the life she hated. She left her ambitions. She left a man burning while he screamed her name.

She did not look back.

Not once.

SAVING THE WORLD

SOLYANA

DUSK DEEPENED, THE RED MOON creeping ever closer.

Erval's dark presence over Mothmar, the looming shadow of his impending rule, stretched wider with each passing moment. The hoofbeats beneath Solyana beat like the drums they use to honor their dead, their echo bouncing in the empty space of Gamaliel's absence.

She embraced the burn of the wind and the aches in her muscles. It was not Mothmar's fate that fueled her charge toward Thonethren. Rhuth waited there, danger surrounding her on all sides. Solyana would recover her sister, then she would return for Gamaliel. Erval was Phineas's problem, and Pallah Ahren's. She would not bear the weight they carried any longer.

Phineas used his Tala with the horses, allowing them to slow as they approached the hills that served as a natural border to Erval's domain. The three of them sat on the hillside, the blanket of night descending upon them, and both men kept keen eyes on any movement—searching for Halldora's men.

"You understand?" Phineas had asked her with genuine awe once they both had a chance to tether the stoat.

"I guess so." Solyana had shrugged. "It feels entirely too simple."

The old steward had nodded sagely, his eyes searching the sky. "Sometimes the greatest truths are."

It had become clear over their time together that Phineas no longer wanted to follow the Taka Reu but felt trapped within it. It was an honor to watch him come to understand something new, something greater.

Now, Solyana herself scoured the darkening sky in search of the path of Leídín. Although, according to Jonas, one didn't actually need to find it; it just helped make the conversion happen faster.

She had trod a distance away, letting the glow of their fire fade to a pinprick of light in the waving grass.

"How could we have had it wrong for so long?" she asked the skies, her braid whipping out behind her in the warm wind. "Somewhere along the way, someone altered our truths, placing us in boxes, separating us from each other. Forming communities turned into forming walls. If we had only known... How much pain and suffering could have been avoided?" Pressure built behind her eyes, the accumulated mistakes of prophecies, falsities, and selfish lies rearing to heights that threatened to overwhelm her. The truth so simple, so gentle, it hurt to accept it.

"We were never meant to split into Heitt, Fera, and Tala. We were meant to have access to all. You are generous. You never intended for us to be without."

The Celestials spoke nothing audible, but Solyana could feel their presence in her soul. It wasn't about worshiping each deity separately, but all the Celestials as one. It made sense to her now.

"I believe in you," she whispered to the skies. "Please forgive my selfishness and guide me." Eyes on the velvet cover of night, Solyana spotted it: the Leídín. It offered a slight pulse of light as she traced the heavenly pattern with her eyes. Something fresh and new entered her mind and wound its way to her heart, bringing her understanding—peace.

She breathed in, taking it to heart. "Thank you, Jonas," she said, hoping in some illogical way he would understand through the skies. She wondered then, for the first time, if they would be reunited or if their paths were destined to be split forever.

She hoped it was the former.

Her hand flew to her face as it tingled and burned, her scar rising to the surface. She whimpered as it flared, and then beneath her fingertips, it dissolved, as if it had never been. Her scar was gone. Forever? She didn't know. But she remembered the words said to her, that the scar was the combination of both the Taka Reu and the Celestials staking their claim. Perhaps now, worshiping the true Way, it finally released her for good.

"I've got it!" Solyana called out as she returned to their camp. Ahren stood beside Phineas, and the three met in the middle. "I think I understand. It's not manipulation, like we've always thought. It's a petition."

Phineas nodded, and Solyana noticed his eyes held glistening tears.

"Did you find it, too?"

He nodded, removing his spectacles to wipe his eyes. "I did!" He released a cry and a chuckle in tandem, and Solyana couldn't help the grin that spread over her face as well.

"I haven't," Ahren said, arms crossed.

Phineas placed a hand on Ahren's shoulder and gave it a squeeze. "We'll try again. But first, the Red Moon is almost upon us. We have yet to see Halldora's men, but I know they're here. I can feel them. And if I can sense them, Erval might be able to, as well."

"Not if they've been drinking the tea," Ahren pointed out. "Or if they picked up on what you taught them."

"True." Phineas nodded and replaced his spectacles on his face.

"How do we get into the castle?" Ahren turned to gaze at the jagged silhouette of Thonethren's castle in the distance. It sat in the center of the city, like a large stone island protruding from the sea.

"He's expecting us. He knows the three of us are together and are coming. We should simply...enter," Solyana said.

"Indeed." Phineas nodded, but one glance at his face told Solyana he was worried. "But I hate to go in blind." He tapped at his chin. "Perhaps I should find Jothan first."

"Jothan?" Ahren asked.

"Erval has been training a new steward. He would know what, if anything, is happening. He would know where the Brextant is being positioned."

"And you still plan on destroying it?" Solyana asked.

"Yes." Phineas nodded, his hands beginning their rasping. "Perhaps Jothan would know of your sister as well."

Solyana straightened, fists clenched at her sides. "Then what are we waiting for?"

Suddenly, the night felt darker. As if dusk had not been mere moments before. The three of them, faces turned up toward the moon, watched as the bright coin in the sky began to disappear from view. The stars shone brilliantly, and Solyana's mouth fell open as she realized it was happening.

The Red Moon.

A cry rent the night. Far below, where the slope of the hills flattened toward the walls of the city, Solyana spotted movement.

"There!" She pointed, and Phineas crouched against the hillside to overlook the city grounds.

"Halldora has launched her assault," he said, his voice lacking all emotion. "We're too late."

Solyana turned to him, his entire face shining with sweat. "We are not too late. We shift our plans. Instead of walking in, we sneak in, grab Rhuth, and get out."

"And Pallah," Ahren said with a bite to his voice.

Solyana nodded, tension rising in her gut. The closer they got to the castle, the more she realized how little each of them cared for each other's priorities. In truth, they were all diving headlong onto different paths.

Phineas's eyes met her own. Solyana found sorrow there and something else she couldn't name. His lips parted as if to speak, but he seemed to think better of it and closed them again.

He still held secrets. Far too many for Solyana's liking.

"We need to go before the army strikes at full strength. We don't want to get lost in the fray," Ahren said, half rising, ready to run. "Ready?"

"The eastern tower. I'll lead the way." Phineas motioned for them to fall in line behind him. "Your eyes be upward."

"And be filled with light," Solyana and Ahren responded.

Then the three took off into the dark, two intent on saving sisters, one seeking to stop a king.

Together, they might just save the world.

BREAK

GAMALIEL

GAMALIEL WOKE, EYES BLINKING at the single lantern left burning on the bedside table. The hearth was cold, and the house held the tension of the unfamiliar. Soft breaths came from beneath him.

"Vinur?" he croaked.

His faithful friend rose from beneath his cot and rested his chin on Gamaliel's chest, tail wagging, a high-pitched whine emanating from his throat. As he had done countless times before, Gamaliel tethered to his Tala companion. But then he froze. Someone had left something in Vinur's mind.

He searched it out, his mind reeling, until the source of it filled him with warmth. Solyana. He latched onto it like a man desperate and information poured through the tether, revealing her plans in detail. His eyes scanning the dark space before him, Gamaliel could imagine only the worst. The boat, the waves, a hidden cave, then riding into Thonethren—all without him.

Clenching his fists, he released a growl of frustration. She had left him. Again.

He was alone.

Memories surfaced, dredged up from the depths of depression and despair he had sunk to the past five years. Sweat broke out over his skin and his chest heaved. His tongue, dry in his mouth, throbbed, begging for a drink. The temptation washed over him, overwhelming and all-encompassing. His fingers curled around an imaginary bottle before reaching up to pull at his hair, the pain grounding him as he lay flat on the cot. His eyes squeezed shut, and he took quick breaths, mind spinning out of control.

Vinur whined and nudged his side with a cold nose.

"I can't do this," Gamaliel told the wolf, cracking an eye open to find Vinur circling his cot. "I don't know how long she's been gone! She could be dead! I can't—"

The wolf growled, almost a reprimand, and launched himself wholly atop Gamaliel, who cried out in surprise.

"Vinur!"

Pain lanced through his body and he made to shove Vinur away, but the too-small wolf evaded him and crawled carefully up his chest to tuck his head beneath Gamaliel's chin. Then he released a sigh, his breathing setting a tempo for Gamaliel's own.

The tracker wrapped the wolf in his arms and wept. Finally, after what seemed a long time, his breaths slowed, and his mind returned to him.

"It's okay, boy," he whispered to his faithful companion, calming them both. "It's okay. I'm okay."

He prodded his shoulder and, to his shock, found the pain to be minimal. A deep ache yet remained, but nowhere near the lancing pain he remembered... How much time had passed? He looked around.

Too much. And now Solyana was gone.

But was he truly too late?

He tethered Vinur again, this time sifting through the information more carefully. There! Solyana had only left last night. And this time, he didn't fault her. He couldn't. He would have slowed them down. According to the information she'd left with Vinur, the soldiers would have—

A sound outside the window drew his eyes. He could hear the sea, waves crashing onto rocks. And layered just above it, footsteps. Soft enough that Gamaliel, who had tracked enough game in his life, knew they were trying to hide—and failing.

Vinur growled, hopping back to the floor, all friendliness gone.

He held his tether firm. Where was his staff? He searched the room and found it leaning against the opposite corner. Legs shaking with the effort, Gamaliel retrieved his weapon and pressed his body against the wall.

A face appeared in the window below his elbow and Gamaliel held his breath. He encouraged Vinur to keep still, hoping the soldier would assume nothing but a fuzzy blanket was lying on the floor. His memory was scattered from the last few days, an assortment of cave smell, barking soldiers, and quiet. But he knew from Solyana's message that the queen marching on Thonethren had sent men to find her.

And if they couldn't find her, surely they'd be happy to take him instead, the perfect ransom to draw her out. And Gamaliel wouldn't allow that. He clutched his staff to his chest, preparing to do what he had to do to keep her safe.

"It's empty!" the man in the window said through a layer of glass. "The witch was telling the truth." He pulled away and Gamaliel breathed a sigh of relief as the sounds of two sets of footsteps marched away.

Witch? Gamaliel shook his head, the pieces of understanding shifting into place. He slipped two fingers beneath his tunic to find the flesh there cleanly stitched.

His last true memory was of the swishing reeds of a hillside meadow, Solyana's hair in his hands, their lips closing in to kiss. Then nothing but pain, in his body and in his heart.

His vision swam, and he sank to his knees, tears burning behind his eyes. "I don't know what I'm supposed to do, Vinur," he said through gritted teeth. "I'm in no shape to keep myself safe. How am I supposed to save Solyana before time runs out?"

Vinur trotted to his side and placed his chin in his master's lap, his ice-blue eyes conveying more than Gamaliel knew was possible.

"I'm too weak," he told the wolf.

Vinur huffed.

"I don't even know where I am or how I would even begin to make it to Thonethren."

The wolf tilted his head to the side.

"Well, yes. Solyana did leave me that message. But I can't get in a boat and swim to an underwater cave."

Vinur released a soft whine.

"She left on horseback then..." Gamaliel rubbed his eyes. "The stables."

Getting to his feet again, he went to the window and looked out to see a stone pathway that ran parallel to the sea. The other side of the path steeply inclined until stairs, set into the rock, splayed to other homes and huts scattered across the cliffside.

"Can't get horses down those paths very easily. They must be at the top."

Vinur got to his feet and sneezed.

"These soldiers aren't looking for a single man but the three of us together," Gamaliel continued to the empty room and the wolf at his feet. "I just have to make it up those stairs."

He squared his shoulders, feeling a thrill of fear and determination worm its way through his being.

Though he was able to walk, his whole body was weak. It would take every bit of strength simply to make it to the opposite end of whatever town he was in. But Gamaliel was nothing if not stubborn. Solyana would be meeting the king of Thonethren in a few days' time, and Gamaliel had every intention of standing at her side. Tracking and trapping, hiding and seeking, he would guide himself by the sun and stars and protect his own.

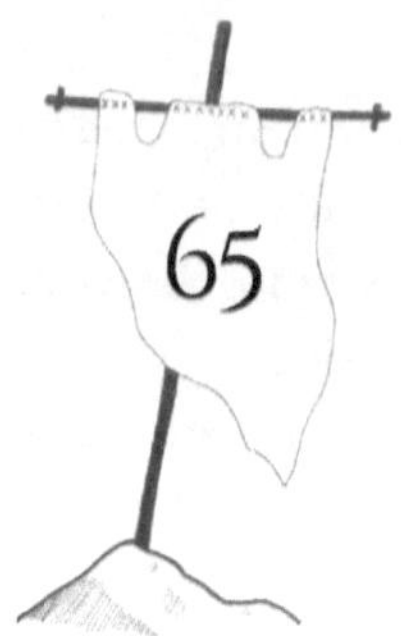

BATTLE OF THE BEASTS

HALLDORA

CLAD IN HER BLACKENED metal armor, Halldora sat straight on her mount, surveying Thonethren through her visor. Like an unblinking eye, her city was structured in distinct rings: farms and hovels on the outer perimeter circled the city itself. The castle proper lay at the very center, surrounded by a wall. And like the lid of that eye, in the north, stood Mount Hekla, ever watchful, always present.

Halldora would give her a show tonight.

Spread behind her like wings were her cavalry, and behind them, the foot soldiers. At the very back stood her archers, each man instructed to use their Gifts, to hold nothing back to retake their city.

A small team had been sent in. Not to negotiate, as General Ivan had suggested, but to see what forces her brother had gathered to meet her. They would secure the wall in such a way that when they reached it, it would crumble like stale bread in her palm.

Unlike her brother, she was no monster. She did not wish to see the people of Thonethren slain for her sake.

Rage burned through her veins as she remembered so long ago when he had thrown her from this same kingdom. She was eager to pay him in kind.

A pair of antlers approached from down the line, and Halldora squinted at the elk coming toward her at a trot. On its back was the blonde woman with braids over her ears, the rest of her hair tumbling behind her. She wore war paint and black kohl that lined her eyes and traced from her lip to her neck.

"I trust your people are in place?" Halldora asked in lieu of greeting.

"Your western and eastern flanks are covered by my riders."

Halldora bristled at the curt speech, but this was not the time to demand titles or vie for ownership. The nomads would learn such truths after the war was won.

"Is the Crimson Chief in place?" Maral's gaze slid to Lake Illgres that lay behind them, past the expanse of the geyser field. "I see no ships."

"No word." Halldora did not elaborate.

The Chief's insistence on following the Way had led them away from the battle. She sneered. Religion and the blind obedience it drew from its followers would never cease to draw Halldora's ire, unless she was using it to her own advantage, of course.

"It doesn't matter. We're stronger without him."

"I can leave a group by Lake Illgres, if you wish. We could relay any information if—"

"It's handled," Halldora snapped. "Is that all you came for?" She sat straighter in her saddle.

"No. I came to tell you my Riders have sensed animals outside of our army."

"I'm sure there are many animals in the surrounding wood." Halldora kept her eyes on the gaps between houses, waiting for the return of her men or the falcon she had sent with them.

Maral hesitated a moment before giving a small bow. "I can't help but wonder what happened to Orson."

Halldora's lip quirked. "He's dead."

Maral blinked beside her. "Dead? How do you know?"

She opened her mouth to reassure Maral when something caught her attention. Formerly lit in pale moonlight, the city before her dipped into a rust-colored red, the color of blood. The moon was shifting. As if heralding the celestial change, a mighty sound, almost like wind, tore through the outskirts of her men. Maral looked over her shoulder, searching for its cause.

"What is…" Halldora's words died in her throat as what had started as a whisper of air grew to a roar.

It was not wind, but a war cry. One Halldora recognized.

"Behind us!" a soldier cried out.

"Orson!" Maral seethed, wheeling her mount around before bolting away to shout at her men. A geyser burst to life to her right, almost knocking her headlong from her mount. "They know we're here! Watch your backs!"

He wasn't dead?

A falcon shot above the grounds, bathed in red moonlight. Halldora tethered it quickly and understanding poured into her mind, pooling like acid.

"Men!" she shouted, turning in her saddle. An arrow whistled past and embedded itself cleanly in the neck of the soldier to her left. Halldora wiped at her eyes, sprayed by his blood.

The soldier made no sound but slumped in his saddle before sliding to the ground. Eyes wide with the news of her team slaughtered at the wall, enemies surrounding her, Halldora kicked her horse into a run. Ivan had been with the group at the wall. It had been his idea to meet Erval on the geyser field, and now he wouldn't be here to see it. What was supposed to have been a head-to-head battle had turned into a short game of cat and mouse, and she had foolishly cast herself as the rodent.

"To arms!" she called out as her horse tore down the line. "Orson and his Beast Riders are nothing but dogs! Turn in line and strike!"

Another whistle, the arrow this time grazing her shoulder, bounced off her armor and spun out of control before sticking into the ground.

Archers recovered, her men returned the volley. A wall of wood and fletching soared into the barren field like deadly rain. Orson's men were in full view now, layered in armor and dark paint, sitting astride beasts twice the size of Maral's. Soldiers in the armor of Thonethren stood in rows on either side across the geyser field. Steam rose from the pock-marked ground, mixing with the dark *aska* that swirled around each rider.

Orson laughed so loudly Halldora could hear him from her position. The arrows took point on him as if he'd purposefully drawn them toward himself. Then, moments before Orson became a permanent decoration on the grounds outside the city, the arrows shattered, raining harmless splinters against the mighty polar bear beneath him and anyone in his vicinity.

Her foot soldiers scrambled to get through the archers, who were retreating to safer positions. She watched helplessly as hundreds of her archers and foot soldiers were slaughtered as the beasts and their riders fell upon her ground men. Halldora drew the sword from her side and screamed as her cavalry launched forward. She peered down the line to see Maral's riders bathed in the red of the moon, gaining ground as they wove around to charge their enemy.

The stallion beneath her rose up on its hind legs, and she grasped at his withers before he landed hard to the earth. This would be named the Battle of the Beasts, and she would be its victor.

"Queen!" a voice barked from behind her as her horse landed back on all fours. She turned to find General Ivan, forehead smeared in blood, running full-tilt toward her.

"Ivan!" Relief coursed through her, new energy filling her veins.

"Our spies have been dead for weeks! The enemy has been feeding us lies." He panted, his sword drawn and dripping blood. "He knew we were coming all along and has had Orson's men and maybe a third of his soldiers waiting out in these fields for days. The rest surround the castle wall itself. My Queen," Ivan said as he drew his visor up and she saw for the first time the fear in his eyes. "With Orson alive and allied with Erval, they outnumber us *ten to one.*"

The screams of her men as they died in droves blotted out all thought. All this time, she had been so sure her brother would fall to his pride, when her own arrogance now threatened the loss of everything she had worked so hard for. She did not numb herself to this feeling of failure; she embraced it and bore its weight. She had not trained for her men positioned entirely backward on the battlefield, and it would cost her. It would cost her greatly.

Halldora raised her visor, meeting Ivan's gaze in full. "Why am I here, Ivan?"

"To win back your seat, my Queen," Ivan responded.

Her gauntleted hand pulled her visor back down as the battle crashed closer. Orson was advancing.

"I'm here to kill my *häfan* brother." She reached down, extending her hand to help Ivan to mount her horse. He hoisted himself up and behind her before Halldora gave the mount a firm kick, ripping the reins to the side as her stallion bolted off into the night.

Charging forward, Halldora wove and leapt over the remains of her men. Maral would keep them back—she had her own issues with Orson to fuel her fight with him.

A crack sounded beneath the ground, so loud her head rattled in her helm. A geyser burst before her, causing her stallion to scream as he rose again on his hind legs. She could feel Ivan slipping off behind her, his fingers grasping for purchase at her waist. Then she was flying, bucked off by her mount before he tore away. She landed hard on the ground, feeling the earth shifting beneath her. She used Fera, tethering to it and gasped. A greater tether than her own was latched to the very ground—multiple tethers.

"My Queen!" Ivan got to his feet and extended a hand to her.

She took it, letting him assist in pulling her to her feet. "They're tethering the ground! They're trying to open a hole! Help me, Ivan!"

Her general dove in with his own tether, latching to rocky soil, and she was encouraged to find it easier with his support. But it wouldn't be enough.

"There's too many of them," he said through gritted teeth.

"No, no!" She heard it then, the rip in the earth, as if the Mother Below was opening her mouth, intent on a feast.

Rocked to the ground again, Halldora was on her knees, Ivan beside her, both staring in horror as the entire contingent of archers fell into the gaping maw and whatever dark fires lay beneath. Then it sealed back up again, as quick as it had opened, burying her men alive.

She had sorely underestimated her brother. And for it, these men who had supported and trusted her were paying with their lives.

She would have to live with that.

If she lived at all.

SECOND CHANCE

RHUTH

THONETHREN WAS CRYPT SILENT.

Rhuth's eyes scanned the perimeter of the city, Ember pressing solidly against her leg. The fox shook as if she could sense the evil present here, as if she knew the cost of coming. She could see the movements of the townspeople in the streets and between houses, their quick and quiet steps, scared of waking a sleeping giant.

Pallah crouched beside them, one hand on her smilodon, the other pressed to the ground cleared of snow. "He's here," she whispered as she rose to stand. "I can feel his power through the earth. His Taka Reu has become the lifeblood of this city, so ingrained as it is."

"Is he controlling everyone here?"

Pallah shook her head. "Not with his Mann Tala. That's far too many people for him. He could have issued an ordinance. Though I wonder why..."

Fear twisted Rhuth's gut.

Magnus gave a low, clicking growl, and Pallah placed a hand on his head, stroking his ears.

"The wall is gone," she said. "It used to wrap around the city itself and now... I bet he built one around the castle itself instead. Selfish bastard."

Rhuth turned around to face the geyser field and the woods beyond. Her creatures were biding their time, ready to enter the city if any trouble arose. The moon was a sliver in the night, a celestial smile that Rhuth hoped was kindly.

"Do you think he knows we're here?" Rhuth asked.

"There's no telling," Pallah whispered and began picking her way through the city. "But I don't like how quiet it is."

They went on in silence, the click of Ember's paws the only sound accompanying them as they trekked between houses and shadows. "You drank your tea today?" Pallah asked breathlessly over her shoulder.

"A little late to ask me now," Rhuth responded. "But yes, every day."

"Good."

They continued on, weaving their way through the southern parts of the city. The stone spires of the castle peeked through the rooftops, backlit by stars, as they scuttled closer and closer until they were through the open gate and into the castle grounds itself.

"There should be guards..." Pallah began, squinting in the darkness. "But where are they?"

"Can you feel them with Lakimi Fera?"

"I don't want to use the Taka Reu this close." Pallah scowled. "He'll know."

"I meant with the Way."

Pallah released a huff but then closed her eyes. Rhuth did the same, intent on finding the men if Pallah couldn't.

Rhuth had never tried to dowse people before, only animals. It was odd, searching for her own kind, but as she poked and prodded through the castle halls with her Fera, she grew increasingly more anxious. Where was everyone?

Then she found them. *All of them.* Packed tightly into one room in the castle; the guards, servants, and stewards all huddled together as one.

Eyes flying open in unison, Rhuth and Pallah stared at each other. "They're all together," Rhuth said. "Some kind of trap?"

"Inconsequential. We're powerful enough to see our way through regardless."

"Your confidence is less reassuring and more frightening."

"It doesn't mean I'm wrong." Pallah ushered her onward until they were pressed against the side of the castle itself. "We need to get to the basement. If the Brextant is anywhere, it's there."

"And Solyana?"

Pallah stopped short. "Yes, yes. We'll find her."

"But you said—"

"I know what I said," Pallah snapped. "But this is bigger than your sister, girl. Without access to the device, we will have no chance of truly stopping him. It all must be destroyed." With a whirl of her cloak, Pallah ducked into the castle through a low window.

Rhuth followed as they snuck in, the halls eerily quiet. She had known it was a possibility Pallah had told her what she'd wanted to hear. But she had begun to believe—she'd *wanted* to believe—that she wasn't being lied to. That Pallah was a changed person, inside and out.

But more than their claimed or true purposes here, what bothered Rhuth more was the state of the castle staff. Why was everyone in one room? The question pounded at the back of her skull, an incessant theory their arrival was known. Erval knew they were here.

"I really think it's a trap, Pallah. We should get out while—"

Pallah's hand flew up, silencing Rhuth, but her pace didn't slow. Rhuth's brow furrowed as she tiptoed behind the priestess. Silently, she pressed into the connections she had with the animals surrounding the outskirts of Thonethren.

Be ready, she told them. In return came a pulse of assurance.

Lanterns issued steady light as they traversed the halls, making their way to a spiral staircase. Pallah wasted no time shuffling down it, and Rhuth had to skip a step or two to keep up. Their animals kept to the sides, keeping in time at a loping run.

No guards. Not a single one to hinder their advance. Fear wound its way up Rhuth's legs and into her hands, making them shake.

The light faded until it ended at a door, though Rhuth couldn't spot a handle.

"How do we—"

"Sh." Pallah commanded, stepping close and dropping her knapsack to the floor. With an outstretched hand, she closed her eyes, and Rhuth could feel it, Pallah's use of Malmur Fera with…not the Way. It was the Taka Reu.

"You're using the Taka—"

"Shut up, girl!" Pallah snapped, eyes still closed. "I have no time to fritter about with powers I am unfamiliar with. It ends here. I'm taking no chances." Something deep inside the door shifted, the sound of some internal metal rods sliding and clicking into place. "Make yourself useful," she said through gritted teeth, "and make sure all those people are staying in that room."

"But you promised—"

"Do you want to live or not?" Pallah glared.

"Yes, but if it's a trap, we should—"

"Of course, it's a trap." Pallah breathed. "You think we got all this way without him knowing we were coming? You think he hasn't been preparing this whole time?" She released a derisive snort. "Now do what I told you." She pointed behind them.

Eyes wide, Rhuth nodded and reached out again, feeling the presence of all those people. Her stomach squirmed.

"Hurry," she whispered.

Pallah had known all along? Rhuth should have guessed, a woman so ancient would not be fooled. Not so easily.

The door emitted a loud *click* and swung inward, revealing darkness beyond. Pallah's shoulders heaved up and down, her breaths becoming ragged.

"Age before beauty," she said before stepping into the darkness, her double axe slung over her back, and Magnus at her side.

Rhuth followed tentatively, Ember trembling beside her.

The room was smaller than Rhuth had expected. The stone lining the floors wound in a circular pattern that spiraled toward the center, where there sat a chair. Though it was no ordinary chair. This chair filled Rhuth from top to bottom with fear. From its clawed feet to its winged back, it stood at the ready. The arms were lacquered and beautiful but harshly adorned with leather straps, matching others near where ankles and feet would rest. A cap hung from the top, attached to some kind of tubing that wound its way around the back of the chair and ran along the ceiling until it escaped out a small hole in the wall.

"What am I looking at, Pallah?" Rhuth's voice shook, and she couldn't find the will to make it stop.

"This is the device. The Brextant. It sucks the years from a person and transmutes that energy, allowing Erval to tether to countless human lives. He's really improved it in the years I've been gone."

Rhuth's eyes went wide. "Human?"

"Yes. He's Mann Tala, as you know. But he can only tether to one person at a time... and depending on their age, were likely to become lost to insanity." Pallah unstrapped the staff from her back, giving it a quick spin to eject the axe heads on either end. "I think destroying this the old fashioned way will be our best bet."

"Wait! Won't they hear us? And even if we break it, couldn't they simply build another?" Rhuth's analytical mind flew through the list of why this was a bad idea. "Shouldn't we locate Solyana first, before you do anything?"

Pallah took a step forward, knuckles turning white on the staff.

"What about Ahren?" Rhuth was desperate now, grasping for anything to keep the woman from doing something that could risk her finding her sister. "Your brother could be here, and Erval could take his ire out on him!"

Pallah reared back, ignoring Rhuth's pleas, and swung at the machine. It cracked into the side with a resounding crunch that sent Ember and Magnus scrambling into the shadows.

"Pallah! Stop!" Rhuth lunged forward, gripping the woman from behind. Pallah threw her off and Rhuth fell to the floor.

"Ahren isn't here!" Pallah pried her axe from the chair. "Solyana isn't here!" She swung again, the sharp blade slicing through leather and splintering wood. "Can't you understand? Your sister left less than a year ago. The world is choking with ice. She *failed*, Rhuth. She lost. And do you know what that means? *We lost, too!*"

"You lied to me." Rhuth hated how small she felt, how weak her voice sounded. "You just wanted me here, for what? Backup? To use me for my power?"

"Of course, it was for your power." Baring her teeth at the girl, Pallah leaned in close. "But in all this time, you've proven incapable of teaching me. Just like your sister, you're a failure. And I have no need for you now."

Rhuth blinked back tears. What had she expected? A feral animal always turns in the end, doesn't it?

"It doesn't matter. We're all just puppets, being pulled by the strings of—"

"Hello, darling," a voice crooned from behind Rhuth.

Pallah's lupine face drained of color. Standing over Rhuth, her double axe in hand, Pallah looked over Rhuth's head as a dark smoke-like substance began to drift up from the ground to snake over Pallah's skin. Magnus crouched low, his black eyes filled with murder.

The click of heeled boots made a slow circle around Rhuth, and she squeezed her eyes shut. She was going to die here; they both were. This man, if he was anything as Pallah had described, held no light inside of him. And Rhuth believed it, feeling his darkness wrap around her like a physical blanket, suffocating her until she was breathing quick and fast on the floor.

"Who did you bring to visit? You're a bit late for dinner, I'm afraid. But I can have Jothan set another plate for breakfast in the morning." He finally made his way around, coming close to Rhuth's line of vision.

The man was unexpectedly beautiful. In every hard edge of him, he held an allure that made Rhuth finally understand. The way he spoke, the way he walked, the look in his eyes, which combed over Pallah with something like concern, drew her in like a cold traveler to a cookfire.

Pallah's face, which had been white moments before, was turning an unseemly shade of red. Her nostrils flared as her eyes flicked to the man beside her, though she kept her head still.

"Wait, don't tell me." Erval folded his arms over his chest and cocked his head from side to side. His neck popped, and he sighed. "This is Rhuth, right? The sister of sweet little Solyana—may she rest in peace."

Rhuth made no sound, locking the scream inside her away. Her eyes caught Ember, slinking around the perimeter of the room. *No*, she told her. *Don't do anything foolish. This man will kill you.*

"I see you added a woman's touch to my machine." He walked to the chair at the center of the room, running his hand over the gouged and bending wood along its side. "Just in time for you to adorn it." He swept his arm as if asking Pallah to dance, bowing at his middle and presenting the machine next to him. "If you would be so kind."

"I think it would look better"—one of Pallah's hands curled around dark smoke, and the other gripped her double-headed axe—"with your body strewn across it!" And she launched herself at him.

Rhuth scrambled to her feet as Erval dove out of the way just as Pallah's axe swung, sinking again into the chair at his side, splinters of wood ejecting from it.

Pallah screamed, her hand outstretched toward Erval, but Rhuth saw his face, and cold terror sank its fangs in deep.

The king of Thonethren was smiling. "Which Fera are you attempting to use on me, Pallah? Lakimi? Bein? Blou?" He shook his head. "I'm afraid they won't work."

Rhuth called Ember to herself, and the fox scrambled to her side. *Come to me quickly,* she told the animals surrounding the grounds.

Magnus snarled and leapt at Erval, but the man simply raised a hand, and the animal hit an invisible wall before slumping to the floor.

Eyes wide, looking more panicked than Rhuth had ever seen her, Pallah shifted her weight, gripping her axe in both hands. "How?" She reached down, pulling up stones from the ground and the walls surrounding.

Rhuth tried to run, but her feet slipped on the shifting stone. She raised her hands over her head as the entire basement began to rearrange.

Erval's arms extended, the walls and ground stilling. "Ah, ah, ah," Erval clucked. "There will be no attempts at suicide today. You see, after so many years of trying to eradicate the tea from Mothmar, I realized the impossibility of the task. Instead, I've learned to work around it and partake as needed."

"No," Pallah whispered.

"I can enter minds quite easily, now I've got the hang of it—even with the tea in place. How do you think I knew you were coming?" He did a half turn on his heel and threw Rhuth a grin. "It's been lovely seeing all you can do, dear." He winked.

Had he been in her mind? Nausea roiled in her gut, and Rhuth fought for control of her body.

"It won't be long until I can use the full strength of Mann Tala, with or without the consumption of your pesky tea." He waved a hand. "What was your plan in coming in here? To destroy my machine first and me second?" He laughed, and if Rhuth hadn't known better, it would have sounded like true joy. "Where you have been hiding all these years? While you've been doggedly suppressing your Gifts, I have done everything I can to grow mine. My power is boundless, Pallah. You will—"

A flurry of feathers and talons whipped toward him as, like a tornado, three falcons swept into the room. Thrown off balance, Erval stumbled backward, covering his face with his hands. Rhuth stood, picking Ember up in her arms, and turning to run. She scrambled out the door before smacking into the chestplate of an armored figure. Ember fell, and Rhuth landed hard on the stone floor.

"Is this the one?" the guard asked another standing beside him. "Ew, look at her eye."

"Nasty scar, that is. But no, it's the other one."

Rhuth, still connected to the cast of falcons in the room behind her, felt the first of their lives stamped out, and she gasped. "No!"

The guards eyed each other, and one shrugged. "Grab her."

"No, please!" she screamed again as a second bird's life was smothered. Without being in the room, Rhuth couldn't tell what was happening. A guard reached down and picked her up, though she kicked and screamed against him. "Ember, run! Pallah! Pallah!"

"Hey, quit!" The guard gripped her, but she continued banging against his armor, clawing his head, biting his ear in her teeth. "Hey!" He twisted her, slamming her stomach and chest against the wall.

Then there was a flash of pain at the side of her skull, and nothing but darkness.

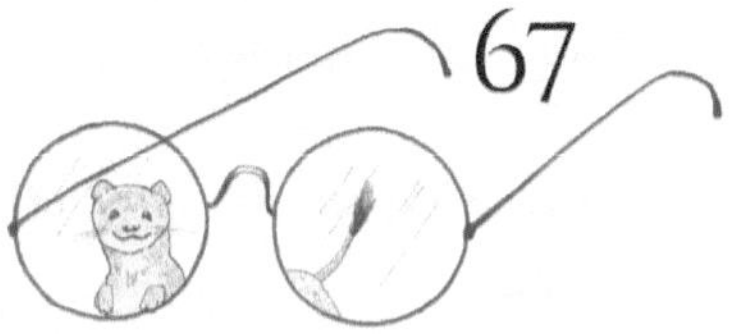

THE CASTLE

PHINEAS

THE TASTE OF IRON lingered in the air as the battle Phineas's master had waited his entire prolonged life for raged close. He crossed through the hovels and homes of Thonethren, Solyana and Ahren on his heels. Finding his way into the castle wouldn't be the hard part. No, the hard part would come later.

His soul warred inside him. Having established his newfound connection with the Celestials, it wasn't just the ends that were important to him; the means mattered, too. And leading these two children into mortal danger was giving him more anxiety than he'd experienced in years.

Yet he saw no other path.

Parts of the city rose up in flames, and Phineas led his small party away from those sections, hoping they could stay in the darkness and avoid any skirmishes until they reached the castle grounds.

The ground rumbled suddenly, and Phineas stopped, holding up a hand, his breath coming in heaving pants. "Wait! If that's an earthquake, we need to—"

"The building!" Ahren cried out, pointing above them. And he was right. Thren Temple swayed before them like a tree in the wind.

"Come on!" Phineas called, trusting the two would stay behind them as they ran away from the bending bell tower. It cracked, and Phineas turned, his robes whirling around him. He threw his hands out. "Celestials help me!" he cried, feeling foolish and free all at once. The stones stopped their freefall, hanging above the heads of his wards as they scrambled out from under the debris. Once they were clear, he dropped the crumbling tower, taking off again toward the castle, now only a few blocks away.

"You're certain you know what we're doing here?" Ahren voiced between puffs of labored breath.

Phineas kept moving. "We get in, destroy the Brextant, and get out."

"And find—" Solyana and Ahren began in unison, but Phineas finished their sentence.

"Your sisters, yes." Phineas glanced back at them, but he kept running.

Though he wished no ill will toward these two, he also knew the strength of the man they were standing against. He knew they were simply no match for him, no matter how many Gifts they controlled. He knew they would never find anyone that Erval wished to remain hidden. And this thought gave him pause.

"But we destroy the machine first," he said over his shoulder.

Another rumble shook the earth, and beneath the Red Moon, the silhouette of Hekla rose, as if to hold the celestial coin of light like a chalice in its hand. Dread pooled in Phineas's gut as memories came unbidden to his mind. Erval held plans close to his chest, closer than Phineas had originally assumed. He thought he was Erval's truest confidant, when the king's plans were, in fact, far more advanced than Phineas ever knew.

Long ago, Erval had attempted tethering to the mountain itself—a constant tether, unhindered by the use of other Gifts. It had failed at the time. Phineas wondered now if he'd done it, if Erval had figured out how to keep one hand on something so powerful, while the other gripped the smaller things in life.

He squinted. Was that smoke brewing near the top? No, only clouds.

"Phineas!" Solyana's voice cut through his thoughts as a building to their right burst into flames. He dodged, following the two to the left, around the chaos. The castle was before them, only a wall standing between them and the grounds.

"Any idea where this machine is?" Ahren asked, his breaths coming in gasps. He pushed a lock of his hair out of his eyes. "What part of the castle?"

"We have always kept it in the basement." Phineas pressed himself to a wall, and the other two followed suit as a platoon of soldiers marched by. "We discussed moving it to the observatory. He proposed it might work better from a higher vantage point."

"Does it?" Solyana asked.

Phineas shook his head. "It shouldn't matter. But I think Erval has been tinkering with it behind my back, though I've told him countless times not to mess with my inventions. It wouldn't be the first time he's changed something without my knowledge."

"So, it could be at the very bottom or the very top of the fortress?" Ahren raised an eyebrow. "How convenient. Do we split up?"

A thrill ran over Phineas's skin. Yes, they had to split up. Ahren couldn't be with him when they found it—he needed Solyana alone.

"Yes, I'd say that's best. But let's focus on getting inside first. I'm hoping there won't be many more guards here, with all the fighting happening in the south of the city."

Sneaking up to the wall, Phineas was glad to see his suspicions proved correct. There was a hidden door along the eastern end of the wall, and he brought out a small ring of keys from his pockets. Fitting one into the lock, he turned it, and the three of them shuffled through onto the manicured pathways of the castle grounds.

"This is a servant's entrance. We should be uncontested through here."

They pushed aside hanging vines that draped along the side of the castle, and after fitting another key into another hidden door, they entered, the noise of battle and fire behind them drowned out once the door sealed shut.

Phineas pushed his spectacles farther up his nose. "Alright, Solyana you're with—"

"Me," Ahren said, cutting Phineas off. "We're finding our sisters together."

Phineas's mouth formed a thin line. "I think that's unwise. You two don't know the castle. Perhaps we should just stay together."

"We can follow instructions. If Erval has taken our families, where would he keep them?"

Phineas did his best to hide his exasperation. "I never saw either of your sisters here. The king doesn't make a habit of keeping people's relatives. They could be in the guest wing; they could be in the prison."

"And where is the prison?"

"A carriage ride away." Phineas pulled out a cloth and wiped at his forehead. "We stay together, or Ahren goes alone. But you"—he pointed at Solyana—"are staying with me."

Ahren and Solyana exchanged a glance, and Phineas felt something twist inside of him. Had they discussed something behind his back? Perhaps they all held their own secrets.

"It's fine, Ahren," Solyana said. "I'll go with Phineas. Find Pallah, and look out for Rhuth as well."

Ahren stepped closer to her, catching her elbow in his hand. "I don't think that's a—"

"There's no time."

Phineas tried not to look at them, hoping they would do the work for him.

Ahren sighed. "Fine. Where do I go?"

"The basement," Phineas filled in. "If it's locked, you'll know you've found it." Phineas reached into the hooded folds of his robes. "Take him," he said, handing Ahren a tiny, copper-coated stoat.

Ahren's eyes bulged. "How long have you been hanging onto this guy?"

"They're loyal things; he hasn't left my side. I'll connect to him and call him back once our job is done."

Nodding again, Ahren tucked the stoat into the pocket of his cloak.

"Now go. The stairs are that way." He pointed.

Ahren took off, and Phineas and Solyana came behind. But when they reached the spiral stairwell, Ahren descended, while Phineas and Solyana went up.

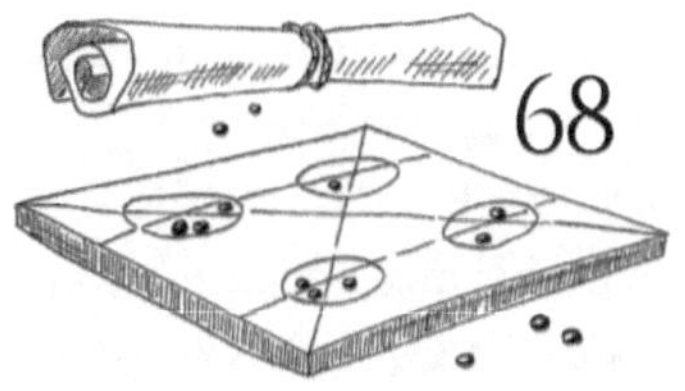

EVEN IF

JONAS

HEART IN HIS THROAT, Jonas listened to the carnage of the battle from his place at the front of the dinghy. All those prepared to go aground and fight had piled into five smaller boats, and the rest of the fleet stayed at the ready in open water. Fridmey had left her mother in charge after a tearful goodbye.

Jonas, too, had felt his emotions rise as he watched the mother and daughter hold each other, foreheads pressing together.

"Your eyes be upward, daughter," Koláme had said to her.

"And be filled with light." Fridmey squeezed her mother tight.

Guided by Fera, their boats cut easily through Lake Illgres. Thrill and terror coursed through Jonas as the city loomed before them. Fires were feasting on swathes of Thonethren, all eyes taking in the massive flames, save Rorhan. His brow was set in resolution beneath hair tied in a high knot, his chest heaved beneath a leather cuirass, and his hands twitched at his sides where Jonas knew his daggers lay.

Jonas glanced down at his thin arms, more suited to holding a quill than steel. His cuirass, too, didn't quite tighten completely over his torso. A creeping doubt spread into his heart. What if his belief was not going to be enough?

He took a deep breath, the time for theological ponderings long past. Looking up at the sky, the stars that formed the Leídín itself pulsed in his vision and his insides warmed.

"I'm sending two of my own with you and Rorhan." Fridmey clasped his shoulder and gave a firm nod. "Once you are clear of the field, we will bring the sea to their door."

Jonas wasn't quite sure what that entailed, but he could guess. His fear must have shown on his face because Fridmey squeezed his hand.

"Don't worry, Jonas. The Celestials recognize their own. Anyone using the Taka Reu won't be so lucky."

The bottom of their boats scraped the pebbled beach as they came to shore, the shouts of battle cut by blasts of steam from across the field. Soon, all boats were towed up the shore and the people formed into lines. Fridmey spoke from the front, loud and clear, a woman in total control of her bearing.

"Men and women of Greater and Lesser Mothmar! We come to this battlefield, not merely to save our land, but to beat back the darkness from whence it came! For we are people of the Way! And WE WILL TRIUMPH!"

A roar shook Jonas all the way down to his bones as the people surrounding him cheered, fists held high.

"Raise the tide!" Fridmey chanted.

"Raise the tide!" the people shouted in return.

The Crimson Chief's eyes found Jonas's, and she nodded. Jonas turned to see Rorhan and two of Fridmey's soldiers on either side of them.

"Are you ready, brother?" Rorhan's eyes were on the battle raging, coming closer.

Jonas thought of Gamaliel and Solyana, probably holed up in the castle now, of which he could only see spires rising in the distance. Then he thought of Lone and Marin, and he set his shoulders. "You'll have quite the story to tell Marin," he said to the big man.

Rorhan smiled. "My little *elskan*." He nodded. "Now, get behind me Jonas."

Jonas did as he was bid.

Then they were off, keeping to the perimeter of the battle, trying to avoid any and all fighting. Soldiers locked together in the center, swords and beasts alike, Gifts and Taka Reu creating a bloody spot in the otherwise barren field. A stream of steam gusted from his left and Jonas focused on striking one foot in front of the other. If he stumbled or slowed, he felt Fridmey's man behind him, hand on his back, encouraging him forward. Rorhan led them well, and soon they were at the midway point, seemingly undetected as they were such a small group.

But then a grizzly bear broke away as it chased a moose and a woman on its back. It stumbled in front of them, foaming at the mouth, fur tufted and torn from its sides. It swiped at the woman; Jonas recognized Maral's colors from Takanah. The moose lowered its head and charged, and the woman atop it shoved her hand forward. The grizzly's back legs sank into the dirt, where it attempted to wrench itself away.

Jonas's heart leaped in his chest—he could feel the woman using the Way! Jonas gathered his strength and readied himself to request the earth to swallow the bear completely, but before he could even form the thought, Rorhan gave a war cry.

A streak of white in the night, the big man tore toward the bear, his daggers flashing in his hands before he released them into the grizzly's eye and neck. He launched himself in a jump that brought him on top of the bear, as if to ride the bellowing thing.

One soldier stayed with Jonas while the other wove through the clash of bodies, her hands balancing stones above her palms. She released them into two soldiers, throwing them to the ground with a crunch of metal. The grizzly shuddered and shook, Rorhan sliding off its side as it flickered, dark Taka Reu smoke floating up and away from the form that shifted from beast to lifeless man.

Jonas's stomach almost expelled his dinner.

"Keep going!" Rorhan roared, and the soldiers ushered Jonas along as he ripped his gaze from the beast turned man.

They followed the perimeter north only a few minutes more when Jonas heard it: Fridmey's attack. With the bulk of the battle behind them, Jonas turned to find Fridmey and her men charging up from the lake, arms lifted as Lake Illgres was no longer behind them—but above them. The water formed into that same dragon he'd seen on the open ocean, the people manipulating it as one. It flew over their heads and crashed into the fray before coming back up toward the sky once more, maw open and drowning their enemy.

Jonas wished he could close his eyes to the carnage, but it was still visible even in the red-dark.

"Come on!" Rorhan cried, tugging on Jonas to continue.

Jonas was a Seer, and it was evident in the pressing truth of his future. It pounded on him incessantly, a warning bell of what was to come. His legs, growing weary as he ran, took him straight for that future, one where he had little control, one that he had seen in terrifying clarity.

He did not fight with weapons and Gifts; he bore the burden of a different kind of battle, one that warred in his mind and his heart. Steeling himself, Jonas surrendered as enemy combatants were felled around him. He would submit to the will of the Celestials; he would do his part, and they would win.

Even if Jonas did not.

A SACRIFICE

SOLYANA

THE GRAND CASTLE OF Thonethren was probably beautiful when it wasn't under attack. Solyana could see the evidence of it as she wove her way through the massive stone and wood structure, following on Phineas's heels. The architecture spoke of talented Stein and Vior Fera who had worked in tandem to create a testament to the kingdom's prosperity at the base of Mount Hekla.

Phineas took a corner hard, and Solyana caught a glimpse of a pair of soldiers ahead. She ducked away quickly, panting with her hand over her mouth. They passed by at a jog, their voices drifting over her like a wave.

"He finally put on the armor, but he killed the guy who told him to do it."

"I'd rather take my chances at the front, thank you very much."

Solyana glanced over at Phineas whose eyes were resolute. She had thought she'd grown to know Phineas over the time they had traveled together, but seeing him inside this darkened castle only made it starkly evident the man was an ancient mystery, much like his master. She took some measure of comfort from his newfound worship of the Celestials through the Leídín. His acceptance of the new faith and rejection of the Taka Reu had to be some proof of his loyalty.

They pressed on, shuffling up stairs and through flame guttering hallways until finally, the man before her slowed, his shoulders heaving with panting breaths.

He glanced back at Solyana, his hand on the door before them. He peered over his spectacles. "You brought the green, Solyana."

She blinked. What did that have to do with anything? "Well, I suppose. Though, as you know, it was done incorrectly."

"Ah, but the Celestials have forgiven. You have the power of Heitt, Fera, and Tala now... The Leídín."

"As do you." Solyana weighed her words carefully. "What are you getting at?"

Pale blue eyes still locked on her own, he took a heaving sigh before pushing open the door to what Solyana finally understood was the observatory.

Plants hung from different spots along the ceiling, which was made entirely of glass. The Red Moon shone directly over them, a reflection of the battle raging below. A large cage sat at the perimeter, something moved inside and Solyana caught the flash of eyes. The circular room held devices Solyana couldn't even attempt to name. However, the ornate chair in the center captured her attention more than anything else.

Phineas stepped up to it, fingers tracing along its grooves and edges. He checked something on its winged back, crouching low near its base before standing again with another labored sigh.

"This is it, isn't it?" Solyana whispered. "The Brextant." She produced a flame in her hand and held it aloft. "Step back, and I'll burn it to ash."

Finding her eyes again, Phineas's gaze held something unknowable. Whatever he was thinking, it sent a chill down her spine and caused the flame in her hand to flicker and die. "Phineas?"

"Yes, so sorry." Cast in red shadows, the old steward gave Solyana a sad smile. He stepped to the side, motioning for her to continue.

Every warning bell in Solyana's mind sounded, but she raised her hands and produced a flame. Then, eyes on her work, she used the Way to burn a fire brighter than she'd ever summoned. The chair was consumed, flames licking up as if to touch the glass dome far above. When finally she thought it was complete, she closed her fists, cutting off the supply.

Not one bit of ash dusted the floor.

No hint of smoke bit the air.

The chair was unharmed.

"I...I don't know what's wrong. Maybe if we do it together, we can..." But the words died in her throat as she got a look at the man standing across from her, hands worrying over one another. "Phineas?"

"It cannot be destroyed, Solyana. Not like this."

"Then tell me!" Solyana shouted before gaining control of her voice again. "Tell me how."

"Erval is a paranoid man. He would not abide an omnipotent machine without any type of protection. To be worked, one must be *willing* to be used up for his purposes."

"Yes, you've told me." She released a pent-up breath, allowing a margin of peace back into her heart. "And there's no one we know that has those years built up, so..." The words died on her lips as she caught the look in Phineas's beady eyes. "You can't be serious."

Phineas gave a sad shrug. "It is not a desire of mine to die upon that seat. But Erval is like a brother to me, no matter his wrongs. I am afraid my heart would betray me."

"Then to destroy it, you want me to...kill you?" Cold fear poured through her, freezing her in place. "Phineas, I—"

"Oh, please." He removed his spectacles and cleaned them on his robes. "He would simply raise up another. Plus, there's Pallah. She, too, may still hold the desire to do this for him." He shrugged. "I don't know. But destroying it? Ah," he said as he began to pace, one finger held up in thought. "This is the interesting bit. After the Brextant was given an ugly scar from an attack, he asked me to make it indestructible. We never found the assailant, but I bolstered the machine. Though I left one fail-safe, one sure way to destroy it if the time came." He turned to Solyana again, closer this time. "Someone would have to sit on it who is intent on saving Mothmar, someone a part of the prophecy, and their years would be spent snapping every tether until the chair was dismantled from the inside out."

"Then this is something you must do, Phineas," Solyana said with urgency.

Phineas sighed. "It was supposed to be me. But I am not part of the prophecy. You see, I've already tried." He motioned to the machine. "It wouldn't accept me. Something so dark and steeped in the Taka Reu needs something of total opposition. A curse had to be set in its heart and only a prophecy, or someone linked to it, can destroy it. It's how curses work, dear girl."

Solyana took several steps backward, knowing now exactly what was being asked of her.

"Ahren is another option, of course. Or Pallah." He clicked his tongue. "But like I said, I wouldn't trust her to choose this path over Erval's. I am only sure about you."

"If we kill Erval, then this machine won't matter." Solyana straightened her shoulders, clenching her fists at her sides. "Let's find him and then—"

"It can't be done." Phineas's voice held no inflection, as if he had given up long ago. He gave Solyana a sad smile. "Do you think this is the first war to knock on his door? The first prophecy he's meddled with? This man is ancient and evil in a way that even through all of our many years together, I've never been able to fathom. His heart is the truest black. So black, I am afraid even if we were to kill him, other atrocities would be set into motion. Things that could never be undone."

"But—"

"The best chance we have is to put him off! With the destruction of the Brextant, we will gain at least another few centuries. Your family would be safe, your people—they would be safe! Do you think it took me so long to craft the Brextant because it was hard?" Phineas scoffed. "I was buying time. Be the saint they believe you to be, Solyana. It wouldn't be just a name or a title, it would be truth. I would be sure of it. On my honor, I would be sure to write the history books in your favor."

"You have no honor," she seethed as she strode forward, pressing her palms to the thing. "Mighty Leídín, Celestials above, aid me!" Then she asked for the sun itself to consume, the wood in the chair to splinter, the metal fixings and leather straps to crumble to ash. Fire burst from her hands, a column so hot that the flame held no hint of orange or red but was only pure white. With the Way, all curses would be broken, surely.

She screamed, her rage at the injustice of it all pouring out of her hands and onto the object before her. Finally, when she worried the floor would catch fire, she stopped.

The chair stood, untouched.

A noise sounded in the hall, causing both their heads to turn. Panic shot through Solyana like an arrow, and suddenly hands were gripping her shoulders and shoving her backward. Her feet ran, keeping her from falling until cold metal hit the backs of her knees, forcing her to sit.

"Phineas!" she screamed at him, but his pale blue eyes wouldn't look at her. He stared just above her head, tears in his eyes, he strapped her arms in place with quick precision. "I'm not a willing participant, unless you lied about that, too!"

"You clearly care about your home, your friends, your family," he said softly before leveling his wet gaze on her and squatting before her. "I'm so sorry, Solyana." He gave that sad smile again but this time the tears rolled down his plump cheeks. "Erval is simply too powerful. This is the only way."

Solyana called on the Celestials again but found the leather straps stayed fast, no fire shot from her hands to burn the man before her. She searched the floor, utterly baffled.

"Lakimi Fera," Phineas said contritely. "Keeping you from drinking the tea was for more than just Erval, as you should understand by now."

Shouts in the hall reached them again and Solyana pulled at the restraint, though there was no give. In fact, the moment she sat in the chair a coolness came over her—a depravity of Gifts. It lined her very soul, stealing her access to any power.

"What have you done, Phineas?" Her eyes grew with panic as she tried to rip her hands away.

"The chair, too, holds technology to keep your Gifts at bay. It's truly some of my best work. It's regrettable—"

The door to the observatory crashed inward, slamming the wall behind it. Storming into the room, staff in hand, wolf at his side, was Gamaliel, his hair whipping out behind him, his chest and face smeared in blood.

"Gam!" Solyana's heart leapt to her throat.

He strode forward, eyes only for the man who was bent over her like a crooked rat. Gamaliel's shoulder's rose and fell with heavy breath, the staff in his hand gripped knuckle-white. Vinur growled beside him.

Phineas straightened and released a withering sigh. "Please, Gamaliel. Allow me to explain—"

Gamaliel punched him.

Solyana's heart leapt to her throat, and she felt an incongruous laugh bubble up, but it died in her chest.

Phineas, glasses askew on the floor and nose bleeding, raised a hand toward Gamaliel, anger and rage a mask over his features. The hunter slid backward on his feet, arms flailing. Solyana pulled at her restraints before remembering the wolf in the room.

"Vinur!" He was growling at the cage near the wall but loped to her side when she called. He bit at the leather strap at her wrist. When she looked up again, the men were locked together, grappling with Gamaliel's staff.

"I don't want to hurt you!" Phineas screamed. "She has to do this—to save everyone! You don't understand what will happen if—"

Gamaliel ripped the staff from his grip and knocked it across Phineas's face. The steward went down hard.

Raising his hand again, resolution seemed to come over the old steward and Solyana cried out.

"Gamaliel, run!"

She could not bear to watch her love ripped to shreds by this man's Fera or burned by his Heitt. But still, whatever curse the chair held kept her Gifts from surfacing, and she was left helplessly trapped.

The air hung with tension, but with Phineas's outstretched palm lingering in the air, nothing happened. Gamaliel raised an eyebrow and charged. Phineas screamed, falling to the ground beneath Gamaliel's weight. He covered his face.

Understanding came over Solyana, and she praised the Celestials even from her position on the chair. "He can't use his Gifts! He worships the Way now, and they won't give him access when he's doing something so wrong!"

Phineas was shaking on the floor, head in his hands. "I'm so sorry. It's all over. It's all over," he repeated again and again. "He'll come for us now. It's over."

Gamaliel ran to Solyana. He strapped the staff to his back and was kneeling by her side, unclasping all the leather ties Phineas had managed to secure.

"I know you're considered a saint, but you weren't doing this *willingly…*were you?"

"Never." Solyana tried to capture his eyes, but they remained on his work, his face a mask of concentration. "Do you hear me?" Hands now free, she reached forward and held his face, drawing his gaze. "Never, Gam. We made a promise, didn't we?"

Deep brown eyes shining, Gamaliel's full lips parted slightly as he searched her eyes. "Until the very end?"

"Always." She wrapped her arms around his neck, his going around her waist. They breathed each other in, before their lips met and moved together, desperate for closeness. Solyana would never leave him again. It was by his side she belonged, and where she would forever stay.

BROTHER

PALLAH

A HREN WAS HERE. PALLAH felt her brother the minute he entered the castle. Not by any means of a Gift but by a simple bond of blood. She would know her brother anywhere. Her heart hammered against her ribs, and tremors made every muscle quake. Decades of waiting for this very moment, only to be terrified now it had arrived. She could only speculate what he must think, how he must feel toward her. A cutting twinge of anxiety made her wince. She had become so soft with age.

Four years had passed since she and Rhuth had arrived in Thonethren, intent on Erval's demise. It had been the second time in her life she had attempted to battle the man. And the second time she had underestimated his skill, the true depths of his desire for power. She had been foolish. And now, was she paying the price, but so was Rhuth.

Erval hadn't used her on the Brextant, not yet. The damage she had done to the machine had merely put off the inevitable. And every time Erval came for a visit down in this basement, Pallah had held her breath, expecting it to be the time she was fitted to the chair. Every time she was left alone. He had promised her long ago there would be consequences should she stray from his side, should she prove ungrateful.

And now he made good on those promises. And here she was, locked in a cell, languishing in a never-ending night with no one but him to visit. For how long, she wondered. For she would live a long time. Would he ever force her onto that machine? Or was his skewed love for her enough to keep her trapped?

Never had she imagined she would ever see her brother again. But he was here. She was sure of it. As sure as she knew he would never forgive her. Who had rescued him from his place on that far off mountain? She could only hope it had been someone kind, someone who could have shown him some semblance of family in her absence.

Straightening the sleeves of her overly formal dress, for Erval had always liked to adorn her, she sat primly on her singular chair, willing her legs to stop trembling.

She heard someone stumble down the steps, almost fall, but catch themself. Her lips quirked, and she was surprised by the tears in her eyes. Her little brother was here. What could she say to him? What would he do?

Perhaps he would spit in her face, or worse...pierce her through with some weapon. The smirk remained on her lips at this thought. It would be an honorable death. By Ahren's hand, she would accept it.

The door clicked and creaked as it slowly pushed inward. Pallah retreated into the corner of her cell. Perhaps she had been wrong; it had to be Erval. It was her time now to take her seat upon the Brextant. Who else could open the—

Standing in the doorway, torch flickering in one hand, her double-headed axe in the other, was her brother, Ahren.

His face was a mixture of apprehension and confusion, as if he had expected someone else. Then she knew why. She was currently guised as a woman in her thirties, not someone he had ever seen before, especially not in this dimly lit room. He, on the other hand, looked just as she'd left him, though a little older, a little broader.

"Ahren?" she croaked. "Is it really you?"

He surged forward, and Pallah couldn't even cry out. He'd come to kill her, of course. After all she'd taken from him, how had she ever expected anything else? She closed her eyes.

But he embraced her. His torch and axe clattering to the ground, his arms wrapped her close to himself, his face buried in her neck. Pallah choked on her surprise, her eyes wide as she slowly came to understand what was happening. She wrapped her arms around him, too.

"I thought you would hate me," she said, her tears spilling.

"Never," he said gruffly as he stroked her hair and pulled her head tighter against him.

Pallah let herself cry, his scent bringing back long forgotten memories of home, of White Wood and Eldfall, of fires and festivities under the moon.

He pulled away from her, taking her in. "How long have you been in here?"

"Four years, I think." She shook her head. "He's done something with this room, layered it with something that stops Gifts from being used while you're inside it."

Ahren glanced around and then motioned toward the torch on the ground, trying to pick it up with his Fera. Nothing happened.

"Fascinating," he said, and then bent down to pick it up along with the axe. "This is yours." He handed her the weapon, and she took it reverently.

"I didn't think I'd ever hold this again." She pumped the axe once, and the heads slid back into place on either end of the staff. "Or you." Wiping at her eyes, she motioned toward her brother with the staff. "How did you get here? How are you still so...young?"

"I could ask you the same." Ahren gave her the lopsided grin she'd known so well. "We have a lot to catch up on after we defeat this king of yours."

Panic seized Pallah by the throat. Ahren? Intent on defeating Erval? No. "We're not defeating anyone. We need to leave."

"We need to regroup," Ahren corrected her. "I didn't come here alone, and we'll stand a better chance of getting back through that battlefield outside with help." Ahren took Pallah by the hand and started moving toward the door. "Come on."

"Battlefield?" Pallah halted. "Who attacked?"

"Halldora, Erval's sister. And a few others who have banded together with her." Ahren tugged on her arm. "We have little time. We're going to destroy the Brextant, kill Erval, and get out of here before—"

"No," she commanded. "Who is here with you?"

Ahren narrowed his eyes. "A girl, Solyana. And Phineas, Erval's steward that has turned against him."

"Solyana?" Pallah's mind sifted through the new information like sand in a sieve.

"She's looking for her sister—"

"Rhuth," Pallah filled in. "Yes. She's here. If anyone can pull her from Erval's grasp, it's her. And Phineas is here, too?"

"Yes, but—"

"No, this is good. Perfect, actually." Pallah nodded, the pieces fitting together. "Solyana can save Rhuth, and Phineas can take down Erval. You and I need to get somewhere he won't find us. There are ships on the west coast, other lands away from Mothmar. He'll never find us if we sail. His connection is with the Mother, with the depths of Hekla…" She held Ahren's hand tighter. "It's not safe here. It's not safe anywhere he can reach. Let's go while we can. I'll call Magnus. We can start a new life. We can—"

But Ahren wasn't following, his hand stiff in her own. She turned back, fury and panic winding its way up her throat. "Ahren!"

He shook his head, his lips pressed tightly together. She dropped his hand, the embers of fury burning.

"We are leaving, Ahren. I'm not doing this again." She closed her eyes, trying and failing to connect to her smilodon, Magnus. She clenched her jaw and turned back to Ahren. "I'm not leaving you. I'm not saving you for later; you're coming with me now. Here, in this moment!" Pallah, a few steps above her brother, stared down at him, his face flickering in the light of the torch he held in his hand. He still held a bit of that lopsided smile, his eyes twinkling with something like…love. But not just for her.

"The last time I saw you, you asked me if I trusted you, and I said yes. This time, I'm asking you…to trust me. Can you do that?" His stark blue eyes searched hers.

"I-I..." Her mouth opened and closed. "But we just found each other again!" She could feel him sliding through her fingers, unable to reclaim the relationship she'd lost so long ago.

An explosion rocked the castle. The walls and ceiling of the basement spewed dust and debris as the noise reverberated through the stone floor.

"What's happening?" Pallah almost screamed.

"Looks like the fighting has pushed back to the castle." Worry crossed over his face. "Pallah, I'm not leaving without my friends. And I'm not leaving without my sister. Can you finish this with me?" He ascended the steps until he was level with her, holding out his hand for her to take.

Her palm slid into his, and she gripped it tight. "I trust you." Then she spotted two shiny black eyes set in a whiskered face peeking from within her brother's mess of hair.

"Ahren! There's something on your head!"

"Ah, yes. Phineas's stoat. You said Rhuth is here?

"We were captured together, though I haven't seen her in years." Guilt reared up inside Pallah, though she tried to squash it.

"Do you know where she is?"

Pallah shook her head. "Honestly, if he's held onto her this long, she'll probably be with him."

Ahren gave a stiff nod, and the two of them began climbing the steps.

"Did you say you were going to destroy the Brextant?"

"Yes. Phineas and Solyana should've done it by now."

"Erval will be on them then; we need to hurry!"

Eyes wide, Ahren turned and leapt up the stairs two at a time, the guttering flame in his hands leaving Pallah to scramble behind him in darkness.

Another explosion sounded as they continued past the next floor and onto the final level. Coughing the dust out of her lungs, Pallah cast around with wide eyes, searching for the guards that would drag her back to her cell at any minute. She opened her palm, calling upon her fire, her soul aching to feel her Gifts once more. But nothing happened, as if the room's stifling power clung to her even after leaving its threshold. She gripped her staff and stepped beside Ahren, taking long strides to match his own.

Her brother stopped short as a group of three soldiers raced around the approaching corner. In less than a second, their hands flew to the hilts of their swords, one extending his arm to attempt to latch onto Pallah's staff. She could feel the tug of his tether.

Gifts or not, she would not let them harm her brother. She fought the soldier's hold, spinning in a tight circle, and with the scrape of metal on metal, the dual axe heads slid into place. She kept her momentum, taking two steps out of her spin, arcing the axe down on the first soldier, slicing him from shoulder to navel. She kicked the second, his sword extended but not quite far enough to reach her. The first soldier's body fell away, her axe coming free, and Pallah spun the opposite way, catching the third man in the middle. One more step brought it out to swing at the neck of the man she had kicked as he came closer to engage.

She pumped the staff again, and the blades shifted back into it, leaving the soldier's neck open to bleed. He fell, joining his comrades on the floor. Chest heaving, she turned to her brother, his mouth hanging open.

"This is certainly a step up from your hatchet days," he said with some of the old humor Pallah had missed so much.

"What else does one do when they're alive forever?" She wiped at her brow with the back of her arm. Both were sticky with sweat.

"Are your Gifts working now?" Ahren asked.

Pallah tried again, this time a flicker of light coming into her palms as she held them up.

"Taka Reu?" he asked, his brow furrowed.

"What else?"

Ahren gave her a sad smile. They continued on, reaching the main dining hall, which was damaged beyond recognition. The table was smashed, chairs were strewn all over, food sat spoiling on the ground. The balcony doors were flung open, and Pallah was tempted to run out to see what was happening outside.

"Let's take the stairs in the hall. We'll go to the observatory," Pallah said, and Ahren seemed relieved at the suggestion. "If Erval is anywhere, it'll be there."

BAIT

PHINEAS

HE WAS COMING. PHINEAS could feel his presence like a damp cloth over his face.

You've been keeping secrets, Phineas. The king of Thonethren strode into his steward's mind.

Phineas released a long breath as he watched Solyana and Gamaliel embrace across the room. He closed his eyes, focusing his mind to slow down before opening it fully to Erval. If the man wanted full access, he would get it now. There was no more reason to hide.

How far you've wandered after a mere few weeks away.

He had done his best to avoid this mess. All his plans had come to ruin in this moment. The king would see now, see the love Phineas hadn't been able to dispel for the man who was like a brother to him, the desire to see him safe from the consequences of his own actions. But alas, here he was, left to ruminate in the quagmire of his thoughts with Erval on the sidelines, watching him drown a slow death.

What were you thinking, Phin? Erval sighed through every corner of Phineas's mind. *Honestly, you disappoint me.*

Phineas squeezed his eyes shut, his hands rasping over each other faster and faster. Erval was too powerful; this had gone too far.

Destroy my Brextant? Or destroy me? You know better than to attempt anything so unwise. If nothing else, who would hold back the red tide?

Dread drained into Phineas's gut and pooled there. Erval's words turned over in his mind, trying and failing to find traction, sliding like slippered feet over bloodied stone. He had been a fool. Of course Erval had a hold on it, the mountain itself. The red tide. Denial was a powerful thing, and Phineas had succumbed to its comforts. No, Erval couldn't be destroyed, this he believed in fullness. But now he knew, *knew* for sure, the king was bent on releasing the fires of Hekla on his own people—his own home—*if*, and only if, he were so threatened.

That's my smart boy. Then Erval untethered him, and Phineas inhaled after having held his breath so long.

Yes, there had been so many groups before who had attempted to take down his master. None had come so close as this group, this culmination of battles and prophecies and the people behind them. How far was too far to push him?

They would all be dead before they could find out.

"Solyana!" he heard his own voice cry out.

The double doors to the observatory blew open, shards of wood and glass shooting throughout the echoing room. Phineas scrambled backward like a fat crab. He was not ready to face Erval. He would never be ready.

Peering through his fingers, he watched the king of Thonethren stride into the room, flanked three guards, Jothan, and a woman.

Her attire matched Erval's, the pair dressing in form fitting black leather. She even bore a cape made of the same lightweight velvet that Erval wore. It waved behind her effortlessly. On her shoulder there rode a falcon, and her face—*häfa*, her face—a jagged scar marred the skin from temple to chin, her right eye nothing but puckered flesh.

Phineas made no attempt to move as Erval's male and female companions shifted into defensive positions. Gamaliel stepped in front of Solyana with his staff, and Solyana raised her hands, flames held in her palms. Then her fire guttered and fell away, a gasp coming from her lips.

"Rhuth?"

But the woman stood stoic, her single kohl-lined eye narrowed at the intruders. The falcon on her shoulder ruffled its feathers and cocked its head, beak splayed in a screech.

"What fun." Erval stood head and shoulders above all but Gamaliel. He steepled his fingers before his lips, a smile spreading across his face. "I've waited for this reunion for so long. Postponed plans, sequestered schemes—all for this!"

Jothan and the other guards kept to the perimeter of the room, circling it until they reached Phineas at the back. Phineas peered up at Erval's new steward.

Jothan sneered down at him. "How the mighty have fallen."

Phineas ignored him, his eyes swinging back to Erval.

"Solyana!" Erval said. He took a stride in her direction, but Gamaliel side-stepped to block him. Erval raised his eyebrows. "Hello, handsome." He made a small gesture with his hand and Gamaliel screamed, then crumpled to the ground like a smashed doll. He struggled but to no avail, restrained in a heap on the floor. Erval looked at Solyana. "I've kept my end of the bargain. Where is Ahren?"

Solyana dropped to the floor to kneel beside Gamaliel, but her eyes were on her sister. "What have you done to her?" Her voice shook, and Phineas couldn't tell if it was from fear or rage. "Rhuth! Look at me!"

But the girl's eye slid from one person to the next, and no recognition lit her gaze.

"She's been with me a while now." Erval chuckled. "I've found her to be quite the companion. She was strong in her Gifts, but everyone comes around sooner or later."

"Rhuth!" Solyana pleaded, ignoring Erval. "It's me!"

Erval stepped closer to Rhuth and ran a finger down the scar over the right side of her face. "I'm not sure she can come back after all the work I've done rearranging her mind. A very long time ago, a dear friend of mine told me about using Tala to craft Mazes in animal minds." He glanced at the cage in the room that held the smilodon. "It took me a few years, but I figured out how to do it neatly in a human. Rhuth might be able to hear you, but her soul is very much somewhere else. Still, she's a lovely shell for me to guide and decorate." He smiled at Rhuth, but then it faded. "A pity really. Her power was unlike anything I had ever seen." He tutted. "But too risky, I'm afraid."

Solyana's eyes landed on Phineas's, and he shook his head, hoping she understood. He had lied about quite a few things since joining Solyana and her friends, but of Rhuth, he'd had no idea. Erval had hidden her and his knowledge of Mazes well. The revelation of his own ignorance was like trying to swallow a lemon, too large and sour to get down his throat.

"I've kept my end of the bargain. The question is, Solyana, have you kept yours?"

Solyana's eyes twitched toward the exit.

Erval smiled as his attention swung toward the observatory's broken door. "Join us, won't you? Into the light, please. Everyone's days of skulking and hiding are over."

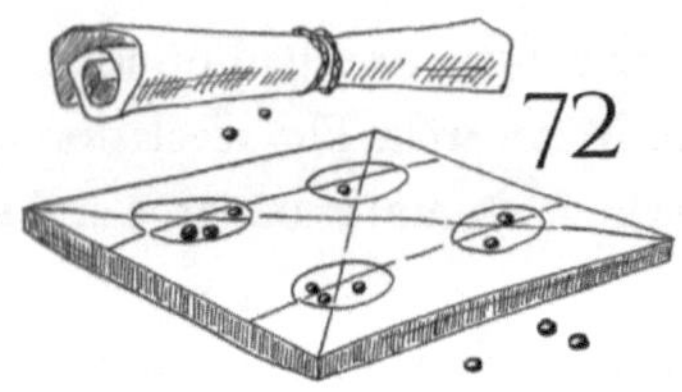# SON OF THE STARS

JONAS

INTENT ON SLIPPING INTO the castle unseen, Jonas and Rorhan separated from Fridmey's two guards who rallied outside the castle walls. The fighting had moved with them as soldiers and Beast Riders clashed with weapons and Gifts alike. The castle itself was rocked with flames and projectiles as the soldiers from Halldora's army seemed intent on winning, even if the cost meant rebuilding Thonethren from the ground up.

A boulder caught Jonas's eye as it soared above them and slammed into the turret to their right. Ivy tore from the stone, which crumbled to pieces, leaving an indent in the side of the fortress.

Jonas peered through the smoke and debris. It was hard to tell in the red-hued night which way the fighting was going. Halldora's forces, if they were succeeding, would undoubtedly push Erval's troops and Orson's beasts back toward the castle.

Rorhan seemed to be following the same line of thought. "They will be coming back this way, to protect their king and castle."

Jonas opened his mouth to agree when his vision went dark. Something in his chest lightened, and he felt himself drift upward. Placed inside a vision both like and unlike his own, he felt his connection to his body grow thin.

He opened his eyes to see himself at a great distance below, as if he were a bird flying overhead. His small form stood at the base of a mountain, hands raised to the sky, speaking something—though Jonas couldn't make out his words. The mountain itself was exploding. Rolling dark clouds of ash, malevolent bursts of orange, and red liquid fire spewed rock and debris, raining down in slow motion, with Jonas at its center.

"Run!" he screamed at himself, but the words were a muffled whisper to his ears.

The other Jonas kept his lips moving, his eyes closed to the onslaught of death only moments away from taking him.

Jonas could do nothing but watch. He had no Gifts, no way to change the tide. His own Heitt useless, there was only Jonas and the fire mountain intent on killing him.

He gasped. This was his dream. But having it while awake made it all the more clear. He had never been given this vantage point before, always having been the boy below, surrounded by fire and ash. Why was he being given this view now?

The moon! He found it, still red, though Jonas was sure it wouldn't be for much longer. The Red Moon only lasted for about two hours, which meant...this would happen. And it would happen very soon.

He saw no friends, just the boy and the mountain.

He blinked. Something flashed behind him, then fell to the ground. He couldn't make it out.

Then a voice—not audible, but something deep and rumbling in his soul—spoke to him. It gave him a new name, and with it, Jonas knew three things:

The Leídín had spoken directly to him.

He would fulfill this vision.

And he was not just Jonas anymore... he was something more than himself. He was the Son of the Stars, and he was not afraid.

BY BLOOD AND BY TIME

SOLYANA

SOLYANA HAD SPENT MUCH of her life wishing for more, for something to make up for her lack of Gift, her lack of purpose. What a fool she had been. What she wouldn't give now for a hunt deep in Shadow Wood, her family gathered for a meal, for her disappearing footprints in the snow.

Rhuth stood across from her, mere footsteps away. But she was not the same girl Solyana had rocked to sleep. She was not the same girl whose hair Solyana had braided, or whose face had been marred by an untethered falcon. This girl was a stranger, all hard lines and cold glances. How had Solyana failed her so completely?

Gamaliel had been allowed to claw his way to standing, his shoulders rigid and still beside her, protecting her through his own pain. She was unsure how he'd made it to her, or how he was surviving his wounds. Selfishly, she was glad he was here, though she knew it would cost him.

Erval had turned to face the door, to welcome the new arrivals to the room. Solyana didn't have to see them walking in to know who they would be.

"Pallah, darling," Erval crooned. "Introduce me to your brother!"

Priestess Avi, though a far younger version than she remembered, walked in with her staff. Seeing the woman now, Solyana was struck by how well she seemed to fit by Erval's side. How had Solyana seen her as anything but the devious snake she turned out to be?

The woman turned, her colorless hair sliding over her shoulders, but she stopped when she spotted Rhuth.

"What has he done to you?" she said, just loud enough for Solyana to hear. Then her eyes found the cage and the creature inside it and something in Pallah's expression broke.

Erval waved an impatient hand. "You're two minutes too late; I won't repeat myself. Jothan can fill you in later. Right, Jothan?"

"Yes, m'lord," Jothan said coolly, his arms crossed as he stood guard over Phineas. Solyana tried to catch Phineas's eye, but the stout steward would only look back and forth over the tiled floor.

"What a glorious reunion!" Erval clapped his hands as he spun in a slow circle, taking everyone in. "The girl who brought the white, the girl who brought the green, and everyone they damaged in between." He chuckled. "I would make a good bard. Jothan, make a note. When all this is over, we're going shopping for a suitable instrument."

"You'll certainly have the time to practice!" Jothan gave a tinny laugh.

Erval leveled his gaze at the young steward. "Phineas, what's my rule about quips?"

Phineas licked his lips. "The king, long may he reign, is witty enough in his own right, and has no need for any lesser additions."

Erval's face fell further. "I've missed you, Phineas. It's such a shame."

Erval crossed the room, making his way to Phineas's side. He held his steward under his gaze like an artist studying a painting, the rest of the room waiting on the man with bated breath in the stretching silence.

"What say you, Phineas? Shall the king forgive? Should I grant you a chance to prove yourself faithful?" He held out his hand.

Phineas grasped it, and Erval pulled him to his feet, a grin making the angles of his face sharper. "Good man!" He tucked the squat steward beneath his arm and gave his shoulders a squeeze. "There's still good in this world. Now," he began with a slight nod. The guards who had entered with Erval sprang into action, closing in on those in the circular room. "I need everyone still."

Then the king's hand flung out, releasing a few metal orbs that cracked against the tiled floor. Solyana jumped back as whatever it was started ticking. The devices popped open, revealing blooming metal flowers, and an inky blackness began to pour from it. *Aska* billowed, not quite smoke but not quite liquid, as it rolled over the ground and wound its way over their feet and ankles, locking Solyana and Gamaliel in place.

Solyana could feel the power of the Leídín drain from her body, an emptiness akin to despair filling her, similar to when she sat on the Brextant. She stared into Gamaliel's dark eyes, but he was looking at her with similar fear.

Pallah and Ahren were trapped in the same, their feet locked firmly to the ground.

"Do you remember these, Phin?" Erval bared his teeth in a smile that did not reach his eyes, giving the steward another hard squeeze. "We shelved it a while back; they were too unstable, would attach to any living being too close."

The guards each took a tentative step backward.

"It took a while, but I balanced them, no thanks to you. So busy, you were, with the Brextant. Right, Phin? My busy little bee? My loyal steward?" His speech got louder with each word. "I didn't want to lie to you, Phin, but there is so much I've had to keep from you. And it's a good thing I did, isn't it?" Erval spun the steward to face him. Phineas stiffened. "First there was the tea. It took me a long while and lots of practice to get around that particular annoyance, but I did it." He smiled.

Silence hung in the room.

"Really? You're not curious? Well, Phin, it's you I have to thank." Erval released his old steward to carefully unbutton his dark satin vest, revealing a pendant hanging from a thin gold chain about his neck. "You tried to hide it from me, you clever little weasel. But you're simply not as good as I am at managing who knows what." He tapped the side of his temple. "I call it the Mörstant. It's been tricky keeping this one from you, but I've had it for so long I thought it time to share." He cupped the shining pendant in his hand, bringing it up so all could see. "I can use as many Gifts as I like with this. And while the Brextant"—he motioned to the chair at the center of the room—"allows me to use one Gift with multiple tethers, this lovely device allows for the use of several Gifts, each with their own tether." He looked at Phineas again. "And it doesn't steal my years to do it! Our minds together, truly a marvel of innovation. We make a good team."

Phineas's face was nothing but a blank canvas. Solyana wished, not for the first time, that she could peer into his mind and see his thoughts on display. Had he given up? Was he biding his time? Did he truly wish to return to Erval even after finding the Way?

"My sister felt so protected by that tea. Did you see her face when Orson and his Beast Riders came out from—" Erval's speech was cut off from his own laughter until he gathered his breath and bearing again. "By Hekla..." He wiped his eye. "That sight will hold a special place in my heart. As will you, Phin."

Erval rested his hands on Phineas's shoulders, then gripped the steward's shirt until his knuckles went white. "This was supposed to be a gift for Pallah!" He dragged Phineas over to the Brextant, placing a foot behind his heel to drop the rounder man into the ornate chair. "But I'm afraid my steward has incurred my wrath just a bit more. Poetic, isn't it? The inventor, victim to his own invention."

The guards behind Solyana, Gamaliel, Ahren, and Pallah took hold of them, ensuring no interruptions to their master's work.

Phineas's face was a mask of terror as the straps tightened around his wrists and ankles of their own accord, surely manipulated by Erval's Fera. The king fitted the headgear himself, pulling the straps so tight that Phineas let out a cry of pain.

Keeping one hand on Phineas's shoulder, Erval lifted the other like an offering, closed his eyes, and grinned up at the glass ceiling and the red moon beyond.

Hopelessness spread through Solyana as she realized there was nothing she could do to stop the inevitable. A prayer she had offered long ago, the only thing she could offer, slipped through her lips. "Please," she whispered to the Celestials. "If you have any affection toward me, change our fate."

Gamaliel squeezed her hand. The two of them watched as Phineas began to shake, his mouth falling open in a silent scream. How long would it take to latch onto every soul in Mothmar? Hours? Minutes?

Then she felt it. Like an intruder slipping in through an unlatched window, Erval entered her mind as she was sure he was entering all those in the room. A slow creep of total allegiance rolled over her, and her hand dropped from Gamaliel's. This was how it was always meant to be, she knew then. Why had she ever bucked against it? Yes. A total freedom to do as King Erval pleased. What joy, what power. She reveled in his tether, in his desire as it coursed through every bit of her. She would serve him until her last breath, whenever that would be.

A slip of darkness launched itself from Ahren's head, and Solyana blinked, confused. First believing it to be a shadow or quick moving *aska,* but it was Phineas's stoat, scrambling across the floor toward him.

The king, eyes still closed, ecstasy on his face, didn't see it.

Solyana opened her mouth to warn her king when something deep, far deeper than even the king had grasped hold of, refused to comply. Frustrated with herself, she shook her head and looked up again, but the stoat was gone. She looked wildly around, then spotted it.

"Sire!" a guard barked before she could and rushed forward, kicking the metal orbs, they closed and rolled away.

The stoat shot from the back of the chair at Erval. It landed on his arm, scrambled upward, and launched itself wholly at his face.

Erval screamed and stumbled backward. Phineas went limp. Solyana came back to herself, bile rising in her throat. Her eyes caught the orbs rolling a distance away and felt the power of the Way fill her once more. The last few seconds felt like a dream she couldn't fully recall, but she took in what was happening quickly.

Though Phineas had tried to strap her to the machine just before, he had done it to save the rest of Mothmar. Skewed though his reasoning was, she knew, deep down, he was their most powerful ally. He only needed to believe they could win. Gamaliel was coming to himself beside her, his hand grasping at nothing where her hand used to be.

Lacing her fingers through his, she steadied herself and called upon the Leídín. She asked the straps of the Brextant to loosen and without hesitation they listened. Phineas, shaking and far older than he'd been just a minute ago, pulled his hands and legs from their restraints and tore the headgear from his brow.

He took two steps away from the Brextant just as Erval flung the stoat from his face. Gamaliel twirled his staff and Phineas, hand splayed toward the remaining orbs, made a fist and the last of them clapped shut and rolled away.

The room erupted.

The guards were on them and Solyana and Gamaliel turned in unison. Flames at her fingertips, Solyana shot them at the guard to her left. Vinur tore away from Gamaliel's side as he blocked the sword arm of the second guard, grunting at the force of the impact.

The guard beneath her flames screamed and fell to his knees. Something deep inside of Solyana wrenched, and she thought she might vomit, but channeling energy through the Leídín above, she bent her knees and used the man's weight against himself, shoving him away from her until he was breaking through the glass at the back of the room. His screams faded to silence as he fell.

Ahren called out for Gamaliel, panicked and raw. The guard behind Ahren gripped him by the hair and shoved a knee into his back. After using his staff to dispatch the guard trying to subdue him, Gamaliel rushed over to help.

Pallah had gone straight for Erval, her metal staff making a loud *shook!* as twin axes emerged from each end. But then Phineas was flying, a tangle of robes and flesh, thrown into Solyana, and the two of them tumbled toward the back wall.

Blinking, Solyana sat up, her head pounding and wrists aching where she had tried to catch the man twice her weight.

"Phineas!" she screamed, but her legs were trapped beneath his bulk. His eyelids fluttered, blood running from the side of his head. She dragged herself from beneath him, drawing her Heitt back to herself.

She stood, ready to launch everything she had at the mad king, but she stopped short. Standing before her, hands splayed to both sides, was her sister Rhuth. Her lips held a malevolent smile, her dark hair whipping around her as she controlled the air in the room.

"No! Rhu—" Hands flying to her throat, Solyana realized what Rhuth was doing. Using Vindur Fera, the girl had effectively stolen the air from Solyana's lungs, rendering her incapable of taking another breath.

Gasping, her vision blackening and lungs screaming for air, Solyana prayed. But not for herself. She prayed for her sister. She prayed that whatever evil had taken a hold of her would release itself, and Rhuth would be free.

That's when she spotted it. On Rhuth's head was a diadem that was far more functional than beautiful. Solyana struggled to breathe as her sister stepped closer, and in the diadem, Solyana recognized Phineas's handiwork. In desperation, Solyana lunged forward, ripping the crown from her sister's head and throwing it as far as her waning strength would allow.

The wind stopped blowing. Solyana's breath returned. Falling to her knees, she gasped for air, clutching her throat. Coughs racked Solyana's frame as Rhuth dropped beside her, one eye closed and the other a scar and memory of years ago.

"Rhuth!" Solyana croaked, pressing fingers to her sister's neck and feeling a strong pulse. The bird on her sister's shoulder hopped close and pecked at Solyana's fingers.

Eyes locking with the bird's, Solyana gave a firm nod. "Protect us."

The bird took to the air and circled the space in the tall observatory before falling fast toward Jothan, who was dashing toward the broken door.

And in this war-torn city, trapped in this blood-stained room, everything fell into place again, right once more. Solyana had Rhuth back, even after everything. She had her sister. And with stark clarity, she realized this was what she had always been searching for. Family, forged both by blood and by time.

A soldier's eyes locked on her own as he charged across the room. She rose to her feet, drew two large flames into her hands, and strode to meet him.

THE RED TIDE

PALLAH

ALL WERE LOCKED IN their own skirmishes, but Pallah had only one path.

Erval.

The name was bile in her throat, threatening to choke her before she could spit it out. Twice before, she had allowed failure. Not a third time.

Clearing the stoat from off his face with one hand, Erval's other palm shot out toward Phineas, who gasped as he was lifted bodily from where he stood. Erval's face was a mask of disgust as he threw his old steward. Pallah ducked as his form flew overhead, a grunt escaping his body as he slammed into Solyana across the room.

She pressed forward, bypassing Magnus's cage, everything inside of her screaming to release him. But her first priority had to be Erval, who maneuvered behind the Brextant, his lupine snarl transforming with terrifying speed to something like amusement. His eyes danced with excitement. She stepped close, only the chair between them, and pumped her staff so the axe heads slid gracefully back into place.

"We've been through this twice now, Pallah. Let's save ourselves the trouble." A feral grin slashed through his features. "I'll win, and you'll try to run and hide."

"You don't win." She walked forward slowly, her staff clasped behind one arm. "You cheat."

"Cheat?" Erval pressed a hand to his breast, fingers resting on the chain of his pendant. "You insult me. But that's all you have is words. You won't fight." His eyes scanned her as he closed the distance between them. "You can't." His last word sprayed spittle on her cheek.

"Pallah!" Ahren's voice rang behind her. She tried to move, but Erval had taken control of her muscles, fixing her beside him.

"Wait, Ahren!" was all she could say.

But she was too late. Erval tethered to Ahren, freezing him in place. In doing so, his tether to Pallah should have released, but with the aid of his new pendant, it merely lessened slightly.

Straining against his tether, she fought to twirl her staff from behind her, its dual axe heads emerging, and she stepped back, the blade on course to shear Erval's head from his shoulders. Too slow. His hand shot out, gripping the staff at arm's length.

He *tsk*ed. "I told you, Pallah. No one is of higher value to you than I." He leaned in close, his demeanor deathly serious. "You forget we are bound. Your life, mine, and the Mother Below."

Pallah's anger flared beneath her skin. "You don't own me! I said no such—"

"But I do!" Erval's hand slid down the staff, shoving it away to grasp Pallah by the shoulders. With three quick steps, her back hit against one of the observatory windows. Only the red-tinged darkness lay beyond. "We performed the Curse of Connection, the three of us." His nostrils flared, and his eyes went wild as he looked at her. "Up on Hekla, so very long ago, we said the rites. We are with the earth. She and us, we and her. The three of us. The lies you tell yourself don't erase the truth."

Memories accosted her. Of shooting high into the air on a block of earth, clinging to Erval as if he were her lifeline. Of being held suspended over the mouth of Hekla, terrified he would simply let go. Of Erval plucking his hair and releasing it into the mountain, forcing Pallah to do the same.

Erval chuckled. "You remember. You gave your life to the Mother Below that day... You gave your life *to me*." Then, louder, to be heard above the tumult and cries of pain, "I *am* the mountain! You destroy *me*, you destroy *everyone*!" He pried her staff from her hands, eyes shifting to the blades that sank back into its frame.

Pallah used Bein Fera to latch onto Erval's wrists, shoving them backward with a snap.

He jumped away from her, his cape swishing behind him, his face a strange smiling mask that held only fury beneath. "You can stop it," he said as he swung the staff over his head. The axe heads emerged as the falcon that had been shooting across the room came for him. A clean stroke separated the creature in half, his eyes never leaving Pallah. "You see, Pallah. If one of us dies, the mountain erupts." He splayed his free hand like a tiny explosion.

Erval was a liar, this Pallah knew. But she also knew he could use truth as a weapon. And in this, Pallah was terrifyingly certain he was being honest. She remembered that day too well, the distinct connection it had formed. The unending desire to be near to him, near the Taka Reu in tandem, and she wondered then if that simple and horrifying moment up at Hekla had changed her life far more than she had ever known.

"I see it in your eyes," Erval crooned, stepping closer to her with her axe. "You understand now. You're stuck with me *forever*." Distracted, his hold on Ahren lessened, and her brother lunged forward. He swept up a sword from the floor and charged at Erval.

Pallah had only seconds before Erval would sense him and kill him. She extended a hand to the side. He would not take her brother, not after she had fought for so long to get him back. Not Ahren.

Palm extended, she used Lakimi Fera to shove Ahren backward. He went flying. Erval's eyes flicked to the boy and confusion rippled through his features. She kicked out, planting her foot in Erval's chest and tried snatching her weapon from his grip. In the same moment, she extended her palm toward something else in the room. It rushed to her, and she shoved it into her cloak. But Erval's grip was steel, drawing her close to himself as the two of them fell near the break in the glass.

The wind knocked from her, Pallah looked up to find Jothan's hands extended toward them, seated on the ground, his face contorted with fear. Using the Gifts acquired from so many years of Taking, Pallah manipulated Erval's body until she was over top of him, fighting against his power, shifting her staff until one blade was pressed beneath his jawline and his hair blew in the windy night through the broken glass.

She couldn't handle them both, not with Jothan's tether working like a wall to keep Erval in the building.

"Jothan!" she screamed. "Let go of him!" But the young man only strengthened his power. Pallah's mind whirled, trying to figure out how to lay everything in place with only seconds of margin. She shifted her tether, releasing Erval and tethering Jothan's throat. She constricted his airway, and his eyes widened as his hands went to his neck, clawing at his skin. But precious seconds were lost as the blade of her axe jerked forward and Pallah felt a lance of pain and cold ice tear through her middle, at the same place she had been struck through the last time they had fought.

Erval's bejeweled fingers gripped her shoulders, flipped her over, and he straddled her. She released Jothan, sure he was dead, and was just able to tether her weapon, slicing Erval's jaw before it was torn from her grasp, flipping tail over head, embedding itself into the wall.

Squirming beneath the weight of him, Pallah's green-gray eyes found Erval's that had probably been a color long ago but now were only pools of darkness. She tried Heitt but her fire sputtered to nothing.

"Not again, *tik*," he spat, and she could feel him siphoning away her flames even as she produced them, making it impossible to gain ground.

Her strength was waning. She could feel it as blood leaked from her middle. She caught sight of the pendant around his neck.

"Now be a good girl and go to sleep," he hissed in her ear, so close to her that his cheek pressed solidly against her own.

She could feel him prod with Blou Fera, trying to find the balance of awake and asleep.

Not again. Not again! She would not be his plaything. Fera! She latched onto his body, shoving him hard. He stayed put, but his grip lessened, and it was enough to take in a stream of air. If she could only get him closer to the gaping break in the glass. Even if Erval dragged her down with him, she would do it. Ahren would have to find it in himself to forgive her one more time.

"Don't be a fool," Erval whispered into her ear. "You're going to die, Pallah. And I'm the only one who can save your brother from the tide."

No, he wasn't. Erval had made sure of that, that day on the mountain. *She* would protect Ahren.

Erval's body weight lifted slightly under her power, and Pallah brought her knees up beneath him. Clawing his cape over his shoulders, she pulled, while simultaneously kicking both feet into his pelvis. His bottom half went sprawling up and over her head as she followed through, swinging overtop of him and ripping the pendant from his neck. Momentum carried them crashing through the broken glass as she connected to the pendant with Malmur Fera and shattered it pieces.

"Pallah, no!" she heard Ahren scream. She reached back with a palm, pulling her axe to herself. It crashed through the break in the glass and rushed toward them as they fell together.

Pallah spun, the wind hitting her full in the face as Erval cursed and spat. She reached out, gripping her staff as it caught up to their descent. The wind grew to a roar as Erval slowed himself using Vindur Fera. Then he shoved her away from him as he suspended himself in the air.

But she was ready.

Arcing her axe over her head, pushing herself up with her Gifts, the blade slid solidly into his neck before he stopped it with his Fera. Then he dropped like a stone. She clutched the other end, latching onto that same metal, pushing it faster toward the ground. Removing one hand from her staff, she fished for the orb she'd stolen from the floor of the observatory and latched it securely to Erval's side. It unfurled, *aska* pouring over the king.

The castle grounds rushed up to meet them. She felt his tether break, his ability to use Gifts stolen. Pallah twisted away, releasing her weapon, catching herself with Vindur Fera just before the king smacked the ground with a sickening crunch. She landed hard, rolling to the side, her intricate dress now only torn and bloodied cloth. Rising to her feet, she gazed down at Erval under the dim light of the red moon. His handsome face was covered in blood and his eyes held a fury that was slowly winking out.

Then, unexpectedly, he blinked at her...and smiled. "We still did it." His speech was labored.

She retrieved her staff from beside him and pumped it, retracting the axe heads with a scrape. "It's over," she told him, hoping it was true.

"You lost." She could hear the battle raging at the front of the castle and around the wall. They would be here shortly.

Erval took a gurgling breath. "We still did it." This time, the choice of words sank deeper, and Pallah's gaze snapped to Hekla rising high above them.

The ground beneath her feet gave a low and terrible rumble.

"What have you done?" Her voice shook.

Erval held his neck, still spilling red beneath his hands. "It will be beautiful." His eyes flicked up as if to look behind him to the mountain before settling on her again. "And you, my greatest protégé, will Take me and begin again." She couldn't help her jaw from dropping open in disbelief, a new fear shook her to her core. "Take me, Pallah. You would truly live forever. I know that's all you ever wanted. Time. You never cared about domination." He coughed wetly. "But maybe you could figure out how to get that cat of yours to live...to live..." As if the conversation had become too much, Erval went quiet, though he still watched her.

Pallah shook her head as traitorous tears squeezed from her eyes.

"You're a wolf, Pallah. A wolf living among sh—sheep." His words began to stutter and slur as the *aska* from the orb continued wrapping him in a vice. "We're alike in that. Can't stand to leave things wasted. Don't let these years disappear!" he bit with a tone that held a finality.

Tracks of tears running through the dirt on her face, Pallah sniffed as she stared down at this man she had loved and hated for so long.

"Pallah!" a new voice cut through the rumble of the mountain and Erval's pleas. Pallah whipped around, peering through the darkness to catch a glimpse of her brother leaning out of the window she'd just fallen through.

Her vision clarified just enough to catch her brother's eyes, pleading and raw with emotion. Though she was exhausted, she *could* heal herself. Then she would climb the stairs to the observatory, grab Ahren, and get out of Thonethren. It wouldn't be impossible to keep just the two of them safe, surrounded by her many Gifts, to get them out of this place before it all went up in flames.

They could have a good life, the two of them.

But Rhuth was also in that room.

Pallah had failed her so wholly, saving her would be the least she could do. But then Rhuth wouldn't leave without her sister, who Pallah had also disappointed. The girl was probably just as stubborn as Pal—

Hekla roared.

"Pallah!" Ahren screamed again.

"Pallah," Erval crooned.

All noise dimmed in her ears and resolve settled in her gut.

She threw her Smilodon Tala tether into the building behind her, switching between it and Malmur Tala to break her cat out of its cage. She would need her friend one final time.

Pallah got to her feet, her hand finding the wound in her side as she stumbled away from the dying king. She would leave him to die, a victim to his own trap. Blood poured through her fingers, and unable to use her Heitt, for she didn't want to lose Magnus, she prayed she didn't bleed out.

"Take me!" Erval gave one final cry of desperation. But Pallah would not sully herself further. She ignored him easily, catching Ahren one last time.

"Goodbye, brother," she told him for her ears alone.

Holding her side, she ran north, hearing the cries of her brother behind her until his voice was lost to the night.

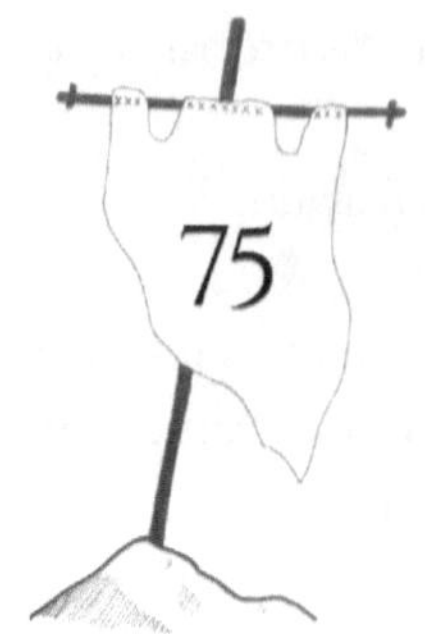

RAZE & RUIN

HALLDORA

CAKED IN BLOOD, STICKY with sweat, Halldora's skin tingled as she sliced through another soldier at the wall. His body slumped and his blood was swallowed by the red-drenched ground. She wiped at her forehead, shoulders burning. The battle around them had pushed toward the castle, trampling over the dead as it went.

The mountain rumbled.

General Ivan sheathed his sword and came to stand at her side, his eyes cast warily into the distance.

Halldora removed her helm, her heart stuttering as she stared at the awful mountain, the truth of her brother crystalizing into reality: Erval truly knew no restraint. He would use the one weapon no one could combat.

"Ivan," she said slowly.

"My Queen."

"Hekla wakes."

He whirled toward her, the whites of his eyes belying the panic he kept from his speech. "What are Your Majesty's orders?"

At that moment, the volcano erupted a black belch of smoke and ash.

"It's too late," she whispered. "We're already too late."

Years of building her army, planning her attack, hoping to win back her kingdom: all of it ended here. If Hekla erupted, there wouldn't be a kingdom to win. Halldora turned, the sound of thundering paws and a battle cry approaching from behind her.

"Hold him back, Ivan," she said to the man at her back as she donned her helm. "There will be nothing to rule if we allow Erval this last victory." She took off at a run, boosting her strides with Vindur Fera, switching to the ground beneath her feet to propel her forward until she made her way through the fray.

Slicing through Erval's men, she rallied her soldiers around her, blasting through waves of men with her Lakimi Fera, siphoning the air from their lungs with Vindur, and slicing through the rest with her sword.

Blood-stained and panting, she made her way to the very back of the castle, Hekla on full display to the north. Her men trailed far behind her, unable to keep up at the speed with which she flew. Halldora, alone behind the castle, stopped cold in her tracks. There, in the gardens of her old home, surrounded by broken glass, was her bloodied and broken brother.

The battle raging beyond dimmed as she knelt beside him, taking in what was left of her family. His eyes flickered open. She pulled off her helm, hair sticking to her sweaty forehead, and watched his eyes and mouth widened in unison like a landed fish.

"Hello, brother," she said softly. "What a mess you've made."

He gurgled.

"Don't you worry. Your sister will take care of everything." Pulling one gauntlet off, then the other, Halldora positioned her hand over Erval's form and murmured the ancient words of Taking into the night. A rush of cold, a flood of darkness; the souls of thousands upon thousands tore through her being. She couldn't think, couldn't breathe as all of the life and Gifts Erval accrued became her own. It took longer than any Taking she had done before. When finally it was over, she gasped, sucking in air in great heaves.

She had won. This was her victory. Thonethren was hers.

The mountain began to spew in earnest.

She spit in his face.

"You selfish bastard." She wiped her mouth. "Handing me nothing but ashes." She sat back onto the ground, and horror widened her eyes as she watched the mountain explode.

Worn through, she called to her men as they rounded the castle. "Protect your queen! Defend the New Kingdom!" And as her men hemmed her in, she connected to the volcano itself, beseeching the Mother Below and finding her to be more terrifying and formidable than she could have ever imagined.

"Gods, save us all," she whispered behind a wall of shields. "Save us all."

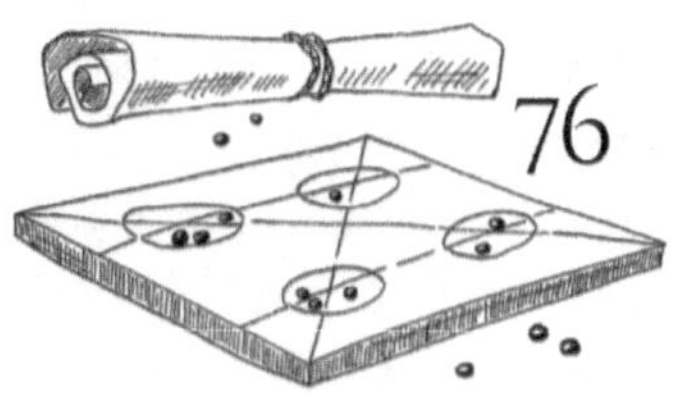

MOUNT HEKLA

JONAS

"Something is about to happen," Jonas said, his vision ending, his senses returning to him.

"Where did you just go?" Rorhan asked.

"They spoke to me," Jonas said, eyes focusing on the peak of the towering mountain in the distance.

"Who?" Rorhan's eyes were panicked. "Jonas!"

"It's okay, brother," Jonas said. "Get into the castle, find Solyana. And give Lone and Marin my love." He took a step backward.

Rorhan's eyes narrowed beneath stark white eyebrows. He looked up at the castle, then back at Jonas once more. "You are doing something reckless. I am going with you."

Jonas stopped his friend, planting a small hand on Rorhan's broad chest. "No, Rorhan. I must do this alone. You have people to protect here and back in Endirinn."

Rorhan opened his mouth to argue, but Jonas interjected.

"I'm serious. If something were to happen to you, Lone would blame me. And she scares me more than what I'm about to do."

The big man grinned and shook his head. "I will see you when this is over."

Jonas kept his voice from breaking. "Tell Gamaliel—"

"No." Rorhan's voice was uncharacteristically hard. "You will tell him yourself." His eyes glistened in the red moonlight.

"But—"

Rorhan drew him in, squeezing him so hard the breath escaped from his lungs. He returned the embrace, careful not to let the waiting tears complete their journey.

With a grunt, Rorhan released him, scruffed up his hair, and disappeared through a rubble-strewn hole in the wall that led to the grounds of the castle of Thonethren.

Jonas took a breath, looking up at the stars scattered across the sky. He spotted the Leídín almost immediately and felt the constellation itself call him north. Shoring up his tether, he turned, latched to the terrible mountain, and took off at a run.

North of the castle was an entirely different atmosphere than that of the south. The civilians of Thonethren had gathered, trying to get away from the battle, women and children clogging the streets. The occasional Beast Rider or soldier passed, bringing the remnants of fighting their way. Jonas yelled as he went, warning the civilians to get beyond the walls, to find cover. But the people ignored him, probably thought he was a lunatic. With no way and no time to convince the people, he kept moving. Legs pounding over the cobblestone streets, his lungs screaming at him to stop.

From behind a war-torn house, a massive direwolf appeared, ridden by a man adorned in a few furs and leathers. Jonas pulled up short, momentarily giving way to fear. But the man slowed his mount until the direwolf crouched before Jonas.

"The Way has sent me to you." His hair was pulled back in a knot at his neck, his face streaked with sweat and blood. He bowed his head, revealing a staff strapped across his back. He leaned down and opened up his palm.

There was something about this man that reminded him of Gamaliel, and for that reason more than any other, he decided to trust him. He reached up, grasping the rider's hand, and was pulled up onto the beast.

"North, to the mountain!" Jonas cried in his ear. The man gave a stiff nod, and they took off.

Careening wildly between civilians and soldiers alike, Jonas hung on for his life, but he was grateful; the time it took to reach the mountain was nothing what it would have been had Jonas continued on foot. As the wolf slowed to a stop near the base of Hekla, Jonas slid from its back and turned quickly back around.

"You must go now!" he called to the man, who sat on his beast, eyes wide at the fiery tumult about to rain down upon them. "Leave this place!"

"I can't leave you here alone!" the man said. "You are a child of the Way; I will not abandon you to your death!"

Jonas locked eyes with him, wondering if he knew him. "What is your name?"

"Reynir."

It sounded familiar, but Jonas couldn't place it. "Thank you for helping me, Reynir. I am only fulfilling what the Way needs me to do. My friends, Solyana and Gamaliel, are in the castle; go now and help them!" Then he felt it, the rumble of the mountain, stronger than before. The man, eyes wide, mouth parted, gave a final nod before his direwolf scrambled away, flying back through the city.

Jonas turned to face Hekla, the towering mountain looming in the night. The second he locked eyes on it, the top of it exploded.

ALL LIGHT

PALLAH

COVERED IN SWEAT AND blood, ash and smoke falling all around her, Pallah gripped Magnus as he tore up the mountain. She kept one hand pressed to her wound, not wanting to disconnect from her smilodon, afraid their time apart would make her tether falter.

But after plunging from the castle to the mountain's base, Magnus was slowing, exhausted and choking on smoke. She hated Erval for keeping him. The king's need to seize and trap all Pallah loved—no. She shook her head to clear her mind, she would not think of that man now. She would not waste one more second.

Finally, she slid from the smilodon's back and transferred her tether to the Mother Below, fully expecting Magnus to bolt. He didn't. Instead, he pressed tight to her as she took one slow step after the other. And it made her think of another cat, who chose her even when he had the chance to run.

Two other tethers were connected, keeping Mothmar from utter desolation. The first, she didn't recognize, though it bore a semblance of Erval, and within moments it untethered itself. The second felt like the valley in which she'd hidden for so long. It felt like scrolls and parchment and rows of tomes. Her steps carried her a bit farther, the smoke billowing around her until finally she reached the base of the mountain. Spent of everything but the will to save the last of her family, Pallah found the person responsible for slowing the mountain's eruption.

Though she could only see his back amidst the smoke and debris, she recognized Jonas, the boy scribe whom she had taken under her wing long ago, relegated to the library beneath the Temple Celestial. Now he was here, older, his strong arms lifted to the mountain, his tether, one made of light, was more powerful than anything she'd ever felt aside from one other.

Rhuth.

The Mother Below pushed against them both, daring them to defy her. Pallah pulled her staff from her back, clutching it as heat blasted her face. How could one convince a deity to stop? One didn't, she realized. There was no negotiating with something so unbound by time and space. They would all die here because of the reckless actions of a man bent on arresting immortality and total control—a man pursuing godhood.

Rage ran up her tether, almost knocking her from her feet, but Magnus was there, keeping her steady. The Mother Below loathed that desire, for who were these people but ants to be squashed? And she would do so. Now it was not only rage but something deeper...desire. She longed to consume, to take the years and Gifts from the people of Mothmar just as Erval had been doing for so long—just as *she* had done.

Pallah blinked as ash fell onto her lashes like snow, realization hitting her full on. The Mother Below was coming for the debt she was owed. After so long of their Taking, she was ready for her recompense. The years and Gifts, meant to return to dust and give life to the ground beneath their feet, had been stolen for centuries.

Hand pressed to her wound, Pallah's thoughts went to Rhuth again and the girl's unwavering faith. She had been so sure that Pallah, too, could turn from her deeds and seek the Celestials. Yet, in the moments when it could truly make the most difference, Pallah failed.

Was it too late now? Here on the doorstep of death, was she so stained that she couldn't walk forward in light? Her tether tightened, displeasure rippling the connection between her and the mountain. The sky was clogged with smoke and ash, no visible Celestial for Pallah to lock her eyes on, nothing tangible she could see. And yet...

"I beg of you!" she cried out to no ears but her own, and whatever god that was above inclined to her. "Father of the Day, Mother of the Night, Children of the Sky! Whoever you are, whatever you are! Save them!"

The earth beneath her feet rumbled, as if the Mother Below disagreed. Pallah continued her petition, her voice growing weaker as her lifeblood ran through her fingers and onto the ground at her feet. She felt it then, the shift in power, the change in direction for where her beliefs lay. Her hold on Hekla became something of a vice, instead of a joining of hands, something that would take her solidly in its maw and consume her.

Here, at the base of Hekla, she would die for her brother. And not just him, she realized; she would die for this boy Jonas, whose tether, she only now felt, held something new and fresh, like a mark. It told her he was a man of old. She would die for Rhuth. She would die for all the people she had wronged.

Would her imperfect, selfish blood be enough to sate?

Perhaps not forever. But for now…it would work for now.

"Take ME!" she screamed, the last of her life calling out for resolution, the last of her blood hitting the ground. She sank to her knees, burning winds and ash lashing her flesh. She heard the boy suddenly, his voice ebbing and flowing over the tumult and wind. Then, as if she were tied to the Brextant itself, the Mother Below drew her years and Gifts from her.

Pallah collapsed to the ground and Magnus tucked himself around her. She clutched his fur as she laid on her side, breathing through the end. Sacrificing herself may not right all her wrongs, but it would save her brother. It would have to be enough. As a final act, she reached out with a shaking hand toward the brave boy before her, siphoning the last of her strength and healing into him as smoke and ash hid him wholly.

Then she closed her eyes, tucked herself into Magnus's warmth, and pictured Ahren.

She was safe…and nothing could hurt her anymore.

She was wanted…for this purpose, to save.

She was cherished…by her brother, who had never stopped loving her.

And that was enough.

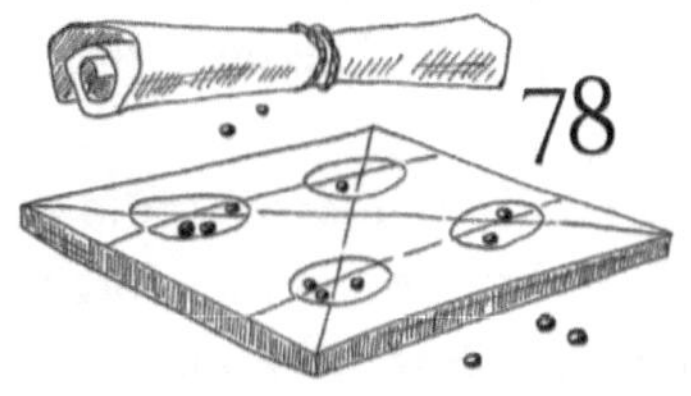

A MARKED MAN

JONAS

THE DREAM THAT HAD plagued Jonas was coming to fruition as his skin was blasted with hot air. This was it. For so long he had foreseen his end and—something fractured. He blinked, confused as his nightmare, so predictable and constant, now shifted in its end. Jonas did not feel so alone. He looked behind him, squinting through the smoke and ash, but saw no one.

He turned to look back at the mountain when, for the second time that night, he was propelled into what he could only understand was a vision.

A small hut set in a rocky outcropping.

Four children burst out of its door.

Jonas looked at his hands which clutched a crooked staff topped with tinkling bells; behind him brayed his flock.

One of the children, a small girl, broke away from the others and ran to him. "Papa!" she cried, pushing her curly red hair from her face to reveal a dark birthmark. "Look!"

She raised her hand and, in her palm, a small flame danced.

An earth-shaking explosion rocked Jonas back to the present; he fell to one knee. What could it mean? A possibility of his future? Was he the shepherd in the vision?

Impossible.

He shook his head to clear it, eyes on the mountain before him. This mountain would consume him, as he always predicted it would. No, whatever he had seen, it was but a flash of longing…a desire unfulfilled. And in that recognition, he voiced his own need to repair, to impart, to forgive.

"Gamaliel," he said aloud. "I'm sorry I couldn't help you more when you needed me these last five years. Please forgive my ignorance." Fire and smoke billowed from high at the mountain's top. It would be mere moments before it came for him in its fullness.

"Solyana," he continued. "I'm sorry I couldn't get to you sooner. That you've been made to do these things you were never meant to do. You're the strongest person I know."

Molten earth welled and began its descent. Jonas extended his arms toward the burning rock, attuning himself to the stars, keeping his mind open to their leading.

"Ahren!" He pulsed his hands forward, and the flow's momentum ceased, then redirected toward the back side of the mountain. "Ah!" Jonas let out a squeal. It was working! "Ahren, take care of Gam. He needs a friend after I'm gone!" He pulsed his hands again, wrapping a flurry of wind around the ash that had begun to rain down to dissipate it.

But he was becoming exhausted. The erupting mountain was so large and he so small. How could he keep this up, alone as he was?

The ground rumbled and shook, and the mountain took on the next stage of attack as the Mother Below seemed to take a breath before exhaling death and fire. The mountain exploded a second time, and Jonas stumbled backward, eyes wide, his whole body shaking.

This was it. Whatever happened inside the castle, whatever battle they thought they were waging, it was nothing against the unadulterated power of the earth itself. He recognized it then, the moment his dreams always ended, the same moment his vision from the Celestials had faded. He had seen the mountain burning, seen himself speaking, though he had been unable to hear his own words. He had said his last goodbyes, though there was no one to hear him. But he had always thought, as a Seer he might—

Jonas's spectacles dropped from his face as a gust of hot air blew over him, threatening to melt him on the spot. His eyes were tugged upward toward the Leídín constellation. His hands extending upward, he fell to his knees.

"Wiped clean, the hearts and land of the people of Mothmar will be made anew." Jonas's voice rang loud and clear to his ears, though the rush and rumble of the onslaught of heat roared around him. "Born from the Sacrifice of the Red Tide comes a time of silence, of waiting, and of preparation. The beginning of the abide is here. The Mother rests, and the Children quiet. When hearts slide backward—one will rise again." He took a breath, preparing himself for the inevitable. "You will know this one by the mark. Known by the fruit of the one who bears this prophecy."

Jonas crumpled to the ground as fire and ash consumed the very place he stood.

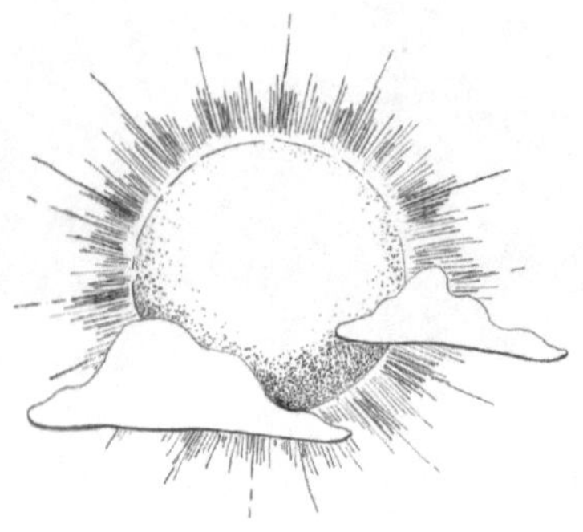

BRINGER OF THE GREEN

SOLYANA

DRESSED IN EMBROIDERED ROBES, Solyana sat on the edge of her ornate bed in the Temple Celestial, back in the valley of her people. Her hands clutched a small scroll, careful to keep it hidden from the curious mind behind her. Gentle tugs signaled her sister's work on Solyana's braid. How many times had Solyana done the same for her Little Fyug? Now, here they were again, as if time had never passed. And yet, so much had transpired.

Exactly a year ago today, she had run from the castle of Thonethren only for Hekla to stop its burning and all Gifts to have ceased. Now the people, gathered outside her window, expected an answer. She could hear the thousands who had traveled from Greater and Lesser Mothmar, buzzing like the bees her mama had tended to this spring, as they awaited her descent.

She would address them today as their priestess.

With the death of Erval, Halldora had claimed queenship over Thonethren while Greater Mothmar had pledged their allegiance to Maral. Lesser Mothmar would continue to rule themselves. A pact was produced where the safety of Solyana and her friends was promised and religious equality enacted. The crown would no longer determine Thren Temple's teachings. Although Halldora was no perfect ruler, she had no

Mann Tala, and her stance on religious freedom held firm as she ushered in her New Kingdom. But, just to be sure, Solyana had asked her older sister to see to the Brextant. Directly following the battle, the Crimson Chief had sailed far into Kana Ocean, where she tipped it overboard and it sank deep beneath the waves.

Solyana allowed herself a small peek at the scroll, ruminating on the last line. She hadn't stopped thinking about it since she received it via carrier bird three days prior and had only shared it with one other. A final gentle tug on her scalp signaled Rhuth's finishing touch as she tied off the braid and laid it over her sister's shoulder. Solyana tucked the scroll back into her silken sleeve that trailed to the floor.

"There," Rhuth said softly. "You look perfect."

Turning, Solyana smiled at her younger sister, fighting the tears that threatened to well in her eyes. It had cost so much to get here.

A knock came on her door.

"Come in." She straightened her shoulders, only to relax them when Gamaliel's head poked through the opening.

"She ready?" He grinned at the both of them.

"Yep." Rhuth hopped off the bed. "I'll leave you two." She slowed as she reached Gamaliel. "That is, unless you want me to tame that." She picked up a lock of his hair and flung it over his shoulder.

Gamaliel swatted her away. "My hair will remain unbraided, thank you."

Rhuth grinned and closed the door behind her.

Solyana smiled at Gamaliel, her heart fluttering in her chest. "I'm glad you two get along."

"I don't have much choice in the matter, do I?" He teased, crossing the room. He was dressed in formal wear, looking quite handsome with Vinur trotting at his side. "Do you agree with Rhuth? Are you ready?" He caught her face in his hands and kissed her, slow and sweet. "Priestess Solyana?"

Scrunching her nose, Solyana pulled away. "Not sure I'll ever get used to that title. I prefer saint instead."

"Saint Solyana it is, then." He sat beside her, pulling her hand into his own, and searching her eyes. "Do you know what you're going to say?"

Solyana had spent much of the last year scouring the scrolls of the Temple Celestial for answers but had found nothing. She shook her head. "I've been keeping something from you."

Gamaliel's dark brows rose as he sat beside her.

"I wanted to be sure it was valid... I didn't want to raise your hopes only to find out it was fake." She carefully produced the scroll from her sleeve and placed it in his hand. "Phineas and I both believe it to be credible. Gam...just..." She waved him on to read, covering her mouth with her hand. He unfurled it, eyes wide with concern and read aloud.

"Wiped clean, the hearts and land of the people of Mothmar will be made anew. Born from the Sacrifice of the Red Tide comes a time of silence, of waiting, and of preparation. The beginning of the abide is here." He looked up, wariness mingled with hope evident on his face, then returned to reading. "The Mother rests, and the Children quiet. When hearts slide backward—one will rise again. You will know this one by the mark. Known by the fruit of the one who bears this prophecy."

Gamaliel gasped, one hand reaching for Solyana's. "It's signed, Son of the Stars."

"I know," she said quietly.

"Jonas?"

"I think so." Solyana nodded. "I'm not sure how or why. But over the last few days, the best guess Phineas has come up with is that with the nature of this prophecy and the eradication of Gifts, so would be the consequences of losing them."

"But how could Jonas survive?"

"Our working theory is that Pallah survived the fall from the observatory, killed Erval, if he wasn't dead already, and stopped Hekla herself. Phineas believes she found Jonas there, and as her last act, saved him."

"What delivered the message?"

"A carrier bird. I couldn't tell where it was from."

"So," Gamaliel said, deflating. "All of this is speculation. It could be just that—only a message."

Solyana shrugged. "I happen to know someone who captains a ship. Maybe she could give us a ride. I feel like Endirinn would be as good a place to start as any."

"I don't think priestesses generally travel away from their temples." Gamaliel grinned.

"Probably not," she said and nudged him with her knee. "But saints do."

"I promised Rhuth and Ahren I'd sit with them. See you soon." He kissed the top of her head and left the room, Vinur following behind.

Solyana reached into a pocket of her robes and pulled out an iridescent pearl. She rolled it in her fingers for a moment before rising to her feet. They had a life here, back in the place she grew up, which held a pool of memories, both bad and good. But things weren't fully right. Jonas was one piece of that puzzle, her father another, and the prophecy the last. She tucked the pearl back into her robes for safe keeping.

She would leave her people again. But they didn't need her as they once did. There was Rorhan and Lone, who'd had a baby boy just a few moons ago. Rorhan had insisted on naming him Jonas. Mama was Chief of the valley and Rhuth was getting better by the day, her time with Erval having rooted deep. Ahren was good with her, having had endured a similar time separated from those he loved for so long. They had bonded close over the last year.

Phineas, who had repented of his wrongdoings, had been a loyal advisor over the last year, but now he primarily raised goats and made his own cheese. He had come back to his roots after so long away from a life of tending and caring, and Solyana was glad of it. Without the use of the Taking, and victim to the Brextant, Phineas had aged far more rapidly than a year warranted. His years would be shortened without the Taka Reu, though he didn't mind, content as he was with the Way.

Solyana strode through the door and down the stairs into the sanctuary of the Temple Celestial, solid and sure of her footing in this world. No longer was she a girl uncertain of her place, lacking a Gift and a purpose.

Bringer of the green, leader of her peoples' hearts, and soon to be wife—she touched the feathers woven into her hair that signified her betrothal—Solyana Marusda donned her circlet and opened the double wooden doors to the faces and applause of her people.

Her eyes scanned as she approached the center of the steps, finding her family and friends gathered together. Gamaliel beamed at her. Phineas and the copper-colored stoat on his shoulder squinted in the morning light. Lone held a squirming Marin in her lap, while Rorhan cradled baby Jonas. Mama and Fridmey stood behind Ahren and Rhuth, each looking expectantly at Solyana. Rhuth's eye held Solyana's gaze for a touch longer, and she grinned.

Solyana took courage.

"People of the Way! Your eyes be upward!"

And in unison, thousands of voices replied, "And be filled with light!"

Thank you, dear reader, for investing so much time in the world of Mothmar. Though this story has concluded, there are a few short stories compiled together available via the QR code below! If you'd like to keep up with all things by me, Amanda Auler, there's also a place to sign up for updates at the code as well.

Also, if you enjoyed Son of the Stars, please rate it on Amazon and Goodreads. It really helps get the book in the right hands!

Your eyes be upward,

Amanda Auler

All the links!

ACKNOWLEDGEMENTS

How does one end a trilogy? To say goodbye to characters and an entire world crafted from one's imagination? Well, speaking from my limited experience, I'd say it is equal parts sadness and relief...and a bit of annoyance. In fact, *Son of the Stars* was probably the most frustrated I've been with a book yet. Untangling the threads of plot and motivation felt impossible on more than one occasion. The story shifted and transformed over the course of a year until finally becoming its final form that you hold in your hands today. I do remember twice writing myself into a corner and frantically calling friends to talk things through until we figured it out.

And we did, we figured it out every time.

Each book in the trilogy has a bit of my walk of faith layered into it. But this book in particular I found myself allowing my characters to explore what understanding truth means. It was an odd thing, as books feel a bit like children in a way, to watch my characters grow up and ultimately choose either darkness or light. A few times, I found my eyes blurred with tears as I saw my own walk with the Lord reflected in their journeys. Writing is funny like that. You often don't know you're writing your soul into your book until it's over.

I began the Mothmar trilogy when I was fresh into motherhood, a single baby on my hip. I was struggling with my new role as a stay-at-home mom and desired creative output. Writing became my freedom. It was a connecting point to who I was as a child and who I wanted to become. And now, four kids in, with my youngest just barely a year old, I've completed what I've set out to do. My skills, style, and goals have grown over the years, and every time I feel the itch to go back and edit my first book; I pause and allow it to remind me where I've come from.

People have inquired as to how I've had the time to write these three books while rearing children. I usually say something along the lines of, "Lots of late nights and early mornings!" or "You have to really want it!" And while those things are true, the deeper answer to that is I have a really great support system. And that's what these acknowledgments are about, so without further ado...

Thank you to my parents and in-laws—Super Grandparents—who have volunteered weekends, appointments, sleep, and food to watch my kids so I could get some work done.

To my husband, who tells me to skedaddle on his days off so I can write. And then has dinner waiting for me when I come home. He also is half the brains for these books so...are we technically co-authors? Maybe.

Writing can be a solitary event, if you allow it to be. But I am thankful for the group of people who have stood alongside me to help make these words a story. Angela, Kayla, Moriah, Manda, Andrea, Moon, Emma H., and Emily B. your efforts were not in vain. I appreciate all the time it took to read and send me your notes.

To all the Kickstarter backers who helped get this book where it needed to be. THANK YOU!! And special thanks to Samantha Keil, Angelo D., Mike McCue, Iqra Shafi, Emma Swink, and Isabel K.

To all the editors and illustrators I hired to bring *Son of the Stars* to life, I am so thankful for your expertise. You can find their names in the copyright section.

The farther along in this journey I go the more I want to separate myself from the internet, funny enough. So, thank you to my street team, ARC readers, and all readers, who consistently share and spread the word about *The Mothmar Trilogy*.

And finally, to my Heavenly Father, thank you for putting in me this desire to write. I am ever thankful.

Until we meet again (and all that comes before it),
Amanda Auler

Amanda Auler lives in Sanford, North Carolina with her husband and four growing boys. Though Amanda writes for every audience, her roots in Christianity shine through her work as she explores themes of redemption, forgiveness, and grace. When she's not writing you can find her baking cookies, drinking too much coffee, and staying up past her bedtime to watch anime with her husband.

Amanda's Links